IRREGULARS

A Shared-World Anthology

Nicole Kimberling
Josh Lanyon
Astrid Amara
Ginn Hale

Irregulars
A Shared-World Anthology
By Nicole Kimberling, Josh Lanyon, Astrid Amara, Ginn Hale

Published by:
Blind Eye Books
1141 Grant Street
Bellingham, WA. 98225
blindeyebooks.com

Edited by Nicole Kimberling and J.D. Hope
Cover Art by Sam Dawson
Authors's Portraits by Dawn Kimberling

First Edition March 2012

ISBN: 978-1-935560-16-6

No Life but This is dedicated to Krishna—writing isn't the same without you beside me.
—Astrid Amara

CHERRIES WORTH GETTING

Nicole Kimberling

"We must not look at goblin men,
We must not buy their fruits:
Who knows upon what soil they fed
Their hungry thirsty roots?"
The Goblin Market
— Christina Rosetti

For reasons unknown to Agent Keith Curry, food carts proliferated on the mostly rainy streets of Portland, Oregon, like they did in no other city in North America. Their awnings sprang up like the chanterelles in the Pacific Northwest forest, sometimes filling an entire parking lot.

Keith preferred visiting these eateries because many had permanently rented parking spaces and settled down like oysters cementing themselves in place. The parking lot near his hotel supported one of these colonies so he thought it might be as good a place as any to begin his investigation, though he didn't expect to find much.

Rarely did venues like these serve human flesh.

Hidden places, places with concealed entrances, front businesses with makeshift kitchens, art galleries—he found contraband in places like these, but the average health department certified cart?

Probably clean as a whistle.

Keith stepped up to the cart—a converted Airstream that sold nothing but grilled cheese sandwiches—and ordered a "Kindergartner"—American cheese on white bread. A slight vibration came from his wrist and he glanced down at his watch. It was a prototype designed to alert a human wearer of the presence of extra-human beings. Now the numeral seven shone blue, which indicated that a faerie had come within fifty feet of him, setting off his proximity alarm. Briefly, he scanned the people queueing up to the food carts, wondering which customer hid a fae nature. Business heels lady? Sparkly hippie juggler, busking? Little blond kid eating a snow-cone? It could be any of them—or maybe all of them. Probably more than one faerie was abroad, actually, this close to the upscale condos in the Pearl District. Faeries didn't concern him this time around. What he needed to watch for was the red three that indicated the presence of goblins.

He returned his attention to the amiable, bearded guy currently buttering the bread that would shortly become his sandwich.

"You mind if I ask you a question?" Keith asked.

"Go right ahead." The bearded guy slapped the bread down on the food cart's small but impeccably clean flatiron and applied the cheese.

"Do you know where a guy can find any flesh joints around here?"

The cook laughed. "There're too many strip joints to count, man. Just google 'stripper.' You can get any kind you want."

"I don't mean naked ladies. I mean bloody protein."

The cook looked up at him in mild disdain. "Not really my style."

"Not that into meat?" Keith asked casually.

"Not into performance art shit," the cook replied. "I believe in cooking food, not eating it raw in front of a smoke machine while some pretentious dick plays lame beats."

"So you've never been to the Theater of Blood Carnivore Circus?"

"One of my buddies went to it, but I don't really remember where he said it was. Like I said, it's not my thing."

"Do you think I could convince you to call him and ask? I'm only in town for a few days and I want to experience the entire Portland food scene before I put up my report."

At this the bearded guy perked up.

"You a food critic or blogger or something?" He handed Keith the sandwich. It smelled amazing—like something his mom would have served alongside a bowl of canned tomato soup.

"Or something." Keith winked. Generally speaking, restaurant reviewers did not reveal themselves to people whom they were to review. The grilled cheese guy understood this and nodded sagely.

"If I call him, he might remember."

"I'd appreciate it." Keith took a bite of his sandwich, made a show of savoring it before pronouncing, "Delicious."

"You should try it with our spiced turkey." The cook tilted a pan to show him half of a roasted bird, concave rib bones visible. "Just roasted it with harissa and preserved lemon. Want a sample?"

Keith's stomach lurched slightly, as it always did these days when he saw a carcass.

He held up a hand in refusal. "None for me, thanks. I'm a vegetarian."

Keith ate his sandwich and the grilled cheese guy phoned his friend, who came up blank. Too drunk, he said, to remember where he'd been. But he'd seen the poster for the show when he'd been clubbing downtown. Maybe, he said, it was still there. Keith thanked the cook and headed east, walking the length of the central business district to reach the Willamette River. Huge clubs of every persuasion, including gay clubs like C C Slaughters and Silverado, dominated the streets. Since it was lunchtime, few were open.

Portland's old town, like every other urban center in the midst of being gentrified, was a perfect combination of swank and sleazy. Genuine homeless alcoholics loitered on sidewalks next to trust fund students merely posing as alcoholics. Wingtips mingled with Converse.

The combination of Portland's art, music, and food scenes made it the perfect place to hide a blood orgy. Even when civilians happened upon the carnage, they often simply believed it had to be some kind of performance. Keith had investigated orgy sites where there had been twenty or more witnesses all standing and watching some victim being dismembered just because a cameraman was filming it. The presence of a camera implied fiction and a sense that some authority was in control.

That was right, at least. But few spectators ever asked themselves who that authority might be.

Keith didn't blame them—the spectators. They couldn't know how many monsters existed in the world. Hell, his own agency, NIAD, went out of the way to make sure they didn't know. The NATO Irregular Affairs Division, often simply called the Irregulars, had been tasked with the duty of policing otherrealm traffic, beings, and artifacts.

NIAD policed NATO territories, providing justice for the wronged and infrastructure for the hundreds of thousands of unearthly refugees, diaspora, and émigrés who now lived hidden within NATO borders.

The array of agents employed by the department included rumpled old magicians, witches in business suits, and faerie lawyers as well as a wide variety of extra-human consultants. But the people who did most of the work were regular old human agents, like him.

Keith turned onto SW Stark Street and walked slowly, scanning the brick facades for arcane symbols hidden in the graffiti. He pulled his NIAD-issue glasses from their case and put them on. Through the enchanted lenses, he could now see that a few faint faerie signs marked the building. They were remarkably like hobo signs: circles, slashes, and arrows indicating what a passing extra-human might encounter. The building directly in front of him was marked "cream left out".

Not surprising. It was an ice cream parlor. But Keith noted it all the same. If the owners left product out intentionally to feed passing extra-humans, they might have some other-realm connections. If this had been New York or Boston, the whole bottom six inches of the building would have been scribbled with vulgar Gaelic epithets left by leprechaun gangs. Here only a couple of marks had been left at ankle-level and they looked like elf work. Apparently one could find work with a shoemaker nearby. He walked up and down the street. Here and there other spirits had left their mark. He found some ancient Japanese cursive left by displaced yokai that had been overwritten in English by a local Native American salmon spirit.

At last he came to a telephone pole plastered with flyers and handbills for various shows, crudely taped and staple-gunned over one another. One caught Keith's eye. Carefully, he peeled aside a flyer advertising a Dykes-n-Dogs singles meetup (canine companions welcome) to reveal the words:

Theater of Blood

Carnivore Circus

One Night Only!

Lulu's Flapjack Shack

A quick map search revealed that the restaurant was located on the city's east side. The sun was setting now. As Keith predicted, his proximity alarm started to gently flash as more and more extra-humans emerged from their lairs, homes, and office buildings. Blinking green nine: vampires. Yellow two: pixies. Red three: goblins.

Across the water, the city's east side with its hipster bars and award-winning restaurants beckoned, but Keith's days of gourmandizing were long gone. Besides, the east side of Portland was known to contain the largest naturalized goblin population in the world. If he was going to go asking questions there, he'd need backup. Preferably backup that both spoke the language and understood the treaties that existed between humans and goblins.

Because of the necessity for human flesh for certain historic goblin rituals, NIAD, in conjunction with other human governments, had struck a bargain: ten death row inmates sent to the goblin realm every year, no questions asked. In return for this, the goblins had agreed to an extradition treaty that had curbed the ability of goblin human-hunters to disappear on the wild white mountainsides of their snowy kingdom. Keith could see how, when the deal was made a century prior, it would have seemed like poetic justice to render up a sinner to the tortures of hell.

The program had been largely effective, but not completely. Certain goblins still chose to hunt human beings. The only time Keith had ever used his mage pistol against a hostile was when he'd neutralized a pair of goblin butchers in an abattoir in Chicago. He wasn't excited about the prospect of using it again. Avoiding direct conflict, through use of the greater communication skills provided by a translator or community liaison, would provide the most desirable outcome.

At least that's what the NIAD field operations manual assured him and he was willing to give it a try, if only to sidestep filing the mountain of paperwork required by investigating agents who discharged even a single, laser-etched incantation bullet.

He phoned the field office for backup, then headed back to his hotel, stopping only briefly at a supermarket to purchase bread and cheese.

❧

Keith's room at the Mark Spencer Hotel was small and not at all hip, but it had the two things Keith needed most—a bed and a tiny kitchenette. He laid his mage pistol on the small square of counter next to the range and started dinner. He heated the warped nonstick skillet that had come with the room and laid one piece of buttered bread down in it, hearing an appealing sizzle. He added a couple of slices of havarti and another slice of buttered bread and waited. He didn't really watch his food so much as he listened to it—smelled it. Behind him the television let him know about events currently taking place in the Willamette Valley. There was a brewer's festival and a triathlon, perfectly representing Portland's twin obsessions: the culinary arts and outdoor recreation. The open window let in a pleasant summer breeze.

Keith was pondering his chances of still being in town for the brewer's festival when he felt a slight vibration from his wrist. He glanced at his watch. The numeral three glowed red—goblins close by.

There was a knock at his door. Out of habit, Keith switched off the range and shifted his skillet off the electric element. Mage pistol in hand, he moved to peer through the fish-eye lens. Outside his door he saw a tall, well-muscled man wearing the standard black trench coat favored by their department, despite the fact that it was nearly eighty degrees outside. He had lustrous black hair and blue eyes and a jawline perfect enough to get him a job selling any men's cologne on earth. The man smiled and held up his NIAD badge. The circular insignia of the Irregular Affairs Division gleamed dully in the yellow hallway light.

Gunther Heartman. Keith cracked his knuckles. It was a bad habit and also a tell, since he did it only when extremely irritated, but he found he couldn't stop. Gunther worked in the San Francisco office as a field agent and member of the strike force. He also did do-gooder double duty as a community volunteer, coordinating the annual human returnee Christmas party. Held in San Francisco, this party was arranged for the benefit of humans who for whatever reason had been away from earth for too long to be normal. Some had been hostages; others, lost in amateur magic-using accidents only to be retrieved years later, addled and hopelessly out of sync with everyday human life. Still others had never lived on earth at all and were dealing with the problem of having been repatriated against their will. It was a mixed bag of scratched and dented individuals who needed further socialization before being allowed to roam free in the general population.

Gunther had convinced Keith to come in from HQ to participate the previous year. And because Gunther was a good-looking man, Keith had been happy to oblige, on the notion that he might find opportunity to seduce him. He'd taken the red-eye from DC and six hours after landing was running a little table where he helped the human race's long-lost weirdos create, decorate, and ultimately eat the most disturbing Christmas cookies imaginable.

Still covered in sprinkles and colored sugar, they'd had sex for the first time. Keith had thought he was in love at the first taste of Gunther's mouth, but he'd played it cool, returning to DC on the next flight.

Gunther had phoned him about a week later. He'd been in DC for some meeting. They'd met, screwed, and parted that very night.

This pattern repeated itself a few times as the two of them casually entered each other's orbits, only to be pulled away again the next day. That suited Keith fine for a while.

Then, just like that, Heartman had ended it.

He'd ended it just as Keith had been about to suggest that they try to see more of each other.

Keith pulled the door open, but not far enough to let Heartman enter. "What are you doing here?"

"You called for me."

"I called for a goblin linguist."

"And here I am," Gunther replied. "There was no one else available so they sent me."

Keith gave a resigned sigh and pulled his NIAD-issue utility knife from his pocket. He folded the identification light out and focused the beam. "Light verification please, Agent Heartman?"

"I suppose it's too much to hope that you'd feel comfortable calling me Gunther." He offered his ID again.

"Let's just keep it professional." Keith shone his light across the plastic surface. Text previously invisible revealed itself, including Agent Heartman's species: naturalized goblin.

Keith's breath caught in his throat. He hadn't known that, though he could see how Gunther would have failed to mention it.

Oddly, Gunther's photograph didn't shift under the light to show any other image. It looked just like he looked—like an actor who would have been cast to play a hot federal agent in some action film. The lean planes of his face would have photographed well from any angle. Probably even upside down.

"There's no secondary ID photo here," Keith remarked.

"There wouldn't be. I'm transmogrified." Gunther took a pack of Lucky Strikes filterless from his inside pocket, folded one into his mouth, and began to chew.

"It says naturalized here." Keith stared hard at the ID and then at Gunther. Was this some sort of trick? Another creature casting a masking spell to look like Gunther? Keith surreptitiously adjusted the light to pierce illusions and, without warning, flashed the light into the other agent's face.

Gunther winced and held up a hand against the piercing white light, but his countenance remained exactly the same.

"Although I am fully of snow goblin descent, I was transformed to be compatible with this world while still in utero." Gunther kept his voice low and glanced around the empty hallway as he spoke. "This isn't a glamour or masking spell or any other kind of illusion. My real body has been irrevocably reconfigured."

"Right," Keith muttered. "I've heard of that."

Gunther said, "Do you think we could continue this conversation in private?"

"Oh, of course." Keith stepped aside.

Gunther sauntered through the doorway, sidestepped the bed, and seated himself in a high-backed chair by the television. His eyes immediately honed in on the skillet.

"Are you cooking grilled cheese?"

"I was." As Keith returned to the range and flipped his sandwich over, his deeply ingrained sense of hospitality took over and he found himself asking, "Want one?"

"Sure." Gunther gave him a brilliant smile, showing his perfectly white teeth. "I'm always hungry."

Chapter Two

Snow goblins were, for Keith's money, the scariest looking of the species. Their pure white bodies seemed to be constructed entirely of bones, talons, and teeth. Only red slits marked their eyes and nostrils. They spoke in growls. They drank pure kerosene on the rocks and called it moonshine.

In so far as Keith knew, Gunther Heartman had never scared anyone. Not even accidentally. He was polite, well meaning, and easygoing to a fault. Even when Gunther had ended his relationship with Keith—if you could describe a disjointed series of one-night stands a relationship—he'd been nice about it. "I think you might still be struggling with some issues," Gunther had said, "and I don't think being with me is necessarily helping you. I don't think I'm the right man for you. And I know you're not the right man for me."

At the time, Keith had consoled himself by thinking that at least Gunther had had the guts to give him a real reason, instead of the old "it's not you, it's me" line. Keith had always wondered why Gunther thought he wasn't the right man for Keith. Now he thought he knew. Not only was he not human, he was exactly the sort of extra-human American who had destroyed Keith's previous life.

But that didn't bear thinking about. Keith turned his attention fully back to cooking. Almost casually, he remarked, "I didn't realize that you were of goblin descent."

"There's no reason you should have."

Except that we've slept together at least a dozen times, Keith thought. Aloud he said, "I suppose there are quite a few of you on the West Coast."

Gunther nodded. "About six thousand. More than half of them were reengineered while they were still in the womb, like myself."

"It's odd that you never brought that up before," Keith said.

"Is it?" Gunther gave him a meaningful look, though what meaning he intended Keith to take away was not clear.

"Yes, it is." Keith flipped Gunther's sandwich. "So, have you always looked human?"

"I haven't just looked human, I've been human. I went to public school, ran track, and got my first job washing dishes at Kentucky Fried Chicken just like everybody else." Gunther popped another cigarette into his mouth and chewed slowly. He fished in his pocket for his slim, yellow tin of lighter fluid, popped open the red safety cap, and took a swig. Thin, flammable vapor floated from his breath as he said, "I enjoy being human."

"I bet you do," Keith said dryly.

The other man gazed at him with a mild, pleasant smile and then said, "Correct me if I'm wrong, but you seem slightly uncomfortable. Is it because you just found out I'm a goblin?"

"No," Keith said.

"Is it because of our previous relationship?"

"Yes." Keith took his sandwich, cut it in half, and offered one plate to Gunther, who accepted it with a strange half bow. Keith took his own plate and sat on the edge of the bed.

"I really didn't mean for you to feel awkward—" Gunther began.

"Let's just focus on the task at hand," Keith cut him off before he could launch into another well-meaning speech. While they'd been seeing one another, Gunther's reflexive urge toward humane action had been one of the qualities Keith admired. Now that same quality not only irked but confused him. "Did you get much of a debriefing?"

"Not much," Gunther said, puffing around his first mouthful of hot, gooey cheese and bread.

"We've had three dead, butchered human carcasses here in Portland in the last six months."

"Any evidence of serial killing?"

Keith shook his head. "FBI says you can never rule that out completely, but our informants say that human protein has appeared in a couple of different goblin venues in the city. The summer holy days are coming up. I think some members of Portland's extra-human American community might be stocking up their pantries."

"For the goblin solstice feast, you mean?"

"That's right," Keith said.

"And so you're thinking that this is the work of some reactionary cadre of old-time religion goblin butchers, therefore you requested a native speaker to assist when you go talk to the community?"

"In a nutshell." Keith thought he sensed a certain reluctance to comply emanating from Gunther but chose not to address it. Not yet, anyway. Clearly the two of them made for a less than ideal team. But if they could get through the next couple of days, they could both go back to their respective offices on opposite sides of the continent, no harm done.

"What about other known human predators?" Gunther asked.

"There are three registered vampires in the area. I'm planning to interview them as well, because there was some exsanguination present, but there's nothing to connect them to the crimes at this moment."

"So what do you have to link this to goblins?" Gunther asked.

"The timing and the state of the bodies. It's circumstantial, I know, but these really look like goblin killings," Keith said and from Gunther's brief expression of distaste he guessed Gunther understood what he meant.

"I might have something more solid soon," Keith added.

"Such as?"

"Maybe a venue. Lulu's Flapjack Shack hosted a show recently that has all the hallmarks of a hide-in-plain-sight blood orgy. I'm heading over there in a few minutes and I'd like you to come along."

"Yes, certainly." Gunther took his remaining sandwich triangle, folded it in half, and, despite the magma-like cheese, ate it in three bites. He then said, "Do you mind if we stop to get another pack of cigarettes on the way? I'm out."

Lulu's Flapjack Shack inhabited a space that had certainly been continuously used as a hospitality venue since linoleum had been invented. Mismatched vinyl booths lined the dining room walls and small tables filled the center space, creating the feeling of being in a pastiche of all diners that had ever existed anywhere. Keith couldn't tell if this was sophisticated and subtle interior design or the result of buying fixtures piecemeal.

According to the sign, Lulu's was open twenty-three hours a day—the one hour closure occurring between four and five a.m.

Presumably, this was when they mopped.

At nine thirty p.m. the dining room was at about half capacity. Mostly the patrons seemed to be in the pre-legal phase of adolescence. Groups of five or six shared plates of french fries and pretended to be adults. At the diner counter, intermittently spaced single older males competed for the lone waitress's conversational attention in between bites of all-day breakfast.

"Where do the bands play, do you think?" Keith asked Gunther, mostly to make conversation. The notion that the goblin currently setting off his proximity alert was standing right next to him disturbed him more than he wanted to admit, even to himself.

"Banquet room." Gunther pointed down the long counter to a lighted sign at the back.

Gunther turned out to be correct.

"I don't like the fact that it's called The Banquet Room." Keith's watch buzzed gently, number three still glowing red.

Gunther glanced at it. "Is that some sort of prototype?"

"It's a sensor. It's coded to alert agents to the presence of extra-humans." Keith gave Gunther the brief rundown on the prototype and its codes. "It's meant to be more subtle than other types of sensors. The downside is having to memorize the codes."

Gunther nodded and said, "So what's it say now?"

"At least one goblin within fifty feet. But that is most likely you."

"You know, R&D really needs to get on developing a way for agents of other-realm origin to avoid triggering those things before they take it out of the prototype phase. I could see how that could go really wrong in a strike force situation with limited visibility."

"I'll make sure to include that in my report on how it functions in the field," Keith remarked, somewhat dryly. Strike force was never an assignment that Keith had coveted, but there was a certain inevitable comparison of masculinity that occurred between agents when one was a member and the other wasn't.

"I'd appreciate that, thanks." Gunther headed back into the restaurant and Keith followed with caution.

The Banquet Room had been designed when restaurants still routinely catered banquets, sometime way back in the early imitation wood paneling era. Like most banquet rooms of this ilk, it offered no windows and only one emergency exit in the back.

Essentially, a perfect space to hold a blood orgy.

Whoever had converted The Banquet Room into a bar had kept the basic fixtures and furnishings. The room seemed largely set up like a banquet room as well, with long tables lined by inexpensive, wipe-able pine green dining chairs. Large mass-produced nautical-themed paintings dotted the wall. Toward the front of the room, where head tables would have been, was a small stage, a ten-seat wet bar, and a tiny dance floor.

Few patrons were in evidence—just a few young guys at the bar watching cartoons on closed-captioned television and a couple who seemed to be hiding in the corner table. Keith gave them the once-over. But upon closer inspection, the reason for their furtive behavior became clear. He wore a wedding band and she did not.

He seated himself at the bar next to Gunther. Catching sight of himself in the mirror behind the bar, Keith had the unfortunate experience of comparing himself with Agent Heartman physically. There was no contest whatsoever. Gunther was taller, broader, and somehow looked good slouching beneath dank, yellow light. Whereas Keith, sitting in shirtsleeves, tie slightly loosened, resembled nothing more than an off-duty county health inspector. Only the tattoos on his arms revealed that there might be any aspect of his personality that an average person could find interest in.

The bartender set a bowl of popcorn down between them. The man resembled Gunther in the powerful proportions of his body, but his coloring differed notably. He had red hair, small, narrow eyes, and a mouth that stretched too wide to be attractive, especially when he smiled.

"What can I get for you?"

Gunther ordered pink vodka on the rocks. Keith stuck with beer—microbrew. The bartender stepped aside to pour their drinks. Gunther began to amiably munch the popcorn. After a few bites he remarked, "This would be a good venue."

"Yeah, that's what I thought. No windows. Drain in the floor."

"I was thinking more for seeing a band," Gunther said. "The décor seems dank and lowbrow for a real goblin feast."

"Have you ever been to one?"

"Do I not have a mother who would be disappointed if I failed to attend?" Gunther tossed a yellow kernel into the air and caught it in his mouth, then slid his gaze slyly around. "I feast every year. Not how you're imagining it, though. My family's feasts take the form of barbecues generally conducted in the garden. The most unsavory item generally present is my godfather's fifth of substandard rye."

"What protein did you cook?"

"You know, a less polite man might find that question, and its implicit assumption, somewhat offensive." His tone shifted slightly, lowering to a near growl.

Keith bristled. "Maybe a less polite man hasn't seen the same kinds of things that I have seen conducted in places much like this."

Gunther folded. His easy manner returned. "I suppose not. I imagine that as the primary investigator for cases like these you've grown naturally suspicious of individuals of my heritage."

Keith lowered his voice to a near whisper. "Look, last year, in Dallas, we busted a group of upper crust gourmandizing sickos who were human right down to their Manolo Blahniks. Before that we collared a real, live child-eating Russian baba-fucking-yaga. But in this particular case, I happen to suspect goblins, all right? If you can't deal with that maybe you should request reassignment."

The bartender turned back and plunked their drinks in front of them. Keith slid the tattered flyer out in front of him and said, "I was wondering, did you happen to be working on the night of this show?"

The bartender glanced down and grimaced. "Yeah, I was. Hell of a mess they made." Then, with a bartender's eerie prescience, he inquired, "You two cops?"

"I'm Agent Keith Curry. This is Agent Heartman." He briefly opened his NIAD ID, then closed it again. For most people, just seeing a badge—any badge—was enough to get them to talk. The bartender was no exception. He nodded, stiffening only slightly. Keith continued, "And you are?"

"Jordan Lucky Greenbacks. What is this about?"

"Just a routine inquiry." Gunther gave the bartender an easy smile. "Are the owners in?"

"No, they don't work nights."

Keith took over again. "How long have you worked here, Mr. Greenbacks?"

"Three years," Jordan said.

"Tell me, does the management ever close this room for private parties?"

"Sometimes."

"When was the last time?" Keith removed a black notebook from his pocket and flipped it open.

"Around Christmas last year there was a private party," Jordan said.

"So around the winter solstice?"

"It didn't have anything to do with any solstice, winter or summer." Jordan's tone sharpened. His expression snapped instantly into defensive hostility. He stared straight at Gunther. "It had nothing to do with...our community. It was a fundraiser for the fire department."

Keith raised his eyebrows fractionally. Jordan could have been referring to the gay community, but Keith seriously doubted that.

He wondered if Gunther had already perceived that Mr. Greenbacks was trans-goblin as well. And if so, how did the two of them recognize each other? Psychic power? Smell?

"So, are the owners of this club part of you and Agent Heartman's community?"

"No, they aren't," Jordan said in an insistent whisper. "And they don't know anything about it or about me. I haven't broken the Secrecy Act—"

"Of course you haven't," Gunther said. "The reason we came here was to ask about this particular show. We want to know what you can tell us about these bands."

"Nothing except, you know, the obvious." He looked directly at Gunther as he spoke.

"Define *obvious* for me." Keith took a sip of his beer.

"Some of the musicians were—" he gave another slight gesture in Gunther's direction, "—also part of our community. Obviously you know that already or you wouldn't be here."

Keith allowed himself a tight smile, then said, "Did you happen to get any names?"

The bartender shook his head. "It was a popular show, I was running the whole time. I didn't even have time for a smoke break. You could ask our booker, Samantha. She'd probably have some contact information for them."

"Is Samantha here?"

"No, Monday's her day off."

"Let's get back to the band. Did you notice anything special about any of them?" Gunther asked. "Physical characteristics? Anything?"

Jordan shrugged again. "It was just a metal show. They drank cheap beer and played really heavy, brick in your face metal but didn't do anything..." He leaned forward, whispering to Gunther, "...anything magical. They sang in goblin during the refrain, but that was all. Hardly anybody even recognized it."

"That and made a hell of a mess." Keith circled back around to the front of the conversation.

Jordan paled slightly. His fingers tightened imperceptibly around the white bar towel.

There it is, Keith thought, that telling expression of information that has been omitted. "What was so messy about the band?"

The bartender swallowed. "They did some theatrical stuff on stage."

"Such as?" Gunther prompted.

"They drank some stuff that looked like blood. Poured some of it over the crowd." The bartender busied himself with wiping the already clean bar. "A lot of metal bands do things like that."

"Did it look like blood or was it blood?" Keith pressed.

"I don't know." The bartender refused to look at him. "I'm not some kind of expert."

"You cleaned it up, right?" Keith folded his hands, prepared to wait all night for the answer. "Blood has a fairly distinct odor, color, and texture."

"I—" Jordan looked to Gunther.

"It's all right," Gunther assured him. "We just need to know about this band. We don't have any reason to believe you are connected with them. Are you?"

"I'm not," the bartender said quickly. "They said it was cow's blood. They poured it out of these gallon jugs that said USDA on them."

Keith nodded. Though strange from the standpoint of an average white-bread American, beef and pork blood were standard ingredients in everything from the Filipino blood stew called *dinuguan* to *verivorst*, the blood sausages Estonians considered crucial for any Christmas feast. It was entirely plausible that the blood had its origin in livestock. It was also possible that they had simply refilled empty containers with human blood. Without a DNA sample and test, it would be impossible to tell.

"How long ago was this show?"

"Last week."

"Has the mop head been changed since then?" Keith asked.

"I don't think so. The laundry service hasn't been here yet. Do you want to see it?"

Keith followed the bartender back into a dank supply cup board. As predicted, the mop head was still attached to the mop handle, sitting in a yellow plastic bucket.

Keith detached the moist, stinking thing and crammed it into an evidence bag.

"We're going to have to take this with us." He wrote Jordan a receipt, returned to the bar, and sat down next to Gunther, who observed the bagged mop head with silent curiosity.

"I'm going to find out exactly what kind of blood the band was pouring out at the show," Keith explained.

Gunther nodded. "That's what I thought."

"Then at least we'll know something about this case," Keith said.

Gunther nodded again. Jordan returned to ask them if they needed another round.

"Not right at the moment," Gunther said. "So, you don't remember anything else about the band? Any detail at all?"

Jordan paused thoughtfully, seeming to come to some painful decision before finally speaking. "The bassist had a Portland Saturday Market sticker on his guitar case. He said he worked there. I remember it because I wanted to know if he knew my friend Spartacus, who sells hard cider in the beer garden."

"Did he?" Keith asked. The Portland Saturday Market was one of many markets heavily run by goblins—an earth-based offshoot of the Grand Goblin Bazaar.

"He did," Jordan said. "Everybody knows everybody there." A man at the end of the bar suddenly hoisted his empty aloft and began, rudely, to clack his ice as a way of indicating that he'd like additional service. Jordan gave him a professional smile and a nod before saying, "Is there anything else?"

"Tables at the market here are hereditary, aren't they?" Gunther asked.

"Of course. There's a waiting list you can get on, but my friend Spartacus told me it's years long. He only got in because he took over for his mother. He's been studying with cider makers in England for the last few years. He's really a genius. I have it on tap here. I'll pour you one. You'll be blown away."

Gunther accepted Jordan's largesse with grace and some formal-sounding word in goblin that Keith didn't understand.

Keith eyed the cider sparkling in Gunther's pint glass. Apart from their ritualistic taste for human flesh, goblins were well known for the astonishing quality of their fruits. Doubtless this particular cider would be the best he'd ever had. More than that, he wouldn't be able to stop thinking of it. Tasting goblin fruits ruined the flavor of all lesser fruits forever. Eating goblin fruit and then returning to mundane varieties was like having the opportunity to make love to your soul mate for one night, then forever more being relegated to meaningless one-night stands.

He'd once eaten a few slices of a goblin peach. Those soft crescents had been the most amazing flesh he'd ever put in his mouth.

Barring Gunther's flesh, that is.

But again, that didn't bear thinking about.

Now before them sat a glass of goblin cider. If he drank it no other cider would be enough ever again. Disappointment would be frequent and yet the temptation of goblin fruits pulled at him. The desire to have the best in the world, even just one time, was one of the very personality traits that had attracted Keith to cooking in the first place.

And somehow, even though his suspicion about food had grown to what could rightfully be called paranoia since he'd joined NIAD, alcohol remained the chink in his armor—especially when he'd just had other alcohol.

Temptation won.

Keith asked, "Mind if I try your cider?"

"Not at all. It's really good, but I'm not much of a hard cider man." Gunther slid the pint over. Keith wondered if the taste of goblin fruits actually affected goblins.

As he suspected, the cider was amazing. Better than amazing. A feeling very much like orgasm zinged over his tongue, electrifying every taste bud with tangy, juicy sweetness. He laughed for no reason. Tears had filled his eyes. He closed his eyes and gave an involuntary groan of pleasure.

"If I'd known you were going to like it that much I'd have brought one with me to the hotel," Gunther remarked.

Keith opened his eyes to find Gunther gazing at him with the sort of openly homosexual public appreciation that Keith found nerve-wracking, even though he'd been out since he was twenty. Reluctantly, almost involuntarily, Keith found himself returning Gunther's smile.

Chapter Three

The Portland Saturday Market was part beer garden and part DIY art fair. Rows of white, eight-by-eight tent canopies inhabited Ankeny Plaza—a brick-paved space in Waterfront Park on the bank of the Willamette River.

Gunther walked with a spring in his step. His black trench coat was draped across one arm in the fine, sunny morning.

Since Keith and Gunther had parted the previous evening, conflicting thoughts and feelings had been twisting through Keith's brain like a dough hook working relentlessly at a fifty-pound batch.

On the one hand, he wanted Gunther. That had never changed. On the other hand, Gunther no longer wanted him. That had also not changed. And yet, the intractability of the situation did nothing to dissuade either of them from smiling at each other when they had met in the elevator that morning. Or from flirting mildly with each other in the car on the way over. Keith found himself admiring Gunther openly as he peered ahead at the market like a child approaching an amusement park.

"My parents used to bring me to this market every weekend," Gunther said.

"You grew up in Portland?"

"No, Oakland. My parents still work as translators for the San Francisco field office, but there's a portal at Fisherman's Wharf. There were always a lot of other trans-goblin kids to play with here and my parents could visit with their fellow dissident diaspora. Usually people brought sandwiches. Sometimes potato salad. And every now and then one of the men would surreptitiously share his flask of naphtha."

"Replace the naphtha with vodka and it would be exactly like going to a picnic at my grandma's church," Keith said, smiling.

"I've never been to a church picnic, but there was a feeling of community here that we didn't always have in Oakland. Coming to the earthly realm was quite the sacrifice for my parents."

Keith glanced at Gunther sideways. "How do you mean?"

"Well, to make a decision to leave behind the shape of a Luminous One and condemn their only child to wearing the flesh of a homely little human, of course. I retain some goblin characteristics, but there's really no chance of me finding a nice goblin boy to settle down with while I've got this meaty body." Gunther shook his head. "Just too unappealing."

"So that's what you're looking for? A nice trans-goblin boy?" As soon as the words were out of his mouth, Keith regretted them. Why was he showing all his cards and behaving like he had no game whatsoever?

Gunther stopped, standing as if affixed to the green grass by tent pegs, regarding Keith with a slight, sardonic smile.

"I thought you said you wanted to keep it professional between us," he said.

"You're right. That was cheap of me," Keith conceded. "Let's just get to work."

Like many places used for congregation by the extra-human American community, the goblin markets were linked through a series of portals. One could walk into a portal in Portland, step through a door, and emerge in Brooklyn or London or Mexico City. In Keith's experience, in markets that were open to the human public, like this one, the portals were generally disguised as out-of-order toilet stalls. Any human brave enough to open the stall door would be treated to an illusion so unappealing as to dissuade casual entry.

Keith knew some Irregular agents who were so comfortable with magic that they used goblin market portals to avoid airline security lines when traveling between the coasts. But being neither a magician nor a mythical creature, Keith had never felt too secure with that sort of travel.

As they walked across the damp grass toward the rows of small, white pavilions, they passed a line of blue portable toilet stalls. Two displayed signs expressing that they were out of order.

Keith put on his glasses and noted, with interest, that Gunther did as well. Immediately hidden text all around him was revealed. One port-o-let was marked Fisherman's Wharf while another read Grand Goblin.

Hidden signage on stalls sprang into view as well. One table, selling handcrafted glass, advertised that their product was fair trade—made by elves who received a decent living wage.

"What do elves consider a living wage?" Keith whispered to Gunther.

Gunther just shrugged. "Their own pair of pants?"

They moved through the rows of canopies. Keith followed Gunther's lead, stopping when he stopped, simply listening as his fellow agent softly inquired about the weather and other knuckle-poppingly irrelevant subjects.

Gunther bought a basket of Rainier cherries from a girl named Agnes, then stood there, munching them in front of her, chatting about rain and the phases of the moon and gardening. Just when Keith thought that Gunther had given up investigating altogether he noticed Agnes's bike—or more specifically, the Carnivore Circus sticker adhered to it. Even without the glasses he'd have been able to see it.

Agnes seemed to know and have an opinion about everyone in the city.

"If you need some help with your garden, I can put you in touch with some gnomes," she told Gunther. "They're really great guys and work for peanuts."

Keith's patience thinned.

"Look, we aren't here looking for discount day labor. We need to know where to find meat." Keith flipped out his wallet, flashing his badge. "You know what I'm talking about."

Agnes's lip curled. Her silver septum piercing glinted. "I know what you mean, and I think it's disgusting. You agents are all the same. You think we goblins all just waiting around to become cannibals."

"Hey now, that's not true—" Gunther began.

"You're worst of all—standing there with juice from my produce on your lips while taking *the man's* coin to continue the unfair profiling of your own people."

Vendors in the booths around them started to take notice. The lanky man selling recycled sweaters in the stall next door drifted over. Keith suppressed the urge to reach for his mage pistol. It would only escalate the situation. Besides, Gunther didn't seem ruffled. He munched cherry after cherry, an affable smile on his face. Keith guessed that he was accustomed to dealing with this sort of aggressive reaction.

"We're not here to bother you, miss. I'm sure nobody here has anything to do with the murders that have taken place in the last year," Gunther said. "But we have to check up on every possible lead, you see? We need to speak with everyone who might have heard something about these crimes. Sometimes people aren't even aware that they know important information."

"But why come here first? Why not ask the bloodsuckers? They eat people all the time," Agnes said.

"We will be following multiple lines of inquiry," Keith said. Then following Gunther's lead, even though it went against his personal grain, he said, "I apologize for being abrupt earlier, miss. But three people are dead. Butchered right down to their bones. Imagine what that must be like for their families to see when they come to claim the bodies."

"But it's not goblins," she insisted.

"How do you know for sure?" Gunther cocked his head slightly. "Have you heard anything about the murders? Anything at all, gossip or speculation? People talking in bars?"

"Have you ever seen this before?" Keith pulled the Theater of Blood Carnivore Circus flyer out of his pocket, unfolded it, and showed it to her.

"Never," she said.

"Are you sure?" Gunther asked.

Agnes clamped her mouth shut and shook her head. She covered her face with her hands and said again, "It's not goblins. It can't be goblins."

"You have a Carnivore Circus bumper sticker on your bike, miss. Now I'm going to ask you again: what do you know about this flyer?" Keith persisted.

"Nothing," she said, from behind her hands.

Guilty, Keith thought. *Or at least not entirely innocent.* She knew something. Keith wondered how hard it would be to drag her to the Irregulars field office.

"The Carnivore Circus isn't involved," the lanky man suddenly said. "We're just a band, that's all."

Keith's attention snapped immediately to the lanky man. "I take it that you're in this band?"

"Yeah, I play bass."

"And your name is?" Gunther flipped out his notebook.

"Lancelot Paddington, but my band name is The Lancer."

Agnes laid a hand on his arm. "You shouldn't talk to them without a lawyer."

Lancelot shrugged. "I've got nothing to hide."

"So tell us about your band," Gunther said.

"We're a three-piece metal band. All goblin. Our influences include The Stooges and Three Inches of Blood. We've got an EP out right now. Last week we made a date to talk with a local label—"

Keith cut him off, "Tell us about why someone would think your band has to do with these murders."

"This flyer," Lancelot pointed at the grimy paper, "it's for two different acts. The first one was Theater of Blood. They sucked."

"Sucked blood?" Gunther prompted.

"No," Lancelot said. "They drank it out of these cheap plastic goblets that looked like they came from the dollar store. They had no style, couldn't wear makeup, and didn't know how to play."

"Do you know what kind of blood it was?" Gunther glanced up from his notes.

"They said it was human."

"Why didn't you report this to our agency?" Keith asked.

"They were humans. All of them," Lancelot said. "And they were such poseurs I figured that they had to be lying about the blood. I thought they were trying to impress us because we eat raw meat in our act. A lot of guys get intimidated by that. They think they have to be more macho than us."

Gunther's eyebrows shot up. "You eat live meat on stage?"

"No, nothing like that." Lancelot backpedaled. "We just get really hungry when we're shredding and sometimes snack."

"So you eat raw but not live meat?" Keith clarified.

"Right. Beef mostly. Sometimes, if it's a really big venue, we eat goat because the bones look more, like, human."

"Don't tell them that," Agnes said.

"No, it's okay, Aggie. The first time we did it—ate raw meat, I mean—it was just what we brought for lunch. We were in the green room at a club snacking on frozen hamburger patties and chewing butts between sets and the bartender came back and caught us. We claimed to be from Ethiopia."

Keith wondered how that had gone over. Lancelot was white as vanilla ice milk.

"Ethiopia…Nice one," Gunther murmured, a hint of a smile curving his lips.

"Yeah, the bartender—his name is Jordan—Jordan said that he liked our sound but our stage show was boring. It was his idea to incorporate eating raw meat into the act because it would seem hardcore. He came up with the new name too. He's a good guy. He works at Lulu's Flapjack Shack. See Spartacus over there? The guy with the cider? Jordan is his first cousin."

"Yes, we've met Mr. Greenbacks," Keith said sourly. "So he came up with your new name?"

"Carnivore Circus. Before that we were called Grand Coulee Mayhem Tennis Project," Lancelot said sheepishly. "I guess I was drunk when I came up with that."

"So did Jordan set up the gig with Theater of Blood?" Keith asked.

"No, that was our manager, Milton. I can give you his phone number only…" Lancelot shot a sideways glance at Agnes. She was on the phone with someone. Perhaps Jordan, but most likely a lawyer.

"Only…" Gunther prompted.

"Milton doesn't know we're trans-goblins and I'm worried that if he found out your guys would put some forgetting mojo on him and then he'd forget he's supposed to be getting us a record deal."

"We will make every effort to conceal both your and our identities," Gunther said.

"Thanks, man." Lancelot nodded absently, his attention distracted by a pair of yuppies perusing his recycled knitwear with some interest. "Would you mind if I get back to my stall now?"

After they released Lancelot, Keith was ready to go, but Gunther insisted on seeing the rest of the market. He bought a dozen light bulbs from one table and three bottles of hot sauce from another. A few vendors gave them nervous smiles as they passed by but most stared stonily or looked away. Before leaving, Gunther stopped by and bought a Carnivore Circus CD from Lancelot, which seemed to smooth things over somewhat. Lancelot shortchanged Gunther three bucks. Keith wondered if that was malice, nervousness, or bad math. There was no real way to tell.

Their last pass was through a row of food vendors. Keith was hungry but at the same time deeply distrustful of food—any food—prepared by goblins. Fortunately, there was Spartacus and his cider. He bought one and found a place at one of the picnic tables.

"It seems like it's getting to be lunchtime," Gunther remarked.

"I'd have thought you already filled up on cherries."

"Merely an appetizer," Gunther said. "Can I buy you lunch?"

"Nothing here looks that great to me," Keith said.

A smile twitched at the corner of Gunther's lips. "Let me take you to lunch in my neighborhood."

"You mean to San Francisco?"

"Home of some very famous vegetarian restaurants including one little five-star hole in the wall called Verdant. We could be there in half an hour."

"It takes that long to get through the portal?"

"No, but traffic between Fisherman's Wharf and Fort Mason isn't that great at this time of year. What do you say?"

"Portaling to San Francisco for five-star lunch sounds less like a business arrangement and more like a date."

"So what if it is?"

"Now who's not keeping it professional?"

Gunther stuffed his hands in his pockets and shrugged. "Neither of us seem to want to, so why should I adhere to some pretense?"

Keith shook his head. "We've already done this, Gunther. It didn't work the first time and it won't work now."

"We never had a proper date before, just a series of booty calls," Gunther said. "So let me make it up to you the old-fashioned way."

Keith had to admit the temptation. And not just the temptation of going on a date with Gunther. Verdant was legendary. While he'd worked as a chef, he'd never given much credit to the vegetarians in his field, nor had he been any great star. The chef at Verdant was both. And he did want Gunther to make it up to him. Hell, he might even be able to figure out what Gunther found so inadequate about that series of disconnected sexual events that he'd wanted to call them off.

"Wouldn't we need reservations?"

"The chef owes me." Gunther leaned forward and whispered, "Pixie trouble. You know how capricious they can be. One little misunderstanding and they're curdling your cream and luring you off Lands End in the dark. But it's all sorted out now. So how about it? We can be down there, done, and back again before this place closes."

Keith was about to refuse. Then the alcohol kicked in, relaxing him enough to say yes.

❧

Verdant was located in an airy space alongside the marina in Fort Mason. From its wide windows, Keith could survey both the marina and the Golden Gate Bridge beyond.

The chef, a friendly faced brunette with close-cropped hair, greeted Gunther as a VIP and seated him immediately.

The menu was elegant, filled with heirloom vegetables, local wine, and cheese.

The price tag was breathtaking. Keith, in fact, had to take a deep breath as he automatically calculated price-point to food cost.

It actually wasn't that bad, for the location and for what they were getting.

And besides, he wasn't paying.

Like every fine dining establishment that Keith had ever been to, the tables were small and relatively close together. But no one was seated alongside them, so once the appetizer had been delivered, their conversation could continue unimpeded by the presence of civilians.

"So, who do you like for the murders?"

Gunther glanced up, a look of slight confusion on his face. He set his fork down and said, "I don't know. I wasn't thinking about it."

"What were you thinking about?"

"My lunch. My companion." He gave a warm smile, as though it was only right and natural that all knowledge of his current mission should be put on hold just because someone set a radicchio, apple, and pomegranate seed salad down in front of him. "I was wondering, was being an agent your first career choice?"

"No, not at all," Keith said, laughing. "I was a chef with no aspirations at law enforcement and no knowledge of the other realms."

"I wondered," Gunther remarked.

"Why?"

"When we—" Gunther seemed to struggle a moment before finding the words he wanted. "When we were seeing each other before, you seemed to be uncomfortable with extra-human Americans."

Keith shrugged. "I hadn't been with NIAD that long. And the few experiences I'd had—especially with goblins—had been extremely negative and personally painful."

"I imagine they were." Gunther poked at his salad, seeming to consider and then discard some worrying thought before saying, "So when you cooked, did you work in other people's restaurants or did you have your own?"

"Other people's at first. I followed the tourists from place to place. Finally I managed to get the capital to open my own place—

a former diner with twenty seats and the ugliest gray linoleum ever manufactured."

"I sense this is when you had your first other-realm encounter," Gunther said.

"It wasn't for about a year. I busted my ass making that place. I was surprised that all my teeth didn't fall out from grinding. I got this gray streak during the opening." Keith touched his temple self-consciously. "I'm thinking of dyeing it. I'm only thirty-four."

Gunther shrugged. "Premature gray is standard in our line of work, I think."

Keith nodded. "Very true."

"You were telling me about how you joined NIAD," Gunther prompted.

"One day one of my customers came by with this special request. He had this family obligation. Some kind of religious feast he wanted me to cater. He'd provide the meat and all I had to do was cook it for this special summer banquet. I asked, 'what's the meat?' He told me it was special pork from Sweden."

Gunther nodded grimly. He took a forkful of salad.

"Right away I knew it wasn't pork. The bones were all wrong, but I needed the money and I just didn't think about it that hard."

"What did you think it was?"

"I honestly didn't know. Some endangered creature, I suppose. I figured if it was already dead it shouldn't go to waste, right?" Keith shook his head. "I was an idiot."

"You weren't an idiot. You just didn't know what you were dealing with."

"Even without the extra-human angle I knew there was something sketchy about that meat and I went ahead and cooked it anyway. I used to try and figure out what it had been. I ran down all those endangered Chinese delicacies, trying to figure it out—looking at the bones of sun bears—seeing if they matched. And I knew for a goddamn fact it had to be illegal, but the money was too good to say no. I kept thinking, 'At least I'm not dealing coke, right?' It never occurred to me to look at the bones of one of the most widely dispersed animals on the planet."

"How did you figure it out?"

"I got a piece of protein that had some skin attached and found a tattoo. No caribou, cow, or sun bear tattoos *Mom* on their arm." Keith wiped his lips with his napkin.

"Had you eaten the flesh?"

"Of course I'd eaten it. How was I supposed to tell how it tasted without eating it? I'd eaten a lot of it."

Gunther sat in silence. An unspoken question within him. Since Keith knew exactly what the question was, he said, "It's okay. You can ask me. Everybody asks me."

"How did it taste?"

"Really delicious." Keith pushed his soup plate away. The spinach, chard, and escarole soup had gone down easier than he expected, considering the conversation. "The best meat I ever ate. The last meat I ever ate, as it turns out."

Gunther, too, finished his first course and set his fork aside. "That doesn't explain how you got involved with the Irregulars."

"No." Keith waited politely for the slim, pleasant-seeming waitress to take his plate before continuing. "I reported what I'd found to the police and a couple of agents contacted me. They wanted to set up a sting operation and I agreed. That's how I found out that my customers were goblins."

"That must have been a shock."

"Finding out that everything I'd previously believed to be a myth was a pretty big shock, yeah. During that time, the agents assigned to the case communicated with me extensively. They and I both realized that there wasn't anyone at NIAD who had specific knowledge of cooking or restaurants, while at the same time, there was still this problem with human-sourced protein. I suppose the agents who contacted me had planned to recruit me from the moment that they introduced themselves, but I'm not disappointed. I do good work. Important work."

"Don't you miss cooking?"

Keith found himself smiling. Melancholy drifted through him. "I do miss it. I miss the companionship of the kitchen, the creative aspect...I suppose what I miss most is the solvability of all problems."

"How do you mean?"

"Well, when you're cooking during a dinner service, it's a pass-fail situation. Either you get the food out right and on time or you don't. Problems don't linger. At the end of the night you've done all you could and tomorrow is another day where you get a fresh chance at success, no matter how big the fail might have been on the previous day."

"I see," Gunther said, nodding. "Our job is not like that at all."

"No, it isn't." Keith folded his hands, observing the sunset across the bay. "It's not so bad though. I'm the first and only specialist in the detection of contraband food items. I like the idea that I can make a difference."

They spent the rest of the meal engaging in the sort of harmless chat that they'd never bothered to make before. He found out that Gunther's high-school track specialty had been hurdles and that he had majored in sociology with a minor in anthropology before signing up with NIAD.

Finally, during coffee and dessert, Keith got the courage to ask the one question he wanted answered.

"So why exactly did you call off our previous arrangement?"

"You made a few offhanded comments about goblins that I didn't care for," Gunther said simply. "At the time, I was offended. I couldn't say I was offended because I hadn't told you about myself, so I just called it off."

"Why invite me to lunch today then?"

"I guess I just remembered how sexy you are. And I felt like I'd been unfair."

Keith drained the last of his coffee. He tried to remember what he might have said that could have been offensive. With no small degree of horror, he realized that he'd said plenty. Shame verging on mortification churned through his chest.

"I don't want to sound like I'm making excuses for myself, but I wasn't all that stable at the time. I was still in the humans versus monsters mindset."

"Yes, I remember." Gunther's expression remained neutral, even somewhat blank.

"I guess what I'm trying to say is that I'm sorry if what I said hurt you. I'm not all that smart and it takes me a while to adjust sometimes," Keith said. "But I do know it's not all cut and dried. I do now anyway."

"That's good to hear." Gunther glanced at his phone. "We should probably be getting back to the market if we want to use the portal."

❧

Back in Portland, the market was just wrapping up. Their rental had a parking ticket tucked lovingly under the windshield wiper. Keith stuffed it into his pocket to commune with the other three already crammed in there.

"Anything else on the agenda for this evening?" Gunther asked.

"On demand and a shower for me. Unless you feel up to interrogating vampires after nightfall. In which case you're free to take the rental." Keith wiggled the key fob at Gunther.

"Actually, I was hoping to borrow the car to pick up a box of legendary Bauer & Bullock feijoa jam *alfajores*. Apparently, they're the most addictive cookie ever made. I need to bring back a farewell gift for another agent."

"Someone retiring?" Keith had often wondered where old agents went to retire once their crime-fighting days were over.

"No, just moving. Promoted to directing the Vancouver field office. You might remember him from last year's Cookie Jamboree? His name was Rake? Great big fellow?"

Keith had a sharp recollection of an enormous hulk of a man hanging around near the cookie decorations eating sprinkles and silver dragees when he thought no one was looking.

"The mountain with the sweet tooth."

Gunther chuckled. "Right. He was my first partner when I was a rookie. He loves these cookies with a profane passion."

"I've never heard of them, but I'm not really a big bakery guy."

"They're actually sold at a steakhouse. It's supposed to have an excellent bar as well. If you'd like to come along, I'll buy you a drink for keeping me company."

Keith hesitated. Although he'd have never admitted it to anyone, Gunther scared him. And not just because he had turned out to be a goblin. Keith wanted Gunther and that desire had led him to break two cardinal rules he'd long held sacred—never date anybody twice and never stay friends with a guy who dumps you. Keith didn't want to be a chump all over again.

Apparently sensing his reluctance, Gunther said, "Or I could drop you off at the hotel if you'd like."

"Hotel sounds good. I'm beat." Keith tossed him the keys and headed to the passenger side.

As he pulled up to the curb in front of the hotel Gunther said, "I'll be having a drink there anyway. You could come by if you change your mind."

Keith gave a noncommittal nod and left.

Once he'd made it back to his hotel room and gotten through a dicey, but necessary, cold shower, he had time to regret his decision. He decided that, on closer reflection, he did want a drink.

Maybe, he thought, he could still catch Gunther at the steakhouse if he took a cab there.

Finding Bauer & Bullock's webpage was easy. It was splashy with a lot of photo carousels showing beef searing on different apparatuses. The one hundred and forty-three seat restaurant was apparently the choice for the Portland business diner looking to impress a client. Keith had always hated joints like these, even before he'd become a vegetarian. White guys in business suits eating slabs of meat and steak frites while talking about money always curtailed his appetite.

But Gunther had gone there, so now Keith wanted to be there too. He decided to check out the bar menu.

Pleasantly, though somewhat predictably, the website informed him that the bar stocked over five hundred different whiskies. He picked up his phone and was just about to dial Gunther when the image on the carousel changed from a sizzling grill to a photograph of the owner.

The face was familiar but her name even more so: Cindy Bullock, wife of Trent Bullock, whom Keith had arrested for cannibalism less than a year before.

He decided to pass on the whisky after all.

Chapter Four

Gunther arrived at Keith's hotel room early the next day. The coffee maker had just started to gurgle and fill the hotel room with the scent of morning. Keith had neither dressed nor shaved and still wore the ragged old Misfits T-shirt and shorts he'd slept in.

"I just got an email from the lab." Gunther set his laptop down on the small hotel desk. "The blood sample taken from the mop head at Lulu's Flapjack Shack contained a mixture of human and bovine blood," he said.

"So the killer is stretching one with the other?" Keith set about making coffee.

"Or there might have been two separate sources of blood," Gunther said. "In addition to that, traces of methotrexate were present throughout the fibers, which would indicate that it has been combined with the blood mixture," Gunther went on.

"Is that some sort of exotic new food additive?"

"It's a prescription drug used to treat rheumatoid arthritis."

"Weird." Keith hunted through the cupboards for coffee cups. "I don't know what to make of that at all."

"Nor do I."

"Did you get your cookies?"

"Last box of the night," Gunther said.

"How did the restaurant seem?" Keith poured two cups of coffee and pulled the room's remaining chair up alongside his partner.

"Busy. Crowded bar." Gunther glanced up. "I sat down and had a superb whisky sour. When you failed to appear to keep me company I decided to while away the time google-stalking you on my phone."

"Why?"

"Idle curiosity." Gunther's response came with such flirtatious ease that Keith initially mistook it for sarcasm.

"Did you stumble across anything good?"

"Your freshman yearbook photo. And a fine mullet you had then too. I particularly like the vaguely stoned look on your face and the ripped Whitesnake concert tee." Gunther looked pointedly at Keith's Misfits shirt. "Good to know you haven't changed too much."

Keith momentarily choked, embarrassed by the accuracy of the statement, but he recovered. "I was also wearing red parachute pants, but you can't see those."

"Nice." Gunther smiled. "Do you still listen to metal?"

"Sometimes." Keith took a sip of his coffee. Too harsh. He returned to the counter to swirl more sugar in.

"I always wanted to make some kind of rebellious adolescent statement on school photo day but never had the nerve," Gunther said. "I was always afraid that if I was anything but absolutely harmless and normal I'd be found out, charged with breaking the Secrecy Act, and sent away."

Keith was ashamed to realize that he'd never thought of what it must be like to grow up with that kind of isolation. Sure, he'd had the experience of hiding the fact that he was gay from people, but that was different. At any point he'd had the freedom to tell anyone which gender he preferred to sleep with. The Secrecy Act mandated silence on pain of deportation.

Lamely, Keith said, "That must have been rough."

"It's a unique way to experience childhood." Gunther's tone told him nothing.

"Don't feel bad. My wearing a Whitesnake T-shirt was more an act of laziness than rebellion."

"For you, maybe, but my mother dressed me in slacks and a tie every day of my freshman year," Gunther said. "My classmates all thought I was a Mormon."

"I imagine you learned to fight pretty early, dressed like that."

"Some, but I also became adept at hiding other clothes in my backpack and changing in gas station bathrooms." Gunther punched a couple of keys and entered the NIAD database. "I never really had to learn to fight so much as how not to kill people. Humans are fragile."

Keith's discomfort rose to an intolerable level. He wondered what offhanded remarks he had made about goblins. Had he called them butchers? Animals? Sick fucks? Any or all of those pejoratives was possible. He hadn't been in a good way when he'd met Gunther before—angry and full of rancor.

He sat down on the bed and said, "I did look up the address of the bar you were at."

"You did?" Gunther's expression brightened briefly before dimming again. "But you didn't come."

"It's not because of you," Keith said quickly. "It's because of the restaurant's owner. Bring up Trent Bullock's file in the NIAD base and you'll see what I mean."

Gunther complied and took a few minutes to read through the details of Keith's recent bust.

"So although the meat that these people had been eating was goblin sourced, the diners were all human?" Gunther finally asked.

"It surprised us too, but then after we reviewed supper club, we realized that these same sort of people whose demand fueled the mermaid flesh trade were branching out into this chic cannibalism. They were foodies gone very wrong."

"This is the case you were mentioning at the Flapjack Shack, wasn't it?"

"Yeah, it is. Bauer & Bullock is owned lock, stock, and barrel by Cindy Bullock, now Trent's ex-wife, since he went into Beaumont," Keith said.

"According to the file, Beaumont was just a stopover on his trip to the goblin high king's summer solstice table."

"As the main course, yeah," Keith said. "The wife was in Argentina researching sources for her new restaurant venture for the entire duration of my investigation. We had our South American counterparts monitor her movements while she was in their country, but her exploits were purely beef or beefcake related. We couldn't nail her on anything."

"Okay, so Bullock's widow is here slinging steaks. And?" Gunther asked.

"And it occurred to me that there are a few things we don't know about this case."

"Such as everything?" Gunther gave a derisive snort.

"Such as: where does the butchering take place?"

Gunther shook his head. "I don't know. I'm not sure anybody would risk the sentence for cannibalism if they actually knew the law and I'm fairly certain that Cindy Bullock is familiar with it."

"I'd like to say that I agree with you, but when it comes to carnal pleasures like food, people will risk anything. Trust me on this. I want to question Cindy and take a look around the restaurant kitchen if I can. Even if she isn't involved in these murders, I guarantee that she is still in contact with at least a few of her old cronies." Keith drained his coffee and stood to get himself another cup.

"All right, but apart from the Dallas connection, do we have any reason to question the Bullock woman?"

"At least three ex-employees have called her a bloodsucker and a harpy," Keith offered.

"Do we have any hard evidence of either of those?"

"No, and it's pretty common for an ex-employee to call their boss a bloodsucker."

"That is a very tenuous connection. I don't think any judge, even one who was in the Irregular loop, would issue a search warrant based on accusations of harpydom," Gunther remarked.

"I realize that, but I don't see any reason not to see if we can shake something out of her," Keith said. "We'll hit her place on the way back from the vampires. Did the lab happen to know anything about what methotrexate is used for aside from arthritis?"

"It's a very strong antimetabolite with potentially fatal side effects taken only by people in the advanced stages of rheumatoid arthritis or psoriasis. It's a human drug with no known magicial applications." Gunther paused, musing before he continued, "Maybe the victim was taking it. We could have a look at missing persons to see if any of them had a prescription for methotrexate. At least that way we might be able to identify one of the three unknown deceased, if nothing else."

"Can you do that in the car on the way to visit the vampires or would you like to stay back here?"

"My phone is mighty," Gunther said. "And I wouldn't want to send you off to visit vampires on your own."

"I'm twice as likely to be eaten by a shark as a vampire."

"While that is true, I'll just tag along anyway. After all, it only takes running across the right hungry individual and suddenly you find yourself contemplating lunch from the perspective of a hamburger."

"How do you know the vampire wouldn't just gobble you up as well?"

"I have it on the highest authority that vampires hate the taste of trans-goblin body fluids."

"Whose authority would that be?"

"Ex-boyfriend," Gunther said simply.

Keith gaped, unable to mask his sense of revulsion. Like most teenagers, Keith had once found vampires sexy. And why not? Films portrayed them, generally, as hot young people in leather. The true form of the vampire was more Nosferatu, less model-turned-actor. To Keith they resembled humanoid hagfish. Because of the necessity of hiding their extra-human nature from the population, all registered vampires wore glamours to disguise their pale, pointy faces and hide their bulbous eyes and round, jawless mouths.

The idea that Gunther had managed to have sex with one both fascinated and revolted him. Finally, he said, "I'm not sure I'm liberal enough to have a romance like that."

"You mean because of his true physical appearance?" Gunther asked.

"Right." *That*, Keith thought, *and the fact that you qualify as a main course to him.* Aloud he said, "Did you ever see it?"

"Yes, of course. But not often. He was self-conscious about his appearance, but it would have been shallow of me to insist he always disguise himself."

Shallow? Keith supposed so, but it might also be considered crucial by anyone who was made nervous by the prospect of sticking his dick into the mouth of a creature with more than a hundred and fifty razor-sharp teeth.

Gunther must have seen the skepticism on his face because he said, “I enjoy dating challenging men.”

“Why did you break up?”

“He insisted on polyamory,” Gunther answered. “That and he kept wanting me to call him ‘master’. Ultimately, I was not that interested in pursuing a vampire-style relationship. Too hierarchical for me.”

Chapter Five

The three registered vampires living in the Willamette Valley ran a business called Azalea Point Creamery. They produced goat-milk artisan cheeses sourced from their own, humanely pastured herd. As Keith's rented sedan moved up the long, tree-lined drive, Keith's proximity alert buzzed. Blinking green nine.

Keith shut it off. Gunther glanced up from his phone.

“These individuals have no priors,” he stated.

“I know. Procedure says I have to interview them, though, so here we are.”

“What's your feeling?”

“My gut says they don't have anything to do with it, but rules is rules and I've got to interview them anyway since evidence of exsanguination has been found.” Keith pulled up alongside a long, corrugated tin goat shed. Three farm hands were at work there, forking hay and soiled wood chips out of the shed. The goats seemed to be out back in an enclosure. He wondered if the farmhands knew about their employers' true nature. Most likely not.

Keith put the car in park. “Do you ever wonder why these guys come here?”

“The vampires?” Gunther kept his voice low. “Probably the same reason as everybody else. They want the chance for a better life.”

“I suppose so. It just seems like a lot to have to put up with—concealing your physical form, having agents routinely hassle you.”

Gunther shrugged. “It depends on what they had to put up with in their own realm, I guess.”

Keith casually unsnapped the holster of his mage pistol and said, "Well, I guess we should go wake them up."

The farm hands watched but did not intervene as the two of them walked to the front door and rang the bell. There came the slight whirring noise of the camera mounted above the door focusing and a groggy male voice on the intercom said, "Can I help you?"

"Joe Sounder?"

"Yes?"

"NIAD. We'd like to ask you a few questions." Keith held up his ID and the door popped open. They entered a small porch thickly hung with blackout curtains. Overhead lights switched on automatically. Gunther closed the door behind them. From a speaker somewhere above, Joe said, "Please make yourselves comfortable. I'll be right up."

Keith walked into the living room, which, apart from the blackout curtains, looked perfectly normal. He took a seat on the overstuffed beige couch. Gunther remained standing, apparently performing a survey of the numerous photographs of goats hung on the walls.

Joe appeared shortly thereafter. For his glamour he'd chosen the form of a fit, if slightly weathered, middle-aged man. His soft brown hair was rumpled, but attractively so. He wore a blue bathrobe over a set of striped flannel pajamas.

Keith introduced himself and Gunther.

Joe nodded, stretched, and scratched his head. "I was wondering when you fellows would be coming around. You want to ask me if I know anything about the Cannibal Killings, right?"

"Just a routine inquiry," Keith assured him. He glanced down at his black book. Joe was listed as having two concubines. "Are Julie and Janice also still residing at this address?"

"Janice is visiting one of her friends in Boise. Julie is still asleep downstairs, but I can wake her if you'd like." Joe started back toward the hallway.

"I don't think that will be necessary at the moment," Keith said. "Have you heard anything about the killings?"

"Just what's been on the news. We don't get into town much."

As Joe sat down the cuff of his pajamas rose up to expose Joe's ankle and reveal the plastic tracking device all registered vampires wore. Keith noted it. "I guess I just assumed it was goblins. They've been coming around here looking for meat for the summer solstice. I told them I don't raise meat goats."

"Do you know anything about this?" Keith displayed the Theater of Blood Carnival Circus flyer.

Joe shook his head and shrugged. "Looks like some kids playing monster to me."

"Tell me a little more about the goblins who came looking for meat," Gunther said. He stood with his hands in his coat pockets, looking genial and harmless. Clearly his interrogation technique was based on gaining trust rather than inspiring fear—just the opposite of Keith's.

"Every year we get inquiries. Mostly over the phone, but sometimes guys will come out here to the dairy right before solstice hoping to make a last-minute deal," Sounder said, chuckling. "They're the same kind of guys who shop for all their gifts on Christmas Eve, you know?"

Gunther nodded. "Some things are universal constants."

Keith scowled slightly. He was himself one of those eleventh-hour shoppers.

Sounder cocked his head to one side, thinking. "There were three of them who came around just recently though. Young guys. I thought it was strange, them being so young."

Gunther nodded, then pulled out his phone and, after a few moments, turned the screen toward Sounder. "Is this one of the guys who came by?"

Keith didn't know why he was surprised to see Lancelot's face smiling out of Gunther's phone. He had been just about to show Sounder a photo of Lancelot himself. He shouldn't have supposed that Gunther would be a less thorough investigator than himself, but somehow he had.

He supposed he did still have some issues with goblins after all, if his unconscious assumption was that because of his race, Gunther wouldn't pursue all avenues of inquiry impartially.

The thought sobered Keith. He hadn't considered himself to contain the capacity for bigotry.

Sounder peered at Lancelot's picture carefully, squinting slightly against the backlit screen.

"Yeah, he was one of them," Sounder replied. "Seemed like a little bit of a kook."

"Can you remember exactly what he said when he came?" Keith leaned slightly forward, keen to catch the inferences of Sounder's delivery. Glamours made reading body language difficult, but the sound of a person's voice often communicated information the glamour erased.

"Well, let's see…They asked how much it would cost for two whole goats. I told them that we didn't sell meat goats, like I told you. And then the kooky one wanted to know if I ever heard of any vampires who drank blood on stage."

"On stage?" Gunther gave Keith a sidelong look.

Sounder nodded. "It was a really strange question. That's why I remember it."

"It does seem somewhat random," Keith remarked. "Why do you think he wanted to know?"

"I have no idea," Sounder said.

"What did you tell him?" Gunther asked.

"I told him that only an idiot would risk a run-in with NIAD over something like that, and I don't associate with idiots." Sounder shifted on the sofa and stifled a yawn. "Not if I can help it, anyway."

"And then?" Keith prompted.

"Then they left," Sounder said. He flashed a faint smile. "I think they might have been offended."

❧

During the drive back to Portland, neither he nor Gunther spoke too much. Keith was sunk in his own thoughts. Interviewing the vampires, which had seemed to him to be borderline harassment at first, had yielded a piece of information after all. Goblins had been there looking for meat. The arrows were all lining up and all confirming Keith's original suspicions.

He supposed Gunther's silence could also be attributed to this information.

They made good time and got into the city and to the Bauer & Bullock Steakhouse right in the thick of the dinner service.

Stepping into the dining room, Keith was struck by both the smell—searing flesh—and the décor—the predictable, yet still imposing combination of dark wooden paneling, leather, and massive proportions. The whole place looked like a supersized fantasy of an old-time gentlemen's club. Even the silverware was slightly too large.

Keith made his way to the host station, where he very discretely flashed his badge at a fragile-looking young host and asked to see the manager. It would do no good to antagonize the staff, especially if this turned out to be a dead end.

The busboy disappeared upstairs, only to return a few seconds later, Cindy Bullock in tow.

Bullock was a skinny, stylish woman with kinky blond hair and long, bony arms on which she wore a multitude of designer bangles. She took one look at Keith, crossed her arms, and said, "Agent Curry," by way of greeting.

"Hello, Ms. Bullock," Keith went on, undeterred. "This is my associate, Gunther Heartman. We'd like to ask you a few questions."

"About?"

"About your meat supplier," Keith said. "Who might that be?"

Cindy's expression darkened. "We serve grass-fed organic beef sourced from USDA certified local ranchers. You can read all about them on our menu. Additional information can be found on the website."

Keith jotted down the address of the website in his black book, though he already had it. He wrote slowly and precisely. He wanted Cindy to squirm a little. She clenched her hands. The large rings on her fingers glittered.

"You have a really impressive selection of whiskies," Gunther commented.

Cindy's initial bright response at being complimented dimmed with suspicion. "Yes, we have a discerning clientele."

"Do you do much catering?" Keith swept in with another question.

"A fair amount," Cindy replied.

"So you've got, what? Three jobs a week?" Keith asked.

"I'd have to look at my calendar. It's upstairs in the office if you'd like to follow me."

"Actually, what I'd really like to take a look at is your kitchen." Keith started for the kitchen door. Cindy rushed ahead of him.

"I'd really rather you didn't go back right now, Agent Curry. You know we're right in the middle of dinner service. If you could just wait—"

"Oh, I won't be in the way," Keith said. "I've been a chef. I know how to keep out of the way."

Cindy placed herself between him and the kitchen door. She flung her arms out, bracelets jangling, ringed fingers flashing. "I must insist, Agent Curry. You have no right to go back there. This is my place. You have no right!"

A dishwasher who had been rounding the corner carrying a rack of clean plates stopped, reflexively backtracking at the sight of Cindy in what looked like full rage.

Keith's lip curled in disgust. Why was it that the completely insane gravitated so heavily into the hospitality industry? "Listen, ma'am, I can go get a warrant if you want, but I assure you that you don't want me coming in here during dinner service with a bunch of uniformed officers, right?"

"Are you threatening me?" Cindy lunged forward, skinny body flexing like a viper preparing to strike. "I know why you are harassing me."

"Neither Agent Heartman nor myself is attempting to harass you. All we'd like to do is have a look at where you do your butchering. That's all." Keith kept his tone calm, businesslike. "We can go get a warrant if you like, but all I need to do is look at your product."

"Well, you can't." Cindy crossed her arms, raising her chin triumphantly. "I won't let you because I don't have to and you know it."

Keith shrugged. "If that's the way you want to play it, ma'am, then we will. I'll be back with a warrant, a health inspector, and a representative from the state liquor board. I might bring an auditor just to get it all over with at once." He turned and started toward the door. He needed to get out of this joint anyway. The smell of char-grilled meat was beginning to seriously nauseate him. He saw a slight motion out of the corner of his eye.

"Son of a bitch!" With a jangle of expensive bangles Bullock smashed her fist directly into his jaw. He staggered back a step, pain exploding through the side of his face. In a moment, Gunther had caught her right arm, but she still lashed out with her left, raking her nails across his neck.

"That is really uncalled for, ma'am," Gunther said, tightly twisting her arm around her back and slapping one handcuff on. He caught hold of her left hand and managed to get it in the cuff, but Bullock bolted. Keith stuck out a foot and hooked her ankle. She went down, screaming and cursing, on the damp tiled floor. Gunther wasted no time; he cuffed her ankles, then brought them up and hogtied her.

The kitchen had gone silent as the whole kitchen crew gaped at the scene. The dishwasher seemed to be working hard to suppress a smile.

Gunther leaned down and said very loudly and very close to her ear, "You are under arrest for assaulting a federal officer." Then, to Keith, he said, "You want to go have that look around now or wait till the police get here?"

"Yeah, sure." His jaw throbbed. He glanced at the dishwasher. "Show me to the meat locker, kid."

The dishwasher led the way back into the kitchen. They passed a busy line of grills. Flames and smoke leaped and billowed around the cooks as they tended the orders. Then they entered the back kitchen—a small, clean space whose walls were lined with steel prep tables and banks of shelves holding dry goods.

"The big one's right there." Tentatively the dishwasher pointed back toward a heavy door. "But there's another smaller one for the really expensive steaks that's padlocked."

"Who's got the key?"

"It's a combo lock." This came from a burly Black guy who had followed them from the line. Keith thought he might be the head grill man. "Ms. Bullock is the only one who knows it."

"Of course it is."

After a wait of approximately ten minutes, Portland Police Bureau arrived with a car to transport Ms. Bullock and a pair of bolt cutters for the padlock. Being a member of the strike force, Gunther could have probably performed a spell to open it, but there were far too many bystanders and it was just easy to use a human tool. By the time PPB carried Bullock away, the deep bruise on Keith's jaw had begun to darken, but he refused to show any pain in front of the restaurant's staff. There was still no way to tell where any of their allegiances lay.

Keith entered the meat locker. He already felt ill. Very quickly he found himself fighting to avoid retching. Two naked bodies hung suspended upside down from chains, throats cut, blood collecting in buckets on the floor.

To the left, on a stainless steel rack, were more remains. This one had been skinned, cut apart at the joints, and separated into several metal hotel pans, but Keith recognized the anatomy immediately.

Gunther's cookie search had led them straight to the abattoir. Plainly, the butchering had taken place here. For all his commentary about humans not abandoning their carnal pleasures easily, Keith would have never seriously thought that Bullock's wife would have the sheer stupidity to continue her Thyestean feasting after her husband had been caught. Yet, here she was.

Keith stepped back outside for some air. Gunther waited outside.

"From your face I gather that you've found something?"

"Have a look for yourself," Keith suggested.

Gunther held up a demurring hand. "I trust you. What do you want to do now?"

Keith scanned the faces of the kitchen staff and of the servers who were looking anxiously on. It would be impossible for all of members of staff to be innocent. Cindy Bullock's manicure made it clear that she never picked up a kitchen knife.

"Put a uniform on this door, clear the dining room, and call for a paddy wagon. We're detaining and questioning all staff. We'll also need to find the names of any not on shift tonight and have PPB bring them down to the station. Particularly the butchers. Someone with skills skinned those carcasses. I'm thinking we're looking for one front of the house person and one or two members of kitchen staff who were in on it with Ms. Bullock."

Gunther gave a slight salute and departed the back kitchen. Keith walked up to the line but didn't walk through. Each and every one of those five guys had at least one knife. Plus, they'd be more cooperative if he respected both their territory and hierarchy. He held up his badge. "My name is Keith Curry. I'm a federal agent. Who is the person in charge here?"

Unsurprisingly, it was the Black guy who had spoken first. His name turned out to be Baratunde and he was the chef. He outweighed Keith by at least forty pounds but seemed overall even tempered. "I need to ask you to shut this down and bring your people out to the dining room to be interviewed."

"What about the tickets?" He indicated the unmade orders with a wave of his tongs.

Keith shook his head. "Shut it down. For tonight, anyway. We're already clearing the customers. This is a crime scene."

The other man nodded slowly. Behind him, Keith could see one of the cooks texting someone. "And I'm going to ask to hold your phones for the time being, starting with his."

Baratunde whipped his head around to fix the young cook with a glare. "Damn it, Jesse. Bring that here. Haven't you got any sense?"

Jesse cowered as he handed over the phone. "I was just texting my girlfriend to say I'd be late, chef."

"Your woman can wait."

Keith found it sentimentally amusing that as an agent he inspired less fear than the chef.

Baratunde collected the phones into a square plastic refrigerator insert. As he handed them to Keith, he said, "Jesse's just a dumb kid, sir. He wasn't trying to disrespect you."

"Sure, I understand." He waved the chef into the back kitchen where they could have relative privacy.

"I'm going to ask you straight out. Have you ever been in this locker?"

"No, sir. It's Ms. Bullock's private refrigerator. No staff is allowed in there."

Keith leaned back against a stainless steel prep table. "You and I both know that somebody must be allowed in. Ms. Bullock is not cooking for herself."

This drew a slight smile from Baratunde.

"Not my staff." The chef's tone was final. "None of my boys have ever stepped foot in there."

"Who then?"

"There's a private catering company that uses this space on Monday nights when the restaurant is closed. Forbidden Pleasures, I think they're called."

Of course, Keith thought. "Do they share all this equipment?"

The chef nodded. "It's part of their rental contract. They clean up fine, but they're hell on the knives."

"Do you have contact information for this company?"

"No, sir. We're not allowed on the property on Mondays. Not even me."

"Did you ever think that maybe Ms. Bullock was hiding something?"

"Sure," the chef said. "Look at that big-ass lock."

"What do you think is in that refrigerator?"

"Heroin." The answer came without pause and with certainty. "Or maybe coke. Some kind of drugs anyway."

Keith nodded thoughtfully. That is exactly what he would have assumed in this guy's position. He said, "Do you read the newspaper?"

Baratunde's eyes narrowed slightly. "Sometimes. I'm more of a talk radio man, though."

"Have you heard anything about the Cannibal Killer?"

The chef's face paled to the color of ash. He swallowed and said, "Some."

"Inside that walk-in, lying in stainless hotel pans that you probably use every day, are the butchered remains of at least three people," Keith said. "You can see how I want to know more about this catering company that shares your kitchen, right?"

The chef did not immediately answer. Keith wondered briefly if he had misjudged Baratunde. Maybe he truly had been complicit. Then, with no warning, the man lunged sideways and puked loudly into the trash can. The uniform didn't look very much more well, but he, at least, hadn't been eating off the same dishes used to process human protein. Keith waited while the chef splashed his face with water and stood, leaning on the hand sink, breathing deeply. Finally, he said, "Sometimes the caterers have leftovers that they leave in our refrigerator for the staff to eat."

The cause of Baratunde's abrupt illness became sharply clear. "And?"

"This morning they left some posole in our walk-in. I—for lunch—" Tears rimmed the chef's eyes. Whether they were the result of impending further illness or horrifying remorse, Keith could not say.

"Is there any left?"

Baratunde nodded. "Ms. Bullock and I were the only ones who ate any. Nobody else wanted hominy. She kept talking about how back in the day the dish was made with human flesh."

"You better show me. We'll need to test it."

"I just need a second." He leaned far over the sink, jaw working, plainly fighting the urge to vomit again.

Keith said, "Take your time."

It only took Baratunde a few deep breaths to recover before he was able to lead Keith into the main walk-in, a long, narrow space. It was supremely clean and well organized. The chef plainly took pride in his profession.

"This is it." He handed Keith a long insert of quasi-congealed stew, taking obvious care not to touch the contents.

Gunther ducked into the walk-in. "We've got the dining room cleared."

"Thanks." Keith glanced at him and then at the chef, whose eyes were still glassy. The big man's hands shook slightly. Keith remained placid while he removed a small vial from his pocket.

He pulled a piece of flesh from the stew and squeezed a couple of drops of tincture onto it. The tincture shone blue. He looked at the chef and said, "It's pork. We should keep it anyway. The container might have prints we can use."

The relief that swept across Baratunde's face was that of a condemned man released at the last minute.

"Thank the Lord."

"I'd appreciate it if you'd go and see how your crew is doing."

"Yes, sir." He went, smiling.

The second the door closed, Keith crumpled the meat in a napkin, whispering, "I'm sorry—whoever you were."

Gunther drew closer. "I thought blue meant human."

Keith nodded. "The chef doesn't need to know that though. He doesn't need to have that knowledge on him for the rest of his life—that he's a cannibal. It's bad enough that he's going to lose his job when this joint shuts down. Working here isn't going to be a resume builder, either. We'll still send it to the lab—just for documentation. And prints, like I said."

Gunther said, "Do you need a minute?"

"No, let's just go get this over with."

Chapter Six

Interviews at Bauer & Bullock went quickly. Few staff knew much about Forbidden Pleasures. Keith called it quits around nine, when his jaw started hurting him too much to pay attention to their uninformative answers. He decided to save Bullock's interview for the morning, when he was less tired and after she'd spent the night in jail.

Once they reached the hotel, Gunther went to the ice machine to make up a pack for Keith while Keith himself poured two vodka shots and drank them both in quick succession.

Returning with a softball-sized bag of ice, wrapped in a clean white towel, Gunther said, "By the way, it was bison."

"No, the carcass in the fridge was human. Trust me." Keith held the ice pack to his jaw, wincing at the cold against his tender flesh.

"I mean the preferred protein at my family's midsummer meal. It was bison. You asked and I never answered." Gunther sat down beside him on the bed. Keith's proximity alarm buzzed and buzzed again, warning him of Gunther's closeness. He pulled it off and threw it on the nightstand. He didn't need the watch to know how near the other man sat. Every part of Keith's body seemed to be responding to the nearness—to the smell of Gunther's faintly spicy cologne, to the knowledge of his sheer masculinity.

He needed to get laid and that was a fact.

Gunther said quietly, "Is your jaw hurting you a lot?"

"It hurts enough." The bruise did hurt, but if he was honest, the real wound had been mainly to his pride. He said, "Getting hit by a crazy, slap-happy bitch isn't what I wanted from this evening."

"I admit I had other hopes as well." After this remark, Gunther lay back and fell silent. Keith glanced sideways, wondering if the other man had somehow fallen asleep. His eyes were closed, his fingers laced behind his head. His abdomen rose and fell slowly. His expression had softened. His mouth looked supremely kissable. Keith imagined himself leaning over and tasting Gunther's mouth, wondering if the taste of tobacco still lingered there.

And for so many reasons that was the stupidest impulse Keith had had in years.

Without opening his eyes Gunther said, "Are you hungry?"

"I'll make myself some grilled cheese in a minute."

"That's pretty much the only thing you eat now, isn't it?"

"Pretty much."

Gunther shook his head. "It doesn't seem like that could possibly be good for you."

"Says the man who ate two and a half packs of cigarettes today."

"I didn't say my diet was good. I'm just saying that you might want to take a multivitamin."

"I ate an orange last week," Keith said. "Grilled cheese is easy when you're cooking for one."

"Why don't you include me in your dinner plans then?"

"I don't cook meat anymore." Keith felt like a complete weakling admitting this but also knew that Gunther probably didn't truly understand how pathetic this made him seem in the professional cooking world.

"I didn't say it had to be meat." Gunther opened his eyes, regarding Keith with a steadiness that made him look away.

"You're a goblin. Meat is what you want."

"You know we prefer to be called Luminous Ones. And I think we don't know each other well enough for you to know what it is that I want."

"You're telling me that your favorite food isn't meat?"

Gunther shrugged. "When I was a little kid my favorite food was Christmas lights. I used to eat them right off the string like candy."

"You're shitting me."

"Not at all. My godfather used to bribe me with them so I'd stop sucking all the butane out of his lighter. So while it's true that I haven't eaten many vegetables, I'm feeling very game today. So how about it?"

"I don't really want to cook," Keith said.

"What do you want to do then?"

"I don't know."

"You must want something."

Though he knew Gunther was still talking about their dinner plans, Keith felt so demoralized and tired and maybe slightly drunk from the vodka shot on an empty stomach that he found himself saying, "What I want, Heartman, is to fuck you and not have to talk about it afterward."

Gunther didn't immediately respond and Keith realized he'd gone too far so he added, "That's just about the only thing that would make me feel okay about today."

Gunther sat up and then stood up. Keith stared down at the mottled brown carpet, expecting the other man to take his coat and go. He heard the rustle of fabric.

Soon I'll hear the click of a hotel door closing, Keith thought. Instead he just heard more rustling. He glanced up and to his astonishment realized that Gunther had shed his sport coat and tie. His cuffs hung, unfastened, while he worked the buttons of his dress shirt open.

Stupidly, Keith asked, "What are you doing?"

Gunther pulled a slow smile, looking him straight in the eye as he shrugged out of his shirt. He wore a white undershirt that molded to his flat abdomen. His biceps and forearms bulged, angular masses of muscle. "I'm preparing to make you feel better about today."

Keith gave a dry laugh. "Okay, nice one. You got me. How about we get Thai takeout from that joint around the corner?"

"Afterward." Gunther stepped out of his shoes and unbuckled his belt.

With a weird mix of pleasure and fear, Keith realized Gunther wasn't joking. He said, "I don't have anything…for that."

"I do. Inside pocket of my overcoat." He dropped his pants. Even in white boxer-briefs and black dress socks, Gunther looked amazing. He didn't keep either of those on for very much longer, though. Nor did his undershirt remain in place. Naked, Gunther's pale body seemed like it could have been cut from paper. His legs were heavily roped with muscle. Though his chest was mostly bare, a fine line of dark hair ran from his navel to his groin. His cock, like the rest of him, seemed perfectly proportioned. Long, uncut, and resting on a pair of the most even testicles Keith had ever seen.

Gunther stepped closer. Keith set his ice pack aside and rested his hands on Gunther's hips.

Gunther shuddered and murmured, "Chilly."

"Sorry." Keith ran his palms up over Gunther's abdomen, then around to his back, sliding down over his round ass, the tips of his fingers lightly brushing the tender inside flesh.

Keith watched Gunther's face as he gently explored Gunther's body. "You really were perfectly made."

"Through no effort of my own, unfortunately. But thank you." Gunther rested his hands on Keith's shoulders, spreading his legs slightly, allowing Keith greater access. Gunther's cock was fully erect now, the head bobbing very near Keith's face. He nuzzled the shaft, cheek pressed against Gunther's abdomen.

Gunther said, "I hope you will invite me into your bed soon."

"In a minute." Keith caught the head of Gunther's cock, sucking it, tasting it. Now that he knew Gunther was trans-goblin he half expected some vile Zippo fuel flavor to assault his senses and kill his desire. But Gunther tasted just like he had before. He tasted just like he looked—perfectly human, while simultaneously being inhumanly perfect. Gunther arched into him, just slightly.

Keith stood and nibbled Gunther's lower lip, sampling that flavor too, though he'd never truly forgotten it. How could he? Spicy, fragrant, rich, and slippery. Luscious as drawn butter. Gunther's lips parted, soft and passive to Keith's explorations. His hands rested lightly on Keith's sides, as if they were waiting to receive a permission slip before even attempting to touch Keith's chest.

Keith supposed that that was exactly what Gunther was waiting for, given Keith hadn't even loosened his tie. Cheek pressed against Gunther's throat, he said, "Lay down with me."

Gunther said nothing. He merely climbed onto the mattress and stretched out on his stomach as he had numerous times in the past.

At the small of his back, Gunther had a tattoo. A small triangular blackwork design with a point that dipped down toward the cleft of his ass. It was just about the last thing Keith expected to ever have the pleasure of seeing again, but once he did, he could not get his clothes off fast enough.

Face resting on his folded arms, Gunther watched. He said, "I have a condom in my inside jacket pocket."

Keith picked up the jacket, felt inside the pocket, and laid the foil packet on the bedside table, along with a small tube of lube. He lay down next to Gunther and ran his hand along the other man's back till he reached the tattoo. He traced the inked lines, wondering what, if anything, they meant.

Keith had tattoos of his own. He'd never met a chef who didn't. His were slightly more embarrassing, though piecemeal, work that dotted his body like pictures scattered from a scrapbook. On his right shoulder, a Jolly Roger from his pirate phase—on his left, a Celtic maze, and on his inside left forearm, a line of black stars stretching from his wrist to inner elbow—a remnant from his club period.

"I always liked this." Keith gently traced the lines of Gunther's tattoo.

"It's goblin script." Gunther looked slightly embarrassed. "It's how you write the word 'love.' I got it on my eighteenth birthday."

Keith chuckled, ran his hand down over the curve of Gunther's buttock. "And you say you're not rebellious."

"It's my one and only display. I'd seen a picture online of a man who had a tattoo right there and I thought it was beautiful so that's what I got. Imagine my surprise when it turned out to be called a tramp stamp." Gunther smiled up at him from under his lashes. "Will you still kiss me?"

"Why not?" Keith bent to press his mouth against Gunther's. The other man's lips were hot and soft and supple. Keith didn't think he'd ever kissed a man who seemed so relaxed and willing to let him take the lead. The very compliance seemed suspicious. Why in the world had Gunther taken his ludicrous bait? Had their positions been reversed, Keith would never have offered his own body—especially not to a guy like himself, with such questionable views and obvious anger issues. It seemed impossible that they should be here together this way. And yet, here they were.

By nature Keith was not a rough or aggressive lover. He never had been. He'd played at it, sure. Lied about it to the straight guys he worked with who didn't really understand that being gay wasn't about plundering ass after ass after ass—not to him anyway. He'd bragged with some bravado over slaying this or that twink at the bar. But inside he'd never thought about sex that way and he couldn't think about it that way now. He gave it his best, turning the ritual of condom and lube into teasing play, taking time to make sure Gunther was comfortable, relaxed, and overall eager to accept him into his body. Keith murmured small compliments, telling Gunther how beautiful his body was—how hot inside—as he lay, chest pressed to Gunther's back, fingers entwined with his temporary partner's, hands flexing and contracting, mirroring the push and pulling of their bodies.

Gunther responded with more generosity, if it was possible to supersede the hospitality of allowing Keith within his body.

Keith wound his arm around Gunther. Feeling Gunther's questing hand, he laced their fingers together once more.

Friction became slick heat and he could no longer tell where his skin ended and Gunther's began. Dizzying scents and sensations flowed through him. The carnal pleasure of Gunther's skin far exceeded anything he'd ever known before or since he'd last had this man. Whether it was a trick of his goblin flesh or actual love, Keith did not know and he did not care. He thrust into Gunther's responsive flesh, kissing and consuming him as if he'd been starved and alone for years only to stumble upon some lush, wild bacchanalia.

No number of kisses or fevered thrusts seemed adequate to slake Keith's craving. He longed to consume Gunther utterly, selfishly. Gunther bucked back against him, then began a tense and shuddering climax. The beauty of seeing Gunther's pleasure, feeling the other man's delicious hunger, drove Keith to the blinding, inarticulate edge of sheer avarice. Then all at once ecstasy was upon him, rolling through his taut muscles, drawing tears from his eyes.

Afterward, Keith lay alongside Gunther and drifted, waking only briefly when Gunther rose, collected his clothes, and silently departed.

Chapter Seven

Keith was up and out the door at six the next morning. As was his habit, he walked the block and a half to Whole Foods and bought a doughnut. But rather than returning immediately to the hotel, he found himself, for the first time, pacing the aisles. Soon he had an armful of ingredients—eggs, heavy cream, milk, butter, spinach, nutmeg, gruyère, which he toted back to the hotel in a newly purchased green reusable bag. Without allowing himself to think about what he was doing, he began to cook. First came the crepes, completed one at a time and layered with sheets of waxed paper to keep them from sticking together. After that he prepped creamed spinach filling and grated gruyère. He brewed coffee. He waited, surfing through television channels until his proximity alert informed him that Gunther had exited the elevator. Then he bounced to his feet and began to assemble breakfast, filling the first crepe before he heard a knock.

Gunther's manner was exactly the same as it had been the previous day. No casual observer would have suspected from looking at Gunther that they had made love less than twelve hours ago in this very bed.

Really, the only person displaying a change of behavior was himself.

Keith decided not to think about that at all.

"Want some breakfast?" he said. "I made crepes."

Gunther smiled. "Yes, please."

"Do you like spinach?"

"I've never really had a spinach crepe before, but I probably do. So far I like everything except banana pudding."

Keith folded filling into the four remaining crepes and handed the plate to Gunther, along with a fork.

"Aren't you going to have any?" Gunther asked.

"I already had a donut."

"So you made these specially for me?"

"I wanted to cook something this morning." Keith knew that this wasn't really an answer, but he wasn't ready to actually think about an answer either. He didn't want to plumb the murky depths of his own motivations. It was perfectly reasonable to want to make breakfast for a man you had sex with the previous night. The urge toward hospitality contained no special significance. And yet, he found himself carefully scrutinizing Gunther's reaction.

Again, nothing special. He was a chef. Chefs all wanted to know how their food had been received. He paid no special attention to Gunther, nor should he.

If he told himself this enough times, Keith thought, certainly he would eventually believe it.

Suddenly, Gunther glanced up, noting Keith's stare. "These are amazing, but I really feel awkward eating them all alone."

"I'll get myself some coffee." Keith rose, poured himself a cup, and to change the conversation, asked, "So do you know many other gay goblins?"

"Trans-goblins," Gunther corrected, then added, "No, hardly any. During the transformation process virtually anything can be determined about a baby. Few parents want to give their child an orientation that will make their human lives less easy. My parents were the exception to this rule."

"Are you telling me that you were made gay on purpose?" Goblins, Keith thought, truly were a breed apart. Apart from common sense, mainly. But then he caught himself in his own disturbing condemnation. Why shouldn't parents want a gay child? Goblin or not?

"My parents thought my godfather was the ideal human, so they wanted me to be as much like him as possible. I joined NIAD to follow in his footsteps. You've probably heard of him. Half-Dead Henry?"

"The Undead Bum?" The words leaped from Keith's mouth before he could jam his foot in to stop them from escaping. "I mean—"

"No, you got it right: the Undead Bum." Gunther took a forkful of crepe and chewed it thoughtfully. "You remind me of him, somewhat."

"How's that?" Keith tried to keep his tone neutral, but he couldn't help but be slightly offended by being compared to a famous hobo.

"Your tattoos. The way you don't seem to be able express yourself emotionally. And your terrible diet. Henry eats cold chili right out of the can. Are you sure you won't have this last crepe? They're very good."

Keith hesitated, on the edge of turning back from a second

refusal. Again that unthinking inspiration struck and he just said, "I would, but I'm too lazy right now to lift a fork."

"I could feed it to you," Gunther said. "That's what you want me to do, isn't it?"

"God, no. I'm not a little kid. Give me that." Keith took the plate and fork and ate the crepe in six bites. It tasted better than he expected. He wiped his mouth and, finding Gunther staring at him, leaned across the table and quickly kissed him.

"Are you—"

Keith held up a silencing hand. "I haven't changed my mind about talking about it."

"I didn't think you had. I was about to ask if you wanted to question Bullock now."

"I think it's about time. Is she still at PPB or was she moved to the NIAD detention facility?" Keith asked.

"I'll call." Gunther did so. Keith listened absently, while finishing the dishes. He heard Gunther say, "I see."

Gunther's tone alarmed him and Keith turned back to see that his partner's expression had grown dark. He said, "What is it?"

"Bullock was dead in her cell this morning. Suicide. I guess she knew the penalty for cannibalism after all."

Chapter Eight

While Gunther spent the day visiting homes and interviewing members of the local trans-goblin community, Keith remained in his hotel room, staring at his own laptop, sifting through tens of thousands of pieces of text.

Looking.

Searching for any connection.

Keith made grilled cheese, brewed coffee.

Around ten p.m., Gunther returned. "Find out anything interesting?"

"Samantha Evans, the booker from Lulu's Flapjack Shack, has gone missing. Her mother reported her disappearance to the PPB and they sent out an officer to investigate, but according to the

PPB report, her boyfriend says it's not uncommon for her to take off for a couple of days without telling anyone," Keith said. "What about you?"

"I had to drink seventeen cups of tea, but I did manage to catch up on every piece of trans-goblin gossip for the last fifteen years. Lancelot, our goat-seeking goblin musician, has recently lost both his parents in a boating accident."

"A suspicious accident?"

"Not at all." Gunther leaned back, closed his eyes. "Nothing even remotely suspicious about him. Everybody loves him as far as I can tell."

Gunther yawned mightily. Keith waited for him to continue. He did not. A minute later Keith said, "You can take the bed if you want, Heartman."

Gunther complied, lurched up out of the chair, and flopped onto the bed limp as a side of salmon slapping down onto a chopping board.

Thinking that he should persevere, but tempted beyond all reasonable measure, Keith made it ten more minutes before joining Gunther on the ugly bedspread, then between the freshly changed hotel sheets.

Approximately five hours later, at 3:06, PPB called them out to take a look at a foot.

The foot in question had been found lodged under some fallen wood near an observation point in the Smith and Bybee Wetlands Natural Area. The foot was pale as wax. It had four toes—all of them very long. Each greasy white digit ended in a horn-like yellow talon. The most striking feature of the foot, though, was its NIAD vampire-identification bracelet looping the burned and slimy ankle stump.

"We called this cuff into the office and they gave us your number," the police officer said. "I would have called the department of wildlife myself. Since it doesn't look like a human foot."

"It's not a human foot." Keith knew he stated the obvious but felt the need to say something. "Don't worry, I've got the gear to take care of it."

"Who found this?" Gunther asked.

"And ornithology professor from PSU. He was trying to set up in a blind before sunrise to observe the waterfowl when he ran across it. We sent him home. We wouldn't have called you except for the cuff."

"It's no problem," Gunther said.

"Do you mind if I ask what that thing is?"

"It's an animal limb. We'll know more about it after it goes to the lab in San Francisco." Keith opened up a lightproof bag and prepared to remove the evidence from the scene. They'd need to buy some dry ice on the way back to the hotel to keep it fresh during shipping.

"It doesn't really look like any kind of animal around here," the officer remarked. "I've hunted here all my life, you know."

Gunther stepped smoothly between them. "I strongly suspect that this is part of a highly endangered animal."

"Endangered animal?"

"Yes, the Argentinean four-toed sloth. Have you ever heard if it?"

"No. I've seen a sloth in Costa Rica before, but never heard of the Argentinean one."

"Well, until recently, they were considered extinct. I'm actually collecting money for habitat preservation right now. Do you think you'd be interested in helping with a donation? Anything at all would be appreciated."

The officer demurred, claiming to have left his wallet in the car, and sidled away.

"What would you have done if he'd given you money?"

"That guy? It was never a possibility," Gunther said, smiling.

Keith crouched down. The stench of decay filled his nostrils. He gloved up and gingerly picked up the limb. After wiping the goo away he read out the serial number on the tracking cuff while Gunther typed it into the database, via his phone.

"Janice Sounder," Gunther pronounced. "No surprise there. The question is—is the rest of Janice alive somewhere?"

"I don't think so." Keith finished bagging the foot, then poked at the ground with his pen. Though footprints and rain marred the scene, traces of ash remained. "I think she burned here."

"Wouldn't there be clothes left behind? Or remnants anyway?"

"Only if she was wearing them." Keith beckoned the PPB liaison forward. "You say the foot was found in the woodpile?"

"Yes, sir."

"Was any of the wood around it burned?"

"Yes, sir. We have those in evidence. We're testing them for traces of accelerant. We did find some metal as well. Some fragments of silver and also a piece of metal we think might have been a wedding ring, sir."

"Why do you think that?"

"It was gold and about the right shape."

Driving up the road, Keith could see a small procession of nondescript black SUVs approaching. The forensic team had arrived, probably via some sort of portal. Through his NIAD glasses, he could see the faint blue tracers still clinging to them.

"Well," he said. "I suppose we need to go turn this over to the team."

By the time they'd relinquished Janice's foot to the Irregulars forensic team and signed all the requisite papers, it was seven a.m. Keith was hungry and on the delirious level of fatigue. He pulled into an old-school donut shop called the Tulip Bakery, glanced over to Gunther, and said, "You want to go in or should I just get a dozen and head back to the hotel?"

Gunther leaned back in his seat, eyes closed. "I trust you."

Tulip Bakery turned out to have the sort of donuts he remembered from his childhood back east. No coffee-milk, in fact, and no coffee at all. He got an assortment of cakes and raised and a couple of maple bars. He set the box in Gunther's lap—the other man didn't open his eyes but held the box instinctively as Keith pulled out of the parking lot, heading back to downtown.

"Okay, so we've got the butchery venue and we've got one dead vampire who was supposed to have gone to Boise but never made it." Keith rubbed his face, not relishing the drive back. "There is no reason to believe that these two occurrences are connected except for proximity."

Gunther reclined his seat. "Let's say, for the sake of argument, that they are."

"All right."

"What if Janice was somehow connected to the killings—maybe not as a killer, but as a purchaser of blood?"

"Why kill her then?" Keith asked.

"Maybe she wanted out. Maybe she was blackmailing the real killer."

"I don't know. The Sounders have been here for a hundred and forty-five years without a single incident," Gunther pointed out.

"Okay, let's go at it from another angle. Who was Janice meeting in Boise?"

"A vampire named Silas DuPree. According to our office there he hasn't even left his house for the last fifteen years." Gunther cracked an eye long enough to paw a coconut twist out of the donut box.

"How does Silas survive?"

"Blood delivered weekly by courier." Gunther took a bite of his donut. "He's basically a shut-in."

"Where does he get the money for the home delivery blood-mobile?"

"He wrote a series of romance novels featuring sexy reclusive loners. Before that he performed on stage, but that would have been in the pre-electricity era." Gunther inhaled at least half his donut in one massive bite. "Damn, these are good. Any coffee?"

"There's some cold stuff from yesterday in the cupholder if you don't mind my backwash."

Gunther looked like he might make some sort of droll remark, then seemed to think the better of it. He slugged back Keith's left-over black with two sugars, then fished around in his pocket for his cigarettes.

They turned and were heading straight into the rising sun. Keith scowled. More than likely this was the last sight that Janice Sounder had seen. "Did our office actually send an agent to speak with DuPree or did they just check the computer tracking system?"

"I don't know." Apparently reinvigorated by fried dough, Gunther adjusted his seat back to alert passenger position. "Are you thinking that he's not really there?"

"I'm thinking that a vampire can survive losing a foot, no matter how it gets removed."

"That's true," Gunther said. "And speaking of surviving losing a foot, we've also just seen that a foot can survive losing a vampire."

"What's your point?"

"It's really convenient that we should find Janice's ankle cuff still attached to her foot. I think she might have deliberately shoved her foot out of the sunlight when she knew that she was going to die."

"It's not like the sunlight would have destroyed the cuff. We would have found that eventually via the GPS tracking."

"But what would that have looked like? Just a ring of plastic. It's nothing that anyone would call the police over," Gunther said. "Someone needs to contact Janice's friend in Boise directly."

"I'd like to do it myself."

"That's just what I was thinking. I'll call for air transport." Gunther applied himself to locating his phone.

While Keith focused on staying awake so as not to kill them both in a tragic car wreck, Gunther spent the next few minutes arranging for a plane to take them from Portland to Boise. "A NIAD plane can take us at four and bring us back tonight."

Keith nodded.

Gunther finished off his donut, then paused thoughtfully. "That was pretty good. Could have used some hot sauce though."

"I could use a nap and shower."

To Keith it seemed inevitable that they would end up having sex again. They were both too exhausted to feel inhibited and also pumped up on half a dozen donuts each. It felt natural in the surreal, sugary morning to invite Gunther into his room, then into his shower, then finally into his bed.

Afterward, Gunther lay next to him, his chest heaving. Keith stared up at the hotel ceiling for a few minutes, catching his breath.

Gunther said, "Want something to drink?"

"Anything that contains alcohol."

Gunther rose, opened the refrigerator. The chill and artificial light flowed out across Keith's damp skin and silhouetted Gunther's perfect body as he grabbed a beer and twisted the cap off. He handed it to Keith, then delved back into the refrigerator. From inside the door, he chose a bottle of Dave's Insanity Sauce, unscrewed the top, then tipped his head back and chugged the entire thing, ending with a satisfied sigh.

He climbed back into the bed and pressed his lips against Keith's cheek.

Keith lay awake as Gunther fell into a doze, feeling the slight warmth of pure capsaicin left behind in the shape of a kiss and wondering what the hell he was going to do now.

Chapter Nine

For the first time in two years, Keith dreamed about his old restaurant. He had thought that he would dream about it more than he did. It was as though even his subconscious mind remained too wounded to venture back into his own kitchen.

He knew he was in a dream. The department had trained him in lucid dreaming, trances, and astral projections as part of his basic course. But knowing one is in a dream and being able to control that dream world remained two different activities.

He stood behind the long, old-fashioned counter, regarding his sole customer, who sat drinking coffee and reading the paper. A snow goblin. A creature of made of angular bone with smoldering red slits for eyes. The goblin turned a page of paper, took a sip of coffee, and then shook a few dashes of hot pepper sauce into the liquid. He said, "I think we should check out that film festival."

"Can't. I'm working."

The goblin folded the paper shut and said, "Not everything is about food, you know."

"To me it is. This is my whole life. It's everything I know." He became aware of the fact that he hadn't finished his prep work for the dinner rush. Customers would be coming in hungry and wanting to be fed. Shadows moved outside his restaurant's front window, some stopping to read the menu posted there. Somewhere in the background he could hear the sound of the dishwasher playing reggae and clanking dishes together. He had to get to work. Keith went to pick up his chef's knife from the cutting board, but he couldn't find it. Instead his mage pistol sat atop a neatly folded bar towel. How could he have left it sitting out? He lifted it and slid it into the holster under his left shoulder. The goblin, Gunther, glanced up.

"You look good wearing that," he remarked, tapping a cigarette out of a pack. "It suits you."

He felt a slight bump, then a hand on his knee. The restaurant dissolved. He opened his eyes to see the inside of a plane cabin. The private plane used by agents on assignment. Gunther sat across from him, leaning forward, shaking his knee slightly.

"We're touching down," he said.

Outside Keith could see the flat expanse of the Boise airport. The evening sky had gone the color of cantaloupe and cured ham, tinged at the edges with lavender. A Provençal-flavored sky, Keith thought.

"I was dreaming," he said blearily.

"Was it prophetic?"

"No, just a normal dream." Keith shifted in his seat to pull on his coat. "You were in it though."

"Was I?" Gunther sat back, apparently pleased by this information.

"You were made of bone."

"How did I look?"

Keith thought of telling him. Frightening. Strange. The shape of his nightmares. Instead he said, "Good…You looked good."

❧

As was standard, a government car was waiting for them—a big one. Keith had never been to Idaho before. As far as he could tell everything had been made to accommodate at least a family of six. Especially the cars. Or rather, the SUVs. They crowded the roads and lined up in neat rows in the ample parking lots.

DuPree's house was located in a section of the old town called The Bench, which was what the natives called the one bluff that bisected the city. Houses there were, like everything else, large. Even DuPree's old arts and crafts style home, which must have been a mansion when it had been built in the early forties.

The house looked exactly like a place where a vampire would live. Surrounded by a wrought-iron fence posted with pressed tin Keep Out and Beware of Dog signs.

"Do you think he really has a dog?" Gunther asked.

"If the dog is as old as the sign, it must be a revenant by now." Keith pressed the button mounted on the front gate. He expected a voice to come at him from some hidden intercom speaker. Instead the front door opened fractionally. A man's pale face peeked out. He appeared to be in his mid-fifties with thick, gray-streaked hair and a thin, beaky face.

"Who's there?" The voice was thin and reedy.

"NIAD." Keith held up his identification. He didn't know if DuPree could read it in the dark. Probably. "We have some questions to ask you."

DuPree crept from the door, looking furtively to the now-dark sky, then toward the neighbors on either side, before he slunk down the sidewalk toward them. He was dressed in a black turtleneck and slacks, which made his spindly limbs seem even more spidery.

He gave Keith a long, suspicious look, then turned to Gunther. DuPree sniffed the air obtrusively, his mouth half open. When he did, his expression brightened considerably. He whispered, "You're trans-goblin, aren't you?"

"Yes, sir. Gunther Heartman." He, too, showed his ID.

"Oh, good." DuPree seemed inordinately relieved by this. He unlocked the gate and Keith started through. DuPree leaped back.

"Please don't come too close, Agent Curry. I don't mean to be disrespectful, but I have a phobia of humans." His voice shook slightly.

This was new. Keith didn't think he'd ever heard of anything so ridiculous in his life. A hunter being afraid of his prey.

"May we come inside," Keith said.

"I certainly can't stop you, can I?" DuPree remarked. He said this without particular malice, just making a statement of fact.

After waiting for DuPree to lock the gate behind them, they followed him into his disheveled old living room. Books and papers were everywhere: stacked on tables and chairs, forming leaning, waist-high towers against the wall. Most of the furniture seemed to have been acquired in the forties as well. There were a couple of deco beige couches and silver modernist lamps.

"Please sit down." DuPree indicated the only clear couch in the room. He kept well away from Keith. "Can I get you a soda? I have several flavors."

"No, thank you. Would you mind showing your cuff, please?" The vampire's nervousness was making Keith edgy. Gunther didn't seem phased by it. "We need to verify that it's working."

"Could Agent Heartman do the cuff verification please? I mean no offense, Agent Curry, but if you come too close I might hyperventilate." DuPree said this apologetically.

Gunther smiled easily. "Sure."

He approached DuPree with no obvious caution or concern and this seemed to settle the vampire somewhat. Once Gunther had established that DuPree's cuff was both present and sending out the correct signal, he took his seat beside Keith on the couch.

DuPree remained standing, hand on the mantelpiece of his empty fireplace. "What can I do for you?"

"We're here about Janice Sounder. Her husband said she was supposed to be here visiting you." Gunther took the lead.

"Yes, but she never arrived. I phoned several times, but she isn't answering her cell," DuPree said. "I even called her awful master, but he says he hasn't seen her. I'm terribly worried about her."

"Why is that?" Keith asked. He didn't miss DuPree's use of the word *master*—nor did he miss the fact that DuPree didn't seem fond of Sounder. DuPree also appeared to be under the impression that Janice was still alive, but he could just be casting a good glamour. A person couldn't trust body language when an extra-human's real body wasn't visible.

"Because she hasn't arrived." DuPree seemed to feel he was stating the obvious. "She was flying on a night flight, but you can never be sure about airplanes these days. Flights get delayed. I've been checking the news to see if there were any cases of spontaneous combustion."

"What is your relationship to Janice?" Gunther asked.

"She wrote me a fan letter about ten years ago," DuPree said. "We started a correspondence. At first neither of us knew the other was a vampire, but after a couple of years we discovered we were kindred spirits, so to speak."

"And Mr. Sounder knew you two were writing letters?" Keith pulled out his notebook.

"Yes, of course. Janice had a very traditional concubine relationship. She keeps nothing from her master." DuPree seemed displeased as he said this.

"Do you think her master had a problem with her writing to another vampire?" Gunther asked.

"No, I don't think so. I don't think she would have written to me if he had." DuPree paused, alarm rising up through his expression. "What do you mean by 'had a problem'? Why are you speaking in the past tense? Has something happened to her?" DuPree started forward toward Gunther, then recoiled slightly as he remembered that Keith was also present.

"I'm sorry to inform you that Janice Sounder has been killed," Gunther said.

"Was it Sounder?" DuPree asked.

"We're looking at a variety of suspects. Why would you think it was Sounder?" Keith kept his voice very neutral. He had perceived that, though he was more comfortable playing the heavy with Gunther taking the more sympathetic angle, DuPree truly was experiencing a tremendous degree of distress. He didn't want to shut the vampire down with ham-fisted tough guy talk, no matter how easily it came to him.

"Because Janice and I had planned to leave this realm together. Surely you must know. I've filed all the paperwork. Oh, Janice…" DuPree crumpled down to the sofa facing them. A thin red tear trickled down his gaunt cheek. "She didn't even have a chance to file her papers, did she?"

"No record of a petition exists as far as we know." Gunther rose and handed DuPree a handkerchief. "When you said you and she were kindred spirits, what did you mean, exactly?"

"We were born into the same cult. Polygamists, you know. That's why we were all exiled here. I had thought that that was common knowledge."

"Not as common as you might think," Gunther said.

"So you have concubines as well?" Keith was a little at sea. How could this information not have been covered in basic training? Then again, there was so much information—so many realms. Realms upon realms upon realms, all stacked atop one another, existing at once in layers.

DuPree sniffed and wiped his eyes, leaving Gunther's handkerchief streaked with blood. "No, I came as a concubine to my mistress."

"And where is she?"

"Gone. Burned along with my two brother concubines. It's why I'm so afraid of humans, you see?" DuPree spoke to Gunther. "I've seen such horrible things. And the mass media just reinforces all stereotypes about us. Encourages our murder."

"Mass media doesn't cover actual vampire deaths," Keith remarked before he realized how callous his statement sounded.

"Have you seen a vampire movie?" DuPree demanded. "They're horribly violent. Full of wooden stakes and decapitations." DuPree choked on his last words. A sob escaped him.

Keith felt his sympathy for DuPree unexpectedly rising. Was it actually possible that Janice Sounder's death had been merely a case of spousal abuse? Much more gently he asked, "Do you think that Sounder would kill Janice for leaving him?"

"Why not? She was his property, wasn't she? In his mind anyway. In her mind too, at first. But after living among humans for so long, Janice had started to have her own ambitions. She had decided to write her own mystery novel. I thought she had tremendous potential. When we returned to our own world we were going to write together."

Keith was momentarily too stunned by the idea that the vampire realm had a publishing industry to think of a follow-up question. Gunther saved him.

"Do you think we could read part of Janice's novel?"

DuPree shook his head. "She had only just started writing it. She'd written only short stories before—mostly about farm life and rearing goats. But those killings in Portland had given her inspiration. She was asking me a lot of questions about how the police investigate crimes. I didn't know the answers, of course, because I write only romance. I believe in love, you know."

Keith exchanged a glance with Gunther.

"Were you in love with Janice?" Gunther asked.

"Yes, oh yes." He broke off again, sobbing.

"What do you think happened to her?" Keith asked.

"I think that Sounder found out that she planned to leave and..." DuPree said, lifting his face from Gunther's now-scarlet handkerchief, "and he burned her. That's what happened to her, isn't it? That's how masters punish disloyal concubines. And it's never investigated."

"We're investigating it now," Gunther said.

"But you'll never prove it," DuPree said. "How could you? There won't be any evidence. Like those poor girls who get drowned in Saudi Arabia or honor killings of rape victims in Pakistan. No one cares what happens to concubines. One less vampire—that's all anyone ever thinks."

Gunther stood. "I assure you, Mr. DuPree, that we will see this investigation to its conclusion. In the meantime, I'm afraid we will need you to remain here in Idaho."

"Do you really think I am a suspect? I haven't left this house in two decades."

"No," Keith said quickly, causing DuPree to start. "But if Sounder is behind it, we will need your testimony."

"Please...I just want to leave this place. Meeting Janice, I finally had the courage to try and start again. Even if..." DuPree took a deep shuddering breath, but then recovered. "Even if Janice won't be with me physically, she'll be with me as the beautiful, shining spirit that she was."

Keith said, "We'll be in touch."

Once back they were back en route to the airport, Keith said, "That was not what I expected to happen."

Gunther shrugged. "As it turns out, not everything is about food."

Pushing through a profound sense of déjà vu, Keith returned, "It is to me. Plainly, Janice's interest in the Cannibal Killings could not have been coincidental. Coincidences don't leave combusted vampires behind."

"Agreed. We need to pay Sounder another visit. Even if he's not connected to the Cannibal Killings, he's certainly the number one suspect in Janice's death."

"Then we're officially calling Janice's death a murder?" Keith didn't even know how to begin to file the paperwork on that one. Who would investigate? NIAD, he supposed.

"Vampiric concubines are citizens like anyone else, right?" Gunther's phone rang. He answered and after a perfunctory conversation turned to Keith and said, "They found bones from the club booker's body. Same MO as before."

"And?" Even without the déjà vu Keith knew there had to be an *and*.

"They found them in our friendly rocker kook Lancelot's garbage. He's being held at the NIAD detention center."

Chapter Ten

On the way to the NIAD detention center the next morning, Keith picked up a copy of the Willamette Weekly. He did this as a matter of reflex. Weekly papers often gave a better snapshot of the restaurant and bar scene in an area than anything else did. Not that he was sure this case even had to do with food anymore. Janice Sounder's death, at least, appeared to be a jealous master vampire disciplining his concubine.

As a matter of course, they'd ordered a search of Azalea Point Creamery and the Sounder residence. The homicide team was there now, going over the joint with spectrometers and witches. At last report, Sounder and his remaining concubine were both cooperative, but then he didn't have much choice but to be cooperative while the sun shone.

Gunther drove while Keith leafed through the paper. Among the usual local political rants, cult cartoons, and ads for escort services, he found the food column.

"This is interesting," he said.

"What?"

"This food critic is talking about the Bauer & Bullock closure. He's missing the cookies."

"I can see why. They're great cookies," Gunther remarked. "Rake's going to be brokenhearted when he learns he's had his last box."

Keith continued to leaf through the paper, looking for live music listings. Carnivore Circus had a Friday show booked at a club called The Greenhouse. He found no listings for Theater of Blood. Was it because they'd gone underground or because they were just a bad band who nobody wanted playing their club? Hard to say.

As Keith could have predicted, when at last they sat in an interrogation room with Lancelot, they found him not terrified that he would be arrested and tried for cannibalism. Instead, he wanted to know whether or not he would be out of jail in time to make it to his gig on Friday night. Gunther glanced to the legal advocate. She was some sort of faerie with long pink hair and longer legs. She shrugged and shook her head slightly. Gunther turned his attention back to Lancelot.

To Keith's surprise, Gunther's amicable cool evaporated. He let loose a long string of growling goblin syllables that, from Lancelot's reaction, were seriously profane.

"If you could stick to English, I'd appreciate it, Heartman," Keith remarked.

"Lancelot," Gunther snapped. "Disappointing your band mates is the least of your problems right now."

"I know, I just can't think about it. I don't know what to do." Lancelot hung his head in misery. "My legal advocate says I don't have to talk to you, but I didn't do anything. I don't know anything. I don't know what to do."

“Why isn’t your family here with you?” Gunther shot back.

Keith thought it an odd question for Gunther to ask, but then, he supposed he’d underestimated the filial connectedness of goblins.

“My parents are dead,” Lancelot replied. “They were in a boat accident last year. I don’t have anyone else.” Lancelot’s hands shook.

Much as he valued aggressive questioning, Keith didn’t think badgering Lancelot would yield much profitable information. The kid—and he was clearly a kid, Keith could see that now—was visibly retreating into himself. He said, “Would you like a cigarette?”

“I sure would.” Lancelot raised his eyes fractionally.

Keith signaled to Gunther who grudgingly placed his own pack of Luckys on the table. Lancelot took one and chewed the end nervously. He looked up to Gunther and said, “I know you’re disappointed in me, but I didn’t do anything.”

The rest of the interrogation revealed nothing of value. No one could provide Lancelot with an alibi for the time of the murder. He had been at home, alone.

They left Lancelot in the interrogation cell and headed back downtown.

Gunther wanted to walk along the river, so Keith parked and soon they walked shoulder to shoulder along the greenbelt, the Willamette River on one side, the skyscrapers of downtown on the other. Gunther chewed three cigarettes, one after another in silence, before finally saying, “The latest victim of the Cannibal Killer was dumped directly in Lancelot’s backyard. There has to be a goblin connection. Only another trans-goblin would know about Lancelot’s status.”

“But the question is, is the connection to Lancelot or to Carnivore Circus?”

“When I interviewed the other two band members, they alibied out. No, I think the connection must be to Lancelot, but…”

“But?” Keith prompted.

“But I don’t think he’s a killer.” Gunther shook his last smoke out of the pack and crumpled the empty box.

"Are you suggesting he was framed?" Keith sat down on a bench overlooking the water.

"To me it feels like someone is going out of their way to make it look like he is the killer. Not just any old goblin, but him."

"All right, what's special about him? Apart from the fact that he's in a band?"

"He can't make change?" Keith suggested.

"Well, you can't expect that. He hasn't been working at the market all that long."

For the first time, Gunther's reflexive defense of Lancelot's abilities didn't annoy Keith. It was true. He hadn't worked there long. "We know he's an orphan, if you can call a twenty-one-year-old guy an orphan. He owns nothing of value. No car, no savings. His house is rented. He hadn't even finished paying off his guitar. He lives off the nominal cash he gets from his band and his recycled sweater stall."

"Didn't his parents leave him anything?" Gunther asked.

"Just the hereditary table. Lancelot's mother sold handcrafted knitwear."

"There has to be a connection between these things," Keith said. "I'd be willing to bet it's money. Somehow."

"Not food?"

"Food is money," Keith said simply. "In other contexts, food can be love, art, and culture. But in this case I feel comfortable saying that if food is involved, it's in the form of money."

"Agreed." Gunther gazed out at the river. "Maybe if Lancelot needed money enough he would start hunting and selling human flesh, but I don't think it would have been his idea. Maybe Bullock or one of her cronies lured him into it?"

"I don't buy the money angle there. Lancelot's market reporting shows that he made enough cash to support himself," Keith said. "And he has absolutely no connection to Bullock."

"That we've found yet," Gunther countered grimly.

"It's not like we haven't looked. There's none. Zip." Keith flipped his paper open, once again reading the article on the Bauer & Bullock closure, looking for anything he'd missed. What was surprising about the article, from a law enforcement standpoint, was the complete lack of apparent concern the writer had about the restaurant being shut down by the police under suspicious circumstances.

Rather, the author was simply obsessed to the point of torment by the idea that he wouldn't have any more *alphajores* described lovingly as, "A three-tiered sandwich cookie filled with alternating layers of feijoa jam, goat cajeta, and hazelnut pastry biscuit dipped in white and black chocolate for the signature Bauer & Bullock half-moon effect. An Argentinean delight made native to the Pacific Northwest. Local hazelnuts were supplied by Peabody Orchards. The luscious cajeta goat caramel was sourced locally from Azalea Point Creamery."

Keith did a double take. Gunther, who had been reading over his shoulder, seemed to notice the name at the same moment. He said, "Don't I recognize that name?"

"Holy shit," Keith breathed. "It's the fucking vampire after all."

"I don't disagree, but why? And where's the evidence? We already searched his property and came up empty."

"I don't know yet." Keith popped his knuckles in irritation. But the pieces refused to assemble themselves into any sort of picture. "The connection we have is the cookie."

"If only we could interrogate pastry," Gunther remarked dryly. "I suppose we could have it analyzed, but what for?"

"Don't you still have that box you got for your old partner?"

They drove back to hotel under flashing lights and Keith parked illegally while Gunther legged it up to his room to retrieve the souvenir. He flopped back into the passenger seat just as the hotel manager was approaching the loading zone. Keith zipped around the corner into the alley, put on the hazard lights, and said, "Let's see them."

Gunther opened the beautifully wrapped box and handed over a cookie. Keith broke it in half. A delicious, fruity scent floated up. Instantly, his mouth began to water. He wanted nothing more than to put it in his mouth but knew better.

"This jam is not made with feijoa." Keith had experienced this amazing aroma before. He'd confiscated twenty-seven jars once in a quaint teashop in Madison, Wisconsin. "This is heartfruit."

"I don't know what that is."

"It's a fruit that grows exclusively in necrotic human organ meat, specifically the heart and liver. It's incredibly rare. I busted a manufacturing operation last January. A guy who worked at a funeral home was harvesting organs and selling them to a nice little grandma who used them for growing material."

"But Bauer & Bullock sells hundreds of these cookies every week. How could they farm that many organs?"

"Heartfruit is so potent that one fruit can flavor an industrial vat and there isn't much jam in each cookie. I can't believe I've been so stupid. Bauer & Bullock pulled in fifty percent of its take from the sale of these cookies." Excitement rose in his chest. They might just be able to prove Lancelot's innocence. "This isn't about cannibalism. That was just a fringe benefit. It's about money. It's about jam."

"That doesn't connect Sounder," Gunther warned. "Or Lancelot."

"No, it doesn't. But we know Bullock was in a business relationship with Sounder already. Maybe..."

"Maybe it was a trade," Gunther said. "Maybe Sounder traded something with Bullock."

"Like what?"

"If we assume that Sounder provided the bodies for Bullock, which is a pretty good bet, she must have agreed to do something for him. Standard pact," Gunther said.

"You think she or her accomplices, since she clearly had some, agreed to set Lancelot up in exchange for bodies?"

"Right. But there's no connection between Sounder and Lancelot either."

Keith thought about this. Finally he said, "If Lancelot has no direct heirs, who will his goblin market table go to?"

"I don't know. Getting into those markets is really competitive but..." Gunther suddenly smiled. "But I bet they have a waiting list. But that is insane. Killing over a table at a market?"

"It's not a table. The food industry is incredibly competitive. Fifty percent of all food-related business ventures fail in the first year. That table represents market penetration. It's exposure for the product. It's direct sales. It's—"

"It's money," Gunther finished for him. "Regardless, we still have no evidence of anything but a legitimate business arrangement between the steakhouse and the dairy."

"You're right. We need to find the grow operation. Somebody there will know who drops off the ingredient for processing," Keith said. "Is the jam made locally?"

Gunther flashed a smile. "It's Portland. What do you think?"

Chapter Eleven

The manufacturing facility for Cascadia Jams and Preserves was located in a light industrial area in Hillsboro. As it turned out, the flavoring agent for Bauer & Bullock's exclusive house jam was shrouded in such tremendous secrecy that the company's owner, Mike Grady, had to be called back from his afternoon orchard tour in order to speak to them.

Mike was a rotund man with dark circles under his eyes and quick, aggressive body language. Keith had met literally dozens of guys just like him. Cooks with ADD and one-track minds. This guy's brain had been consumed by the idea of jam early on so that every culinary idea that occurred to him, savory or sweet, had to be expressed in the form of jam. Or jelly. Or syrup.

Other cooks he'd met had been obsessed with pizza or hot sauce or ice cream as an expressive format. Keith had often wondered if this kind of focus constituted a form of autism. One-dish thinking combined with inevitably poor social skills created one of the most unpleasant, yet widely dispersed, character types in the culinary world. Often they were very successful business wise specifically because they stuck to one product.

Chances were good that Mike, though ambitious, was too self-absorbed to be directly involved.

Keith knew exactly what would happen next. Mike would try to make them try every product in his entire line while evading their questions about Bauer & Bullock.

"Our newest product is a line of savory honey syrups," Mike said, unscrewing the lid from a tiny jar of golden liquid. "White pepper truffle honey is going to go through the roof. I can feel it. It's just amazing on chicken. Here, try some."

"Sounds great." Gunther politely accepted a toothpick dipped in the fragrant syrup.

Keith demurred. "We need to see the ingredient list for the Bauer & Bullock private label jam."

Mike smiled the typical, sneering smile that all guys like him never knew they were making. "No can do. That's top secret. I had to sign a legal agreement and everything. Sorry, boys."

"I can get a court order, but that's going to bring a lot of unwanted attention to your facility. Especially when it's about to be revealed that Cindy Bullock was butchering humans at her restaurant," Keith said.

Mike paled. "You're bullshitting me."

"Not at all," Gunther said. "In a couple of days anybody with even the slightest connection to Bauer & Bullock is going under the magnifying glass. If I were you I'd start distancing myself now. And I'd start by giving us a full ingredient list for that jam."

"I don't know..." Mike began. His cheeks went gray and waxy.

"Look, would it help you if I told you that I already know what's in it?" Keith said.

"Then you're one ahead of me," Mike said. "It's flavored with a secret liquid compound. She said it was feijoa, but it isn't."

"Who brings you the flavor compound?" Keith asked. "Was it Bullock herself?"

"It's delivered by courier. I just got a bottle yesterday." Mike pulled out a key ring and unlocked his lower right desk drawer. He removed a two-pint plastic screw-top jar that had the words "Bauer & Bullock" written on it in Sharpie. "I have the receipt here. You can have it all."

Mike held up his hands, shaking his head slowly as if denying that the jar had ever been in his possession. This was why Keith didn't like guys like Mike. The cowardly pendulum of their emotions only swung between bullying people and rolling over and pissing on themselves.

With the courier's receipt it was easy to find pickup address—another industrial park only half a mile away—and a business called B&B Extract Company.

Like most industrial parks, this one consisted of a series of low, large buildings whose sides were intermittently punctuated by bay doors. Occasionally a regular door appeared in the corrugated siding, and it was on one of these that Keith found a small, dull sign that indicated the existence of B&B Extract Company.

"You want to ring the bell or just go ahead in?" Keith asked.

"I think it would be wise to let ourselves in." Gunther pulled a skeleton key from his coat and inserted it into the lock. The spells etched into the key's surface blazed to life—first showing red, then slowly turning to green.

Gunther removed the key and Keith carefully tried the knob, moving his hand only slightly, to make sure the knob was unlocked.

Keith opened the door. Inside was a regular-looking front office with an old desk and a couple of chairs. Beyond that was a closed door. The faint sound of music could be heard thumping from beyond it. They moved forward, mage pistols drawn, standing on either side of the door frame. Keith could smell the dense, lush perfume of heartfruit flowers in bloom. The fragrance made him salivate instantly and nearly managed to cover the sweet stink of rotting meat. How many plants did they have in there?

"Please don't let it be trans-goblins running this operation," Gunther muttered.

For the first time since he'd joined the Irregulars, Keith found himself hoping the same thing.

They burst through the door into a dank, humid, sweet-smelling greenhouse.

At the back of the room Keith could see a bank of grow lights. Seven slim heartfruit stalks rose beneath them. Five of these ended in white flowers. The other two had already developed fat, white seedpods.

Three pallid individuals, who had been apparently been engaged in tending the drip-irrigation system, looked up at them in what Keith could only describe as muted alarm. All wore black. Two had fangs. The third wore red cat's-eye contact lenses that Keith imagined greatly impaired his vision. Downbeat electronica pulsed through the air. A stack of Theater of Blood flyers and a staplegun sat on a metal table.

"Yes!" Gunther said into the silence. "Fake vampires!"

Then came a slight buzz at Keith's wrist. Without lowering his mage pistol, Keith glanced at his watch. Numeral nine blinking green.

"I don't think so."

"Are you kidding? Look at them." Gunther waved dismissively at the trio, then said, "You three idiots are under arrest, by the way."

"Master?" The guy wearing the cat's-eye contacts finally spoke but not, Keith thought, to them.

"Blinking green nine, Heartman." Keith kept the mage pistol trained on the three wannabes while scanning the room. In the upper corner of the room, a shadow moved against the ceiling. "Nosferatu. Ten o'clock."

The black shape moved like a spider across the ceiling toward them. Its strange, shapeless jaw undulated. He didn't know if this was Sounder or the remaining concubine.

It didn't really matter.

"Freeze, asshole." He retargeted his mage pistol. The vampire slid along the ceiling, still coming toward them, saying nothing. Saying nothing was a bad sign.

Gunther seemed unperturbed, even slightly annoyed by this. He said, "I order you to stop and identify yourself."

The vampire launched himself at Keith. Gunther threw himself between them. The vampire sank its teeth into Gunther's shoulder, narrowly missing his neck. The three humans bolted, running toward the back entrance. Keith slammed the butt of his mage pistol into the vampire's head. He couldn't risk firing while the vampire was still attached to Gunther. Though trans-goblin, the mage pistol would still have an effect on him.

"Get off him, you fucking lamprey." Keith pried but couldn't loosen even one of the vampire's inhumanly strong fingers.

He wished he'd had the sense to bring a wooden stake or flamethrower.

Flamethrower…

He shoved his hand into Gunther's inside pocket, groping for the flask of lighter fluid there. He got the top off and sprayed the vampire with it, straight into the eyes and down its undulating throat. The vampire released its grip and sprang away out of range of any lighters. Keith brought his mage pistol up immediately and fired. Three spell-inscribed bullets spiraled out, leaving blue tracers. The first shot went wide, but the next two found their target.

The vampire shrieked as the bullets penetrated its flesh, writhing against the ceiling like a vortex of angry smoke. Then, abruptly, the sound ended and a ring of plastic dropped to the floor. Carefully, keeping his mage pistol trained on the traces of lingering smoke overhead, Keith bent to read the name.

He stood and turned back to Gunther, who stood with one hand pressed against his shoulder to stanch the blood trickling out.

Keith holstered his pistol and phoned the ambulance.

Chapter Twelve

PPB apprehended the fake vampires within a mile of the warehouse. Although the transformation from human to vampire was technically impossible, all three fake vampires claimed to have been made Nosferatu by Sounder. None of them was anything but a misguided human.

"Sounder really did a number on them," Gunther said. "He used the administration of methotrexate to induce photoallergic reactions when any of these kids went into sunlight. He let movie mythology do the rest of his convincing. After that he had himself a nice little set of minions."

"And we got this from the remaining concubine?" Keith glanced at the clock. Ten minutes till checkout. Not enough time to have one last hurrah with Gunther. Not that Gunther was in any shape for sex. His shoulder was a mess of stitches and bandages.

Keith gathered up the last of his clothes and shoved them into his suitcase.

"She made a deal. Her lawyer claims that she was acting with Sounder under duress. I believe her." Gunther shifted in the stiff-backed hotel chair.

Keith nodded. "Well, we saw what happened to the concubine who didn't cooperate."

"Exactly. Administration at the Portland Saturday Market confirms that Azalea Point Creamery was next on the waiting list for a market booth. It's hard to believe that Sounder would do all this just for money."

"People have done worse for less," Keith commented. "Ultimately, Sounder only ever saw humans as prey."

"That doesn't explain why Bullock went ahead with it."

"She was just sick, like every other gourmet looking for the ultimate thrill. PPB managed to round up a couple of people associated with Forbidden Pleasures. They've been handed over to NIAD. I'm pretty sure at least one of them will be willing to talk, once they've found out what kind of death sentence they're looking at." Keith zipped his suitcase. Time to checkout. Time for him to head back to DC.

"Want to ride to the airport with me?" Keith squared himself, assembling his expression into professional cool. Gunther didn't appear to be fooled. He reached out, smoothing Keith's lapel.

Gunther said, "So it's over, just like that?"

"I already saw housekeeping lurking in the hallway." Keith knew that wasn't what Gunther was asking, but he'd never been good at saying good-bye.

"There are literally dozens of portals between DC and San Francisco," Gunther said. "It would be easy to pop over there. Maybe you could make me dinner sometime. Or even breakfast, if you're in the mood."

Keith caught Gunther's hand and pulled it to his lips.

"I think I could be in the mood." He heard the creaking of a disinfectant-laden trolley outside in the hallway. "Time to hit the road."

They made their way down to the parking lot, passing by a line of food carts just opening for lunch. Keith felt a familiar pang of loss as he watched them open. He missed that world. He missed it a lot. But then again, being an Irregular wasn't so bad. It had its perks. And watching Gunther slide into the passenger seat beside him, he thought maybe he'd found a regular customer to cook for again.

Gunther folded a smoke into his mouth, then unwrapped the Carnivore Circus CD he'd left on the dashboard.

"Want to find out what they sound like?"

"Why not?"

Massive, heavy beats exploded out of the speakers. Growls and screams like the howling of the damned pounded through the rental. Bombastic blasts of sheer sound vibrated from the speakers.

Above the noise, Gunther shouted, "I kinda like it."

Keith nodded. "Me too. What's the track called?"

Gunther searched the homemade packaging a moment, then said, "Chunderfuck. Next one is: Thy Doom Approacheth, Shit-head."

They listened to the song. It didn't take long, being comprised of only seventy-two seconds of bowel-jangling guitar. Keith turned the volume down. Gunther gave him an inquisitive look.

"I'm not a nice goblin boy," Keith said, then added, "I'm not even nice."

Gunther gazed out the windshield, smiled in that slow way he had, and replied, "I know, but you sure can cook."

GREEN GLASS BEADS

Josh Lanyon

They are better than stars or water,
Better than voices of winds that sing,
Better than any man's fair daughter,
Your green glass beads on a silver ring.
Overheard on a Saltmarsh
— Harold Monro

Never trust a goblin.

Even a child knows that much. But there are times when you've got to take the chance, when the prize is worth the risk—which is how Archer Green happened to be in a drafty warehouse on Quebec Street in Vancouver a few minutes before midnight, waiting with a goblin named Ezra for the Moth Man to turn up.

Why the goblins called the Moth Man the Moth Man was a mystery. He was an albino, so maybe that had something to do with it. That, and his predilection for the bright and shiny, especially things that easily caught fire or exploded. The Moth Man had a way of finding artifacts that were, in Archer's opinion, better left lost. It was probably a strange opinion for the curator of the Museum of State-Sanctioned Antiquities in Vancouver. Not that the ordinary man—or woman—on the street would know anything about MoSSA.

The wind moaned dolefully through the chinks in the old brick walls. Ezra munched agitatedly at one of those violet floral cigarettes he was so fond of. Archer kept to the shadows and resisted checking his pocket watch yet again. He wasn't nervous, exactly—it took a lot to make him nervous—but he wasn't happy either.

"He'll be here soon." Ezra continued to pace up and down before the empty wooden crates with their faded emblems of skulls and crowns, the dully gleaming vats and ducts that looked like nothing so much as a giant steel stomach. "Don't worry."

Archer lifted a dismissive shoulder, but he'd already made up his mind to walk if the Moth Man didn't show by five after. It wasn't that he didn't believe the Moth Man had something worth his time and trouble. The Moth Mans of the realms seemed always to have the inside track on beautiful and rare items before they hit the regular black market. Still, Archer would have preferred to know exactly what he was acquiring before venturing out in the dead of night with a wallet full of cash.

"His merchandise is always worth it." Ezra gulped down the rest of his cigarette and belched an agitated purple puff toward the rafters overhead. "He said he wants to talk to you personally."

Archer threw him a quick look. "Me? Why me?"

"Eh?"

"Your friend. Why should he want to speak to me in particular?"

Ezra gave a smoky laugh. "Don't know. Never asked."

Archer pulled out his pocket watch. Moonlight through the grimy windows illuminated the time. Three minutes after midnight. He snapped the watch closed. "That's it for me. I've an early start tomorrow."

"No, wait!" Ezra cried. "Don't leave. I know he's on his way."

Archer studied Ezra, studied the beads of sweat popping out over Ezra's human features, took note of the anxious licking of tongue over lips. Yep, definitely time to say adieu. Archer opened his mouth, but somewhere to the left of where they stood came a ghostly screech of rusted hinges.

Instinctively, they both turned.

"See. Told you," Ezra muttered.

Archer ignored him, watching warily until at last he spotted a tall figure in a drab overcoat moving through the darkness like a white shadow. The figure moved swiftly, with frequent glances over his shoulder, as though he feared pursuit through the canyons of metal tubes and casks.

"Well! You took your time," Ezra greeted the Moth Man when he reached them at last.

"Can't help it. Thought I was being followed." The Moth Man's voice was high and breathy. His eyes were large and protuberant. They appeared colorless in the gloom. He was taller than most humans, certainly taller than Archer, and very thin.

"Were you?" Archer asked as Ezra scoffed.

The Moth Man shook his head. He eyed Archer curiously. "You're him? You're—"

"No names," Archer cut in.

"No. No, it's just I thought you would be…different."

Archer got that a lot. "What is it you have for me?"

"Have you got the money?"

"Show me the goods first."

The Moth Man reached into his overcoat and pulled out a long, plain envelope. He picked at the flap with long gray fingernails, plucked it open, and held out an old-fashioned Polaroid. He smiled slyly.

"What is it?"

"Take it."

"I don't think so. I don't buy on spec—"

As he spoke, the snapshot gave a tiny pop and green sparks flew up. The Moth Man giggled. "It likes you."

Casting him a doubtful look, Archer reached slowly for the photograph. It seemed to slip right into his palm. He gazed down.

He was looking at what appeared to be a small mound of broken glass arranged on a square of black velvet. The picture hummed against his fingertips.

Wonderingly, Archer raised his gaze to the pallid one so closely regarding him.

The Moth Man gave another of those unsettling giggles. "Er, might I interest you in a strand of green glass beads?"

At that instant the tall warehouse doors rolled up with a rattle like a million eyelids snapping awake. Dazzling white light flooded the building, bouncing off the canisters and tubing in a blinding glare. Navy-uniformed VPD poured into the building, shouting orders. Much worse were the familiar dark-clad agents flanking the locals. The regular law enforcement hung back as the men and women in black fanned out behind the slow rolling green-gray of damping dust that tumbled lazily, almost playfully, through the entrails of the machinery and ladders. They wore spell masks and carried mage pistols. *The Irregulars.* Everywhere you turned these days the Irregulars were underfoot.

The Moth Man gasped in alarm, snatched back the photo, and bolted, his overcoat flapping behind him like failing wings. Archer also bolted—in the opposite direction—ignoring the cries to stop, the shouted warnings, and a few obscenities. He raced for the metal knot of drums and tubing and platforms at the back of the long building. What became of the Moth Man he didn't see, but his words still echoed in Archer's mind as he ran.

Green glass beads…

No time to consider it now, but…Was it possible? Had they turned up after all this time?

The air was thick with holy water and incantations that wouldn't have thwarted a baby brownie. Archer sprang for a sharply slanted ladder, scrambled up, then pelted down a wide landing crowded with mysterious metal silhouettes. Climbing over the rickety safety railing, he leaped across the aisle to another landing. More of a shelf than a landing, but it would do. Below him, the green damping dust billowed up. He pulled his handkerchief out and clamped it over his mouth and nose before dropping down to a large rusted shipping container. He landed with a bang, but what was one more bang in the surrounding pandemonium?

Holding his breath, he sprinted down the scratched and peeling lid of the shipping container, the metallic pounding of his footsteps echoing the beat of his heart. Boom, boom, boom. No time to be subtle. His lungs burned with the need to breathe. The damping dust stung his eyes, but he could still see—an advantage of his half-faerie bloodline. Behind him, he could hear muffled cries falling away.

"Where is he?"

"Where did he go?"

"There he is!"

"That's not him, dumbass! That's a pipe."

Archer dropped to the dusty brick floor behind the container.

Handheld utility lights skimmed the walls of the building and swept the floors. Archer crouched low, breathing hard through the damp silk of the handkerchief. It was not that he was out of shape so much as out of practice. The burst of adrenaline, his human half's response to threat, left him disconcertingly breathless and a little shakier than he liked. This would do him good. If he got out of it. Out of this trap. That's what it was. A trap. But was it for Archer or for the Moth Man? Archer had a suspicion and it didn't make him happy.

Always lovely to be wanted, of course, but that son of a whoring goblin Ezra would regret it the next time they met.

The white beams of the utility lights slid past and Archer took the opportunity to move further away from the approaching tattoo of department-issue boots. Wriggling through a narrow opening between towers of cold and rusted cylinders, he reached up, grabbed for the rough edge along the top of one of the wide vats, and hauled himself up. The soles of his boots slipped on the smooth sides. The muscles in his arms and shoulders, and across his back flared with pain.

Yes, definitely out of practice.

He clambered on top, risked standing upright, and jumped for the landing beneath the giant windows. He almost didn't make it. Nothing like slamming into a hard, splintery surface to concentrate the mind. The fleshy part of Archer's thumb caught on a nail as he dragged himself up and then half climbed, half fell over the flimsy railing. He kept clear of the moon-bright window as he scuttled back, vaguely aware that his hand was throbbing. That was going to hurt like hell later on.

Assuming there was a later on.

For a few seconds, Archer sprawled on the narrow ledge, catching his breath and observing the activity below.

A number of regular police officers now searched the narrow walkways of the warehouse. So many cops, in fact, that they were starting to get in each other's ways. Not so with the Irregulars. They were systematically sweeping the building from one end to the other. Black and silver figures moved quickly up the ladders to the landing across from Archer.

Archer rolled away from the edge and stared up at the rafters far above. What a pity he couldn't fly. But being a half-blood did have its advantages. There were still one or two tricks up his sleeve.

He scooted over to the wall between the banks of multi-paned windows. Closing his eyes, he concentrated on melding with the deep shadows. He pictured the edges of his outline softening, blurring, becoming part of the gloom. Yes, that was it. Fade into the darkness. Let it swallow him…

Footsteps were coming his way. He gathered his nerve and stood, taking a careful, silent step back and flattening himself against the bricks. His heart thumped crazily as the march of feet came closer. Two of them. The beams of their utility lights scudded lightly ahead of them like dogs tugging on leashes.

Archer closed his eyes so that this last telltale gleam would not give him away.

They were nearly on him now. He steadied himself, stilled his breathing, willed his heart to pause.

Down below, the noise and activity continued.

Creak. Thump. Squeak. Thump.

They passed so close Archer felt the sleeve of the nearest brush his arm. His heart did truly stop then, but the agents moved past, slow and deliberate and blind to him.

True faerie glamour. To the casual mortal eye his silent figure would appear to be nothing more than shadows and the outline of post or beam. That was one magic that even the Irregulars with all their special forces high-tech equipment hadn't figured out how to dismantle yet. Too old and too simple perhaps.

Archer remained stone still as the agents continued to prowl the landings and sweep through the puzzlework of aisles below.

"Clear up here." One of the agents who had passed Archer signaled down.

"Check again! He didn't go out the back. And he sure as hell didn't go out the front."

Archer sank further back into the shallow brick recess.

Thump. Squeak. Thump. Creak.

The agents retraced their steps, moving in unison.

And in unison moved right past him. Archer waited to expel a long, soft breath until the two Irregulars had reached the end of the landing and were starting down the ladder. Their boots clanged on the rungs. They muttered their discontent to each other.

Tense, alert, Archer continued to watch, but at last he accepted they had no more sense of his presence above them than would any civilian. He slid slowly down the wall and sat, knees hugged to his chest, waiting.

It was a long wait.

A very long, very dull wait.

They did not give up easily. In fact, Archer wondered at one point whether they would give up at all, if they would perhaps stake out the warehouse entrance and wait until hunger and thirst drove him out in a day or two.

Had they captured the Moth Man? Archer saw no indication of it, which reinforced his suspicions. Ezra, of course, was long gone. Dear old Ezra. But Archer wasn't concerned with Ezra. It was the Moth Man he needed to speak to. He wanted to hear more about those green glass beads. Much more…

❧

The hunt ended at last. The Vancouver police had long since called it quits by the time the Irregulars reluctantly gave up the search and withdrew to the alley outside. The warehouse lights died out, row by row, leaving the great empty barn of a building to the shadows and moonlight. The heavy doors slid shut with a roll like thunder.

Through the dirt-streaked window Archer watched the agents milling dispiritedly. A tall figure appeared in their midst and began to speak. Archer looked more closely and thought he could make out the glittering insignia of a commander.

He swore softly. He'd heard the Irregulars were replacing Brennan. Inevitable, probably, but still too bad. Brennan had been easy to work with. Or work around, as the case might be. No one knew anything about this new man, except that he was not local, not from British Columbia, perhaps not even from Canada. Apparently the rumor that the higher-ups had been worried about Commander Brennan getting slack had been true.

Thus, Commander Spit and Polish.

Archer rested his head against the rough brick and listened to the agents reporting their failure. The alley would have been too far away for human ears to catch a word, but Archer's ears were the least human thing about him. In fact, those small but definite points of cartilage were pretty much a dead giveaway of his half-faerie heritage. The difference wasn't all cosmetic, either. His hearing was as inhumanly keen as his sight.

The commander heard his team out and then reassured them that the night's efforts had not been a waste.

Which meant…what exactly?

Then, finally, the Irregulars departed in an official rumble of government-owned vehicles. The alley stood empty.

Still Archer waited. One could never be too careful.

Another hour passed. The last of the damping dust flattened and its green faded out to nothing. The moon had now slipped down a few squares in the window panes.

Archer walked lightly down the ledge and let himself over the side, dropping quietly onto one of the oddly shaped containers. From there he jumped to the mossy bricks.

A crosshatch of moonlight lay across the open space of the floor. He stuck to the shadows and headed for the rear entrance.

The door was locked, but it took only a few seconds' work to fiddle the mechanism. He eased the door open.

The alley behind the warehouse was silent and empty. The smell of garbage and cold exhaust lingered in the damp air. Nothing moved. Not so much as the flick of a rat's tail stirred the darkness. And yet...unease slithered down his spine. The same unease he had ignored earlier—a few minutes before the Irregulars had burst in.

Archer retreated, slipping back inside the building, slipping back into the shadows, slipping back into the glamour, fading away into the bones of the old building.

He didn't have long to wait.

The door to the alley opened soundlessly. A man stood framed in moonlight. His face was silhouetted; Archer saw only that he was tall and disconcertingly broad.

"I know you're here." The deep voice was conversational, yet it carried. "I know who you are and I know what you are. Why not dispense with these childish games?"

It wasn't a question. He didn't really expect Archer to give himself up. Archer wasn't convinced he even wanted him to give up. There was a certain note in the shadow's voice. Not amusement...something more like anticipation.

Archer kept moving, intangible as a shade, heading for the side entrance. This one was clever and patient, but he couldn't be two places at once, and since he was busy talking to Archer...

"You've had a good long run, but your time is up." The voice found Archer as he reached the door.

Archer waved his hands in front of the lock and felt the tumblers turn, felt the outside bolt slide. He inched the door open just wide enough to step through.

"Another time," he whispered and let the door fall shut.

Just before it sank into the frame, cutting the connection between them, there came a whispered answer to Archer's own whisper, which should have been inaudible to human ears.

"Sooner than you think."

Chapter Two

Scholarly texts are full of information on what faeries will and will not eat. Archer had read many an earnest description of rose petal sandwiches, of button mushroom and wild root soup, of mashed quince and honey. And in fact, he did like honey very much, though he preferred it on hot, buttered English muffins.

He was cramming a honey-drenched muffin in his mouth and trying not to get sticky crumbs on his white silk shirt as he juggled his keys and briefcase when the Irregulars turned up on his Gastown doorstep.

Not the best start to any day, finding members of the elite task force charged with regulating interactions between humans and the inhabitants of all the other realms hovering outside the front door. Archer nearly put a hand up to shield his eyes from all that hardware shining in the sun. "Hardware" as in the buttons and chrome adorning the commander's black uniform, not the high-tech weapons his flunky special agents carried, although they were clearly armed to the teeth.

Archer let the muffin fall from his mouth. He raised his hands—still clutching keys and briefcase—above his head.

Since no one was aiming anything at him, the agents exchanged uncertain glances.

"You can lower your hands, Mr. Green," the commander said dryly after a moment.

He was a big man. Big and brown. Brown hair, brown eyes, brown skin. Built to move mountains. Come to think of it, he rather looked like a mountain. Craggy and intractable. His eyes met Archer's and Archer knew his little performance had been interpreted perfectly. The mountain's expression wasn't amused so much as sardonic. It was the fact that he had any expression at all that caught Archer's attention.

He had thought he recognized the voice; now he was sure that this was Commander Brennan's replacement, Archer's shadow foe of the night before. The knowledge didn't do a lot to improve his morning. Brennan had been careful, conscientious, and occasionally a genuine nuisance, but this one…this one was going to be trouble.

But if there was one thing Archer had learned over the years, it was the human maxim "never let them see you sweat". There had been many wise mortals in the history of the earth, but the man who had come up with that one had been a genius. So Archer smiled at the commander, letting his mockery show, slowly lowering his arms.

The commander's eyes narrowed. He said, "Commander Rake, NATO Irregular Task Force, Vancouver Division. We have a warrant to search these premises."

On cue, the tight-faced agent to Rake's left proffered a sheet of official documentation. Archer took it and studied it.

And studied it.

And studied it.

Eventually Rake caught on and signaled for his minions to proceed. They brushed past Archer and a few moments later he heard the smash of glass in the entryway. Hopefully not Great-Aunt Esmeralda's cloisonné clock. He was not particularly fond of the clock, but it was worth a lot of money and easily liquidated—in lean times he made a habit of pawning it and then redeeming the thing when he was flush again. It was a useful item to keep on hand, that's all.

There was another crash from inside the condominium.

"My tax dollars at work?" Archer handed Rake the warrant.

Rake didn't take the paper. "That's your copy."

"Thank you."

"As a dual citizen of the Glastonbury Faerie Court and the United Kingdom, you have the right to representation from the Glastonbury Court Ambassadorial Corps."

"Dual representation?" Archer took his time folding the document into neat squares and tucking it in his raincoat pocket. Where had the Glastonbury Court Ambassadorial Corps been when he'd been handed off into mortal foster care following the death of his mother? Now, suddenly, he was entitled to dual citizenship? That was rather funny. He said gravely, "Thank you for your meticulous attention to the letter of the law, Commander."

Rake returned, as if by rote, "The laws exist to protect us all, Mr. Green."

Another crash issued from inside the house. Archer's smile tightened. "Great. What does the law have to say about being recompensed for property damaged in the course of an Irregular search?"

"That would depend on what might be discovered during the course of the investigation."

Archer made a rude sound. Commander Rake was sadly out of date. These days nothing in Archer's home would get him arrested, though the French postcards depicting ninetheenth century demons might raise some eyebrows.

"Wouldn't it be faster to tell me what you're looking for?"

Rake was suddenly and, Archer suspected, uncharacteristically urbane. "As a matter of fact, Mr. Green, we'd like to discuss that with you, if you'd be good enough to accompany us to headquarters."

Archer tilted his head, considering. "Headquarters? That sounds serious."

"Just a few questions," Rake said in that same intractable, unnervingly pleasant way.

"Well…the thing is, I'm late for work now." It wasn't that Archer imagined there was any getting out of this, but he hated to make it too easy. He felt certain Rake needed more trouble in his life. Something Archer could offer in great supply.

"That's all right. We've spoken to your boss. Mr. Littlechurch, is it? He said he—and you—would be only too delighted to cooperate with our investigation."

"But what are you investigating?"

"We can talk about it downtown." Rake's tone remained smooth, but there was a glint in his eyes that was almost...derisive.

A frisson of unease curled down Archer's spine. For the first time it occurred to him that he might actually be in trouble. Brennan had had his suspicions, of course, but Brennan had been such a stickler for proof, for evidence. Archer had the uncomfortable feeling that Rake might play by a different set of rules. The same set Archer played by.

Which meant *none.*

He had no choice and they all knew it. All the same, the normal thing to do was to fuss and fume a bit. He offered, "Well, I suppose. If it will help. But it's most...irregular."

He didn't even hear what he'd said till Rake gave a curt laugh. "It is at that. Shall we go?"

They departed with the sound of the Irregulars laying waste to Archer's home.

❧

Archer lived in old downtown Vancouver, the neighborhood affectionately known as Gastown. It was an eclectic and trendy mix of boutiques, cafes, galleries, and overpriced apartments and condominiums. The courtyards and mews had cobbled streets and were lined with old trees and historic buildings. It looked like a well-scrubbed Disney version of the Old World but with all the conveniences of the New.

Needless to say, the Irregulars were not headquartered in Gastown. The black SUV sped silently through the rush hour traffic. No one spoke. The dashboard radio—could equipment that expensive and advanced be called a *radio*?—crackled with news updates from various investigations in progress. It sounded as though another special task force was closing in on a house in Victoria where Chinese illegals, including a vengeful Yóu Hún

Yě Gui, had taken refuge. There were also infrequent bursts of static that didn't come from the human realm. No one in the car seemed to register the transmissions.

It was not particularly cramped inside the official vehicle, but Archer was uncomfortably aware of Commander Rake. Rake was a big man. Not just physically big. He had presence. Still, he kept his muscular length and his muscular presence to his own half of the backseat. Though Archer felt crowded, his personal space was being scrupulously observed. Maybe it had to do with Rake's aftershave, a blend of spicy vanilla and something woodsy. The faerie half of Archer responded instinctively and enthusiastically. He quelled that gut reaction, not that he really suspected the commander of choosing his personal scent based on its power to attract and disarm half-humans.

Then again, Rake didn't seem like the type who left much to chance.

"How did you injure your hand?" Rake asked casually as the tall art deco building that housed city hall appeared ahead of them.

Archer glanced automatically at the white strip of bandage neatly wrapped around the base of his thumb. A few drops of blood collected in a DNA kit by the magical forensics team were as good as the ink on the signature line of a confession. The odds of Rake's team finding where he'd snagged himself on that fucking nail were slim. Slim, but not nonexistent.

He answered coolly, "I cut myself shaving."

Rake eyed him long and levelly. No sense of humor? He said politely, "A close shave then?"

"Very."

Rake's thin mouth twitched, but he said no more, and neither did Archer.

He could have gone on protesting his innocence and insisting he had no idea what all this was about, but he found he had no energy for it. In fact, he'd have felt silly. It wasn't going to be like it had been with Brennan. That was quite clear. With Rake he felt strangely—strangely, because they were obviously destined to be on opposite sides of any and all endeavors—that at last he'd found someone who spoke his language.

The SUV reached the Irregulars HQ and stopped at the security gate. IDs were flashed. The gate opened and the SUV pulled through. They parked in the underground structure and disembarked.

They were all still playing the game that Archer's visit to HQ was voluntary, but as he walked into the elevator with Rake and his boyish subordinate, Archer was uneasily aware that walking out might not be nearly as easy.

Inside, the Irregulars HQ was as generic and nondescript as the outside: blue carpets, white walls, photos of scenic Vancouver. The air was recycled and temperature controlled. Most of the staff bustling down the halls with quiet efficiency were human, but Archer spotted a number of goblin staff members. Even one administrative assistant who was patently Kapre.

In fact, it seemed to him that the extra-human staff ratio had risen since his last visit. He wasn't sure if that was a positive sign or not. The Irregulars claimed to be an equal opportunity employer, but so many of these government organizations merely gave lip service to the concept of diversity initiatives.

"You're set up for Interview Room Three," a well-groomed young woman informed Rake. Rake nodded briskly.

The interview room was new. Not the room itself, the fact that Archer was in it. Brennan had usually conducted interviews in his own office. But this was not an interview. This was an interrogation. That was clear.

A thin, pale woman with sharp features and white-blond hair in a tight ponytail was waiting for them when they entered the room. Her uniform too carried the silver braid of the Irregular commissioned officer. Archer didn't recognize her. Perhaps she had transferred in with Rake. Perhaps he had just never noticed her.

Either way, she was a witch. Archer could sense the energy crackling around her like static electricity on a windy day. Subdued—perhaps even an effort made to conceal her true nature—but he knew her for what she was. A human lie detector.

"This is Sergeant Orly." Rake took the chair across the table from Archer.

"Oh really?"

Rake was unamused by the little joke. He absently straightened his tie, reminding Archer of someone rolling up their sleeves before tackling a dirty job.

Sergeant Orly, already seated, didn't seem to hear. She was going through a thick file. She fastened her pale green gaze on Archer and nodded in greeting.

Archer nodded briefly. He sat down and waited, hoping that he showed neither curiosity nor alarm. He couldn't help wondering about that enormous file. Was that his file? If so, it had expanded considerably since his last visit to HQ.

Orly slid the file to Rake. Rake glanced through it unhurriedly.

Archer grimaced inwardly. He knew this tactic. He let his gaze wander around the barren room. The other two paid no attention to him and he returned the favor, though that sweetly masculine fragrance Rake wore kept feathering the edge of his consciousness.

After a minute or two, though, he couldn't help looking at the file. He felt a flicker of irritation. Did they honestly think he couldn't read that tiny print from across the table? Weren't they familiar with faeries at all? In the middle of that thought, he noticed that the edge of the table on his side was badly gnawed as though by a giant and very nervous rat.

His own unease increased. Very rarely did he find himself at a disadvantage, but he felt at a disadvantage now.

Archer ignored the file they were pretending to so studiously pore over and considered Rake. His suit was tailored, and cleverly tailored at that. It gave Rake's large, powerful body an air of near elegance. Archer could see the blue shadow beneath Rake's freshly shaved jaw. His brown hair was clipped short and inclined to curl and one of his ears was pierced, although he wore no earring. He wore no wedding ring either. No jewelry at all. His hands were big and blunt fingered, but the nails were neatly trimmed and buffed.

Orly leaned forward and spoke into a microphone, giving the time and date of their session.

"Please state your full name for the record," she told Archer.

"I assume you want my actual faerie name?"

Orly and Rake didn't exchange looks, but Archer suspected they wanted to.

"Of course," Orly said, sounding anything but certain.

Archer nodded. "Spider Reedstaff."

"What?" That time Orly and Rake did look at each other.

"That's right. According to the website I play a reed pipe and sing spellbinding songs. I live in a spider-webbed wonderland and vacation in insect grottoes. I can be seen only when the seer holds a four-leafed clover, which I can only surmise you both have stashed on your persons. I wear a tunic made of cobwebs and I have deep green butterfly wings."

"What website?" Orly asked.

"What the hell are you talking about?" Rake's brows straightened into a single forbidding line.

"The fairy name generator website."

Orly drew back. Rake's face twisted into that sardonic expression once more. "You enjoy your little games, Mr. Green," he remarked.

"As do you, if the last five minutes are anything to go by."

Rake's smile was thin and brief. "Let's try this again. State your legal name and occupation for the record."

"My name is Archer Green and I'm the curator of the Museum of State-Sanctioned Antiquities in Vancouver." Most people, of course, had no idea what his title meant or what secrets the museum contained, but Orly and Rake were not most people. In fact, in theory, the three of them were on the same side. But that was clearly a theory Orly and Rake did not ascribe to.

"There. That didn't hurt, did it?"

"Not so far. The morning is young."

"What is your earthly-realm nationality?"

"I'm English."

"What are your ties to the faerie realm?"

"None. I've lived all my life in the human realm." Well, the vast majority of his life. At one time it had even been a sore spot. No longer.

Orly made a notation in the file. Rake asked, "What are your duties at MoSSA?"

"I'm responsible for overseeing the arrangement, cataloging, and exhibition of our collections, much like any earthly-realm museum curator."

Only…not.

Rake said, "The difference is MoSSA's collections contain some of the most dangerous magical artifacts in the universe."

Archer smiled tightly. "They're not dangerous once they reach MoSSA." That actually still was a sore spot.

"True. At least in theory." That was Orly.

Archer ignored her. "In addition to curating the existing collections, I supervise and coordinate our acquisition of documents and artifacts deemed too powerful or dangerous to return to their realms of origin. It's part of my job to arrange for their permanent storage and study."

"That's a lot of responsibility," Rake said.

"I haven't had any complaints so far."

Rake smiled. "As you pointed out, the morning is still young."

"True. Is there some reason you refuse to tell me why I'm being held in custody?"

Rake looked in astonishment to Orly, who shrugged helplessly. "If I somehow gave the impression that you were under arrest or being forcibly held, I apologize. We do have a few questions and most people prefer that we don't interview them at their workplace. That seemed to be the view of your boss, Mr. Littlechurch." The words were right and Rake's tone was sincere, but his eyes were mocking.

"I'll bet," Archer said.

Orly interjected, "You don't get along with your boss?"

"Not at all. That is to say, we get along fine."

Archer could hear the lack of conviction in his tone. He wasn't surprised when Orly made another note in the file.

Rake asked abruptly, "Tell us about your involvement with SRRIM."

Archer managed not to start, warned at the last second by the witch's cautious effort to delve into his thoughts. Fortunately, like her commander, she was strong rather than subtle.

"There's no such organization."

"Not anymore, not officially, but you were once a member of the radical group known as the Society for the Rescue and Restoration of Indigenous Magic."

"That was years ago. I was a kid."

"By faerie standards, yes. By human standards, you were nearly sixty."

Archer said nothing.

"Of course, by faerie standards you're still very young. Which, I think, probably explains a great deal."

Archer blinked. Hopefully it was his only reveal. He could feel the witch still poking and prying at his thoughts, but he sidestepped her. His attention was now entirely on Rake. Rake somehow knew about Archer's past membership in SRRIM and apparently understood enough about faerie physiology and culture to realize…too much.

He said carefully, "I did briefly belong to SRRIM. As you say, I was in my early teens. Obviously my views have changed. I'm curious as to what triggered your interest in my past. The subject of my youthful activism never came up during the hiring process and I've worked as curator for the museum for over five years."

"Yes, I'm aware of that. Of both facts. Nowadays our records are more centralized."

What did that mean? *Centralized* felt like a euphemism for something less benign.

"I don't understand what this is about," Archer said, although he now had a very good idea of what it was all about.

"You're being questioned in connection with the illegal acquisition of a highly dangerous magical artifact."

Damn. Damn. Damn. Archer returned with his best imitation of a fussy museum curator—imitating Barry, in fact—"I thought it might be something like that. I'm aware that many museums are under scrutiny for the illegal purchase of cultural and historical property, but I'm sure you realize our situation at MoSSA is rather different?"

"Oh yes," Rake murmured. "I'm conscious of just how different you are, Mr. Green."

"I'm flattered," Archer said, feeling anything but.

"According to you, your involvement in radical politics was just youthful high spirits. What exactly is your position on the subject of the repatriation of magical artifacts to their realms of origin?"

"Are you asking me as the curator of the Museum of State-Sanctioned Antiquities?"

Rake turned his hand palm up as though inviting Archer's opinion to alight.

"My position is, of course, the official position. These relics do not belong in the human realm."

"Do they belong in a museum?"

Rake and Orly waited for his reply. Archer smiled. "That's not my call."

"You must have an opinion," Rake said.

Archer could feel Orly once again prying at his defenses. He revised his original assessment. She was more skilled than he'd given her credit for. A human would normally not have sensed how much effort it took to get into his mind. He let her read his general discomfort with having missed breakfast and the hardness of the chair.

"I have opinions on many things, but they aren't relevant to the job I'm paid to do."

Orly abandoned the mental infiltration and took over the inquisition. "So it's just a job for you, protecting humanity from these destructive forces?"

Archer sat back in the chair. "I don't understand the question. Do you mean, is it my vocation in life? No. I believe that's your job. Sorry. *Mission*."

"You seem defensive," she observed.

"I feel defensive. I'm dragged here this morning, my plans disrupted, without a word of explanation. Then I'm questioned about what I'm sure amounts to a trivial mix-up. What is it now? A missing signature? The wrong triplicate form? Another misfiled paper?"

"We rarely drag citizens in over misfiled paperwork," Rake said mildly.

"No? Brennan did."

Another one of those silent exchanges, although this time Rake and his sergeant didn't look at each other.

"As a matter of fact, this interview has to do with an artifact known as the Stone of Fal."

Archer raised his brows. "You're joking."

"I never joke," Rake said, and Archer could well believe it.

"I had no idea the stone had resurfaced. In that case, I understand your concern. I'd heard rumor that it was in the hands of a private collector."

"Interestingly, one of your old SSRIM friends, Director Ali Khan Chauhan of the National Conjury Clinic in New Delhi arrived in Vancouver International Airport this morning."

"Ali's here?" Archer said with obvious delight.

Maybe it was too obvious because Rake got that supercilious look again.

"You think he's here to purchase the Stone of Fal?" Archer inquired.

"That's one theory," Orly put in.

Silence followed her words. Archer could hear their wristwatches ticking in counter beat.

Rake's phone vibrated in his jacket pocket. The sound would have gone undetected by most human ears, but Archer—as the interview had already made plain in case he failed to understand—was not human. Not as far as most humans were concerned. Rake muttered an apology, rose, and left the room.

Orly continued to ask Archer various questions, but he wasn't listening to her. He tried to follow Rake's conversation down the hall, but as powerful as his hearing was, he couldn't follow words spoken through cell phone circuits and Rake seemed to know instinctively to restrict his responses to unrevealing grunts.

Rake returned to the room and took his chair once more. Once again, visceral awareness of his heat and strength and fabulous aftershave gave Archer a funny sensation in the pit of his belly. He assumed it was merely nerves, but he would have been happier to be certain.

"The other theory," Rake said, as though there had been no interruption, "*my* theory, is that Chauhan is here unofficially to retrieve the stone in order to return it to the Tuatha Dé Dannan."

"I see." Unwisely, Archer added, "Either way it'll no longer pose a threat to the human realm."

"The problem is, if the stone is not destroyed, it could conceivably at some point be returned to the human realm."

"That seems unlikely."

"And yet it's been drifting along in the human realm for years, isn't that right?"

"That's the rumor."

"I think we all know that it's more than a rumor."

Archer waited.

Rake seemed to weigh various courses. He said abruptly, "Although our search failed to turn up any physical evidence, I believe the stone is in your possession. I believe you plan to return it to Chauhan."

Archer relaxed. He even offered a cheeky smile. "You obviously know nothing about museums or museum curators if you think I'd voluntarily hand over a priceless artifact to a rival."

Rake continued as though Archer hadn't spoken, "Furthermore, I believe that you and Chauhan are both members of whatever SRRIM's current incarnation is, in short, a secret and fanatical organization with a mission to retrieve and repatriate dangerous illegal magical artifacts to their source realms."

He should have laughed. At the very least, Archer should have said, "Me?" in an outraged tone. He did neither. He did nothing. He continued to sit in the hard-backed chair staring across the damaged table at Rake.

Rake's eyes were lighter than he'd originally thought. Or were they? They seemed to change color in the drab little room. Now they were the color of the brown glass that good ale came in, then the color of old honey, next the color of the winter heath on the old Romney salt marshes. They held Archer's gaze without wavering.

"That's interesting," Archer said politely, at last.

He could feel Orly's disappointment. Had she really thought he was going to admit anything? Rake's gaze continued, intent and alert.

"You don't deny it?"

"I assumed you took my denial for granted."

"I'm not taking anything for granted."

"You can take that for granted. Why are you telling me all this?"

Rake leaned back in his chair and folded his arms. He said in a flat, hard voice, "I'm giving you notice. It's over. We both know I don't have enough evidence to arrest you today, but it won't be long before I have what I need. In the meantime, I've reported my suspicions to the director of the museum."

"That…wasn't very nice."

"We're not in a very nice business, Mr. Green."

"Suppose I'm innocent?"

Rake grimaced. "Then I guess I'd owe you an apology. But I'm just an ordinary, everyday policeman, Mr. Green, and that supposition would take more imagination than I have."

Chapter Three

"Furthermore, I don't enjoy starting the day with police knocking on the door, Mr. Green." Barry Littlechurch's prim voice carried down the arched marble hallway and drifted into the exhibit room where Miss Roya and Mr. Baker were cataloging beakers of amber and gold tears reportedly belonging to the Norse goddess Freya. The tears carried no particular properties, but they had been exorcised and relegated to the museum all the same. Official state policy.

Miss Roya and Mr. Baker kept their heads bent over their work, though Mr. Baker's cheeks were pink. He had a severe crush on Archer. Archer thought he was a charming boy, but he hadn't been interested in charming boys since he'd been one himself. And that was a very long time ago.

He replied evenly, "I don't enjoy it either, Mr. Littlechurch."

Littlechurch was a small, slim man with prematurely silver hair swept into a pompadour. His beard was precisely trimmed. His eyebrows circumflexed in perpetual skepticism. "Nor do I appreciate your offhanded attitude. I don't think you realize quite how serious this situation is." The museum director led the way into his office, still complaining loudly.

Archer followed without comment. Just before he closed the door behind them, he threw a look back at Baker and Roya. They hastily returned to their cataloging.

As the lock clicked into place, Barry stopped huffing and puffing. "How did it go?" He took his seat behind the enormous desk positioned beneath the gilt-framed portrait of Carl Peoples, the museum founder.

"It could have gone better," Archer admitted, taking the velvet-upholstered chair on the other side of the desk.

"They released you."

Archer nodded.

"But?"

"They know about my involvement in the SRRIM."

"Of course they know." Barry shrugged, unperturbed. "Knowing and proving that you are still an active member are two different things."

"Not necessarily. Not given the broad spectrum of powers the current administration has given law enforcement agencies like the Irregulars."

"There are no law enforcement agencies like the Irregulars," Barry said gloomily.

"True."

Barry grimaced. "Still. Given your position, I'm sure they'll—"

Archer laughed. "I shouldn't bet on it. I don't think my position is going to protect me this time."

Barry nodded. "What exactly did Commander Rake say when he brought you in for questioning?"

"He believes I'm involved in the effort to return the Stone of Fal to the sidhe."

Barry made a disgusted sound. "That's nothing more than species profiling."

"Well..."

Barry threw him a quick look from beneath his silver brow. "A boy's enthusiasms—"

"They're not merely the enthusiasms of a boy. You know where my sympathies lie."

"Of course. That doesn't change the fact that you're not involved." Barry did not go so far as to ask why Archer had been in that warehouse allegedly meeting a notorious fence, but his gaze was inquiring.

"No. True." Briefly, Archer considered telling Barry the whole story, but this was personal. Truthfully, Barry was better off not knowing.

And Archer didn't want to hear what Barry would have to say.

Barry sighed. "I can see this Commander Rake is going to be a thorn in our side."

"Not necessarily. His interest seems focused on me. That could work to everyone's advantage." Barring his own.

"He plans to nail you to the wall. You're right about that." Barry sighed. "I think he's one of these fellows that takes it all very personally."

"Unlike us."

"I don't know." Barry seemed thoughtful. "Do we take it personally? I don't think I take it personally. This is beyond personalities."

"We're fanatics, according to Commander Rake. He's probably right." Archer smothered a yawn. It had been a long night and a busy morning. "The bottom line is we're out of time. I certainly am in any case."

"This isn't like you."

Wasn't it? Archer liked to think his idealism was tempered by pragmatism. It was one reason he'd managed to fly under the radar this long. "They were waiting for me last night."

"You think it was a setup?"

"Yes." Honesty compelled Archer to add, "I'm not positive, but yes."

"But why?"

"I don't know. It's not as though I pose a threat to anyone."

"A threat? No. Although I suppose the Commander Rakes of the world will always see people like us as threats."

Barry was polite enough to say *us*, but he meant *you*. Archer knew he was right. "I suppose I should think about moving on now that I've been targeted by the authorities." The thought gave him a pang. He had been happy in Vancouver.

Still, it wasn't the first time. He would survive.

Barry was shaking his head. "No, no. Nothing of the kind. Remember how gung ho Brennan was at first? We'll wear this one down too."

Archer thought of Rake, of that big, powerful body clothed in the Savile Row suit. The buffed fingernails and expensive haircut. Beneath that civilized veneer was something not remotely civilized. Oddly, the thought of that unknown excited him. "I don't think so. He's a different breed."

"Speaking of different breeds," Barry said. "I got confirmation this morning that the naga skin will be delivered tomorrow afternoon."

The snakeskin, shed by an Indian demon some eight thousand years earlier, had been under study by the R&D department of NIAD in DC for the past three years. It was be returned to the museum to be cataloged and reshelved and ultimately forgotten.

"No worries there."

"Er…no."

Archer glanced up. "Is there a problem?"

Barry grimaced.

"There can't be. The bloody thing's been exorcised."

"You know the way rumors get started."

Archer's brows drew together. "What rumors?"

"That the skin is…"

"Is what?"

"Showing signs of life."

In the resounding silence, Archer said, "It's just a skin. How much life could it show?"

Barry shook his head. "You know how these rumors get started."

Oh yes. Every legend began life as a tiny, persistent rumor. Sometimes as nothing more than idle gossip.

Barry added, "Nothing that need worry us, I'm sure."

Because they had bigger things to worry about?

❧

The rest of the day passed without incident. At five, Archer slipped his jacket on, grabbed his briefcase, and left the museum. He caught a streetcar and then a SkyTrain to Library Square where he spent the next hour or so browsing book stacks and services.

When he was sure he'd lost the tail that Rake had planted on him, he headed toward Kerrisdale. He crossed the Burrard Street Bridge and turned right onto Cornwall Street. That put him in the Kitsilano neighborhood,were Ezra lived.

"Kits" was an arty-crafty enclave of artisan bakeries, art studios, organic markets, trendy cafes, and Vancouver's Greektown. It was mainly populated by college students and yuppies and yoga teachers. Pretty much the last place one would expect to find a goblin lowlife like Ezra, which was why it was such a perfect place for him to hole up.

As Archer walked he could smell the salty scent of the nearby sea. It reminded him of Romney Marsh. Of home. Home and long ago. He was impatient with himself, but perhaps the sense of nostalgia wasn't surprising given his mission.

Ezra lived in an old apartment building on Vine Street. The scent of lamb moussaka filled the downstairs hallway and tagged along with Archer up to the second floor. Beatles music played from a few doors down.

Archer tapped on Ezra's door. After a few seconds, he knocked again.

The door swung open just as Ezra's goblin face was morphing into more socially acceptable features; the lipless piranha smile transformed into something equally toothy but cheesy and human.

That smile too faded as Ezra took note of his caller.

"Green." His voice came out in a croak.

"I was in the neighborhood," Archer said.

"Oh. Hello. I di—" Ezra staggered back as Archer applied the heel of his hand and the toe of his boot to the door and shoved. "Wh-what are you doing?"

"I thought we might have a little chat."

Ezra took another few steps back and looked around as though seeking an escape way that had suddenly disappeared. "Chat? About what?"

Archer slipped inside and closed the door, leaning casually back against the painted plywood. "Guess."

Ezra shook his head.

"You set me up."

Ezra's human face wavered as his masking spell dissolved and reformed itself in goblin lines. He bit his nearly nonexistent lips, and though he was considerably taller than Archer, he seemed to shrink into himself.

"I heard there was trouble." Ezra gulped. "But it wasn't anything to do with me. How could I know the badges were watching the Moth Man?"

"That's your story? That the Irregulars were following the Moth Man?"

"Of course. You can't think *I'd* work against you."

Archer smiled. "Can't I?"

Ezra shook his head. "I'm no friend of the badges."

"That doesn't mean you wouldn't sell me out to save your own skin. Hell, you'd sell your own mother out if you thought there was something in it for you."

Ezra looked hurt. As hurt as a goblin could look. "That's not true. I've got scruples. Not many, I admit, but I've got'em. Same as you."

Archer considered Ezra's sweaty, misshapen face. He could have been telling the truth, of course. It wasn't impossible. Unlikely, but not impossible. The relationship between fae and goblin had always been…unpredictable. And with the mounting instability among the Irish fae in the Tuatha Dé Dannan Islands and the large goblin mercenary forces there, they were likely to become more so.

Ezra unwisely launched into further protests, finishing, "We all know what you're doing. You and your friends. We're all behind you."

Ezra's intel was out of date—Archer's radical youth was well in the past now—but perhaps that shouldn't have come as a surprise. Archer said gently, "If I were to discover that you *had* tried to double-cross—"

"I didn't! I wouldn't!"

"I have a *very* long memory."

"I know that. You don't have to do the glowing eyes thing. I know! I'm not a collaborator."

He was lying. The more he denied it, the more certain Archer was, but what course would best serve his purpose? Knowing Ezra couldn't be trusted made him a useful conduit for feeding incorrect information to the Irregulars. While it was true Archer was no longer involved in radical activities, his sympathies were largely unchanged and he was privy to the plans and schemes of many whose aims did not align with those of the NATO Irregular Affairs Division.

Besides, Archer wanted something more than he wanted revenge. All day long the thought of the green glass beads had haunted him. If there was a chance they still existed…

"If it wasn't you, then it was the Moth Man."

"Yes." Ezra leaped at this explanation. "That's what I told you. It had to be that freak."

"Where does he live?"

"Somewhere in Downtown Eastside."

"Where?"

"Hastings Street." Ezra babbled out the address.

"All right. I'll pay a call on him. See what he has to say for himself." Archer watched Ezra's fluctuating features.

Ezra's gaze shifted. "You can't trust anything he says."

"Now, now. People say the same thing about you, Ezra." Archer smiled maliciously before slipping out the door.

❧

Downtown Eastside wasn't the hellhole it had been a few years earlier, but it was still no place to be after dark if you didn't need to be. Archer had his favorite places in the DTES. Carnegie Center with its century-old stained glass windows. The Dr. Sun Yat-Sen Classical Chinese Garden with its mirror-like ponds and exotic flowers scenting the smoggy night. Hypodermic needles no longer littered the pavement, but the ratio of drug addicts, prostitutes, and the homeless compared to regular citizens was still too high for most people's comfort. The streets always smelled of blood and urine to Archer, but his olfactory sense was more highly developed than that of a pure-blooded human.

He walked briskly, and though a couple of revenants followed him for a few streets, only the still-living variety hassled him with offers of drugs for sale. At five foot nine and slightly built, Archer looked like easy prey from a distance. Up close, his faerie heritage was apparent, and while the semblance of birth defects was rarely a deterrent, possible—or at least sober—predators veered off.

Archer found the Moth Man's place without trouble. It was an old brick building, a former hotel from the 1920s, converted into a number of single-occupant residences. A musical clash of cultures was being waged in the dingy halls, and somewhere a baby wailed unconsoled. People sat in open doorways, smoking pot and talking loudly. Red-rimmed eyes watched Archer pass, but no one spoke to him.

He knocked on the door next to a tarnished nameplate stating R. Mann.

A double look at the peephole revealed a pale, protuberant eye peering through at him. Archer waited.

There came a sound of sliding bolts, several of them, and then a chain, and at last the door swung open.

"Good evening," Archer said.

Without speaking, the Moth Man nodded for Archer to enter.

Archer stepped out of the hall into a gloomy room full of boxes. The boxes were stacked all the way to the ceiling and marked with the brand names of televisions and stereos and fans. The fans were a little puzzling, but whatever. A chair and table were positioned a few inches from a television set. The television was on, but it was muted. Teenagers danced and sang, silently energetic on a large stage.

"I thought you would come." The Moth Man pulled his chair out. "If you got away from the drearies."

"The…drearies?"

"The badges. *Irregulars*." The Moth Man said the word with contempt. His eyes looked pink in the poor light. If so, they were the only color in his skeletal face.

"You got away all right. From the badges, I mean."

"Sure. I blend in with the crowd." The Moth Man settled at the table in front of the television. There was a plate stacked with pancakes, though where he had cooked them in this tiny stoveless apartment was unclear. He proceeded to pour chocolate syrup over the heap. The syrup pooled on the plate in a brown puddle. "I was just having my supper."

"Don't let me interrupt."

"I won't." The Moth Man neatly quartered his pancakes and then bisected them again. His attention, that which wasn't focused on his plate, was all on the soundless television.

Archer began, "Last night you mentioned…"

"Green glass beads," the Moth Man completed the sentence. He smiled and his teeth were brown with chocolate. The effect was fairly ghastly, but Archer didn't care. All he heard was "green glass beads."

His mouth was dry as he said simply, "Yes."

"Family heirloom, eh?"

"If they're the right ones. There are nearly as many beads in the world as grains of sand."

"They're the right ones."

"How do you know?"

The Moth Man said in a weird singsong mimicry of an Irish accent, “These belonged to a wee slip of an Irish nymph.”

“She was English. My great-grandmother.”

“Even so. These are the right ones. *Provenance.*” The word came out thick with syrup and chocolate sauce.

“Provenance can be faked.”

The big, pink eyes blinked slowly, thoughtfully at him. “You'd know the moment you saw them, wouldn't you? If they were the real thing?”

Archer nodded.

“Well then.”

“Are you saying you have them?” Archer felt almost dizzy at the thought. That in a matter of moments he might see them…touch them. The green glass beads.

“What are they worth to you?”

Name your price. He didn't say it, though. He wasn't that lost to common sense. Instead he shrugged. “You're saying you have them in your possession?”

“No. I don't have them.”

The disappointment barely had time to form before the Moth Man added through a mouthful of pancake, “But I know where they are.”

“Well?” Archer asked when nothing further was forthcoming.

“Weeeellllll.” The Moth Man cleared his throat stickily. “I'll tell you, but I would need you to do something for me.”

Archer narrowed his eyes. “Such as?”

Another sticky throat scratching. “You've got the winged sandals of Hermes in the museum, isn't that so?”

“Where did you hear that?”

“Same place I heard about your beads. I keep my ear to the ground.”

To the underground, more like. Archer said slowly, “It's possible.”

“I want them.”

Archer said nothing for a second or two. “You'll trade information regarding the beads if I'll hand over the sandals. Is that right?”

The Moth Man nodded.

"Do you realize what you're asking?"

The Moth Man hunched his shoulders defensively at Archer's tone. "You're a fine one to talk. You're asking something too."

"I'm not asking for something that poses a threat to anyone else."

"You don't know that."

He had a point. Archer didn't know. No one knew, in fact, because the jewels—if you could call them jewels—were mostly legend.

"You're talking about trafficking in culturally significant other-realm artifacts. That's a federal, international and inter-realm crime."

"It's a federal crime to acquire illegal magical properties, whether intended for sale or not. That doesn't stop you."

When Archer said nothing, the Moth Man said uncomfortably, "Everyone knows what you're up to. You and your friends."

"Do they?" So much for all those years of perfectly blameless and law-abiding existence. "Even so, there's a great difference between acquiring these items in order to repatriate them and turning them loose on the streets."

"Not according to the government. Not according to the drearies."

"According to me."

The Moth Man dropped his fork and sat up straight, goggling at Archer. "No need to take offense."

"I am offended, though."

"Yes. I see that." The Moth Man swallowed noisily. "But the sandals are…are harmless. They'd just let me move about faster, more quietly, see? That's all."

"They wouldn't do you any good anyway. They've been exorcised. Like everything else in the museum."

The Moth Man shrugged. "Maybe so. I'd still like them."

"I don't doubt it. You're not going to have them."

The Moth Man's pale, protruding forehead wrinkled in thought. "What if I were to ask for something else?"

"Something from the museum? The answer is the same."

The Moth Man's expression grew sly. "What if I were to tell someone you came here asking about the beads?"

"What if I were to cast a spell on you and turn you into a moth for real?"

The Moth Man blanched even paler. "No need to get in an uproar. I was only fooling."

"You're a fool right enough."

"Not like I'm planning to make trouble."

"No, you're not going to make trouble," Archer said softly.

The fork clattered against the plate as it fell from the Moth Man's nerveless fingers. "Don't do that!"

"Do what?"

"What you're doing. Magic. I can feel it pressing in on me. And your eyes are all funny and green."

Archer smiled coldly. "My eyes *are* green."

"You know what I mean."

"I know what you mean." Archer stepped forward.

The Moth Man shoved back his chair, nearly toppling a tower of boxes as he rose, keeping the table between Archer and himself. "If you do something to me, people will know."

"No, they won't. If I do something to you, you won't even know it." That was an exaggeration. Archer's mind control abilities were as limited as his ability to cast spells. He knew a few things about psychology, though.

"You don't have to be this way about it." With the table still safely between them, the Moth Man offered a conciliatory smile. "It was a suggestion, that's all. Forget it. Maybe you'll do me a favor in return some time."

"Maybe. I have a long memory."

The Moth Man coughed and then looked wistfully at the half-eaten pancakes in the lake of syrup. "Do you know who George Gaki is?"

Archer stared. Oh yes. He knew who Gaki was. A rich antiques dealer who was reputed to have taken more than a few legal and ethical shortcuts in building his impressive personal collection. A collection that reportedly held magical artifacts as well as treasures from the mortal realms.

What few people knew—and perhaps it had little bearing—was that Gaki was an old and powerful demon.

He said at last, "Are you telling me they're in Gaki's collection?"

The Moth Man nodded. "He bought them at an auction two weeks ago."

"That's not possible. I'd have heard."

"Antique water beads. That's what they were sold as."

Archer was silent. He did remember something about the sale of antique water beads. He'd thought nothing of it at the time. Water beads could hardly be taken for magic by anyone over five years old.

"How were they discovered?"

The Moth Man made a noise that Archer realized was supposed to pass for humor. It sounded like something needed oiling. "The most famous string of beads in the history of the faerie realm?"

And yet they had gone undiscovered for over two centuries. "You're *sure*?"

"Well..." The Moth Man's white lids lowered modestly. "I haven't seen them myself, but a friend saw them. Swears it's them. And Gaki has been boasting in certain quarters that he's got them." His colorless lashes rose. He watched Archer. "You could find out. You have the connections."

"Yes," Archer answered absently. Could it really be this simple?

"Or," the Moth Man said slyly, "you could always ask him."

Chapter Four

There was a pub in Gastown not far from where Archer lived that stayed open till one in the morning on weeknights and served good English ale. No vodkas from all around the world, no dance floor, and thankfully no televisions, plasma or otherwise. Archer found a seat at the bar, ordered a pint of Royal Stinger Honey Ale, and considered what he had learned.

And what his options were.

If it was true, if the beads had resurfaced at last, he had to have them. That part was simple and required no thought. The beads belonged to him. Their existence was irretrievably intertwixt with that of his faerie bloodline. He had searched for them for years. He *would* have them.

Anyway, there was no reason not to have them. What did they amount to? The original love beads. A strand of shining stones guaranteed to win the wearer the heart of anyone he or she desired. How could that pose a threat to anyone? It wasn't as though the possessor of the beads could command worldwide adoration, and the magic worked only if the wearer truly loved.

This wasn't like the Stone of Fal or even Hermes's sandals. This was different. This was personal.

Very personal. A family heirloom, that's all the beads were. Though the loss of them had resulted in his mother being relegated to the human realm and her subsequent doom. Humans thought of magical artifacts as things to simply possess or divest of at will, but in the faerie realm possession and dispossession of such articles meant life or death. Probably in a great many more realms as well.

So there was no need for that anxious fluttering in his guts. He wasn't going to do anything dangerous to anyone but himself. And if he couldn't outwit those overdressed and overarmed meatbags, he deserved to be in danger.

Assuming the Moth Man was correct. Assuming the beads existed at all. And that they were where Archer might retrieve them.

Archer took a long pull on the sweet beer. He felt in his bones that the Moth Man had been speaking the truth. The timing was so perfectly awful that it had to be true. As tricky as it would be to get the beads from Gaki, it would be that much more complicated with the damned badges breathing down his neck.

Ah. And here was another complication. If his intention, no, if even his *interest* came to the attention of the Irregulars, they might—undoubtedly *would*—attempt to confiscate the beads in order to neutralize them. That was basic policy. No magical artifacts left loose in the human realm. No exceptions.

Inevitably this worrying reflection reminded Archer of Commander Rake. The thought of the Irregulars' new officer gave him another of those uncomfortable fluttering feelings in his belly, like a trapped swarm of butterflies. He shook his head at himself and drank another mouthful.

It was a long time since he'd felt anything like that. He had a natural suspicion of mortals when it came to affairs of the heart. Or affairs of the loins. Even if he hadn't…Humans were so short lived. It was asking for heartache, getting too interested in them.

Ah well. He ordered another pint.

The piped music played a slow Irish waltz, "Sidhe Bheag", "Sidhe Mhor". Archer smiled faintly and sipped his ale.

Someone took the bar stool next to him. Someone who took up a fair bit of acreage. An elbow bumped his arm, a muscular thigh brushed his own. The scent of musk and vanilla mixed pleasantly with more prosaic ones. Archer's heart jumped. He turned his head and met the glinting gaze of Commander Rake.

"Here you are," Rake said.

"Commander Rock."

Rake's mouth tugged into a faint smile. He didn't bother to correct Archer.

Archer asked unwillingly, "Where should I be?"

"I thought you might be making for the border."

Archer's jaw dropped. "Making for the border? Why the hell should I?"

Rake still had that amber gleam in his eye, that hint that he was enjoying himself. "You lost no time getting rid of the tail I placed on you this afternoon."

Archer sniffed. "Never send a man to do a Cu Sith's work."

Rake laughed. "True. Where did you go that you were afraid to be seen?"

"Nowhere. I don't like being followed as a matter of principle."

"You're a man of principles?"

Archer shrugged. It shouldn't have stung. What did he care what Rake thought?

Rake ordered a pint before turning his attention back to Archer, and Archer, though he hated to admit it, felt another flare of excitement as that dark, moody gaze turned his way.

"Yes," Rake said. "You're a man of principle—even if misguided."

Archer set his mug down. He said mockingly, "You know me so well."

Rake took no offense. "I do. I've been making a study of you, Green. I think I know you pretty well."

"As well as any man can," Archer mimicked.

"Better than Brennan."

Archer reached for his mug again to hide his smile.

Rake made a soft sound that could have been amusement or scorn. Or both. "This is all a game to you, isn't it?"

"It has amusing elements."

"There's not much of the human strain in you."

There wasn't, no. Archer was tall for a faerie; his ears ended in graceful points usually hidden beneath his dark curls; his green eyes were wide and exotically tilted, but he doubted Rake was referring to his physical appearance.

"Hopefully not."

It must have sounded more bitter than he intended. Rake's eyebrows rose. "Your father was human."

"Yes." Rake had indeed been studying up.

"Is that why…?"

"Why what?"

Rake's tone was bleak. "Why you're willing to gamble with the safety of the human realm."

"That's your theory. I haven't admitted to anything. I certainly wouldn't admit to *that*."

"You haven't denied it with much vigor either."

"There's no point." Rake opened his mouth and Archer added, "Your mind's made up. I saw that this morning."

"True." Rake drank from his mug. He seemed easy and relaxed. "So your father was a naturalist and wildlife photographer."

"So I've heard."

"Your mother was a groundskeeper on an estate in Romney Marsh."

"That's right. Sounds like the start to a risqué joke."

"But you're not laughing."

Archer shrugged. "I'm not crying either. I'm not out to get humanity because my father abandoned my mother before I was born." It was the loss of the beads that had caused all the misfortune in his life. Losing the beads had cost his mother his father's love. Banishment from the faerie realm had done the rest. But that was chance. Might as well be angry with the wind for blowing.

Rake was still watching him curiously. "No?"

"No." Archer gave Rake a sideways look. "If—and I say *if*—what you suspect is true, it has nothing to do with my father or my mother drowning herself or my growing up in human foster care. If I still believed in the goals of the SRRIM, it would be because they're worthwhile goals. These artifacts don't belong to you. You've no right to destroy them. You've no right to them at all. They should be returned to their realms of origin."

"You talk like a child. But then you are a child. You're, what, not quite twenty?"

"I'm seventy-four."

"I don't mean in human years. I mean in faerie years. In faerie years you're still wet behind those pointy little ears."

Archer lost his temper as, no doubt, he was meant to do. "And you're the tool of an ignorant and bigoted government."

To his astonishment, Rake laughed. "Luckily you don't still believe in the goals of the SRRIM." He drained his glass and nodded to the bartender.

"Another?" he asked Archer.

Archer ignored the question. "The Society for the Rescue and Restoration of Indigenous Magic no longer exists."

"Not under that name, certainly. By the way, your pal Chauhan is already on his way back to India. Maybe he just dropped by this continent to pick up a dozen Tim Horton's apple fritters."

"Maybe he did."

Rake's lean cheek tugged into a hard smile. "We'll have a team from NIAD's India field office waiting for him when he disembarks in New Delhi."

"You boys get around. Boys and girls, I should say. Your Sergeant Orly is a witch."

"You noticed. She thought you did."

"Since when does the sticks-and-stones brigade hire blooded witches?"

"Times are changing. The Irregulars are an equal opportunity employer."

Archer sniffed in polite disbelief.

"If that chip on your shoulder was any bigger you'd be a hunchback instead of—" Rake broke off.

"Instead of what?"

Archer was expecting sarcasm at the least. The self-conscious look that flashed briefly across Rake's face intrigued him.

Rake's reply was brusque. "It's no secret the fae are inhumanly beautiful."

"I'm only half fae."

Rake growled, "You're well aware of your...physical attributes."

Archer laughed shortly and picked up his mug. They drank in silence. A silence that, as the minutes passed, softened and grew almost companionable.

Archer swallowed the last mouthful of ale and delicately wiped the foam away with his index finger. He glanced at Rake, who was watching him steadily with a faint, rather odd smile. "Well?"

"Well," Rake said, "I was wondering about those postcards."

"What postcards?"

"The French Victorian postcards my agents found in your bedside table. The ones of aroused demons doing anatomically incorrect things to humans."

Archer's face warmed. He shifted uncomfortably on his barstool. "So?"

Rake's smile widened, even grew rather wicked. "You've a particular interest in demons?"

"It's my job description."

Rake's deep laugh sent a little shiver down Archer's spine. "That particular job description could get you arrested for solicitation in this realm."

Archer couldn't help it. He laughed.

Rake smiled and glanced around as everyone in the bar automatically followed suit in the wake of that peal. He turned back to Archer. "So you…have a thing for demons?"

The phrase sounded odd coming from Rake, almost anachronistic, though Archer couldn't have said why. In any case, oh yes. Archer had a thing for demons. Not that he'd ever been with a demon. He gave Rake a cool little smile.

"Isn't in my file?"

"I'd have remembered that."

Archer shrugged. "I just have a thing for bad boys."

Rake laughed. "But you *are* a bad boy, Mr. Green."

Chapter Five

"Then what happened?" Barry asked.

"Then I finished my beer and went home."

"*What*?"

Archer laughed at Barry's expression. "How did you think that story would end?"

"The man was flirting with you."

"Maybe. Probably."

"He bought you a drink. He brought up your naughty French postcard collection. He was coming onto you."

"He was trying to seduce me." Archer's voice was bored. It was an act. The idea of Rake trying—and succeeding—in seducing him was alarmingly exciting. It was a long time since he'd felt this way.

"That could be very useful."

"If his interest was genuine, but I think…" Archer's voice tailed off. In fact, he did think Rake's interest was genuine. That didn't mean it wasn't calculated. Badges were known for their unorthodox investigation techniques.

"It's just a game for him," he said without conviction.

Barry pointed out, "As it is for you."

"Yes. Of course."

"Intriguing insight into our new commander all the same."

"I don't trust him."

"I should hope not!"

"You know what I mean. There's something different about him. Something I can't put my finger on."

Barry said, "But you'd like to?"

"*Ever* so funny, you are."

Barry chuckled. The phone on his desk jangled. He pressed a button. Miss Roya's demure voice said, "The naga skin has arrived, Mr. Littlechurch."

"Thank you, Miss Roya." Barry rose. "Perhaps Commander Rake is part of the escort. That would add some zest to your day, eh?"

Archer didn't deign to answer.

In any case, Commander Rake was not part of the naga skin escort. There were only three agents, none of them familiar. It was a little unsettling that the local badge brigade seemed to have so many new faces. Too many for ordinary turnover, in Archer's opinion. Recruitment must be up.

The exorcised skin was carried in a small teak trunk carved with cobras and eagles and painted gold. The heavy lid was inlaid with jade and mother-of-pearl.

Barry opened the lid. The skin inside was silvery, almost transparent. When stretched to full length, it would be over eighteen feet. It looked like a pile of tissue paper.

"Any problems?" he asked briskly.

"No problems," the youthful lieutenant reported.

Clipboards were exchanged. Signatures were scribbled in silence. Archer studied the crumbled pile of fragile scales. It seemed to him that he could see two black beady eyes gazing back at him. The next instant the eyes resolved themselves into two holes in the skin.

"Anything wrong?" Barry asked him.

Archer looked away from the skin. He shook his head. "When was the naga exorcised?"

He was speaking to Barry, but it was the lieutenant who replied, "Twelve years ago. We don't refer to it as exorcism anymore. It's called neutralization."

"Of course." Archer's eyes met Barry's. "More than a decade. And there has been no recidivation in all that time?"

"Certainly not!" All three Irregulars scrutinized Archer as though he had sprouted three heads—or was out of the one he had. And no wonder. What he was suggesting probably sounded like sacrilege to them, having, as they clearly did, utter faith in the earthly-realm dogma they'd been weaned on.

Archer shrugged. "Thank you. We'll take charge of it now."

Mr. Baker took the small trunk from the uniformed officer. Archer noticed that despite the rejection of the idea that the naga skin might miraculously reanimate, the Irregulars appeared only too pleased to hand off their charge.

In a small, silent procession they traveled to the display room and the large glass case that had been prepared for the skin.

Archer lifted the lid and Mr. Baker carefully lowered the open trunk onto the large red velvet cushion. Mr. Baker stepped back and Archer slid the glass lid into place and locked the case.

"And that," Barry said, "is that." He gave a brief smile to the agents. "Thank you for your assistance, gentlemen. The naga skin is safely home once more."

The agents snapped him three perfect salutes and turned in unison on their gleaming heels.

❧

There was a great deal of information about George Gaki on the web, but very little of it was relevant or even true. According to various sources, the wealthy antiques dealer and philanthropist was sixty-five and Austrian born. Archer knew for a fact that Gaki was over six hundred years old, hailed from Prussia, and that the only recipient of his philanthropy was himself. Gaki acknowledged no children and was on his eleventh human wife. One thing the news media got right: he was very rich and very well connected. Connected in ways most humans couldn't fathom. None of that mattered to Archer. His only interest was in Gaki's fabled collection of art and artifacts.

The first article that popped up was the sale of the antique water beads through Christie's a few weeks earlier. The auction wasn't significant. The only reason a photo of the beads even popped up on the website was because George Gaki was news.

Archer gazed avidly at the photo in the monitor. The beads amounted to two strands of something that resembled natural pearls in size and luster. But the color was an amazing green like the blazing heart of the first emeralds or the darkest, stillest, deepest water.

Archer's heart pounded. His chest tightened with emotion so powerful it was hard to draw breath. He had to close his eyes for an instant against the onslaught of feeling. At last. *At last…*

His office door opened. Archer's eyes blinked open.

"You haven't forgotten tonight's benefit at the Fairmont, have you?" Barry stopped at Archer's desk. His gaze fell on Archer's computer monitor. "Gaki? What's the old rogue up to now?" His benign smile fell. "Oh hell. Not those damned beads again."

"You knew they'd come on the market. Knew Gaki had bought them." Archer tried to keep his tone neutral, but he couldn't help feeling this was perfidy on Barry's part. A small one, perhaps, but hurtful all the same

Barry looked uncomfortable. "Rumor. That's all it was."

Archer shook his head, turning back to the monitor screen. "There they are."

Barry instinctively leaned forward, peering at the monitor. "That could be any string of old beads."

"It's them. I know it."

"How can you know it?" Barry straightened.

"I do."

"You want the beads to be real so you're telling yourself that they are. Think for a moment. It's too great a coincidence."

"What coincidence?"

"Why, that the beads should turn up at the same time this Commander Rake does."

"You think Rake is working with Gaki to trap me? If the badges knew the truth about Gaki, they wouldn't waste any time on me."

"That's where you're wrong."

"I left SRRIM years ago. I've been a law-abiding citizen of the earthly-realm ever since. Whereas Gaki—"

"George Gaki bends the law for his own personal gain. In the eyes of the government—any government in any realm—that is never as dangerous as political fanaticism."

"But I'm not a fanatic." Archer turned back to the computer screen. "I just want what belongs to me."

"Those beads don't belong to you."

Archer didn't bother to reply.

"Even if you're right," Barry began at last. He fell silent again.

"What?"

"Have you stopped to consider why these beads are so important to you?"

Archer repeated, "They belong to me. They belong to my family."

"Archer."

Archer could feel himself tightening up, getting angry. He forced himself to relax. Summoned a smile. "What?"

"Say you recover the beads? What then? Do you think you can barter your way back into the faerie realm?"

"I wouldn't try," Archer said shortly. When he had been a boy, yes, he had dreamed of buying his way back into the faerie realm, of recovering his family's lost honor. As an adult he had faced the fact that the faerie realm could no more give him back what he yearned for than could the human realm.

Which didn't change the fact that he wanted the beads with all the desperate passion of any lovesick suitor.

They are better than stars or water,
Better than voices of winds that sing,
Better than any man's fair daughter,
Your green glass beads on a silver ring.

"Then what?" Barry was frowning worriedly.

Archer shrugged. "They're a family heirloom. Like Great-Aunt Esmeralda's cloisonné clock."

"*Not* like Great-Aunt Esmeralda's cloisonné clock. The beads are an obsession with you. You've been hunting them ever since I met you."

“Some people hunt first editions,” Archer said lightly. “Some people hunt bottle caps.”

“Most people wouldn’t kill for bottle caps.”

Archer said slowly, “Kill?”

“You might have to kill to get the beads away from Gaki. Have you not considered that?” Barry added, “Your eyes are glowing.”

“I can’t help that.” Archer turned his profile to Barry. “I’m not going to commit murder. Give me a little credit.”

“My dear boy, Gaki will have taken every possible security measure to protect his possessions. He has armed guards patrolling his estate. The choice may not be yours.”

Archer reached out and absently clicked the keypad. The picture of the beads and a benign-looking Gaki disappeared. Archer swiveled the chair to face Barry and offered a smile. “Don’t worry. These things have a way of working themselves out. What time is this gala fundraiser?”

❧

The ghost of a slight girl in a red dress waved cautiously to Archer as he exited the revolving doors into the marble lobby of the Fairmont. He nodded politely.

Formerly known as Hotel Vancouver, the Fairmont was a designated heritage building. It had opened in May of 1939, for the royal visit of King George VI and Queen Elizabeth, but the girl ghost looked circa the forties.

Voices and music drifted from the 900 West Lounge and Archer followed the sounds of celebration past gilt-framed paintings, art deco lamps, and palms in black urns.

A seventy-million dollar restoration in the mid-1990s had secured the hotel’s reputation as the favored hangout for the city’s hoi polloi, and Archer had attended a number of events there. It was not the kind of thing he particularly enjoyed, but taking his turn representing the public face of MoSSA was part of his responsibilities as curator. Barry was much better at this kind of thing, but Barry firmly believed it was good for Archer to “get out and meet people,” as he quaintly put it.

Archer milled around the fringes of the crowd, chatting when spoken to and otherwise smiling pleasantly and thinking of Commander Rake and wondering if the man really had been flirting with him the night before or if Archer was so out of practice he had read the signs wrong.

"What exactly is the Museum of State-Supported Archives?" a portly woman in a purple-flowered gown inquired, referring to the name by which the general public knew MoSSA.

Archer rattled off the usual spiel. "We catalog articles that are difficult to store in the official facilities, but that might be eventually required for study by the state examiners."

"You mean like tax records and deeds and those kinds of documents?"

"Not so very unlike."

She smiled politely, eyes already glazing over. "It sounds fascinating."

"Oh yes! Very much so." Unlike a full-blooded faerie, Archer was capable of lying, but he didn't enjoy it. He was relieved when the woman spotted someone she urgently needed to speak to.

He checked his pocket watch. Barry would expect him to put in another hour. He sighed.

Waiters in red jackets were circulating with trays of champagne, but Archer did not care for champagne. Nor did he care for the caviar on crackers and smoked salmon moving in the opposite direction. He had missed supper and was hungry, but his appetite veered more toward fae than human, and the fae ate no flesh, be it fish, fowl, or animal. Archer went in search of a crudités platter he had spotted earlier.

So it was that he happened to be in perfect position to see George Gaki arriving with his entourage. It shouldn't have come as a surprise, really, that Gaki would attend the fundraiser. He was a major figure on the Vancouver art scene, both as a patron and a critic, but Archer hadn't been thinking his method of approach could be anything so simple as walking up and saying hello.

Eye on his quarry, Archer made his way through the crowd, waiting for the moment when he could introduce himself. In the end, that too was made ridiculously simple. One of the gala organizers spotted him hovering and did the honors.

"Ah! The curator of MoSSA?" Gaki said with interest. "At last we meet."

Gaki was a large, rawboned man, nearly as tall as Commander Rake, and quite a bit broader. His hair was salt and pepper, worn in a style popularized by Julius Caesar. His eyes were a color close to yellow.

"How do you do?" Archer shook hands with the one person in the room, aside from himself, who understood MoSSA's true purpose.

"Better than I expected when I decided on impulse to attend this event. I've been hoping to meet you, Mr. Green."

"Have you?" Was this conversation taking an odd turn or was it Archer's imagination?

"I believe you and I have something in common."

Archer knew of only one thing they had in common and he could hardly believe Gaki would bring up the subject in public. "Oh yes?"

"You're a collector of clocks, are you not? You have a very fine piece, as I understand from Mr. Littlechurch. A large nineteenth century cloisonné clock with cherubs."

Archer relaxed. "Yes. But they're not cherubs. They're fairies."

Gaki's unruly brows rose. "How charming. You're half faerie yourself?"

For a second Archer thought he'd misheard. Had Gaki truly made a reference to the immortal realms aloud? "I..." He couldn't help an uncertain look around, but Gaki's bodyguard was staring into space, and the other guests seemed to be absorbed in earnest conversations of their own.

"Delightful," Gaki was saying, as though unaware of Archer's shock. "Such a rare pairing, but the children are always exquisite. Rarely does the intermingling of bloodlines turn out so fortunately."

Archer colored. Now he was getting angry. Not merely at being appraised as though he was an inanimate object, but at this old fool's arrogant flaunting of the Secrecy Act, which decreed that the human realm should be kept in blissful ignorance of the others.

"As a matter of fact," Gaki observed quietly, "I believe we have much more in common than you realize." He glanced around, rested his large hand on Archer's shoulder, and said in carrying tones, "I assure you, I'll more than match any offer you receive for the clock."

"I'm not going to sell my clock." Archer found he was being steered through the crowd, whether he willed it or not. He tried to regain some control of the situation. "As a matter of fact, I was interested in an item you purchased from Christie's recently."

"You must mean the water beads. Quite a find, I agree. And in marvelous condition. Yes, I imagine you would be interested in those. What a small world it is."

"This one, certainly," Archer said.

"And getting smaller all the time."

They had stopped walking next to a glossy table in the center of the lobby. A giant blue basket with a flower arrangement roughly the size of a small garden allotment sat on the table. They were safely out of earshot of anyone but the bodyguard, who stood a few feet away.

"I'm not sure I understand you," Archer said.

"I believe I belong to an organization that you were once a member of."

Archer's heart stopped. He recovered and asked coolly, "The International Council of Museums?"

"No. Let's not waste time fencing. I belong to the Society for the Rescue and Restoration of Indigenous Magic."

It seemed to take a long time to find the words. "The society no longer exists."

Gaki's eyes kindled with a fanatical light. "But it does— and we're even stronger than before."

"Well, that's nice," Archer said vaguely. "I like to see people getting involved."

"You're very glib about something that I believe once meant a great deal to you."

Archer kept his voice low. "Like many, I remain sympathetic to the goals of SRRIM, but I couldn't condone the tactics being used at the time I left."

"Fight fire with fire."

"That can end creating a bigger fire."

"Let it. Sometimes it takes razing the old to the ground for the new to spring forth."

Archer stared at Gaki's sharp, ageless features. "What are you getting at? What do you want?"

"We need your help."

"What does that mean?" Something clicked in Archer's brain. "Let me guess. The Stone of Fal. I don't have it and I don't know where it is."

"But you could use your position at curator of MoSSA to find it."

"No."

Gaki said good naturedly, "Hear me out."

"I don't want to hear you out. I've already heard too much. This conversation alone could get us arrested."

Gaki ignored that. "If you do this one little thing for us, the beads are yours."

Across the room, Archer could see the woman in purple he had spoken to earlier. She was laughing, but the sound of her laughter, bouncing off the marble ceiling and floor, sounded disembodied and out of time.

"We're not asking you to place yourself in any danger. Just do this one little task. Help us recover the stone. That's all." Gaki was still smiling. "Do it and the beads are yours again. Forever safe from the threat of state-sanctioned neutralization. Think about it."

"I can't do that. I'll pay you for the beads. I'll pay you anything you like. Anything I can."

"The price of the beads is your help."

Speaking the words was physically painful, but what choice did Archer have? "That price is beyond my means."

Gaki made a dismissive sound. "Nonsense. For old times' sake. One last job for your old comrades?"

Archer shook his head.

Gaki seemed to contemplate him for long, solemn seconds. "You disappoint me."

Archer said wearily, "The feeling is mutual."

"There's been talk about you, you know, Green. Certain of your old comrades dislike the fact that you're roaming freely in the world knowing all that you do. Helping us just this once could go far toward proving that there is no need for…worry."

"There's no need for anyone to worry."

"So you say. But then you would. Think about it. It's a generous offer. You say you're still sympathetic to SRRIM's aims."

Archer met and held Gaki's gaze. It wasn't easy. "I'm not going to change my mind."

Gaki's regard never faltered. Then he smiled suddenly and broadly. "Then there's nothing more to be said. It's disappointing for both of us, of course."

"Yes," Archer said huskily.

"I'd have liked nothing better than to see those beads rightfully restored to you. But I always say, if a thing is worth collecting in the first place, it's worth hanging onto forever."

"Forever is a long time."

"No one knows that better than me." Gaki grinned, his teeth very sharp. He reached for a champagne flute from the tray wafting by. "Cheers." He turned his back and walked away.

Archer watched him go. Watched the bodyguard fall into respectful step behind.

He was surprised at the choice he'd made, and yet as he questioned his decision, he realized he did not regret it. It was the right choice.

Not that making it had brought him any pleasure.

He wandered over to the bar and ordered a Yukon Jack on the rocks. He reached for his wallet.

"I've got it," a familiar voice said beside him. Commander Rake's honey brown eyes smiled into Archer's.

Chapter Six

"Why is it you're always trying to buy me drinks?" Archer put his own cash on the counter and the barman swept it up.

"That should be obvious. I want to get you drunk and have my wicked way with you."

"You needn't get me drunk for that."

Rake's eyes kindled with a light that made Archer briefly shy. Rake was not…handsome exactly, but he was striking—or imposing might be the better word—in his severe black evening clothes. There was something about him, some energy, some zest. In the old days they'd called it *virility.* Archer had no idea what they called it these days. These days they didn't seem to make many men like Rake.

"You surprise me." Rake's voice seemed to reverberate right through Archer as though Archer's spine were a tuning fork and Rake was playing his song.

His cock twitched. Elaborately casual, Archer reached for his glass. "I think that's unlikely." He took a long drink and decided it might be wiser to strike out for the shore and safety. "What are you doing here anyway? Following me?"

Rake's eyebrows rose. "Following you? I have people to do that for me. No, attending fundraisers for the Vancouver Arts & Antiquities Alliance is part of my job description."

"Why would it be?" Archer was trying not to be illogically irritated by the information that Rake couldn't be bothered to follow him himself.

"Because deals are made and alliances, if only temporary, are forged at these events." Rake added, "And occasionally the art and antiquities that change hands fall under my jurisdiction."

Archer sniffed in a show of not-so-polite disbelief and sipped his whiskey.

"Speaking of which, you seemed to be having a pleasant chat with George Gaki."

He didn't think he gave himself away by so much as a flicker of an eyelash, but Rake chuckled, a low, growly sound that sent another pleasurable ripple of alarm and anticipation down Archer's spine.

"Something funny?"

"Funny might not be the right word. You do like to live dangerously, don't you, Mr. Green?"

Archer tried to sound bored. He wasn't sure he pulled it off. "Maybe you know what you're talking about."

"Maybe I do." Rake tossed off his own drink, measured Archer from beneath dark, shadowy lashes, and said, "How much longer did you plan on staying?"

Archer grinned. "In a hurry to get home to your pipe and slippers?"

"In a hurry to get home. Not to my pipe and slippers."

"Ah." Archer was surprised at the wrench of disappointment he felt. But of course Rake would have someone tending the home fires for him. Probably throwing another log on the bonfire at this very instant.

"So?" Rake pressed.

"So?"

"How long did you plan on staying here? You've done your social duty and then some, haven't you?"

Exactly how long had Rake been watching him? Archer was amused and annoyed. His usual state of affairs with the commander. The three As: amused, annoyed, or aroused. It had to be more than the aftershave. He tried to keep the edge from his voice. "I thought you paid people to keep an eye on me. What is it you imagine I might get up to tonight?"

Rake's smile was enigmatic. The light from the chandelier picked out bronze glints in his hair; his eyes looked black. He said softly, frankly, so there was no mistaking his meaning, "That's what I'm hoping to find out."

Archer nearly dropped his glass. "You're direct."

Rake's smile widened devilishly. "Yes."

Archer wasn't exactly sure if what he felt was excitement or apprehension. Maybe both. "Isn't this a conflict of interest?"

"Not for me."

He turned that over thoughtfully. It was an important distinction. Assuming he understood what the hell Rake was talking about.

"You're not married?" He was stalling now. They both knew it.

"Not anymore. I ate my wife." Rake grinned and for one truly weird moment his features seemed to waver, his teeth growing sharp and pointed, his eyes glowing red.

Archer laughed and set his glass down. He'd clearly had enough. "Oh dear. Did she forget to warm your TV dinner on time?"

"She was a very good wife. It wasn't her fault. I didn't have a lot of self-control back then and it turned out I liked boys better."

"They do stay fresher longer."

"You're fresh enough." Rake's eyes laughed into Archer's. "Are you coming?"

"Not yet," Archer replied, starting to laugh too. "But the night is young."

❧

Parking was scarce in the West End. Archer managed to wedge his green Beetle between a Saab and a Kia Soul near Stanley Park. He walked the block back to where Rake waited for him in a triangle of lamplight on Chilco Street. The trees were tall and their sweet scent mingled with the ocean smells of nearby English Bay. It smelled like home. Not Gastown. *Home.*

As Archer reached him, Rake pulled him close with a hand curving around the nape of Archer's neck. Rake's mouth descended in a kiss so hot Archer's mouth tingled. Rake's moist tongue flicked out, seeking entrance, and Archer's lips parted. A dark and dangerous heat flooded him as Rake's tongue slipped inside his mouth and stole his breath.

It was crazy to be doing this right here on the street, in the open, beneath the smiling moon and the smaller smiling minimoons of the street lamps. A crazy chance for Rake, certainly, but maybe his self-control wasn't as evolved as he thought because he seemed unable to stop. Archer had no breath for the words, even if he'd had the will.

Rake's lips left Archer's and he kissed him delicately, sweetly beside his unsteady mouth, then trailed across flushed skin to nuzzle Archer's earlobe, rousing shivers in him. Archer moaned.

He felt weak, heavy limbed, as if he had no control over what was happening; it was out of his hands.

Sanity reasserted itself in the form of a pair of headlights that swept around the corner and spotlighted them briefly. They stepped apart. The car zoomed past, exhaust filling the night air.

This was a mistake. Rake was either laying a trap for him or…

Or what?

Archer couldn't think what—the risk seemed to be Rake's, really; he was the one who belonged to an organization that wouldn't take kindly to fraternizing with the enemy—yet Archer still felt it would be dangerous to proceed.

And physically painful not to.

As he stood hesitating, Rake held out his hand. A human gesture, that. An age-old gesture signifying everything from the lack of weapons, an acknowledgment of equality, the implication of solidarity, a binding contract, or even the offer of friendship. Rake said nothing, but that simple move seemed to speak volumes for him. Archer took his hand and they walked in silence up the steps and into the tall, brick-faced, wood-framed building.

Rake's apartment was an elegant one-bedroom suite with a breathtaking view of moonlit English Bay. The windows and that blue view dominated the room, but Archer had a quick impression of modern, streamlined furniture in earth tones, oak floors, granite countertops, and stainless steel fixtures and appliances.

The natural light would be amazing at any time of year and at any time of day.

"Drink?" Rake asked, bottle in hand, from behind the white wood and granite breakfast bar.

Archer shook his head, pacing the room, exploring everything there was to see. Not that there was so much. In fact, the apartment was as tidy as a realtor's model. A few throw pillows in gold and cream, oversized earthenware lamps, small steel bowls with cardamom candy.

"This is nice. Not what I expected."

"What did you expect?"

"Leather? Leather and wood and brass studs." Archer smirked. "Traditional."

"I am traditional, you're right about that." Rake poured himself a drink from the oddly shaped bottle. The liqueur was pale green. Absinth? Archer's nostrils flared. No, cardamom again.

Interesting. But then everything about Rake was interesting. So far. The next hour could change that. Given that Rake was an oversized mortal and in an ultramasculine profession, he would probably opt for the predictable. Archer had no strong inclinations either way. Mortals were often clumsy and brutal in their coupling; so he was mostly curious as to how that precision of manner with which Rake handled himself would translate into sex.

He glanced at Rake, who smiled at him and raised his glass of green liqueur in a small, mocking toast.

Yes, Archer was curious about many things concerning Rake. In fact, the more he learned about Rake—which, granted, was little enough—the more questions he had.

He thought about Rake's accent, similar to his own really, that almost stripped-bare pronunciation that came of years of living in different countries and places. Where *did* Rake come from? How old was he?

Perhaps some of his uncertainty showed. Rake said, "You look nervous. Are you truly only now beginning to wonder what you've got yourself into?'

"Have I got myself into anything?" Archer couldn't fathom Rake's expression. Certainly Rake was amused—by what? There was something else there too. He seemed almost…perplexed as he studied Archer.

Archer moved away, studying the oil painting over the long, beige sofa. An inhumanly beautiful figure sat brooding in a field of flowers. No. Not flowers. Moths. Pale green moths. A cloud of them.

"I know that painting. Or one similar to it. It's by Vrubel?"

"That's right. Mikhail Alexandrovich Vrubel."

"But the painting I know doesn't have moths."

"No. This is a companion piece. Do you like it?"

Archer nodded. Oh yes. He liked it. Too much. It gave him a warm feeling in his belly and a fluttery feeling in his chest. Perhaps Rake had a thing for demons too. Maybe he'd taken up the badge to work out a few kinks. That would be sort of a relief. It would make Rake more…human.

Yes. That was it. Rake seemed almost inhuman in his spic-and-span perfection.

Archer continued to explore the room. The eyes of the demon in the painting followed him. "So where do you keep your pipe and slippers?" he joked.

"In the bedroom, of course." Rake was standing right behind him. Archer hadn't sensed his approach and excitement prickled up and down his spine. Excitement or unease. Archer wasn't completely sure.

"Of course. Where else? You're a traditional guy."

He moved away toward a bookshelf, reaching for a steel-framed photo of Rake in front of the Golden Gate Bridge. He looked virtually the same, in the Irregulars uniform of a decade ago. Odd. He put the photo down again and picked up a geode at random. "The Irregulars must pay better than I thought."

"I don't do it for the money."

Archer threw Rake a mocking look. "No? For the kicks then?"

"It has its moments." Rake drew him into his arms and kissed him, a light, feathery brush of lips, more will-o'-the-wisp than caress. At the snap of electricity, Archer laughed, putting fingers up to his mouth. Rake laughed too, drawing him back again, brushing the soft curls aside to nuzzle him. Archer's breath caught. He expelled it shakily as Rake's hot, wet tongue delicately rimmed the shell of his ear. He shivered, tried to move away, but Rake held him fast. His tongue rasped leisurely over the tips of Archer's ears.

"You know about the ears thing?" a voice that sounded too weak and breathy to be Archer's own inquired faintly. Outside, he'd put it down to chance, but this was too deliberate for chance.

Rake's breath gusted in a little laugh. "I know all about the ears thing." Those heated, moist words seemed to travel right into

Archer's brain, make a sharp left, and arrow down to his groin. The fierce sweetness of his body's reaction nearly made him dizzy.

He wrapped his arms around Rake's neck and kissed him hungrily back. Rake met that demand with voracious enthusiasm. Archer tasted copper, ambrosia, cardamom, and something smoky. Coherent thought fled.

He was unsure of how they got to the bedroom or where along that journey he shed his clothes, but eventually he took hazy note that he was lying naked in a low bed with black silk sheets. Glowing blue lanterns with inked butterflies swung overhead. The butterflies threw giant winged shadows across the walls.

Rake's big hands caught him by the hips, settling Archer on the smooth sheets. He leaned over him, a dark figure in the unreliable light. His eyes gleamed as careful fingers probed the entrance to Archer's body. Archer moaned, squirming. He was no virgin, but his muscles were resilient and passage would be tight given the astonishing size of the bull-like cock between Rake's muscular thighs.

In fact...

Archer's eyes widened. In his entire life he'd never seen a sexual member quite like that one. Not in the flesh.

He opened his mouth, but Rake's fingers, slick with his own hot pre-ejaculate, moved inside him, causing the strangest tingling. Archer murmured wonderingly and then sucked in a sharp breath as Rake guided himself into his body.

Rake took the sound that tore out of Archer's throat as encouragement and he wasn't far wrong, though Archer was transfixed for a second or two with shock. He'd never experienced that peculiar sensation, that mix of stinging and satisfaction—like needles dipped in bliss were floating through his veins and everywhere they stuck came a flash of sheer delight—but he'd read about it. The ultimate one-handed read, in fact. He cried out and Rake stopped at once.

Archer panted, "You're...not...Canadian, are you?"

Rake's eyes turned red. His lips parted in a smile and Archer could see the glint of his sharp incisors. Terrifying. Beautiful. "Don't you recognize the real thing?"

Oh yes, he recognized the real thing. "Demon?" It came out as an inquiry, although that wasn't the real question.

"And you with all those naughty postcards?" Rake laughed down at him and the barbed cock pushed deeper into Archer's body, releasing more of the tiny, felicitous pinpricks.

Hearing that rough, purring laugh, Archer drove back, impaling himself deeply, and it was Rake's turn to catch his breath.

Green and gold sparks danced off Archer's skin and crackled around them. Rake jerked his hips, laughing silently as Archer cried out and arched up. Rake said something in Babylonian. *Lover? Lovely?* Tiny flames leaped in the black-red void of his eyes.

They began to rock, the moon pulling the tide, the tide grabbing for the shore, the melting sand giving way with a final tug at the roots of the mountains...

"Wait. More. I need more." Archer groped for Rake's hand, feeling the callused warmth of his smooth skin, the curve of his long razor-sharp nails as he placed Rake's hand on his groin. "Hold me."

"Like this?" The voice was no longer remotely human, but Archer no longer feared disappointment. No longer feared anything at all.

He wrapped the long fingers around his rigid cock, molding them into a fist. To his delighted relief, Rake slipped easily into the rhythm, and Archer writhed with pleasured abandon, the entire experience heightened by the proximity of the dangerous talons to his tender flesh.

Rake was teasing him now, varying the speed and strength of his thrusts, using hands and mouth with unholy skill until Archer was sobbing, his entire body shimmering green-gold as he swung out into the distance suspended between agony and ecstasy.

Time paused.

"Don't leave me...like this!" Archer groaned. At least he meant to add the "like this." Fortunately his naked little plea was lost in Rake's snarl as he plunged into him, driving Archer toward the peak, pumping his rigid cock in the same rhythm. Archer felt all semblance of control slip away and he squirmed and twisted, trying to draw that indescribable sensation more deeply into himself. Rake's mouth found his ear and he began to lick the upswept point. Something ignited, blazed; every muscle in Archer's body locked. Rake bucked hard into him. It was like being filled with burning glass and at the same time it felt so impossibly, terrifyingly wonderful that Archer feared he would lose what little mind he had left.

Rake sucked hard on Archer's ear and Archer screamed. He felt himself plummeting like a fallen star, giving off sparks as he dropped like a rock into the roaring red light that was Rake.

❧

It seemed a long time later when the red glare faded and the world took shape once more. Lanterns swayed gently above a comfortable bed, blue hearts pulsing. Limp and trembling, Archer lay quietly as Rake softened and slid out of his body. He could see the glitter of his own drying release everywhere: lamps, sheets, Rake's chest as well as his own, marked with it.

"Well, Puck? Better than picture postcards?" Rake's voice was human again, though gruff from his shouts.

"Better." Archer laughed shakily. "Did you just call me a rude name?"

Rake made a dismissive noise, gathered him close to his massive chest. His claws had retracted once more and his hands were gentle. Disarmingly gentle. "Whither wander you?"

Shakespeare. A poetry-spouting demon. A demon Irregular. Archer sniffed in absent disapproval. He was still considering the first question. He felt like something consumed by fire, hollowed out and only the shell left. Whatever he had imagined...Well, imagination could not do this reality justice.

Rake nuzzled his cheek and temple, but, mercifully, was careful to avoid Archer's ears.

"How can you be...?" Archer began finally, troubled.

"A demon?"

"A badge."

It was a moment or two before Rake said vaguely, "If you can't beat them, join them."

Archer raised his head, trying to read the truth in the midnight shadows. There was only the gleam of eyes, the gleam of teeth.

"You don't feel..."

"What?"

"Divided loyalties?"

"No. The mortal and immortal realms must work together or all will perish."

Propaganda. But there was truth in it all the same. Archer had not lived among humans for nearly a century without noticing that for all their fragility they could do a lot of damage. Even without the interference of humans, the other realms had a knack for self-destruction. Remembering how Greine the Usurper had put down the Irish sidhe revolts only too well, he shivered.

Rake cradled him closer, muttering, "Sleep now, little imp."

Archer's smile was wry. So the legends were true in that much at least. Demons were soft and sentimental after sex. With the lovers they didn't kill, anyway. His body still rang with little thrums of pleasure. He humored Rake, snuggling closer still, hearing the muted boom of the eight-chambered demon heart, but his mind continued to flit from thought to thought like a bee sipping nectar.

It was all very well to say the realms could only survive through cooperation, but how had Rake, a descendent of creatures that would once have eaten humans for between-meal snacks, become a protector of mortals?

Come to think of it, how old *was* Rake? Maybe he hadn't been joking about eating his first wife. Archer shivered. Rake growled something in—Babylonian? Sumerian? Hittite?—and kissed the top of Archer's head.

Archer's heart swelled and he kissed Rake back. He liked kissing Rake. His chest was smooth and his skin warm and he smelled of sex and vanilla and he had delivered more physical pleasure in the last half hour than Archer had known in the last half century. The caress was automatic, of course. Just good manners. He appreciated Rake's sexual expertise and it was very nice to be held like this, to fall asleep in someone's arms. Not that he planned on falling asleep. Archer had places to go and things to do.

Not immediately. He could wait a bit. Make sure Rake was deeply asleep. That was just common sense.

What did Rake want from him? Archer continued to mull it over. Was tonight intended as some sort of seduction whereupon, following the fulfillment of a sexual fantasy, Archer spilled all his deepest, darkest secrets and promised to help the badges round up his old comrades? If so, Rake had forgotten to ask him about his deepest, darkest secrets.

He wondered if Gaki had noticed him leaving with Rake. That was liable to send the wrong message.

When he was sure Rake was truly asleep, Archer slipped out from beneath his muscular arm, using a glamour to trick Rake's sleeping consciousness into believing Archer still lay next to him. For long seconds he stood beside the bed and stared down at Rake's relaxed form. There was no sign of the demon now. Rake looked like any weary mortal. Weary and ridiculously content.

Archer found himself unexpectedly reluctant to leave. It would be nice to spend the night, to sleep with the heartbeat of the sea pounding beneath the building, lulling him. Nice to wake tomorrow together and have toast and honey in that sunny room and let Rake cuddle him. Just a little. Perhaps they would talk and laugh and talk some more. Not about world-shaking events. Not about their jobs or politics. Only about matters important to themselves.

He listened to the echo of his thoughts with disquiet. What was he thinking? That fantasy wasn't merely foolish; it was dangerous. And not merely for himself.

He found his clothes in the living room and dressed silently. The wards on the door took a few minutes to figure out. Rake clearly didn't like to take chances. At last Archer opened the door and stepped quietly into the dry, temperature-controlled hall. The building continued to slumber. He walked briskly to the front entrance and let himself into a night that smelled of old wood, plum blossoms, and starlight.

His ears still throbbed, almost unbearably sensitive after Rake's attentions. Archer shivered, remembering. His whole body ached in a distant way, not from the scratches and bites and bruises inevitably resulting from coupling with a demon, but with pangs of something like nostalgia. Missing Rake's touch already—and he had nothing to anticipate because this had been a one-off. He could not risk it being anything else. Thus the walk along the quiet street, moonlight glancing off the hoods of cars, the lamplight slicing through shrubbery, seemed poignant and bittersweet. It felt as though he was leaving home forever as he walked down the deserted street to his car.

Archer jeered at himself as he climbed into his Beetle and started the engine.

❧

Gaki's estate was a tree-shrouded sanctuary in North Vancouver far from the hustle and bustle of the city proper. Archer studied the layout from behind the tall, spiked gates. It wasn't as large and ostentatious as he had expected. A custom-designed Craftsman four-story with a detached garage and large guest cottage. The property was positioned within a protected bay on a private peninsula with a good 650 feet of private waterfront and sandy beach.

The house was well guarded with everything from security cameras to protection spells.

Standing deep in the shadows and well away from the biting iron of the double gates, Archer contemplated the dark windows.

They were there, he knew it. The beads were hidden somewhere in that house. *His* beads. Jewels designed by long ago faerie artisans for Archer's family.

Did the beads sense his presence? Did they warm to life anticipating his touch? Did they know that soon he would have them?

A light went on in the highest story of the house and began to glow green.

Archer smiled. Yes. Soon they would be his.

Chapter Seven

Even before the naga skin came back to life and ate the guide for the tour that had been specially arranged for a group of retirees from the Slovakian NIAD branch office, Archer was having a lousy day. But an eighteen-foot hooded cobra as wide as a Douglas fir loose in the yellow marble halls of the Museum of State-Sanctioned Antiquities in Vancouver took precedence over a sleepless night, running out of honey for his morning tea, and a stolen parking spot.

"Tell Barry to get everyone else out of the museum," Archer ordered Mr. Baker, who had run, panicked, to his office to report the terrible news. "Where's the rest of the tour party?"

Mr. Baker shook his head. His mouth worked. His eyes were stricken. He had been acting as docent for this very special event when the glass case had cracked and then burst apart to release a fanged nightmare.

Archer shoved him out of his office and sent him stumbling toward Barry's. "Never mind. Go tell Mr. Littlechurch."

As Mr. Baker fled, Archer yanked the fire alarm. Bells clamored overhead, the sound ricocheting off the stone and drowning the cries and screams coming from the exhibition hall. He returned to his desk and pressed the silent panic button under the birch top.

That technically ended his responsibility. According to the government employee handbook, he could now lock himself in his office or flee the museum, whichever seemed to offer the best chance of survival. He certainly owed no loyalty to a group of badges, retired or otherwise, but somehow he could no longer think of Irregulars without thinking of Rake. Not that Rake would ever be an elderly, helpless human, but—

The entire building shook as though the roof had caved in.

Without further thought, Archer left his office and sprinted down the hallway, skidding to a stop in the doorway of the exhibition hall. The naga was in the center of the long, wide room, its own display case reduced to debris beneath its coils. The surrounding cases had been knocked over and a number of people in plainclothes cowered behind them—with the exception of one old codger who was waving his cane to try and distract the snake from an elderly lady trying to crawl away.

Six feet or so of the cobra's olive brown body reared up, hood spread, forked tongue flicking out. It swung its massive head, hissing as Archer slid into view.

Archer ducked back, leaning against the wall, heart pounding. That was…one…*big* snake. He swallowed hard, thinking.

"Archer!"

Archer turned his head. Barry wasn't quite running and still looked startlingly dignified given the circumstances, but he was definitely moving faster than Archer had ever seen him move. "The Irregulars are on the way!"

Archer nodded distractedly. He grabbed another quick look.

The man with the cane was hiding beneath a stone bench. Archer couldn't see the woman. The next instant a flick of the snake's tail sent an aluminum-framed walker flying into one of the stained glass windows. The terrified oldsters huddled still further down behind their makeshift shelter.

"What on earth…" Barry's voice was lost in the wake of another crash.

"I'm not sure we can wait," Archer told him.

Barry's eyes went rounder still. "Don't be ridiculous. You can't go in there. We've already had one fatality this morning."

Archer could not have agreed more. Unfortunately… "That… thing isn't going to be satisfied with one little senior citizen snack after a couple of centuries of hibernation."

"No." Barry looked aghast. "Whatever you're thinking. No. We *have* to wait. That thing will snap you up in one bite."

Archer's stomach did an unhappy somersault at that mental image. He didn't like snakes. He didn't even like lizards. Caterpillars were his limit.

"I don't know what else to do."

"We could—we could—" Barry stopped. "How the hell could this *happen*?" He stole a quick look around the doorframe. Whatever he saw caused him to put his hands over his eyes. "Oh my God. It *can't* be happening."

The shriek of tearing metal from inside the hall put the lie to that prayer.

Archer's mouth was so dry he couldn't seem to get enough spit to gulp. He ran through the mental catalog of everything he knew about snakes. It was a very small catalog. Cobras were, at most, a footnote.

"Have you ever heard of an exorcised item reanimating?"

"No. Never. Not like this. Not spontaneously."

"And yet that fucking monster is alive." Archer risked another look around the doorframe. The situation was not improving on its own. "All right. Here's our plan. I'll distract it long enough that you should be able to help the people in there get out."

"That's not a plan! It's suicide."

Archer spared him a quick laugh. "Hopefully not. Think of the paperwork. Anyway, it's the best I can come up with."

Barry shook his head frantically. "*No.* Wait for the ba—the Irregulars. They'll be here any minute." They both looked down the eerily empty hallway to the large doors where Mr. Baker and Miss Roya hovered, trying to see through the etched glass. The alarm bells continued to jangle in surround sound.

A display table scraped and groaned its way across the floor and crashed into the wall. Terrified cries followed.

Barry swallowed. He looked as sick as Archer felt. "You realize that whatever that thing is, it's strong enough to throw off centuries of exorcism. You're…"

"Half-blooded. The thought had occurred." Archer grimaced. "Right. Get into position at the side door while I try something."

"*What*, for God's sake?"

"Something will come to me. *Hurry*, Barry."

Barry whispered, "Be careful, dear boy." He scuttled down the hall and disappeared around the corner. Archer waited, and a few seconds later, he spotted Barry timidly waving from the side entrance.

Archer took a deep breath and stepped into the room.

The cobra's head—large as a dining room table—swung his way. The forked tongue tested the air.

Archer stayed perfectly still, summoning the glamour to conceal him from the snake.

It would certainly have worked with an ordinary snake. The naga continued to weave back and forth, hissing gutturally and tickling the distance with its tongue.

Archer concentrated on melding with his surroundings. It would be easier if he was actually leaning against the wall. As it was, he was trying to blend into several scattered objects. The broken cases, the nearby pillar. He tentatively reached for the snake's mind.

Black.

Venomous.

Void.

He recoiled instinctively. That wasn't right. That wasn't...alive. What was it?

Out of the corner of his eye he saw Barry helping the frail-looking woman Archer had spotted earlier to her feet. As Barry half dragged her to the doorway the snake's head swiveled toward them.

Archer looked around for a possible weapon. The display case with ancient Greek artifacts was turned over on its side, shattered glass from the lid and sides scattered across the marble floor. Amidst the silver arrow points, funeral masks, and shards of black and red pottery, Archer spotted one of Hermes's battered silver sandals. Beaning the naga between the eyes with the sandal was probably not going to achieve much beyond further antagonizing an already irate magical creature.

His gaze lit on another item a few feet further on. Seven wooden pipes bound together with ragged threads and worn leather. Pan's syrinx. Also known in legend as Pan's flute.

Archer scrambled for the flute. The frayed leather gave way beneath his fingertips and two of the pipes fell to the floor, rolling away. Archer rose with the remaining pipes between his hands and blew cautiously. Nothing happened.

The cobra began to rock above him.

Archer blew harder, and a choked, dusty spurt of sound issued from the largest of the bleached, brittle pipes. Archer played a shaky little trill.

The snake leaned closer and closer, its tongue undulating mere inches from him. The yellow fangs glistened with venom.

Archer's lips tickled as he blew softly across the sharp edge of the inner pipes. A sweet ghostly melody slipped out of the syrinx. Archer closed his eyes and tried to remember some of the plaintive tunes he'd learned as a boy. True, the syrinx was a little more complicated than the wooden flutes he'd played, but the basic theory of lip tension and breath control was the same.

He kept his eyes firmly shut and refused to think of his perilous position and the melody turned into the haunting sound of the sea mews and the curlew. As Archer played he could even smell the bitter aromatic scent of the marsh, see the sodden tracts where he had wandered, see again high tide combing silver fingers through the vast surface of sargassum weed floating across the pewter sea, rents and patches of water threading and dappling the reddish brown thatch. He saw the hill of white gravel rising from the heart of the marshes, crowned with ancient thorn trees, accessible only by the old Roman causeway…

Had Barry managed to get the last of the tourists away? Archer was afraid to open his eyes. Even if Barry had succeeded, Archer could think of no way to end his serenade without winding up as lunch for the naga. He was running short of breath, his fingers starting to shake, causing the notes to waver.

The past blurred into the present. Archer swayed, forgetting for an instant where he was. He recovered, stiffening his spine, locking his knees, planting his feet. Already his tune had lasted four minutes.

Despairingly, he wondered how much longer…

He felt a sudden crackling rush of arcane energy that signaled immortal power unfolding around him. It swept up and around him, tendrils slipping through his curls, the space between his elbows and flank, his legs…It surrounded him and then whirled up in front of him, spiraling up like a fountain.

A hand—a hard, human hand—hooked around Archer's right biceps, and he was hauled back, heels sliding on the slick floor as though on ice. He managed to keep to his feet, opening his eyes wide.

Rake kept one hand clamped around Archer's arm. The other stretched before him and white light poured forth as he faced the naga. White light. Dimly Archer took note of the phenomenon of white light from a demon before his attention was restored to the immediate threat.

The snake towered over them, weaving back and forth with increasing speed as though attempting to free itself from an invisible net. Its lashing tail struck one of the supporting pillars, sending a crack like a fork of lightning down its mottled surface.

Archer spied motion on the far side of the room. Sergeant Orly stood behind the naga, wrists crossed in front of her like a cartoon superhero. She was chanting a vanishing spell. Archer could just make out the words above the furious wet growls of the cobra.

He felt power surge through Rake in a torrent of energy that would rightly terrify any sensible creature—not that Archer could currently claim to possess much sense. Uncontrolled, that psychic force could probably knock down the entire building and leave it so much singed rubble, and yet Rake had directed his power with such skill that it had wound safely, gently around Archer like satin ribbons.

Archer's knees trembled. He had nothing to offer in this battle. He had done his share and now there was nothing to do but stay still and not distract Rake.

It wasn't easy. Archer had to fight the natural inclination to move from the center of that force. He could feel Rake's fingers digging into the muscles of his arm, and he found a strange comfort in this reminder of Rake's...not humanity, because Rake was not human...But in his own way he was mortal too.

He could lose this battle. He could be destroyed. They might both die here in the marble halls of MoSSA. It would make a nice subject for a frieze.

He felt a surge of hysterical laughter. But that was better than thinking about death. It wasn't even his own death that worried Archer, but thinking of Rake's ephemerality filled him with a sorrow he was unprepared for. He rejected the thought at once, lest Rake read it and weaken.

Archer risked another look at Rake. Amazingly, he still retained his human form, but it rippled as though Archer were viewing him through deep water. Rake's eyes were black red and his hands were beginning to resemble talons, the nails curving long and ebony.

From across the room Sergeant Orly suddenly cried out and staggered back.

Rake stepped forward, still holding Archer in that excruciating grip. The light emanating from him yellowed and then turned red.

The naga gave a sound that no creature, mortal or immortal, ever gave and lived. There was a horrendous wet ripping sound and chunks of flesh and scales exploded across the room.

Archer flinched, but the bloody shrapnel flew safely past him and Rake, encapsulated as they were behind the barrier of Rake's power.

The air cleared.

Stilled.

It was over.

He felt the outpouring of Rake's power slowing, slowing, ebbing...

For a second or two they stood swaying, still linked, in the wreckage of the room. Somewhere out in the hallway, a woman was sobbing. Voices murmured in comfort. Sirens screamed in the distance. Archer heard only Rake's harsh, heavy breaths.

Abruptly, Rake released him. Archer staggered back, half falling onto a broken display case now tilted on its side. The leather thong holding the syrinx pipes together unraveled and the canes clattered to the marble.

Black-clad Irregular forces poured into the room, weapons raking floor and ceiling, searching for any living remnant of the naga.

"Are you all right?"

Rake's voice was harsh, not quite human. Archer opened his eyes. He watched Rake struggle for control: eyes still black, and the glimmer of fangs behind his tight lips.

He nodded.

"What the hell did you think you were doing?" Rake snarled.

"What the hell did it look like I was doing?"

"Feeding a snake."

Archer's anger spiked and then dipped. He laughed. The sound reverberated lightly through the room and a few of the Irregulars automatically laughed behind their dark helmets.

Rake's expression darkened. His form wavered—then suddenly steadied into human guise as Sergeant Orly reached them.

She and Rake spoke briefly before she turned to Archer. "That was a brave thing," she told him. "Foolhardy. But brave." With an expression of distaste, she brushed bits of blasted snake from her uniform. "And unexpectedly civic minded. I don't know many civilians who would have done what you tried to do. Certainly not among the faeries."

Archer glared at her, though that was perfectly true. "Had you lot done your jobs properly, I wouldn't have had to risk the public image of the faerie by displaying any courage whatsoever."

"That wasn't meant as an insult." Her pale eyes narrowed. "And just what are you insinuating?"

"Insinuating? I thought that was plainspoken."

Rake understood him easily enough. "Bullshit. What you're suggesting isn't possible."

"Says the demon commander employed by the Irregulars."

Orly sucked in a breath. Rake was still, stiller than the herons of Romney Marsh watching the murky waters for shining fish.

"Hold your tongue," Orly hissed.

"Not common knowledge, I take it?" Archer asked. He was a little ashamed of himself for letting temper get the better of his discretion, but he refused to let that show.

Rake moved his head in quick negation and Orly cut off whatever else she intended to say.

Barry bustled up. "It's only fair to inform you, Commander Rake, that I intend to file a complaint at the highest level. Sending a partially exorcised demonic artifact to this institution is an act of criminal negligence. The fact that we had only one fatality today is a miracle."

Rake's eyes turned briefly red again. But he said politely, "I assure you, we're as surprised and unhappy about today's events as you are, Mr. Littlechurch."

"Surprised? Unhappy? That doesn't begin to cover…" Barry didn't pause for breath during the next ninety seconds. Rake and Orly waited in grim-faced silence for him to finish.

When the eye of the storm at last appeared, Rake nodded to Orly, who pinned a tight smile to her face and said graciously from between her teeth, "I promise you, Mr. Littlechurch, the Irregulars will be conducting our own in-house investigation into this matter."

"In-house!" A less civilized man would have spat on the marble floors. "How do we know that won't merely result in another departmental cover-up?"

"You must realize we're every bit as invested in finding out what happened here today as anyone at MoSSA."

"Hardly. It was not your staff in danger of being eaten alive."

Orly's exasperation bubbled over. "*Our* staff faces the danger of being eaten alive or torn limb from limb or *worse* every single day!"

Rake spoke, his voice unexpectedly calm. "Your museum visitors today were retired Irregulars, Mr. Littlechurch. We take any threat against our own seriously."

Barry harrumphed but after a few more minutes permitted himself to be guided by Orly from the hall and all its grim reminders.

The gruesome job of cleanup began. Archer glanced at Rake and found himself under bleak observation. A human would be waiting for thanks, but demons had the same aversion as the faerie to thank-yous.

"Yes?"

Rake opened his mouth, then shook his head. "It will wait."

Archer remembered the circumstances under which they'd last parted and his face grew warm. Hard to imagine now that he had ever lain in Rake's arms, that Rake had taken him in the ancient way, and that afterward Rake had whispered soft endearments to him. Lovely words. Secret words.

Give them me, give them me.

Archer was uncertain as to the etiquette of bedding a demon, but safe to say he had not behaved in a gentlemanly fashion toward Rake. To fuck and run was not good manners in any realm.

He started to speak, though he had no idea what he would say.

Rake's thoughts were clearly running on a different track. "The museum will have to be cleansed before it can reopen."

Rake was not speaking of sponging the walls and mopping the floors, though that had to be done as well. "Of course."

"My team will handle the first phase. After that you'll need to get a private eidolon eraser in."

"Yes. I'll see to it immediately."

Perhaps he hoped that by being cooperative now he could show Rake he was sorry for behaving like a sneak thief in the night. If so, Rake wasn't having any of it. He nodded in curt dismissal and there was nothing for Archer to do but return to his duties—such as they were, given the events of the afternoon.

He made sure everyone had left the museum. Spoke to the media and reassured them that the minor gas leak responsible for the small explosion within the museum had done minimal damage to the paperwork stored there.

He'd have liked to speak to Barry, but his door was still shut, Barry apparently still in private conference with Sergeant Orly.

Archer went to his office to get his briefcase. As he clicked the locks shut, the memory of George Gaki's weirdly benign smile flew into his mind.

There's been talk about you, you know, Green. Certain of your old comrades dislike the fact that you're roaming freely in the world knowing all that you do. Helping us just this once could go far toward proving that there is no need for...worry.

Was it possible that Gaki had seen him leave with Rake, put two and two together, only to come up with five? Was there an other-realm contract out on his life?

Not a cheerful thought.

He picked up the briefcase and nearly jumped out of his skin at the sight of Rake standing in the doorway.

"Guilty conscience?" Rake inquired.

"I didn't see you there."

"I'm not surprised."

Archer raised his chin. "Meaning?"

"You have a blind spot."

Archer leaned back against the desk in a show of casualness. "Everyone does."

"With you it verges on amaurosis."

"Something like amorousness, is it?"

"Not in your case." Rake's voice was dry. "Definitely not."

Archer considered the words and tone uneasily. Rake didn't seem angry. No. Anger was something Archer could deal with easily. This was something else. Something worrisome.

Was Rake...*hurt*?

Archer's eyes widened, considering this possibility. Perhaps Barry had been right. Perhaps there *was* something here Archer could use. But scanning Rake's austere features, he found he was strangely loathe to try. Because he had no idea what to say, he opted for brusqueness.

"Fascinating. Is there something I can help you with, Commander?"

"There's something I can help *you* with."

Archer didn't like the flat way Rake said it—or the chilly dark look of his eyes. "Well?"

"Stay away from George Gaki."

It was a shock, but Archer managed to say, composedly, "Who?"

"You heard me."

Archer's natural mischievousness got the better of him. "I'd no idea it was serious between you two."

Rake's lips compressed further—possibly to conceal his fangs. "In case you haven't noticed, I'm not laughing."

"No? Well, you demons aren't famous for your sense of humor. Especially when it comes to affairs of the heart." He didn't miss the almost infinitesimal flinch Rake gave at the word *demon*. Most definitely not common knowledge. That was some comfort. Though it was still aggravating to think he'd missed something that should have been obvious. But then Rake had had many years to perfect his camouflage.

Rake was not in a playful mood. He said in that same stark, somber voice, "I know about the green glass beads."

It was like being struck by lightning. Archer couldn't have moved, couldn't have spoken if his life had depended on it. Perhaps it did.

Watching him, Rake mimicked, "'Nymph, nymph, what are your beads?'"

Archer was stung into speech. "What do you know of them? What can you know of them? To you they're just another artifact to be exorcised, cataloged, and filed away in some airless, sunless place like this."

"I know the beads are an obsession with you."

Archer made a sound of contempt. He'd have walked away, but Rake continued to fill his doorway. So he folded his arms in a pretense at nonchalance and waited to hear whatever was coming.

Rake said coldly, clearly, "I know everything about you, Archer. Everything there is to know, I know. I've studied you for over a year."

"Studied *me*?" Archer felt an inkling of real alarm.

"Oh yes. I know you're descended directly from the Greenwood branch of the ancient fae court in the southeast of England, although your people have hidden in the Romney Marsh vicinity for the last couple of centuries. I know you're the last legitimate descendent of the wood nymph Thalia."

"So what? That's all ancient history."

"I know your mother was seduced and abandoned by a human, that she took her own life in the River Rother, and that you spent your childhood in human foster care."

"Oh yes," drawled Archer. "And I'm taking my revenge on the whole human race because of it—even though I'm half human."

"No. I don't think you intend any harm to the human race." For a moment Rake looked almost sorry for him. That was intolerable.

Archer scowled. "Then what?"

"Do you not realize that it's well known in the circles we both travel that the curator of the MoSSA will buy any heirloom belonging to the Greenwood connection and that the greatest prize you seek is the necklace belonging to Thalia herself?"

"Green glass gossip," jeered Archer. "You should hear the things humans say about demons."

"I'm not repeating what humans say. I'm telling you what's widely known in the other realms."

Archer shook his head, denying it.

"Yes." Rake was adamant. "And finally, I know, however much you pretend otherwise, that you are one of the ringleaders of the organization formerly known as SRRIM."

"Think what you like. It doesn't make it true. In fact—" Archer stopped himself. Even if some of his old comrades wanted him out of the way, the last thing he was going to do was confirm their suspicions by running to the badges for help.

Rake regarded him grimly. "In fact?"

"Nothing. In fact, you couldn't be more wrong."

"I wish that were true. More than you can know."

Archer had no idea how to reply to that. Surely Rake didn't mean what Archer hoped—thought—he meant.

Probably not, because Rake added flatly, "How long did you think we'd let you run before we nicked you?"

Archer opened his mouth, realized anything he said would be a mistake, and snapped it shut again.

"I transferred to Vancouver for one reason," Rake bore relentlessly on, "and that was—*is*—to catch you red-handed."

Chapter Eight

Given the alarming implications of everything Rake was telling him, Archer was surprised to hear himself ask, "So what was last night?"

Rake didn't hesitate. "Last night was all part of my plan. Last night was seduction."

Archer considered it, frowning. Rake sounded sincere. Which was rather funny given that Archer had been fretting about Rake's injured feelings only a couple of minutes earlier. Well, it just went to prove the old adage about sympathy for the devil.

Into his abstraction, Rake said roughly, "What did you think? That I fell in love with you while poring over your files?"

"Yes."

The unadorned frankness of it seemed to anger Rake. "Then you're a bigger fool than I thought."

Rake's display of temper interested Archer. "Why are you angry at the idea?"

Rake's human visage shifted infinitesimally, proof of strong emotion. But what strong emotion? Aggravation seemed uppermost. "Because it's nonsense. I suppose you're telling me you also fell in love at first sight?"

"Of course not." Rake's human form gave another of those jumps, like fire in the wind. Archer admitted, "I fell in love last night."

Rake said something unpleasant in Babylonian. Or perhaps Hittite. Hittite was especially good for hurtful words.

"Why not?" Archer inquired. "That's how it works for our kind."

"We are not the same kind," Rake retorted. "You're half human. And a terrorist to boot."

The half human remark hurt more than Archer would have expected. His own temper flared. “You’re right. We’re not the same. I was just having fun with you last night. I knew what you were all the time.”

Rake laughed, although it was more of a snarl.

Given the demon propensity for violence, it seemed to Archer time to change the subject. “Why are you telling me all this?”

All at once Rake was human again. Human and rather tired. “Because after what you did today…the fact that you risked your life to save others…I’m willing to give you one last chance. Because surely after today you must realize how misguided—how wrong—you’ve been. You must see now that the path you’re on can lead to nothing but danger and destruction.”

“The path *I’m* on?” Archer gazed at Rake with disbelief. “Today an exorcised artifact came back to life. That’s not even possible. Yet it happened. Either uncontrolled magic is returning to the world or—” Once again he broke off before saying something he would surely regret.

“No.” There wasn’t even a shade of doubt in Rake’s voice. “Blood from the cut on your hand must have touched the skin at some point.”

Archer held up his healed hand. “No. The cut’s long gone. Besides, as you untactfully point out, I’m only half faerie. My blood couldn’t restore life.”

“If the cut is already healed, then your blood carries the old magic.”

Archer shook his head. “I heal quickly, true, but I should know if I had that gift.”

“Then the naga skin couldn’t have been properly neutralized.”

Archer laughed. “Now you’re simply fooling yourself.”

Rake said shortly, “Fine. Let’s agree for the sake of argument that neutralization is not infallible. All the more reason why these items can’t be loose in the human realm.”

Apparently Rake couldn’t see the one other obvious possibility. But then perhaps Archer was the one imagining murder plots where they didn’t exist. “No one wanted them loose in the mortal realms. The intent was to return them to their native cultures.”

"That's not a solution. That's anarchy."

"How can you say that? You, a creature of a magical realm?"

Rake's face colored. "It isn't a matter of either-or. You, of anyone, should know that. The mortal and immortal realms must learn to exist together."

"By destroying the culture, traditions, and history of one for the other's sake?"

"Enough." Rake straightened. "I didn't come to debate with you. This conversation is at an end."

"In fact, it never happened. Like everything else between us that never happened."

Rake stared at him. For a moment Archer thought he might respond to that taunt, to what he was too smart not to hear beneath the cheeky words. But in the end Rake merely said, "I've warned you. If you're smart, you'll take that warning."

Archer smiled. He picked up his briefcase again. "Of course. I appreciate the warning."

He walked toward the door. For a moment Archer thought Rake would continue to bar his way, but just as they were about to bump noses—or as Archer's nose was about to bump Rake's chin—Rake stepped aside.

"Good night," Rake said curtly.

"Good-bye," Archer replied.

❧

When Archer had first entered into foster care some well-meaning person had given him a book called *Flower Fairies of the Trees* by Cicely M. Barker.

"You look exactly like the little fairy boy on page six," the nice lady had said, thereby setting Archer up for a lot of jokes he was far too young to understand. It was a silly book. The fairies in it were all children and they had butterfly wings and wore ridiculous costumes, but in fact, Archer had looked exactly like the little fairy boy on page six. Also known as the box tree fairy. He found the book fascinating and he memorized the box tree poem, which ended with the immortal lines:

And among its leaves there play
Little blue-tits, brisk and gay.

The book had been lost when he had been shuffled off to the next home, but it had eventually turned up at one of the stops along the way of the long journey of national foster care. Archer had reclaimed it with joy. Unfortunately, that copy had belonged to another child. The result of that bitter skirmish was that Archer had been hustled along to yet another strange home and stranger family.

He had bought his own copy of the book a few years later.

Archer paused in unknotting the tangled network of wards and protection spells guarding the hidden entrance to George Gaki's back door. Odd to be thinking of this now. It was Rake's fault. Rake's intimation that Archer was…what?

He'd said he didn't believe Archer was seeking vengeance. So why had he brought up all that rot about Archer's past? Making it sound like Archer was some pathetic orphan child trying to… trying to...

Recovering the book—buying the book—had been Archer's first effort to reclaim his heritage. That was true. But so what? It was natural enough that he'd want something belonging to his family. Family heirlooms. What was so unusual about that? What was surprising there? Great-Aunt Esmeralda's clock, Uncle Cadamus's snuffbox collection, the portrait of Grandmother Philomena. He'd paid for them, paid for every single item.

He would have paid for the beads as well, if it had been possible. Since it wasn't…Well, the beads were his. The beads belonged to his family and Archer was all that remained of his family. The beads were his.

The last of the wards fell away, shriveling to nothing but pale squiggles easily mistaken by the human eye for glow worms. Archer waved his hand in front of the lock and felt it click over, and the door swung silently open.

A sudden prickle across his scalp had Archer glancing over his shoulder, but there was nothing there.

He stepped inside the hall.

It was just a long, ordinary hallway. Hardwood floor, pale walls, framed photographs of generic countryside. At the end of the hall one doorway branched off to the right and one to the left.

The right led to the kitchen, where a security guard sat drinking coffee and flirting with the cook.

Archer veered left and found himself in a sunroom. He stepped around the potted plants and rattan furniture and went out the far entrance. He stopped to listen.

The security guard was still telling a long, dull story only a woman in love would sit still for. Upstairs another woman was singing a department store jingle in her sleep. In another room farther south two more security guards were talking hockey scores.

Archer continued on his way till he came to the long staircase that led to the private room in the faux tower.

The tower door took a little longer to open and sweat was trickling down Archer's temples by the time the last ward fell away.

The door flew open and the row of candles on their rack jumped, flames dancing in the sudden draft.

Archer stepped inside and looked around. There was not a great deal to see. Rich Persian rugs covered the floor and French tapestries partially covered the windows. A gigantic gold-framed triptych of the first demon battles took up most of the far wall.

Archer's gaze fell on a Mesopotamian treasure chest sitting in one corner.

No. Too obvious.

He closed his eyes, opened his mind, and began his search.

Hush, I stole them out of the moon.

Give me your beads, I want them…

A soft humming came to him from across the room. Archer opened his eyes. The flame of one of the fat, squat candles had turned green and was shooting up, licking hungrily at the air.

Archer smiled. In two strides he was across the floor. He pinched out the cold flame, lifted the fake candle from its perch, and removed the lid. The strand of beads spilled out, cool and shining as water.

Archer laughed in delight and held them to his face, feeling the weight of the beads running through his fingers, hearing their silken whisper.

The overhead light came on, dazzling Archer for an instant.

"I must say I thought Commander Rake was indulging in wishful thinking when he told me you'd be paying me a call in the next couple of days." George Gaki, garbed in a luxuriant orange dressing gown and flanked by two security guards, stood in the arched doorway.

It was not Gaki's presence—unwelcome though it was—so much as his words that struck Archer into statue-like immobility.

Seeing his shock, Gaki made a clucking sound, like a sympathetic maiden aunt. "Yes, it seems the commander has had you under observation for some time, Mr. Green. He came out to the estate this very morning to warn me that you've developed a dangerous obsession with an item that belongs to me." He shook his head. "And to think you could have had them for the asking."

Archer said automatically, "The beads don't belong to you."

"I assure you, halfling, in the human realm they most certainly *do* belong to me. And I've the bill of sale from Christie's to prove it." Gaki stared at the beads sinuously twining themselves around Archer's fingers. "The baubles seem to share your misconception. Can it be true? Are you the last of the Greenwoods?"

"In any realm but this one my claim would be recognized."

"But we're in the human realm, where a piece of paper counts more than blood oaths and family ties." Gaki smiled. "The only question now is, since I've caught you, what shall I do with you?"

Archer said nothing. He couldn't seem to think past Rake's betrayal.

"I should, of course, turn you over to the grimly conscientious Commander Rake, but what a waste. Would you like to reconsider my more than generous offer? Before you answer, think. This is what mortals call *an offer you can't refuse*."

"I *am* refusing."

"By all that is powerful, *why*?"

"I already told you. I no longer believe in SRRIM's methods. I'm not even sure I believe in their motives. It looks to me like you're just stealing a lot of artifacts for yourself."

Gaki smiled again, though it was rather pained this time. "I see. I keep forgetting how very young you are. I eat little boys like you for breakfast. That is, I used to. We're all a great deal more civilized these days. By human standards, anyway."

"I know what you are," Archer said scornfully. He was not feeling particularly warm toward demons just then.

"Among other things, I'm an excellent negotiator. Let me help you consider your options. Option one: I call the police. Alas, you'll be dead by the time they arrive. So sad. Option two: I break my diet and have you for breakfast tomorrow."

The security guards glanced uneasily at each other.

"I'm joking," Gaki told them. "I wouldn't dream of breaking my diet. I've lost ten pounds already. Option three: you stop behaving like a rebellious teenager and join us once more. In return, I'll give you those baubles you're holding on to like worry beads. I'll give you other things as well. Lovely things. Things that will make the occasional ping of your half-human conscience all worthwhile."

Archer stared at Gaki's implacable smile. He stared at the guards behind him.

He decided to give option four a try and flew to the star-shaped window. A foot away, he recoiled. There was cold iron in the casement.

Not something one ran across much in modern construction.

He backed away from the window.

"I don't pay you to stand there," Gaki told his security guards.

One guard drew his pistol. The other leaped after Archer who did his best to evade him in the small tower room while keeping an eye on the guard with the pistol. He didn't know much about firearms, but he did know that being shot with a lead bullet would probably be fatal. Not because lead was in itself dangerous to faeries, but being shot with any bullet was probably not going to be healthy.

"This is ridiculous," Gaki said after thirty seconds of watching Archer dodge and duck the much slower guard. "*Shoot him.*"

The guard promptly fired, sending a bullet past Archer's head and into the gold-framed triptych.

Gaki roared and raised his arms above his head. His dressing gown began to tear as fearsomely muscled limbs lengthened and turned black green. The security guards and Archer stopped, staring as if mesmerized, while Gaki's hands curved into razor-taloned claws and his features twisted into something from a nightmare.

The guard with the pistol dropped his weapon and bolted from the room. The other man backed away and knelt, gibbering below the window, as Gaki advanced toward Archer.

Archer's heart pounded in terror, but he couldn't seem to lift his feet from the floor as Gaki stalked toward him. The demon's tail whipped up and the tip was barbed like the tip of a spear. It loomed up over both Gaki and Archer, and Archer remembered the naga skin.

"It *was* you," he said faintly.

The glowing red eyes showed no human comprehension.

He was going to die in the next second. He should have listened to Rake. Except it was Rake who had made his death a certainty. How twisted, then, that his final thought should be a sudden longing for Rake.

The star window shattered and glass blew into the room like silver rain. With it came bits of iron and wood and plaster as the whole wall exploded.

Another demon stood in the ruins of the tower room. Through the opening of where the wall had once been, Archer could see official vehicles parking below. Black-clad Irregular forces rushed the house, battering the doors.

The roar of the second demon sent chunks of the remaining ceiling raining down. His red gaze swept the wreckage, found Archer.

"I thought you'd never..." Archer's voice cut out.

For a fleeting instant, Rake's demon form wavered, showed human.

Gaki didn't miss his chance. He launched himself forward with a bellow. The house shook beneath the force of their collision. Archer sprang clear of the lashing tails, the deadly sweep of shining bat-like wings.

Go, he thought. *Go now. You have what you came for.*

Archer's gaze was drawn to the strands of beads looped around his hand and wrist. He had them at last.

Gaki snarled as Rake's fangs sank into his shoulder. Green blood squirted. He clawed at Rake's face. Rake howled and tried to disembowel Gaki with the talons on his feet. One of his wings knocked the Mesopotamian chest off the platform and box and jewels tumbled, glittering, through the night.

Archer looked at the door. He had to go now. The badges were coming. He could hear the thunder of their boots down below.

He *had* to go. Anything else was stupidity. Madness.

He couldn't go. Not while there was any doubt to Rake's fate.

He jumped out of the way again as Gaki, heavier, broader, managed to flip Rake. They landed on the rack of candles. The remaining tapestries and rugs caught fire and went up in a blazing whoosh.

Gaki's massive head dipped and green blood spurted. Had he bitten Rake's throat? Archer couldn't tell. In terror he leaped onto Gaki's wide back and whipped the strands of beads around his thick throat, yanking them tight.

Tighter.

He used all his strength until he could feel the breath strangling in his own lungs.

Gaki threw him off as though he were no more than a gnat. Archer went sailing and crashed through the remaining section of wall and into darkness.

Miles and miles later, he heard a voice he thought he knew.

"Archer. Can you hear me? Sweeting..." Rake's voice called to him from down a long, smoky tunnel.

Archer tried to answer, but he could never make himself heard across all that distance. He closed his eyes.

Chapter Nine

"Any way you look at it, that was pretty stupid," Sergeant Orly said, folding her hands on the file in front of her. Implication being that this case was open and shut.

Archer shrugged. She was right, and in any case, he didn't have energy for more. The bump on his head had been taped and the hospital had released him back into police custody. In handcuffs and shackles. He'd never been in handcuffs before. Let alone shackles. These were made of special cold iron. They didn't look like much, but they pressed on Archer as though some giant force was crushing him. He could barely walk; running was out of the question—as was escape. But he already knew that.

They were sitting in the interrogation room at Irregulars HQ. Just him and the dour Sergeant Orly. No sign of Rake, but that was a relief, really. Every time he remembered his foolish, impulsive behavior at George Gaki's estate he burned with humiliation. And he was not thinking of his ill-advised attempt to recover the beads.

"Trespassing, breaking and entering, assault, attempted theft of a culturally significant other-realm artifact, trafficking in and abuse of items deemed to pose a malignant threat to humanity." Her eyes held his. "Which is a capital offense."

Yes, even in a country where there was no death penalty, endangering the safety of the entire human realm carried a death penalty.

"That sounds serious. Can I talk to my lawyer now?"

"I wouldn't advise it."

Archer raised his eyebrows.

"I've been authorized to offer you a deal. Confess to the three lesser charges and agree to cooperate in our investigation into the SRRIM and we'll reduce the last charge to trafficking in culturally significant other-realm artifacts. It carries a thirty-year prison sentence, which you'll serve out at the mixed population maximum security facility in Toronto."

"Toronto? That really is cruel and unusual punishment."

She was, unsurprisingly, unamused. "I think, Mr. Green, you'll agree it's to your vast advantage to avoid incarceration in one of the regular high security facilities for the criminally sorcerous."

"I'll wait for my lawyer."

"This deal is good for exactly five minutes. Or until your lawyer arrives. Whichever happens first."

"Even so."

Orly looked at him with real dislike. "You're not getting out of this, Green. We've got you fair and square. We've got a mountain of evidence. Even if your lawyer talks you out of the death penalty, you'll spend the rest of your life behind bars in the extra-human special handling unit in the Northwest Territories. You know what that means. You'll be locked up for the next couple of centuries with everything from Japanese kappa to anthropophagi."

Archer smiled. "The idea of those extra-humans frightens you?"

Orly smiled right back. "They frighten you. I can read that much of your thoughts. And no wonder. A pretty little faerie isn't going to survive long in that hellhole. Especially a half-human faerie. Twenty-four-hour CCTV or not." She looked at her watch. "Time's ticking."

"Where's Commander Rake?"

Orly's face tightened. "He had an a.m. meeting with the mayor."

"Such a busy man."

"Very."

Archer sighed. "Seduced and abandoned. It should be the motto on my family crest."

Orly's face turned red. "Commander Rake is a highly respected officer with an irreproachable record—"

"He's a demon. He ate his first wife. Bet you didn't know about that."

"—and a brilliant future. I don't know what you imagine you can gain by trying to smear him, but you won't get anywhere."

"Whose idea was this deal? Rake's?"

"Correct. This deal was Commander Rake's idea. He felt some consideration should be made, given your service at the museum yesterday. That, and your faerie age."

Archer said bitterly, "And the fact that he believes I can be of help in tracking down and destroying SRRIM?"

"Correct."

Archer sat back in his chair. Between his aching head and the oppressive weight of the iron shackles, he was beginning to feel very unwell. It was tempting to tell Orly whatever she wanted to hear so that he could go lie down. He said wearily, "I keep trying to tell you the SRRIM no longer exists."

"*Last chance*, Mr. Green."

"All right. SRRIM might still exist. I don't know for sure, but I haven't been a member for years. I wouldn't be any use to you. I swear it. I swear it on the green glass beads." He couldn't help asking, "Where are they, by the way?"

Orly slapped the file down on the table. "Last chance. Take the deal or take your chances with the courts."

"All right. The truth is, George Gaki lured me to his estate last night on the pretext of trying to sell me black market artifacts. I felt it was my duty as curator of the MoSSA to examine these items in case they were legitimate. When I arrived at Gaki's estate he began raving about adding me to his 'collection.'"

"You can't be serious."

"I'm perfectly serious. The person you should have in custody is Mr. Gaki, not me. Has my lawyer arrived yet?"

Orly's chair scraped back. She rose. "You had your chance. We'll see if you're still so cocky after a few hours in mixed population."

The door to the interview room popped open.

"Not now, please!" Orly snapped.

The uniformed officer looked apologetic but beckoned to her. Orly exhaled a long, exasperated breath and went outside. Archer tilted his head back and stared at the ceiling, listening.

"We just got the word from upstairs," the uniformed officer said. "You have to cut him loose."

"What?" Archer didn't need faerie hearing to catch Orly's outraged response. They probably could hear it all the way in the holding cells. "What the hell are you saying?"

"He's been sprung. Bail has been posted."

"We're not even finished booking him!"

"The director of MoSSA showed up with a high-powered lawyer."

"*Littlechurch* is bailing him out?"

"Looks like it."

"That doesn't make any sense!"

"I couldn't say, ma'am. He must have called in about a dozen favors to do it."

"We have to stall Green's release. A couple of hours in mixed population and he'll take any deal we throw at him."

"We can't stall. His lawyer is already accusing us of stalling. She's downstairs right now screaming that his civil rights as a protected being have been violated."

"*Protected being*? Since when are faeries an endangered species?"

"It's to do with something called the Sussex emerald moth. Apparently Romney Marsh is one of the last places in the world where you can find them and the moths are somehow connected to Green's family tree and the Greenwood clan."

"I don't *believe* this. Captain!"

A third voice entered the discussion. "Sorry, Sergeant. It's not my call. Now, don't look at me like that. I don't like it either, but we've got to cut him loose. The sooner the better."

Orly began to swear.

"Don't worry. It's a temporary setback, that's all. We've got enough on Green to put him away for good this time."

Archer closed his eyes. He saw Rake bending over him, his face fluctuating between mortal and immortal, his eyes black with pain not his own. Archer blinked rapidly. As tired as he was, he didn't dare let down his guard.

Orly came back into the room. Her smile was closer to a twitch. "Change of plan, Mr. Green."

"Oh yes?" No point reminding people that he had certain advantages, not including a close and personal relationship with the Sussex emerald moth.

"You've made bail." Orly nodded curtly to the uniformed officer who had followed her into the room.

Archer rose, waiting as the cuffs and shackles were removed. Relief at the removal of the cold iron was instantaneous.

He was led out to into the hall and then down to a small room where his personal possessions were restored to him. Through the glass window he could see Barry and a tall, stately black woman with features as sharply aristocratic as a Zulu princess waiting. Barry was pacing up and down the lobby, but he stopped, his face brightening with relief at the sight of Archer walking through the door.

Ms. Sibanyoni explained their legal game plan as Barry ushered Archer out of the lobby and into the elevators leading down to the visitors parking level in the underground garage. Archer listened politely and nodded during the pauses. He had no idea what she was talking about, although he gathered his situation was grim. The leg shackles had been his first clue.

Ms. Sibanyoni finished telling Archer how serious his position was, bade him not to worry, and drove away in her silver Porsche.

"This way," Barry said gruffly, resting his hand briefly on Archer's shoulder.

Archer followed Barry to his car, waited for him to unlock the passenger side door, and climbed in. He let his head fall back.

Barry started the engine.

"Was it bad?" he asked tersely, pulling out of the narrow parking space.

Archer shook his head. All at once he was too tired to move, too tired even for words. Tears smarted in his eyes. He blinked them away.

"I…"

"Yes." Barry's voice was bleak. "You did."

"Sorry," Archer whispered.

Barry shook his head. No apology necessary. "How close did you come to finding them?"

Archer said wearily, "I had them in my hands. For a few minutes."

"Hopefully it was worth it."

Archer's eyes flew open. "How can you say that?"

Barry shook his head. "They arrested Gaki when they arrested you. That's something."

"Good."

"Of course, he's got the money to pay for the best lawyers. Not that Ms Sibanyoni wouldn't put up a gallant fight for you." Barry seemed to be picking and choosing his words. "The badges confiscated the beads as well."

Archer watched him closely. "So?"

"So…you were right. Gaki hadn't purchased any antique water beads. They're the real thing. Carved beads of an unidentified material that's as translucent as glass but harder than jade or emeralds or any known stone."

"Did you think I would be mistaken about something like that?"

Barry said nothing.

The real source of his unease dawned on Archer. "Where are they, Barry? What are they planning?"

"Archer." Barry looked away from the wheel. "You know where the beads are and you know exactly what's going to happen to them."

His heart seemed to drop out of his chest like a bird shot out of the sky. "They can't! They can't neutralize them."

"Of course they can. Of course they will." Barry threw him another of those grimly pitying looks.

"There's got to be something we can do to stop them. Get some injunction against them. Something."

"It's done. Let it go."

"I can't let it go."

"You don't have a choice. And, to be blunt, you've got bigger problems now."

That was the bitter truth. If he'd waited, controlled his impulsiveness, his rebelliousness, his need to possess the beads and all they represented *immediately*, it might all be different now. It would certainly be different now. The beads would still be with Gaki, yes, but they would be safe. Waiting for Archer. Waiting for him to find the right moment for their liberation.

He was not good at waiting for right moments. He never had been. He could blame that on his faerie bloodline. The fae were not an accommodating race.

Archer stared out the window at the buildings and cars flying past as Barry wove in and out of traffic, driving with set face and somber purpose. Not like his normal meandering style of travel at all. It occurred to Archer that they were not on their way to Gastown or the museum. "Where are we going?"

"Stanley Park. I pulled some strings—a cat's cradle worth of strings—and there's a port-o-let there waiting to take you where you need to go."

"But I thought..." Well, no. He hadn't thought. That was the whole trouble, wasn't it?

Again, Archer started to speak, but Barry was still following his own thoughts. "We've got to get you out of the country as fast as possible or you're going to wind up playing house for the next century with a vampire—or worse—in the Northwest Territories."

"I told them Gaki tried to sell me black market antiquities. I think they'll believe it. It turned out Rake was investigating him." Archer added shortly, "He used me and the beads to get Gaki."

Barry snorted. "Don't fool yourself. You were always the real prize. Rake honestly believes that you're still with SRRIM. He used the beads and Gaki to get you." Barry added almost absently, "Anyway, I'm sure the commander has figured out that, unlike a full-blooded faerie, you can lie with the best of them."

Archer thought of Rake. "Maybe. I'd still like to—"

But Barry interrupted, "Don't worry. It's all arranged. We've set up a new identity for you in Brittany."

"Brittany?" Archer echoed. "But I don't know anyone in Brittany."

"Exactly. And no one in Brittany knows you. But there's still a largish faerie presence there. You'll acclimatize quickly, you'll see."

"But..." Once it had been Archer arranging these things. It was confusing to be on the other side. "Don't I have any say in this?"

"Of course. Say whatever you like. So long as it isn't that you want to stay and face trial here."

"No." It struck Archer that he would never see Rake again. All morning he had been seething with resentment toward him, but now when he needed anger the most, it drained away, leaving him bereft.

"You'll be set up in business as an antiques dealer," Barry was saying. "Money is being wired to your account. Am I forgetting anything?"

Probably not. They were not new at this kind of thing, although it was the first time Archer had played the starring role of fugitive. It was not an enjoyable feeling. "What about..."

Barry glanced at him. "What about what?"

Archer gestured vaguely, unable to articulate. He felt overwhelmed by how fast everything was moving.

Barry said quickly, reassuringly, "I'll send your Great-Aunt Esmeralda's clock along with your other belongings. I know what those things mean to you."

Archer nodded automatically. "Rake wasn't there while I was being interrogated."

"He was meeting with the mayor. The word is he intends to have Gaki prosecuted for attempted kidnapping, extortion, trafficking in culturally significant other-realm artifacts, and endangering the health and welfare of a protected being."

Archer spluttered into unwilling laughter. "Can he do that?"

"Who knows. If anyone can, it's Commander Rake." Barry gave him a look of commiseration. "I'm sorry about the beads, but having them wouldn't change anything."

Archer stared out the window. "You can't understand this, Barry."

"Archer, you are who you are and possession of the beads doesn't change that."

Archer turned to him, frowning, but they had reached the turnoff for the West End and Stanley Park.

In a very short time Archer stood in the parking lot where the port-o-let was.

"Thank you, Barry," he said belatedly. "You're going to take a lot of heat for this."

"Yes, but it's a dry heat," Barry said blandly. It was such an un-Barry-like comment, Archer began to laugh. Or maybe he was laughing because the alternative was unthinkable.

He was startled when Barry reached out and pulled him into a hug. Barry was blinking when he released Archer. All this time

Archer had believed Barry didn't care for sentiment, but Barry was the one reaching to wipe his eyes.

"I'll miss you," Archer said. He was surprised to realize how true it was. It was only now dawning on him how much of a home and even extended family he had here—now, when he was leaving forever.

"We've had some high times," Barry agreed, smirking.

"Give Commander Rake my love."

Barry grimaced. "Take care of yourself, my young friend. Be happy. Write."

Archer nodded. There was nothing left to say. He turned and sprinted across the parking lot.

As the blue plastic door closed, Barry's waving figure seemed to fall farther and farther in the distance. After a moment, Archer tugged open the door and stepped onto another continent.

Chapter Ten

"One more client, if you want to see him," Marie said. "American. They always think the world revolves around them."

Archer, feet propped on his desk, looked up from the article about a series of strange deaths in Mexico City. Not that deaths in Mexico City were strange, but when you were fae, and marshland fae at that, you had to wonder about fatally fouled water supplies.

"Buying or selling?"

"He didn't say. He only asked to see you."

Archer sighed. Not that bloody Stone of Fal again. Even if he'd had the faintest idea where the wretched thing was—and thankfully he didn't—he wasn't about to be mixed up in sidhe politics when the simple act of trying to retrieve costume jewelry had nearly gotten him killed.

"Did he ask specifically to see me or to see the proprietor?"

"Propriétaire." Marie was a member of the local korrigan tribe. She was about two feet tall with long silken white hair and red eyes. She reminded Archer of those Danish troll dolls that had been so popular in the sixties. She was his shop assistant and the closest thing he had to a confidant in Saint-Malo. Hands on her hips, she waited for his verdict.

"Tell him I've gone for the day."

Marie went out. Archer went back to his paper.

A while later Marie was back with Archer's tea. A bulky envelope rested on the tray.

"What's this?"

Marie shrugged. "He left it for you."

"Who?"

"The American."

Archer picked up the envelope and examined it doubtfully. He'd had a few run-ins with the local hard cases, but it was hard to believe the drow would hire American muscle. *A. Green* was dashed off in a strong, unfamiliar hand across the face of the envelope.

He ripped open the flap and tipped the envelope. Green stones as cool and silky as running water pooled in his hand and then spilled over, whispering sweetly.

Better than stars or water,
Better than voices of winds that sing,
Better than any man's fair daughter,
Your green glass beads on a silver ring.

Archer caught the rope of green glass beads before they fell to the floor.

He clutched them, feeling the weight of them swinging gently between his fingers. He pressed them to his face and felt the strange chill of them against his eyelids and lips. His throat tightened. His eyes stung. It was all he could do not to weep with joy. It was the shock of it, the utterly unexpected granting of his greatest wish.

It was only then that he realized that, in fact, recovery of the beads was his second greatest wish.

He lowered the beads to find Marie staring at him, puzzled.

"What did he look like?"

"Who?"

"The American?"

"Big." Marie spread her arms. "*Les Rochers Sculptes.*" A man as big as the bas-relief sculptures of sea monsters and giants along the Emerald Coast at Rothéneuf.

"Where did he go?"

Marie shook her head.

Archer dropped the beads onto the tea tray and ran out the door, ignoring Marie's cries to take his raincoat.

The antiques shop was located in the back streets of quiet and quaint Saint-Servan-sur-Mer, part of Saint-Malo. Barry had chosen well. Archer had felt immediately at home amidst the cobblestones and narrow, vaulted passageways and small, enclosed gardens with trees and flowers and mushrooms. Or as much at home as he would ever feel now that he understood that home was, as humans put it, where the heart was.

He ran down the alleyway and out onto the high road.

In the summer months of July and August the area was overrun with tourists who came for the beaches and the blue surf, but this was May and the streets and beaches were empty as Archer sped along, searching for Rake.

Rain bounced off the cobblestones, skipping and zinging down the narrow road.

Why had he done it? Why had Rake brought the beads, unharmed, untouched, to Archer? Why now? Six months later?

And why had he gone away again?

Archer realized he had dropped the necklace on his desk and left it there unprotected, unguarded, but still he kept running, glancing down alleyways, peering through the rain-silvered shop windows.

There was no sign of Rake anywhere.

Couldn't he have waited? Couldn't he have insisted on seeing Archer? After six months couldn't Rake have given him another half hour?

But then Rake had already given him the thing he believed Archer wanted most.

Six months! Even Archer, young enough to be optimistic in the face of all reason, had nearly lost hope that he would ever see Rake again.

True, at the start of his exile he hadn't wanted to see Rake again. He had been angry and hurt. Not merely because Rake had made good on his threats but because of the things Rake had said the last day at the museum, because Rake had tried to pretend that there was nothing between them. You didn't have to read fairytales to know the magical thing that had sprung to life the very first time they had laid eyes on each other.

Love. That was the word for it in the mortal realms. And in the immortal realms as well.

Yes, Archer had been far angrier about Rake's rejection than Rake's attempt to trap and imprison him. After all, Rake had given him plenty of warning—as Archer had given Rake. They were on different sides, that was all. What had been harder to forgive was Rake pretending there was nothing else between them.

But when Archer had time to think—and he'd had plenty of time to think these past six months—he'd known Rake was lying. Lying to himself and lying to Archer, but mostly lying to himself.

All Archer had to do was remember Rake's expression when he had feared Gaki had killed Archer.

That didn't solve the problem of being on opposing sides. But perhaps they weren't really on opposing sides.

It still didn't solve the problem of Rake disappearing again.

Archer rounded another corner and stopped short. Speak of the devil. Demon. Rake stood gazing into a small park ringed by a black ornate railing. His expression was somber, but maybe that was the rain running down the back of his neck.

Having been focused only on finding Rake, Archer realized he didn't know what to say to him. In his mind, the Rake he was pursuing had been the passionate and tender lover of the single night they'd spent together. This Rake was the severe-faced man of their first meeting.

Rake must have picked his signature up because he turned his head and stared at Archer without surprise.

"You're welcome. But you didn't need to run out in the rain to say thanks."

His voice sounded exactly the same. He looked exactly the same. But then why wouldn't he? The change was within Archer.

Archer walked toward him. "Why didn't you wait?"

"I didn't think there was a reason to wait."

Archer reached Rake. The faint scent of vanilla mingled with rain and wet flowers. He breathed in deeply and smiled. "I was afraid you were only wearing that to seduce me."

Rake's brows drew together. He glanced down at himself. "My raincoat?"

"Your aftershave."

Rake's smile twisted. "Of course. The vanilla. I thought that was an old wives' tale."

Archer shook his head. Suddenly shy, he stared at the stone bench and flowers, the statues of little people probably intended to be faeries. "Why did you do it?"

"What? Oh. The beads. You know why I did it."

Archer risked a quick look. Rake was looking at him steadily. Archer said, "I know you think I'm a fool. But when you don't have a home or a family…"

"I know." Rake's face softened. "But it isn't clocks and snuff-boxes that make a home. And family ties aren't forged in silver and green glass beads."

"True. But you take what you can get." That sounded pathetic. Archer said quickly, "How did you manage it? I thought the beads were going to be neutralized."

Rake's expression was strange. "The beads don't pose a threat to humanity. They're not magical."

Archer blinked, uncomprehending. "That's not true." He'd seen that look on Rake's face one other time: in his office at the museum when Rake had said he didn't believe Archer intended any harm. He said bewilderedly, "That's not possible."

"If there is magic in them, it's only for you."

Archer turned away, trying to make sense of this. "But they are magic. I can *feel* that they are."

Rake shrugged.

"They are magic."

"Why does that matter?"

Archer opened his mouth and then closed it.

Rake took pity on him. "With George Gaki busy doing thirty years for trafficking in culturally significant other-realm artifacts,

I appealed for ownership of the beads in the faerie realm. You've been awarded custody."

"You did that for me? After everything?"

"It's because of everything that I did it for you."

It was impossible to turn away from the look in Rake's eyes. Archer had no desire to turn away in any case. He said shakily, "I thought seducing me was just part of your plan?"

"I thought you seduced me."

Archer's irrepressible laugh rang out and Rake laughed too.

"That's right," said Archer. "I was forgetting."

"How do you like Saint-Malo?"

"I like it."

"Do you think I would?"

"I'd make it my business to see that you did," Archer said seriously. "But it's a long commute to your office."

"I don't have an office. I've resigned my commission."

Archer's jaw dropped. Rake's smile was grim. He tapped Archer's cheek lightly. "Close your mouth, sweeting. You'll drown."

"You resigned your commission?"

Rake shrugged. "I was ready for a change. In any case… Change is coming soon for us all."

"I thought so! Didn't I say so?" Archer exclaimed.

"Maybe. But I don't want to hear 'I told you so' for the next three centuries, so give it a rest."

"Three centuries? Is that all you give us?"

"You're very young," Rake said. "You might change your mind down the line."

"Probably not. As you pointed out, I'm a little obsessive."

"It's one of the things I like about you."

"Tell me some other things you like about me," Archer invited.

"Come closer and I will."

Archer lifted his face up and Rake's mouth met his in a honey-sweet kiss with just a hint of a bite. Above them the rain dripped slowly, steadily from the leaves. The shining droplets fell through the air looking like nothing so much as green glass beads.

NO LIFE BUT THIS

Astrid Amara

I have no life but this,
To lead it here;
Nor any death, but lest
Dispelled from there;

Nor tie to earths to come,
Nor action new,
Except through this extent,
The Realm of You.
— Emily Dickinson

The overpowering smell of cooked meat and car exhaust couldn't compare to the explosion of colors emanating from the wall of billboards outside Mexico City's Benito Juárez International Airport. The thick, hot air was rank with jet fuel. Traffic noise battled a trumpet blasting enthusiastically over a car radio.

As he scanned the passenger pickup area for his ride, Deven took deep, calming breaths—just like his therapist had taught him. He wondered how the driver would recognize him. He didn't look much different from the men around him...maybe a little paler, and maybe greener eyes, but they were hard to see through his sunglasses.

"Taxi?" a man offered, waving at Deven as he blinked on the curb. "Taxi, señor?"

"No." Deven glanced around, looking for someone who resembled an Irregulars agent.

They had to know he'd landed. It had required special clearance to get his obsidian knives through security, and someone with authority had clearly pulled strings to procure him a business class seat on an overbooked flight with little advance notice.

"Mr. Shaw?"

Deven turned, squinting against the sunlight.

"I'm on your right," the man said.

Deven frowned. "I see you."

The man's face was pink with sunburn, nose already peeling. His short brown hair darkened in sweaty patches at his temples, but his sleek black suit hid any sweat on his body.

"Sorry, I was told you have vision issues." He held out his hand. "Agent Frank Klakow."

Deven didn't shake his hand. "ID?"

Agent Klakow's smile faltered but didn't fade. "Yeah, hold on." He struggled with his wallet, tight in his back pocket, and pulled out his badge. Deven took hold of it, studying the image. After a moment the agent shone a pen light at the badge and text illuminated around the insignia. The refraction of light bent oddly, but in this case he knew this wasn't an effect of his damaged eyesight but merely a seal of authenticity.

"So, the information I received about your vision was incorrect?" Klakow asked.

"I'm not blind. I have dark-adapted eyes." Deven returned the badge and picked up his duffel bag. Klakow led him to a black sedan. Inside it was air conditioned and shockingly cold.

"Is this your first time in Mexico City?" Klakow asked, sliding into the driver's seat.

"I was here a year ago," Deven said. He watched the agent pull a seat belt across his chest and Deven followed suit, mimicking the man's gestures as he'd learned to do over the last year. "But I stayed for only a few hours before I was repatriated to the US."

Klakow pulled into the stream of traffic. "Well, it's damned hot, that's all I can say for it."

Their car emerged from the concrete landscape of the airport and headed west toward the center of the city.

Deven removed his sunglasses and turned to view the city out the window but found the jumble of images too confusing to look at for long. He closed his eyes.

"Do you need to rest at the hotel before we go to the crime scene?"

"No." Deven didn't open his eyes. He wasn't sure exactly what he could offer the badges as a consultant, but they paid well. And it seemed like the kind of job better served with promptness.

Besides, it was something to do. Something better than running, or reading, or learning how to fish.

Deven sensed that Agent Klakow was staring, so he opened his eyes. The agent glanced at Deven frequently as he navigated the car. His eyes flickered to Deven's neck, but Deven was used to it.

What he wasn't used to was the look of pity that crossed people's features when they spotted the jagged scar where Deven's throat had been slit. It had happened so long ago Deven barely thought of it himself anymore.

"Has anyone briefed you on the investigation?" Klakow asked.

"I know someone was killed and Aztaw magic is suspected," Deven said.

"Two people," Klakow corrected. "One of ours, Agent Carlos Rodriguez, and his younger sister, Beatriz. Agent Rodriguez had come here to spend his vacation with his sister. None of his caseload had anything to do with the area."

Deven considered asking what Rodriguez's caseload typically consisted of, then thought better of it. Participating in the investigation would be hard in any case—Deven had a very good reason to distrust badges—but he would need to overcome his hostility toward the agency if he was going to remain on their payroll.

Klakow turned the car onto an unevenly paved road and Deven opened his eyes. They maneuvered through a densely packed neighborhood. Low single-story structures plastered in faded pastel colors lined the narrow street. All the windows were barred. Bright billboards rose above the structures bearing words in giant fonts.

"The victims' skulls were smashed in with no apparent sign of a struggle." Klakow shook his head. "Rodriguez was one tough motherfucker. There's no way he wouldn't have defended himself unless he was taken by surprise."

"Was there a lot of blood?" Deven asked.

"No." Klakow sounded impressed. "The forensics team commented on that. Several pints of blood seem to be missing."

"That's typical of deaths related to Aztaw magic."

"They use human, not Aztaw, blood in spells?"

Deven nodded.

"So I assume they wouldn't leave something that valuable behind," Klakow said.

"If you know all this, then why did you hire me?"

Klakow smirked. "We know some things about the Aztaw, but you're the only one who's actually lived with them for an extended period of time and has practiced their magic. Hopefully you'll catch details we'd otherwise miss."

The streets narrowed and the buildings grew more dilapidated. Bright yellow tarps stretched over stalls erected on sidewalks selling piles of cheap clothing and household goods. The sidewalks were packed with bustling people. Deven stared, amazed by their sheer numbers. He'd never seen so many human beings crowded in one place.

"Where are we?" Deven asked.

"Tepito barrio. Beatriz Rodriguez's house is a few blocks away."

The buildings looked impoverished, with rusted metal awnings and chipped plaster corners. Power lines drooped down nearly at street level and formed webs across the skyline. Piles of shiny litter clustered over the broken pavement. Dark blue corrugated garage doors shuttered closed blocks of shops.

Deven concentrated on a building corner, finally realizing he was staring at peeling, colorful posters layered upon each other. Deven felt triumph at finally comprehending what he saw, and then confusion. Why would anyone want to look at that mess?

They turned onto Republica de Paraguay. Agent Klakow maneuvered the car to a stop along the sidewalk in front of a two-story, persimmon-colored plaster building. There was little outward sign that a murder investigation was underway—no police tape, no crowds of onlookers as Deven had come to expect based on the television shows he watched. The street appeared nearly vacant.

But as Deven glanced around, he saw other things. Two men in suits down at the end of an alleyway. A dog that watched closely as they got out of the car. There was a smell here too, barely detectable above the overwhelming odor of roasting pork. The sizzling odor of the supernatural world, a smell of sulfur and ozone, pervaded the air like a nearly forgotten memory. It burned Deven's nostrils.

It made him homesick.

Klakow led them to a crooked red wooden door, held open by a man in a suit and sunglasses. Following Klakow, Deven climbed a narrow set of stairs up to the second floor.

"The good news is, you have a great magical forensics team working with you," Klakow said, breathing harder as he climbed the steep staircase.

"You aren't leading this investigation?" Deven asked.

Klakow turned and smirked. "No, though you're going to wish I was."

"Why?"

"Because the bad news is, you're working with Agent Silas August."

"Bad news? Why?"

"August is a complete prick. The only agent who could ever stand working with him was Rodriguez. He was August's partner for the last six years, so needless to say Rodriguez's murder hasn't sunnied August's disposition." Klakow pushed the door open.

Inside the small room were half a dozen people, some in business suits, others in personal protection gear, collecting evidence. Klakow stepped carefully over the chalked outlines of two bodies and pointed Deven toward a tall man standing near the window, speaking on a cell phone.

He was thin and handsome and dressed as if planning to attend an awards ceremony. He wore a tailored charcoal suit and a fitted white dress shirt with the collar open. His black, wavy hair accentuated the distinct angles of his pale face—sharp cheekbones, long nose, and piercing blue eyes.

The man turned and gave Deven a cold, cursory glance without bothering to interrupt his telephone conversation. Deven found himself looking away from the intensity of the man's stare and that's when he noticed the stains on the floor.

Bloodstains formed sprayed haloes around the heads of the body outlines. Dark, serpent-like soot stains marred the floor-to-ceiling mirrored wall. Deven noted the cracked glass in the framed photographs; the burned paper, matches, and a copper bowl dented inward with great force; and shattered pieces of jade ground into the carpet, glinting in the low apartment light.

And covering every surface, hundreds of them, the tiny, broken bodies of dead quail.

Deven's heart began to race.

The sharp clap of a phone snapping shut startled Deven's attention back to the agent.

"I'm Agent Silas August. You the Aztaw expert?" August asked.

Deven felt nervous under such scrutiny. "Yes. I'm Deven—"

"About goddamn time you got here."

"No spell on earth can make the traffic in this city any better," Klakow said. He patted Deven on the back. Deven tensed at the contact. "He's all yours."

August fixed Deven once more with his steely glare. "First impression?"

For a second, Deven thought the agent meant himself. Deven caught up quickly. "This isn't a murder," he said.

"The hell it isn't."

"This isn't *just* a murder," Deven amended. "It's a message."

Chapter Two

Agent August pocketed his cell phone and stared. His glance traveled up Deven's body, eyes locking with his. "The report I got said your eyesight is shit."

"It's better."

"Well then, why don't you use those pretty green eyes and take a look around?"

"I don't need to. I already know most of what I need."

August's mouth formed a hard line. "Explain."

Deven felt inexplicably nervous. He picked up a leather cord threaded with thorns that had fallen near a body outline and held it out to the agent. "Do you know what this is?"

"You're the Aztaw expert. You tell me."

"It's a ritual bloodletting cord. It means someone here performed an Aztaw spell."

"No shit. The question is, what for?"

"The smoke patterns on the walls make me think someone summoned a vision serpent." Deven started moving around the room and August followed him. "You see these snake-shaped scorch marks? The vision serpent isn't really a conscious organism, more a force, and it burns its will into everything—surfaces and beings. The ritual bloodletting with the cord could be for numerous spells, but these markings are the clue that they wanted to see something hidden." He crouched and picked up a shard of jade. Turning it in the faint apartment light, Deven was able to make out the broken image of a serpent glyph. "And this was a token to break the spell and send the serpent back into hiding." He handed this to August as well.

Deven felt self-conscious because he'd spent so much time in the last year being told how things worked. It was rare for him to be the expert in anything. He had to remind himself that this was what he was being paid to do—advise the Irregulars on a culture and magical system they knew next to nothing about.

"Are there ways to end the spell other than breaking this token?" August asked.

Deven nodded. "The spell itself can run its course. The duration of the vision is dependent on the amount of blood used to conjure it. They initiated the curse by pouring their blood in here—" He bent down and retrieved the dented copper bowl. "—and then soaked a paper offering, which they burned to send to the underworld."

August frowned at the jade in his hand but didn't respond. He looked at the other pieces of jade on the carpet.

The silence stretched. Deven felt he needed to continue. "The quail worry me," he admitted. "Quail are watchbirds for certain lords of the Aztaw. Common Aztaw citizens, the soldiers, they don't have magical powers of their own, and they don't control watchbirds. The quail suggest the perpetrator was watched by a lord. And the fact that the birds are dead means the murderer doesn't want his actions carried back to the Aztaw lord who dispatched them."

"Who would the message go to?" August asked. He still stared intently at the shards on the carpet.

Deven shrugged. "I can't say. There used to be nearly a hundred lords of Aztaw. But now most of them are dead. The few remaining lords have had their house powers broken and live in hiding."

Deven realized he'd just summarized over five years of complex Aztaw political history in three sentences, but August seemed not to notice.

He picked up another shard of jade. "Do you know which lords use quail as watchbirds?"

"Not anymore. I've been away from Aztaw for nearly a year. It might help, though, if we took a look to scc what happened here," Deven suggested.

August's eyes narrowed. "What?"

Deven shrugged. "I brought my mirror. We could see the last few seconds of their lives, at least."

Now everyone in the room watched him. Deven swallowed. He was slowly readjusting to human culture but often became nervous in public situations. He set his duffel bag down on the blue carpet and rooted around until he found the cloth-wrapped shard of his obsidian mirror.

As he held the shard in his hand, a pang of deep regret filled him. He thought of Jaguar, the Aztaw lord who had given this to him, along with his greatest power. Now Lord Jaguar was dead and Deven had done nothing about it. Reflected in the mirror, Deven saw the pen he kept wrapped tightly in his black hair and reached up to touch it as if that would make everything better.

"Hey, Narcissus," August called from behind. "Care to explain what the hell you are talking about? How would we see what happened?"

"Can we turn off the lights?" Deven asked. August closed the window shades as another agent hit the light switch, but it was still too damn bright. Pure darkness was nearly impossible in this world, but at least curbing the sunlight cut down reflections. Deven noticed that August carefully avoided stepping on the outlines of the dead bodies. He'd seen this done on television as well. He wasn't sure if this was common crime-scene caution or a human gesture of respect for the dead, but he mimicked the actions anyway.

"This is an obsidian mirror," Deven explained, holding it in his right hand and tilting it up so both he and August could see. The shard was slightly bigger than his hand and about seven inches in length, unevenly edged where the mirror had been broken during a battle with Lord Jade Shield's soldiers. The surface, at the moment, was nearly opaque, revealing nothing but the reflection of those looking into it.

"It refracts time," Deven said. "We can catch a glimpse of the last few moments of Agent Rodriguez's life, assuming we're able to pull a clear image from an object in the room."

There was a muscle in August's pale jaw, Deven noticed, that pulsed when he ground his teeth. "What do you need?"

"Blood would be best."

"Does it have to be fresh?"

"No."

August crouched beside the large chalked outline. He touched the shape almost reverently. "This is Carlos's blood." His voice sounded rough. "This is where he died."

Deven nodded. He knelt beside August and the outline, then reached in his back pocket for his knife.

He switched open the blade and scraped chunks of crusted blood out of the carpet fibers. He piled these in his palm. When he glanced up, everyone was staring at him again.

Maybe it wasn't normal to collect blood in your hand?

"Uh...here," someone said, handing him a plastic specimen cup.

"Thanks." Deven poured the flakes of blood inside. It was too dry to spread so he spat in the cup and stirred the mixture with his fingers, forming a thick, chunky paste. Deven smeared this on the mirror shard, then crouched in the darkest part of the room, in the corner near the bathroom door.

Even the whispers in the room ceased as everyone watched him intently. August's hard expression faltered and he looked almost anxious. "Should I stand by you?"

"If you want to see," Deven said. He held out the mirror.

August crouched beside him, his long legs making him resemble a crane at the edge of a pool of water. He smelled like leather and some sort of pine soap. His thigh brushed against Deven's as they huddled to look into the mirror.

Deven spat on the mirror. The cloudy haze cleared and through the glass emerged an image, as seen from Carlos Rodriguez's eyes.

The first image that arose was the smoky contours of a vision serpent looming against the apartment window. Smoke trailed from its coiling body, but even through the dirty mirror Deven saw the serpent's two distinct heads, one looking into the real world, and the other fixed on the supernatural.

But before the serpent even turned to reveal what it saw, something distracted Agent Rodriguez's attention and he spun to face the apartment door.

Several unnatural, flying female creatures burst into the apartment, bodies dark with sagging skin. They looked identical—skeletal spines and skulls with living, shining eyes, bright as stars, set inside deep eye sockets. The paper-thin, bluish-hued flesh that hung off their limbs like wrinkled shawls ended in clawed limbs more resembling the talons of birds than any human hand or foot. Their breasts sagged above thin grass skirts and serpents slithered like writhing phalluses from between each creature's legs.

Behind them, Rodriguez quickly glimpsed the tiny quail following the creatures, but then he crumpled. The vision clouded over and disappeared.

Deven sat back, feeling a little shaky. He'd expected to see Aztaws, which look nearly human, other than their visible, glowing bones and skull faces.

But these female spirits were new to him. He'd never seen the like, but he had heard descriptions of such malevolent creatures and who they worked for.

It's not possible, Deven thought. *Even in Aztaw, everyone knows he's gone.*

Deven spat on the mirror again. He wiped the blood off its surface with the hem of his T-shirt before remembering that wasn't acceptable here. He turned to see if August had noticed, but August was frozen, staring straight ahead with a look of shock.

"Agent August?" Deven asked.

The man didn't speak. He hung his head for a moment. It seemed like he was gathering strength. When he finally did collect himself together and turn to Deven, his look hardened.

"What the fuck were those?" His voice was rough, angry.

"I'm not sure," Deven said. He wasn't going to voice his suspicion until he had more proof.

August didn't ask for clarification. He stood, quickly wiping at his eyes, before he turned to bark orders at the others in the room. The folks who had been watching in silence burst into activity, collecting the remains of the ritual and tossing the broken birds into a large plastic bag.

Deven leaned against the wall and closed his eyes. The journey from Seattle had taken over ten hours of flying and he was hungry and thirsty. But he pushed these sensations from his thoughts and instead concentrated on the legends he remembered hearing regarding tzimimi, taloned night spirits.

They came at the bidding of the Trickster. They served his needs and hunted at night, feeding on the bones of children.

And they had been exiled over a thousand years ago.

So what were they doing in the human world? And what had they prevented the vision serpent from revealing to Carlos and Beatriz Rodriguez?

"Wake up, sunshine," Agent August snapped, yanking on Deven's arm. "Time to go to the funeral home."

"What for?"

"I want to look at Carlos's body."

Chapter Three

The sunlight outside seemed even more powerful after hunkering in the shadows of Beatriz's apartment and Deven had to pause at the curb and shut his eyes. He fumbled in his duffel bag for his sunglasses. Someone yanked the bag from him and, a moment later, slipped the glasses into his hand.

"Here." August sounded annoyed. "Hurry up."

"Is the body likely to walk off somewhere?" Deven snapped. Once he had the sunglasses on he opened his eyes. He turned and followed August's long legs up to his face. He didn't wear sunglasses. His pale blue eyes stared down at Deven.

"Okay?" August asked. He sounded as if he'd prefer the answer to be no.

"I'm fine." Deven yanked his duffel back over his shoulder.

August walked briskly to another black sedan, a few cars down the road. He slid into the backseat. Deven followed him.

"Morgue," August told the driver.

The man said nothing as he pulled the car into the street. Agent August sank back against the cold leather and rubbed his eyes.

"So that vision serpent," August asked. "It was to see those flying things?"

"No, they were sent to stop whatever it was Agent Rodriguez and his sister were trying to see. The vision serpent shows you hidden layers of the world, things made invisible by magic."

August didn't ask any further questions.

"You were friends with Agent Rodriguez?" Deven asked after a moment.

August stared out the window and didn't answer.

That was Deven's one attempt at conversation, he decided. He leaned back and closed his own eyes, hoping to get some rest.

After several minutes of silence, August spoke. "You have knives in your pockets."

"Yes."

"What for? You're a consultant."

"Habit." Deven wondered how much the Inter-Realm Refugees Office had told the agent. "If we're dealing with Aztaw magic, there are going to be Aztaw lords."

"So?"

"Aztaw lords and I don't get along." Understatement of the century, really, but it seemed to sate August's curiosity and he let the subject drop.

The car eventually pulled up in front of the funeral home. Despite the central location in the city, the building had a lovely garden in the front, which Deven assumed was supposed to soothe grieving souls.

He didn't understand why flowers were supposed to make death less painful, but he didn't voice this thought out loud.

Inside, Agent August spoke quietly with the mortician, who then led them down to the morgue, where two corpses were laid out, covered in white sheets. Deven wondered why the dead needed sheets to cover them—were they cold?

Deven glanced at the mortician, unsure if he knew why they were there. Very few people were privy to the operations of the Irregular Affairs Division, let alone the presence of other realms and extra-human beings. It was one of the reasons Deven found himself a reluctant employee of NIAD—regardless of his feelings toward the agency, they alone had an inkling of his past experiences. He found himself drawn to those who knew the truth and now wondered how much information this guardian of the dead was privy to.

"Juan is with us," August told Deven, as if reading his mind. "You can speak freely." August cleared his throat, then pulled back the sheet covering Agent Rodriguez.

He had been a handsome man in life, Deven decided. His features were rugged and hard, but there was a softness to his expression, even after having died in fear. The back of his head was obliterated, caved in, collapsing the frontal lobe around the man's right ear. His right eye bulged out from the pressure.

The rest of his body was white with death. Several scars marked his arms and chest, but these were old, healed and raised over time. His genitals were purple and nearly buried under his pubic hair. He had wide, thick feet and ugly toes.

But that wasn't what he was looking for, Deven chastised himself. Truthfully, he wasn't sure what he was supposed to find.

When the sheet was removed from Carlos Rodriguez's sister, Deven noticed August avoided glancing at Beatriz's face as he examined her body.

"What's that?" the agent asked, pointing to a red bruise just below her heart. Her skin had turned gray in death, but the bruise stood out, red and garish.

The bruise wasn't large, about the size of a quarter, but it was perfectly circular, as if made with a cookie cutter. Deven checked the dead agent and saw he had the same marking.

"He has one too."

August turned. He reached out and touched Carlos Rodriguez's bruise, which was directly over his heart.

"I've seen a few bodies with these markings before," the mortician told them. "I assumed ringworm, although the skin isn't scaly like a fungus."

"Does it always appear on the chest?" August asked.

The doctor shrugged. "They are always on the torso but not consistently in the same place. There are so few cases, I considered it an environmental anomaly, maybe some form of rash. It's never shown any evidence of relating to the death of the individual."

August stared hard at the marking on his partner's chest. He pulled out his phone and took several photos of both Carlos's and Beatriz's markings.

"Know anything about this?" August asked. It took Deven several seconds to realize the question was addressed to him.

"No," Deven said. "Never heard or seen of any circular bruises on bodies." Deven tilted his head, considering. "Of course, there's little known about the tzimimi so it could be related to their attack, although I don't see how."

"Tzimimi?" August asked.

"Malevolent female night spirits," Deven said. "I've heard of them only in passing. The way they've been described fits with the creatures that attacked your partner. But they're supposed to have been exiled from Aztaw thousands of years ago."

"Why didn't you tell me this before?"

"Because I wasn't sure they're really tzimimi. I'm still not. They were exiled with the Lord of Hurricanes to the realm of light and there would have been no way for them to come back here. It doesn't make any sense. No one has seen or heard from the Lord of Hurricanes or his minions in generations."

August turned back to examine the bodies once more. He reached into the inner pocket of his jacket and pulled out what looked like a pocket utility knife. Deven felt a moment of camaraderie.

But it was quickly apparent this was no normal army knife. It had strange attachments and Agent August frowned as he poked through the various options before picking out a screwdriver-shaped metal prong. He scraped this prong across the bruise on Agent Rodriguez's chest, collecting a strip of skin.

"What's that?" Deven asked.

"It's for spectral analysis," August said. "I can run a check on other-realm signatures when I get my equipment at the hotel."

Deven wanted a closer look at the knife. He'd heard that many Irregulars agents used enchanted technology in place of magical powers but had seen little of it in person.

But by the time he drew near August had already closed the blade and pocketed the tool. He quickly replaced the sheet that covered Beatriz but paused as he did the same to his partner.

"See you on the other side," August whispered. For a moment his eyes looked almost glassy. He drew the sheet over his dead partner's body and strode out of the room, forcing Deven to rush to catch up.

❧

Outside the morgue, the sun was setting and for that Deven felt grateful. It had been a stressful day and darkness always brought him comfort.

Of course, all darkness was relative. Here on earth, he could see perfectly well at any hour, because even without the sun, there were stars and moonlight and street lamps and a thousand other sources of ambient light.

During the decade that he'd spent in Aztaw, darkness had defined everything. The Aztaw themselves navigated perfectly well in the dark, but for the few humans who visited, only the glowing luminescence of Aztaw bones provided contrast on the jet-black backdrop of the flat, endless terrain of the Aztaw realm.

The utter lack of any starlight hampered human interaction with the underworld and had probably contributed to his father's eventual madness.

Agent August sat next to him in the taxi's backseat, silent once more. His body was completely still, eyes shadowed, and Deven would have thought him asleep if it hadn't been for the chronic twitching of his jaw muscles as he ground his teeth.

"Have you been to Mexico City before?" Deven asked, not because he cared particularly, but because it was the question Agent Klakow had asked and therefore he assumed it to be a safe, normal conversation to have.

August nodded. "I vacationed here with Carlos and Bea a few times." He rubbed the heel of his hand against his eye. "I'll have to tell Teresa when I get home. God."

"Teresa?" Deven asked.

"Carlos's girlfriend." August sighed loudly.

"She doesn't know yet?"

"There hasn't been time. I only heard of it this morning and came via the Fisherman's Wharf–Mercado Sonora portal." August ground his teeth and changed the subject. "Commander Carerra in San Francisco will want a report about your little trick with the mirror."

"All right."

"That's something I'd heard of but never seen demonstrated."

"There's a lot of Aztaw magic that could be useful to the division."

"Does the mirror work only for those who've died?"

"No, anyone can use it," Deven said. "It can even tell the immediate future, but that's rarely useful since it shows only a few seconds, and those seconds are usually just putting the mirror back in your pocket."

August smiled at that. Deven was startled by how such a small gesture could transform the man's face, how it made him look, for one moment, beautiful.

But August's smile vanished as quickly as it came. "I'm surprised the Irregulars have allowed such a gap in knowledge about another realm to exist."

"Aztaw isn't very forgiving to human beings. There would be little opportunity to collect data."

"You survived it."

"Yeah, but I'm not particularly better off for the experience." Deven was quoting his therapist, since he had no idea whether or not he would have been a different person had he not moved to Aztaw with his father.

August studied him. "Is that where you had your throat cut?"

"Yes."

"Who did it?"

"Lord Jaguar."

"Why?" August asked.

Why was such a strange question to ask about anything, really. "I was his hostage. He decided to sacrifice me for my blood."

"How did that happen?"

"My father was the first and last NATO Irregular Affairs ambassador to Aztaw and I moved there with him when I was ten. We were under the protection of Lord Knife, who was the most powerful of the lords at the time, and my father established lucrative trade agreements with Lord Knife's house."

"What did they trade?" August asked.

"Human blood in exchange for Aztaw-enchanted weaponry. My father thought it would reduce the number of humans kidnapped from the natural world and dragged down to fuel spells."

"Did it?"

"I was too young to know at the time. And within two years Lord Knife's supremacy was challenged. War broke out between him and Lord Jaguar's dynasty, and Jaguar took me hostage and threatened to kill me if my father didn't end his allegiance with Lord Knife and trade with him instead."

August no longer looked sleepy. "What did your father do?"

"He told Lord Jaguar he'd rather have me killed than betray his allegiance with Lord Knife. He said it presented him an opportunity to prove his loyalty."

August blinked. There was an uncomfortable silence.

"That's pretty shitty," August finally said.

Deven shrugged.

"So Lord Jaguar ordered your execution?"

Deven nodded. "I was held at his feet by a soldier and he slit my throat."

August didn't look at Deven with sympathy, which was a relief. Deven told this story to few people, and when he did, it usually led to displays of pity that made him uncomfortable. He didn't want pity for something that wasn't his doing.

"But you survived." August eyed him keenly.

"Aztaws move slowly. I was able to kick the soldier restraining me and break free. I pulled his ankle and by luck he fell off the sacrificial dais, cracked open his skull, and died. Lord Jaguar was impressed with my reaction and speed and decided my life was worth more than a sacrifice in his ritual. He stopped my blood loss with a time trap and spared my life."

"Is he still alive?"

"No." Deven swallowed. "I regret I lost my opportunity to avenge his death when I fled Aztaw."

August's eyebrows came together. "He cut your throat and you feel guilty about not avenging his murder?" He snorted. "You're more messed up than I thought."

Deven felt his face flush with anger. "He was a great lord and I owe everything I am to him."

"And what is that, exactly?" August's mouth curved into a sneer. "You're clearly not just an Aztaw magics expert. You keep reaching for that knife in your back pocket."

Deven realized he was reaching for his knife and quickly let go, resting his hands in front of him.

"You're a soldier then," August continued, "or, worse, an assassin. When you are uncomfortable your instincts are violent. And clearly you lack the skills to blend in to normal society, otherwise you wouldn't be taking shit consulting jobs for the Irregulars." He shook his head. "You ever hear of Stockholm syndrome?"

Of course he had heard of Stockholm syndrome. His therapist had told him all about it. "You don't know anything about me," Deven said, his anger rising.

"True. Nor do I care," August said coldly. "All I care about is finding out who killed my partner and my friend. If you have skills that help me, then you'll be useful. If you're just an under-socialized nut job who the division's taken on as a charity case, I don't have time for you."

"I'm not a charity case."

"Then why were you included on the guest list of the annual under-socialized nut job Christmas cookie-making party?"

Deven opened his mouth to respond, but August held out his hand. "We're here." He jumped out of the car before the driver had even put it into park.

Deven followed the agent out of the car, rage pulsing through him, deep and irrational.

For one thing, he'd hated that cookie party. It had felt demeaning.

And he despised it when anyone said anything about Lord Jaguar. He was too great to even be spoken of by the likes of these people.

He recalled his therapist's shocked face when he'd first broached the subject of Lord Jaguar's kindness to him. Everyone here saw him as a monster. They didn't understand that, in a world of monsters, Jaguar had been Deven's only friend.

They entered a mundane, industrial-looking L-shaped hotel. "Welcome to the wonders provided by government per diem rates," August commented.

The Bristol Hotel was a nondescript cement structure overlooking a roundabout with a phallic statue in the center. The outward appearance resembled some sort of institution, but inside the hotel was clean and utilitarian. Tiled floors and white-painted walls lent the space an open air.

August gave their names to a young woman behind the counter. She smiled warmly as she handed over two plastic keycards. "You'll be staying in room 210," she informed them with a strong accent.

"We're sharing a room?" Deven asked suspiciously.

August didn't look very pleased himself. "Goddamn budget cutbacks!" He handed the receptionist his credit card. "Any chance it's a non-smoking room?"

"All rooms are smoking rooms," the woman told him.

"Of course they are." August sighed. "I had my luggage dropped off here."

The woman called someone in Spanish and a man returned with five suitcases.

"I had to bring *equipment*," August snapped, seeming to think his luggage required an explanation.

"The branch office doesn't have supplies for you?" Deven asked.

"I like using my own." August nodded to the concierge, who wheeled his luggage to the elevator.

At the door to their room, August palmed the concierge a tip, grabbed his bags, and opened the door. He immediately threw his belongings on the closest bed.

Deven entered carefully, eyes darting to the corners and checking out the bathroom shadows. The carpet was a shocking purple. The bedspreads were plaid and there was a faux wooden headboard nailed to the wall behind each of the two twin beds. The beds themselves were separated by a narrow bedside table with only enough room for the massive lamp and a large-numbered alarm clock.

There was too much furniture for such a small room. Overstuffed plush sitting chairs were huddled around a large round wicker and glass table. There was a wicker counter with drawers and an old television perched on top.

Thick plaid curtains hung to the sides of the windows. Deven pulled these shut. He feared forgetting and having himself jarred awake by the unwelcome glare of morning sunlight pouring through the window.

August immediately began unpacking his belongings, so Deven followed suit. It's what he always did when unsure of himself—imitate others. The technique had managed to convince most of the other humans living in his new home, Friday Harbor, that he was normal, if a little shy.

August had nearly a dozen tailored and pressed dress shirts as well as three complete suits. "You hanging anything up?" he asked, eyeing the paltry collection of hangers in the closet.

"No."

"Good." August grabbed all the hangers and began to organize the closet.

Deven unzipped his duffel and stared down at his two T-shirts, three changes of underwear, a pair of trousers, a razor, and his toothbrush. He hadn't even brought toothpaste. He moved these into a bedside drawer, which opened with a loud protest.

The rest of Deven's bag contained his weapons. He noted that August had placed a mage pistol on the bedside table, and so he figured it socially acceptable to place one's weapons near the bed. He carefully unloaded his extra knives, some burning papers for sending messages to the underworld, as well as a sacred bundle of feathers, pieces of jade, a jawbone, and a segment of jaguar skin. For some reason, that had required a lot of documentation and negotiation with the Irregulars administrative staff to bring along.

Now that he considered it, he could have left it behind. It was really useful only for detecting the presence of his lord, but it had served like a talisman for so many years that he was loathe to be parted from it.

Apparently finished stowing his wardrobe, August unzipped another of his bags and took out a laptop with an external metal box. He set this up on the round table in the center of the room. He jammed the pronged tool from his utility knife into the box, shook out the small plug of skin he'd collected at the morgue, then pocketed the tool. Graphs started moving on the laptop, but August didn't look at them. Instead he flopped dramatically back onto his bed, propped his head against the faux headboard, and started texting someone on his phone.

"You hungry?" August asked, in the midst of his text message.

"Starving," Deven admitted.

"The taqueria a few blocks down the road makes great *al pastor*. I've never tried the hotel restaurant. It doesn't look promising."

"I'll eat anything," Deven said. It was true. He had spent most of his life without the luxury of gastronomic choices. Food had served the simple utilitarian role of keeping him energized enough to move.

Not that he wasn't tempted by the smells he'd already encountered that day. Roasting meat, while conjuring some unpleasant memories, also made his mouth water. And he was still thinking of a fruit stand they had passed that sold watermelons. Deven had recently discovered a great love of fruit and wondered what something as large and green as a watermelon would taste like.

"Why do you wear that pen in your hair?" August asked suddenly.

Deven instantly reached up for the pen behind his ear, touched it, and let go. He knew it was absurd, and his therapist had been trying for the last two months to get him to forego it, but he couldn't.

August's eyes hadn't left his phone screen.

"It means I deserve respect in Aztaw."

"I thought Aztaws just saw humans as sources of blood."

"They do." Deven frowned. "They did. But I was different. I had a job."

August glanced at him with a smirk. "You worked in Aztaw?"

"What do you think, I just laid around, feeling sorry for myself?"

August smiled and looked back at his screen. "With your looks you could have made a great gigolo."

Deven flushed. "Fuck you."

"So my first guess was correct," August continued. "You worked doing something violent."

"I was Lord Jaguar's bodyguard."

"Did you leave Lord Jaguar's side to kill others?"

"...Of course."

"That's not bodyguard. That's assassin. There's a difference, kiddo." August made a face. "Assassins are the worst."

"You have no idea what life was like down there."

"No, and it sounds miserable, so I'm glad for it." August finished his text and eyed Deven. "If it was so awful, why do you miss it?"

"I don't—"

"The report I got from headquarters cautioned there was a likelihood you wouldn't leave Mexico City once you got here. They suspect you're going to try and go back to Aztaw."

Deven felt sick thinking about the possibility. Returning to Aztaw wasn't as easy as August made it out to be. Still, if he was going to go back, this was the place to leave from. Calendars turned quickly here and allowed more options of reentry.

Just the idea of returning set his heart racing. But Lord Jaguar was dead and Deven had made a promise to him. He longed to return with suicidal hunger, but nothing remained for him in Aztaw anymore.

August looked at him, clearly waiting for an answer. But Deven didn't want the agent to know that much about him. Deven was never one to hide his feelings, but he had too much emotion wrapped up in Aztaw to explain to someone who clearly didn't give a shit.

"I asked you a question," August said.

"I don't work for you," Deven replied. "I'm paid to give you advice on Aztaw culture and magic. That doesn't mean I have to answer personal questions."

August's expression darkened. "Look here, pretty boy. As long as you're working on an investigation I'm in charge of, you'll answer *any* question I ask. It's what you're getting paid for. So—"

A knock at the door startled both of them into silence. August stood quickly and warily opened the door. "What?"

A nervous-looking boy in an oversized football jersey placed something on the ground. "A present for you," he said, his words strongly accented, before fleeing down the corridor.

August glanced down at the object. "What the fuck? Maybe it's a bomb." This idea seemed to amuse him and he snorted.

"Don't touch it," Deven cautioned.

August rolled his eyes. "I wasn't going to."

Deven moved closer. At first glimpse it resembled a cheap knockoff souvenir of a Maya clay statue—the kind he'd seen in the airport gift shop. The figure wore a traditional grass skirt and was draped in jaguar skin.

Deven picked it up to examine it more closely.

The figure held a bundle of knives in one hand and a broken mirror in another. There was a pen in his hair. The eyes were closed on the face, but Deven recognized his own nose and the slit across the statue's throat.

Adrenaline and fear rushed through him.

"What is it?" August asked. "You've gone white as a ghost."

Deven thrust the figurine into August's hands and charged after the delivery boy at a run.

Chapter Four

"Deven! Wait, God damn it!"

Deven heard Agent August's footsteps behind him, but he didn't stop. He figured the boy had used the staircase because the elevator flashed that it was still on the tenth floor. Deven jumped the last set of stairs and raced out the door into the lobby, catching a glimpse of the boy as he barreled out the front door of the hotel.

Deven charged after him, knife in his right hand. It was dark, but the city lights were bright enough to still cause discomfort. He charged after the figure, not stopping for anyone or paying attention to what was going on around him. He heard shouts and the charging load of a mage pistol behind him, which he assumed to be Agent August arming himself.

The delivery boy darted down a side alley and Deven followed. It felt good to run this hard, even though the mixture of adrenaline and nausea was familiar in terrible ways. The boy glanced behind him with a look of fear before charging forward at a faster pace.

He heard August curse somewhere behind and turned briefly to look back. August was right on his tail, keeping up, although sweat glistened on his face and his shirt was pulled from his trousers.

The boy tripped over a pile of garbage bags and darted to the right, slowing his pace. Deven gained on him. As they passed under a street light the image of the boy rippled, and for a moment, he looked like an Aztaw—glowing spine and skull visible under a thin layer of translucent skin, teeth gnashing—but as they passed back into darkness he once again appeared as a panicked, out-of-breath Mexican child.

The boy burst into a crowded intersection and Deven had to dodge to avoid being hit by a taxi. Car horns blared all around him. He bolted across the street and was clipped by the side mirror of another car. Pain burst across his hip and he spun to the pavement, a moment of agony searing through everything.

"God damn it!"he heard August roar. August leaned over him, offering a hand. "Are you all right?"

"Hurry!" Deven cried, using August's hand to pull himself up. The first few limps jarred his hip, but he regained his pace, blocking out the pain.

He'd lost valuable time but managed to catch sight of his target darting into a night club. Deven pushed through a crowd of revelers awaiting entrance. He charged into the club.

And instantly froze.

He covered his ears, choking on a cry of fear. The noise was unbearable. A thumping beat reverberated through the two-story dance hall so loudly he could feel it in his chest like a second, frantic heartbeat. The room writhed with wall-to-wall people, arms in the air as they danced, their faces bright and then disappearing in the constant churning glitter of a disco ball, lasers shooting green and red beams of light over the crowd.

Deven stood stock-still, unable to process what this was or understand what to do. Seeing a crowded club like this on television could not have prepared him for the chaos of being inside one. If he couldn't think with such an unrelenting noise beating in his ears, how on earth was he supposed to see?

"Up there, on the balcony," a voice said in his ear. Agent August grabbed Deven's arm, just for a second. "By the DJ."

"Where?" Deven had to shout to be heard. He blinked and tried to focus, but everything was chaos, shooting lights and flashes of skin and sparkling clothing.

"This way." August pulled him to the right. Deven blindly followed, his heart racing. His throat had gone dry in the terror of the moment, but now he forced himself to calm down. The room swarmed with people.

A black metal catwalk formed a square above the dance floor and this was where a man sat behind two massive thumping speakers. Dozens more people crowded the metal walkways and stared down at the revelers. Deven followed August up a black flight of stairs, pushing past women in short skirts and men who reeked of cologne. Deven's arm brushed loose someone's drink and the person shouted at him in Spanish, but he didn't stop. At the top walkway it wasn't any easier to see, but August's body tensed and he threw himself forward. Deven kept up.

At last Deven spotted the boy. August pushed Deven to the left and he went to the right. Deven forced his way through a crush of sweaty bodies.

The boy saw them flanking him on either side and must have realized he was trapped. He grabbed the banister of the walkway and swung himself over, making as if to jump twenty feet down into the crowd below.

Deven would never be able to find such a small kid in that seething mass. He threw his knife before he had a chance to reconsider. The knife embedded itself deep into the boy's throat. If he gagged, the sound was lost to the pump of the music. The boy fell backward off the balcony and landed on the dance floor below with a muffled thump.

Chapter Five

Deven thought the night club had been packed before, when it had been full of young dancing couples. But now the place swarmed with Federales, embassy staff, and NIAD agents. With all the lights on, the flashing, colored lasers were less of a distraction and he could see just what level of chaos he'd created by killing the delivery boy.

Outside the club, dozens of kicked-out revelers complained, along with the club owners. He saw them through the entrance window but couldn't hear them since no one had figured out how to silence the stereo system and blaring techno rhythms continued to blast through the club.

"What the hell did you think you were *doing*!"

Agent August was furious. He glared at Deven over the dead body.

Deven realized he was still in a state of shock. He felt lost in time and space.

A growing sickness filled the pit of his stomach. He should have never agreed to do this job. What the fuck did he think he was doing, pretending to be a normal person?

In the chaos of the crime scene, Deven waited until few were looking their way and bent down to reclaim his knife.

August looked ready to strangle Deven. "What were you thinking, you idiot? You aren't a fucking assassin anymore. *You can't just kill people here.*"

"I know." Deven swallowed. "It was instinct. I didn't think."

"And because you didn't think, a fucking *child* who might have had information for us is dead!" He paused suddenly, glancing over the body. His eyebrows came together and he knelt by the corpse's head.

"I'm sorry." Deven meant it. He believed in doing what he was told and now he'd failed. He'd been employed by the Irregulars for less than twenty-four hours and he'd already broken a cardinal rule.

He didn't know how punishments were carried out in NIAD. In Aztaw the penalty for failure was swift and brutal. But he deserved it in this instance, so he steadied his resolve.

"I apologize." Deven swallowed. "However I can amend—"

"Shut up." August fumbled for something in his inner jacket pocket. "No blood."

"What?"

"No blood on the body. You stabbed him in the neck and he's not bleeding." August pulled out his utility knife and split it open, turning the ends and reattaching them in a configuration that made the device resemble a flashlight. August turned several rings around a small bulb at the base of the knife, and as he adjusted the rings, the light shifted until it was very bright white.

He shone the flashlight over the dead boy, making slow sweeps from head to toe.

"Under a street lamp, I thought he looked Aztaw for a moment," Deven told him. "But I don't know how that would even be possible."

"Masking spell," August answered. "It conceals the true form of those from other realms by transforming their outward appearance. It's a way to make them look human. We often use them in the division." He kept fiddling with the flashlight settings. As he moved the light back over the corpse's face, instead of skin and hair, Deven saw the faint glimpse of an Aztaw skull.

Deven tensed. August made small adjustments to the rings around the light. Now the part of the body under the beam of light was clearly Aztaw.

August seemed to sigh out in relief, and he glanced up at Deven with a small smile. "Lucky for you, kiddo. Aztaws don't investigate deaths of their own here."

"Stop calling me kiddo. I'm only a few years younger than you."

August's eyebrow quirked up, but he didn't respond. Instead he shone the light back in the corpse's eyes. "Aztaw indeed."

"What does that light do?"

"Every type of being has a unique visual spectrum, and this light cuts through transformations and masking spells. I've never seen an Aztaw before, but now with this calibration I'll be able to detect one anytime." August cocked his head and turned the light on Deven, fiddling with the rings until the light burned bright as he shone it on Deven's face.

Deven covered his eyes with his hands, wincing. "Asshole."

"Yep, human." August's mouth quirked up. "Barely."

The music kept thumping, a quick-paced drumbeat that rattled Deven's teeth. His hip hurt badly.

Horrid electrical pulsing screeches emanated from the speakers and someone chanted a word over and over and Deven felt like he would drown in lights and sound. He crouched down, eyes pressed shut, hands over his ears.

Through the noise he heard August bellow, "Somebody cut the goddamn A/V system!" Then after a pause, August's voice again. "Just find the damn plug and kick it out of the wall."

Seconds later the music blissfully stopped. Slowly, Deven uncurled and stood upright.

August was on his phone again. "...at the Cazador," August said. He hunched over the body protectively, other hand covering his exposed ear to hear the phone better. "Most only saw the fall, not the knife!"

August finished his call and frowned. "The director said she hopes he isn't some sort of dignitary in Aztaw that might further sour relations between us and their underworld." He rubbed his hand over his face.

"Do dignitaries often make hotel deliveries?" Deven asked.

August snorted. “Not usually, but when it comes to Aztaws, I’m out of my depth.” He stared at Deven for a moment. “I have to stay until the cleanup crew arrives and takes over.”

“All right.” Deven grit his teeth.

“You wait outside.”

“Thank you.” Deven gratefully rushed out the doors and pushed his way through the frustrated crowd of spectators.

Outside, the air was still warm, but a light breeze wafted down the street. He leaned against a dirty wall and realized how tired he was. Adrenaline still coursed through his body from the chase, but as soon as that ran out he knew he would crash.

Luckily, it took less than ten minutes for the Irregulars’s mortuary team to arrive. They came dressed as a local ambulance crew, but Deven saw the warped, refracted images as they flashed their badges and knew they were more than they appeared to be. Deven remained outside, too afraid of the dance club to return indoors, despite his curiosity. A few minutes later, the dead Aztaw was wheeled out to a waiting ambulance on a stretcher and August followed behind. He didn’t look much better than Deven felt.

“All cleaned up?” Deven asked.

August nodded. “Yeah, no thanks to you.”

Deven took a deep breath. “What will my penance be?”

August shot him a glance. “What?”

Deven motioned toward the ambulance. “I have failed you.”

August rolled his eyes. “Christ. Just don’t throw the knife next time, all right?”

Deven nodded. “I promise to do better.”

August sighed. He gave Deven a thorough looking over. “When was the last time you ate?”

“I don’t remember. This morning? Maybe yesterday.”

August grabbed Deven’s arm. “Come on. We both need to recuperate somewhere normal.”

❧

The Barracuda Diner was Mexico City’s best approximation of an American diner, according to August. And there Deven found himself, at eleven o'clock at night, considering various burger options.

August probably assumed Deven would feel comforted by the familiar food of the American menu. The agent was clearly in his element, a small smile softening his features. But burgers and milkshakes weren't any more common in Aztaw or Friday Harbor than tacos.

Still, if the place relaxed Agent August, Deven was happy to be there.

Besides, it felt good to sit down. Deven's hip protested painfully, but he grit his teeth and soldiered on.

August slid onto the turquoise faux-leather bench seat across from Deven. In the harsh bright lights of the diner his blue eyes appeared ghostly in contrast to the dark curl of hair falling on his forehead. He slumped against the back of the bench seat and glared at Deven. "We need to get you a different weapon of choice."

"I'm good with knives," Deven said.

"I didn't ask your opinion." August frowned. "If your instinct is to defend yourself without thinking, then you need something less deadly than a blade." He cocked his head. "Have you ever used a freeze ball?"

"No." Deven studied the menu, unsure of what to pick. All the choices sounded equally baffling.

"You'd like it. You can throw it, but it instinctively targets living beings and paralyzes them. Works on all but the revenants, of course, and buzz bugs, since they aren't much more than pinpricks of light."

"I'll try it, I guess," Deven said, privately thinking that he would never get rid of all his knives.

"There are other resources we have that are less pointy. I'll show them to you in the armory."

"Okay."

"We'll have to go tomorrow though. The pixie in charge of the armory is particular about odors and you smell."

Deven knew he blushed. He studied the menu intently, but out of the corner of his eyes could see August smirking, missing nothing, taking in the red color on Deven's cheeks without a word.

"Aren't you going to look at the menu?" Deven asked, hoping to distract from his own humiliation.

"I already know what I'm eating." The waitress approached, and August glanced up at her. "Mushroom Swiss, no pickles, fries, Corona."

The waitress wrote this all down.

Deven glanced quickly down at the menu. "I'll have uh...the chicken ranch burger."

"Bad choice," August said.

"It's my dinner," Deven snapped. "And a chocolate milkshake," he added, on a whim. He'd never had one but had seen one advertised on television the other day.

August shrugged, turning to watch the patrons of the restaurant through the mirror on the wall beside them. "So tell me what that was all about."

"What?"

"You freaked because the Aztaw left us a statue. Why?"

"It was a death threat. In Aztaw, soldiers are cremated and their ashes stored in clay funerary figures. The figure resembles the Aztaw soldier and there's a cavity in the back of the skull of the statue to store their ashes. That statue was of me. It was a threat against my life and I had to act."

"I wonder why he threatened only you."

"It may not be related to this case," Deven suggested. "It may be personal."

August's eyebrow raised.

"I told you I don't get along with Aztaw lords," Deven said.

"Enough that they'd actively pursue you if they knew you were here?"

"Perhaps." Deven shifted in his seat. He wasn't sure how much he wanted to tell Agent August.

August scowled. "You knew there's a chance you'd be hunted if you took this job, and you returned here anyway?"

Deven shrugged. "I need something to do now that I'm back in the natural world. It's a worthwhile cause."

"One worth dying for?"

Deven paused. It hadn't occurred to him that a person could engage in something *without* planning it to be one's last act.

August shook his head. "Kiddo, there's very little in this world worth risking your life for. If I were you I'd have stayed tucked up at home."

"You know this job is dangerous, and yet you do it," Deven pointed out.

"Yeah, dangerous, but not guaranteed *deadly*." August frowned. "Nothing's worth dying for, trust me. Life is all you got. You should take better care of it."

"You should write poetry," Deven mumbled, but August just laughed at him.

Their drinks arrived. Deven felt foolish ordering a massive, creamy brown milkshake, while Agent August cradled a beer. It made Deven feel less masculine.

August took a long pull of his beer. He sighed contentedly. "So why are these Aztaws after you?"

"Shortly before Lord Jaguar was murdered in the revolt, he gave me something of his. The revolutionaries, as well as the other lords, want it."

"What were the revolutionaries fighting for? Power?"

"Aztaw soldiers and their families were tired of serving and expending such great resources to keep the lords housed in luxury. Besides, the cost and effort of hunting and keeping human beings to fuel the lords' spells was a great burden on the soldiers, so they rebelled. In the process they killed not only the lords themselves but also the house powers of the lords. The magic was lost forever."

"House powers?"

"Each dynasty had its own house power. It is sacred and unique to each lord. It represents the lord's history, his dynasty and purpose in the universe. The power is tied to a physical object but is sustained with blood. If it is allowed to drain completely it will lose its power and break forever."

August eyed Deven. "Lord Jaguar gave you his house power."

Deven was surprised August figured it out so quickly, but he didn't deny it. "Yes."

"And that's why they want you dead. They want your power."

"More than that." Deven stirred his milkshake. "A house power has never been given to a human being before. Lord Jaguar's gesture upset the natural balance of things in Aztaw. It put me in a position that the other lords feared greatly."

"Why?"

"I'm human, as your flashlight demonstrated. It means I don't need any messy sacrifices to use a house power. I fuel my own spells."

August blinked. "Christ, that makes you stronger than all of them."

"Too strong," Deven agreed. "Their life spans far exceed ours, but I could still rule them for the short length of my own life, so the lords were determined not to let me keep it. And after the revolution, the soldiers themselves wanted to see it destroyed, along with all the trappings of the lords' rule. But I made a promise to Lord Jaguar before he died that I would protect his house power with my life. It represents his lineage, his eternal soul. I swore I would never see it destroyed. So after the revolution I fled."

August stared at Deven quietly. Finally he pushed Deven's shake closer. "Drink up."

Deven had already forgotten the drink. Just recalling the story filled him with such a sense of loss he couldn't ground himself. Everything he knew and cared for had disappeared the day he had given up and run like a coward.

But he'd kept his promise to Jaguar, he had to remind himself, and that was all that mattered. As long as he protected the Jaguar house power, he honored the memory of his great lord.

The ice cream was thick in the straw and Deven sucked hard to get it to move. His cheeks hollowed out and he noticed the way August watched him, almost predatorily, as he pulled the sweet drink into his mouth.

The burst of flavor stunned him. He'd not tried ice cream since he'd been a child back in Virginia and he'd forgotten how cold and creamy the texture was. It burned his tongue and burst onto his taste buds with sweetness. It was almost too sweet, but with each gulp the flavor grew on him.

"This is incredible!" Deven cried, when he stopped inhaling the drink for a breath. He pushed over the shake. "You've got to try this."

August looked amused. "I know what a milkshake tastes like."

"But this is insane!"

August rolled his eyes and grabbed the shake. He took a sip, then pushed it back. "Tastes like shit with beer."

Their burgers arrived and Deven took a careful bite. The flavor overwhelmed him—it was too many things at once. At home he made rice, beans, corn, things he could relate to. This ranch-slathered fried chicken between bread business was too extreme for his untraveled palette; he found it difficult to process.

"Well?" August asked, watching him eat. "How's your meal?"

"It's a bit like the billboards," Deven said after swallowing.

"The billboards?"

"Too much color. Can't process what it really looks like."

August chuckled. "Told you it was a bad choice."

Back at the hotel, Deven's funerary statue was still in the doorway when they entered the room.

Filled with sudden contempt, Deven booted the thing against the far wall. The clay shattered.

August hissed. "Messy." He glared at Deven. "You need more than your weapons taken away, kiddo. You need anger management classes."

"I told you to stop calling me kiddo."

"You start acting like an adult, I may." August unzipped one of his suitcases and removed two more small metal boxes. He stuck the first alongside the door and the second on the opposite wall. He flicked a small switch at the base and a green laser beam shot between the two boxes.

"What's that?" Deven asked, yawning.

"Extra security."

"Is it magical?"

August snorted. "No, just expensive. It's a laser that triggers an alarm if the beam is interrupted. It'll alert us if you receive more care packages."

For some reason that seemed funny to Deven, and he laughed. He closed his eyes and leaned against the bathroom door.

"Let's see your hip."

Deven blinked for several seconds before he remembered he'd been injured. He was so used to ignoring pains in the hot, sterile environment of Aztaw.

"It's fine."

"You got hit by a car." August went back to his suitcase and this time pulled out a small cloth bag. Deven wondered how heavy the suitcase was. August hadn't been kidding about bringing his own equipment.

August stood close. He reached for Deven's hip and Deven instinctively pulled back.

August's expression instantly darkened. "*Oh Christ*. What did that son of a bitch Klakow say this time?" His hand clenched into a fist. "Whatever that asshole or anyone else told you, I'm not *that* much of a shit. I don't fuck guys unless they want me to."

Deven's shock clearly showed before he had time to censure it. August turned away, face burning.

Deven quickly processed what August had admitted. He was still getting the hang of things around here, what was embarrassing and what wasn't. He considered assuring the agent that his reluctance to be touched had more to do with years of living as an assassin than fear of being fondled. But something told him that conversation would go wrong.

Instead he unbuttoned his cargo pants, lowering them and his underwear to reveal his left hip bone. The skin was already mottled dark blue.

August wouldn't face him.

"Well?" Deven asked.

August turned, his face still flushed. It took him a second to regain his composure, and when he did, he frowned at Deven's hip. "Looks nasty. Does it feel like anything's broken?"

"No. It's just bruised."

"Right." August touched the swollen skin briefly, his fingers gentle and cool. Deven found his touch soothing, but before he could consider what that meant the touch was gone. August pulled a tin of something white and creamy from his bag and sank his fingers into the substance. "Don't ask what this is. You're better off not knowing." He slathered the substance over Deven's bruised joint and rubbed it in vigorously, hard enough to make Deven wince. He braced himself, holding his shirt out of the way.

He expected a mess. Instead the ointment melted into his skin and disappeared. He touched a spot where August had rubbed cream in and found his skin dry.

"Better off or not, what is that?" Deven asked.

August was still a little pink from his outburst, but the corner of his mouth quirked up. "Dead marda."

"Who?"

"Marda. They live in the spiral realm. Their bodies have regenerative properties and they heal injuries well."

Deven looked at the cream in the tin. "Are they...harvested?"

"God no, we're not *Nazis*," August said, sounding offended. "We buy their decomposed bodies legally from the families of the marda. We have trade deals with the spiral realm." August studied Deven's expression. "You don't seem to have a good opinion of NIAD."

"They abandoned the ten-year-old son of their insane employee in a dark underworld for thirteen years," Deven said, wishing he sounded less bitter. "It wasn't as though they kept their promise to see to my well-being."

"I guess not." August was still staring at him, his blue eyes sharp, calculating. He finally nodded. "You can pull your pants up now."

Deven quickly buttoned his trousers, feeling his own cheeks flush red.

"Get some sleep. We've got a lot of work tomorrow."

Deven dropped onto his bed and kicked off his boots, turning his back to the agent. He didn't bother changing clothes—he removed the knives in his pockets that made sleeping difficult and closed his eyes.

Chapter Six

Deven rarely dreamed about sex.

After all, his experience was limited. Lord Jaguar had granted him access to one of his human sacrifices prior to her demise, and that had been a humiliating and awkward encounter that had gone nowhere.

On San Juan Island a visiting tourist named Christopher, who was about Deven's age, once spent an afternoon fishing with him and later the two had drinks and he had done marvelous things to Deven's body. But that was it for Deven. It wasn't as though either experience had proceeded according to his own design.

Which was why it was so strange to wake up with his thoughts heated and a raging hard-on. All night he'd been haunted by the feel of a human caress, the soft, wet pressure of a kiss, so rare and pleasing. He wanted to be touched, to be devoured. He yearned for human contact so strongly he nearly gasped as he awoke, blinking up at the strange hotel ceiling.

Light poured into the room from the edges of the curtains. Deven glanced at the clock and saw it was a little past eight in the morning. He was surprised he had been allowed to sleep in so late.

He moved slowly in the bed, willing his erection to go away on its own. He didn't have the privacy to take care of it; although judging by the unmoving form on the bed next to his, he expected Agent August was sound asleep.

Deven swung his legs over the side of the bed and stretched. His hip didn't hurt at all; a quick glimpse revealed only a yellow bruise at the site of impact.

Quietly, he padded to the bathroom. He showered his pixie-offending smell off. Since he hadn't brought a comb, he used his fingers to brush down the damp strands of his spiky black hair. It was getting long, beginning to tickle the nape of his neck, but after years of having his head shaved by Lord Jaguar's slaves, it felt nice to leave his scalp alone for a while. His green eyes looked oddly luminescent in the low light of the bathroom, especially against his light brown skin.

He examined the collection of toiletries August had brought with him and sprayed some of his deodorant on in the hopes of remaining offense-free for the rest of the morning.

He changed into a clean clothes, but none of this roused Agent August, whose back was turned to Deven's bed and who lay curled under the covers like a child. Deven loaded his trouser pockets with gear he thought he'd need for the day—his obsidian mirror, a selection of knives, summoning papers, a book of matches. He made sure his pen was still wrapped in his hair and tucked behind his right ear and pocketed his sunglasses.

He tucked the thin piece of jaguar skin into his pocket last, as if embarrassed. It was almost as if he heard his therapist's reprimands in his head.

There was still no movement from the agent. It was nearing nine o'clock. Bored, Deven decided the man had slept enough and moved to shake him awake.

Deven stopped beside the bed, however, taking in the sight of August asleep. He looked much sweeter without his sardonic sneer. His lips were flushed pink, his eyelashes long and dark against his pale skin. His high cheekbones gave his face a chiseled, statuesque appearance. An explosion of black curls covered his pillow and only a hint of stubble darkened his chin.

He smelled sleepy and warm, and for a moment, Deven longed to stick his hands under the agent's blankets, feel the body heat pocketed there. Aztaws were so cold and bony. As long as he had lived in their world, he had found their touch repulsive. Even when Lord Jaguar had gripped Deven's arm in affection, the contact had been like metal prongs striving to reach bone.

"Agent August," Deven whispered, touching the man's shoulder. He gave it a little shake. "It's nine."

Nothing but the man's slow, even breathing.

"Agent August?" Deven said louder. He shook harder.

August's eyes snapped open. Deven pulled his hand back, ready in case August struck out in surprise.

August blinked at him sleepily. "Hi."

Deven felt something heat inside him. "Hey."

"What time is it?" August's voice was rough with sleep. He rubbed his hand over his face.

"Nine o'clock."

"Forgot to arrange a wake-up call." He sat up, glanced around, and then clenched his eyes shut, looking pained.

"You okay?" Deven asked.

August nodded. "Yeah. Just remembered that Carlos is still dead."

Deven tried to think of something sympathetic to say but drew a blank.

The agent padded to the bathroom, dressed only in a pair of tight boxers. Agent August had a very nice body, Deven realized. He also noted with interest that August, a man who packed a month's worth of clothes, hadn't brought anything but underpants to sleep in.

August disappeared into the bathroom and reemerged wearing a fresh suit, with a white dress shirt and dark black trousers that were so perfectly tailored it looked as if he'd been sewn into them.

"Coffee, then the field office," August ordered. The shower and shave had clearly revived him, for now he was flinty-eyed and full of energy. "And take that damned knife out of your pocket before you kill anyone else."

Deven pulled out his largest blade and left it on the table. He didn't mention the other three he had concealed.

August plugged his phone into his laptop and downloaded the test results he'd run the night before. Like so many other things, the readout seemed to make him angry.

Deven glanced at the scatter plot himself. "What does it mean?"

"No fucking clue." August shook his head. "I've never seen a reading like this, but someone at the office may have an idea." He yanked his phone out of the port and dashed out the door. Deven rushed to keep up.

In the hotel cafe August ordered them both coffees. August's was pale brown with milk that smelled burned. Deven had his black. Coffee had been the great joy of his life upon returning to the natural world. He loved the bitterness and the aroma. This coffee, however, made him long for the small coffee shop he'd grown accustomed to in Friday Harbor.

The thought was an odd one, and he smiled to himself. It was the first time he had considered the Pacific Northwest as a place he might miss.

But he had no time to linger on such thoughts because August was growling at someone on his phone and rushing out the hotel doors. The same black sedan from the day before waited for them in the circular drive of the hotel, with the same driver.

"Embassy," August ordered the driver, sliding inside.

"Hello," Deven offered the driver. The man didn't respond. Deven figured he was used to being barked at.

"72 doesn't speak," August told Deven.

"What?"

August nodded at the driver. "Refugee from starys. No vocal cords. Air too dense for sound waves or something."

Deven studied the driver more closely. He appeared perfectly human. He would never have guessed the man wore a human body as a disguise. The driver met his eyes in the rearview mirror and smiled.

There was a deep chasm in his mouth, like looking down into the pit of hell. Distant echoes of screams seemed to fill the vast red space between his teeth. For a moment, Deven thought he saw the flicker of a small body writhing, impaled on one of the driver's shiny white teeth.

Deven's skin went clammy. He quickly looked away.

August chuckled. "Poor 72. That happens all the time. It's why he's stuck working for us. No masking spell is strong enough to hide how damned *weird* the starys are."

The driver flipped August his middle finger, then pulled into traffic.

The drive to the US embassy was short. Blue uniform-clad and armed security guards surrounded the embassy. The sedan pulled under the green front awning of the building and August jumped out, with Deven close behind. They didn't enter the embassy through the front. Instead, they walked around the building to a blocked-off alley, also guarded by wary security.

There were a few angled parking spaces with cars in them. August stopped beside a nondescript white SUV with tinted windows. He reached into his suit jacket pocket and pulled out a keyless remote. The SUV clicked and the lights flashed.

"Get in," August said. He opened the back door. Deven climbed inside.

There were no backseats in the car. Instead, a gray-carpeted hatch lay on the floor of the vehicle. August lifted the hatch open to reveal a staircase.

"Down you go," August ordered.

Deven cautiously made his way down the steep stairs, hand twitching for his knife. He heard a shrill beep as August locked the car again and saw him shut the hatch above them.

At the bottom of the stairs Deven found himself in a short office hallway. Gray carpet lined the floor. Pictures of eagles and dignitaries decorated the otherwise bland cream-colored walls.

"Why doesn't NIAD have its own office in Mexico City?" Deven asked.

"Mexico isn't a member nation of NATO," August replied. "So our activities have to fall under the purview of the US government while we're here."

August directed Deven through a series of corridors until they reached a solid metal door with a plaque that had NIAD—Mexico City Field Office engraved upon it. August spat on his palm, gripped the door handle, and opened the door.

Inside, it looked exactly like any busy office. Men and women in suits fixed their attention on computer screens, filed papers, and carried boxes. Most were Mexican, but there were other nationalities as well, judging by looks, and a gentleman standing near a photocopier had an unpleasant greenish hue to his skin.

Deven had a sudden urge to shine August's special flashlight in his face and see what he was.

As they wandered through the labyrinth of offices, storage rooms, restroom facilities, and an employee break lounge, a sense of déjà vu hit Deven and he realized he'd been here before. A little over a year ago, when he'd begged for political asylum, he'd been taken here.

But he had barely been able to see back then, his eyes burning from so much light after thirteen years of darkness. Now, however, with the gift of full sight, Deven found the place less intimidating, more mundane. Last year it had represented a great failure—a reluctant refuge that embodied his guilt at leaving Jaguar's dynasty behind in their greatest need.

But now it was only an office. He was relieved that bad memories didn't linger here the way they did in other parts of his mind. Several of the people they passed offered him curious smiles. Some nodded to August as well, but others glanced away from the agent or outright ignored him. He was clearly a man respected and hated in equal terms.

They stopped in a room labeled Magical Forensics that resembled the merging of a sterile laboratory and a junkyard. Advanced, shiny equipment sat upon clean white counters along one wall; the rest of the room overflowed with an assortment of boxed oddities, pouring from their containers like the contents of a child's play box. Little was recognizable; something that resembled a Gatling gun was propped against a wall. Another box seemed to be filled with what looked like dead puppies.

A young woman in a lab coat was busy reading a computer screen when they entered, but she glanced up and smiled at August as soon as the door shut.

"Hi, Elia," August said. "I need you to look at something for me."

"Sure. How are you holding up?" she asked.

"Fine." August's mouth formed a tight line. He handed her his phone. "This is from a bruise on Carlos's body. Can you interpret the pattern?"

Elia took the phone, but her eyes kept darting over to Deven. "You haven't introduced me to your friend, Silas," she said.

"Deven, this is Elia Nogales, forensics. Elia, this is Deven Shaw, a special consultant on Aztaw."

"Hi." Deven hesitated, then stepped forward and offered his hand. Elia shook it softly, a big smile on her face, until she spotted the scar on his neck. The smile faltered slightly as she let go of his hand.

"The analysis matches the spread on an object that came in from Carlos's apartment," Elia said. She lifted a small baggie out of the white cardboard box on the table beside her. "Blood and bone remnants found at the murder site, belonging to Carlos. A fragment of obsidian has a similar spectrum."

"Can you define it?" August asked.

"I'm working on it."

The lab door opened and Agent Klakow entered, wearing the same suit he had on the day before but looking more comfortable in the air-conditioned underground office.

"Local team got the identity on last night's corpse," Klakow said. He offered Deven a smile. "How you doin'?"

"Good." Deven didn't miss the way August's back stiffened at the sound of Klakow's voice.

"Who was he?" August asked.

"Huezartzaw, alias Juan Lopez, registered Aztaw refugee, legally here. His masking spell and movements all check out." Klakow shook his head. "You shouldn't have killed him."

Deven opened his mouth to apologize, but August cut him off. "When I need your opinion I'll ask for it."

"You're an asshole, you know that?" Klakow glared at August, and Deven realized he must have thought August was responsible for stabbing the Aztaw.

"I'm the one—" he started.

"When had the refugee last been to Aztaw?" August interrupted, giving Deven a sharp look.

"He traveled between the Aztaw realm and his apartment in Itzapalapa regularly and had returned from Aztaw two days before." Klakow turned to Deven. "Agents Ortega and Zardo went to his apartment last night. They found pictures of you."

"Me?" Deven asked.

Klakow nodded. "A ton of them. A copy of your flight itinerary too. We must have a leak in the agency for that to have gotten out."

"He was trying to scare me away from descending into Aztaw," Deven said. "He must have had orders from whichever lord he's still loyal to."

August frowned. "Still?"

"Most soldiers supported the defeat of the lords and the rise of the common Aztaw," Deven explained, "but some vassals remained faithful to their lords and dynasties. If this soldier served a house rival to Jaguar's, he might have had instructions to keep an eye out for my return to Mexico City and to prevent me from descending."

"Why?" Klakow asked.

"It's irrelevant to this case," August snapped. He looked to Elia. "So? It's supernatural?"

Elia nodded. She held out a printout from the box. "See the pattern? It looks like filaments were tied to the skin cells, tracing to an unseen source. It's a remnant of magic from a hidden realm, but I can't tell you which one."

"A hidden realm." August frowned. He was quiet for a moment, then turned to Deven. "We need to try and figure out what Carlos and Beatriz were trying to see. That would help us pinpoint which realm to search in for their killer. Can you do the same vision serpent spell?"

"Of course."

"Would we see what Carlos and Bea were trying to discover?"

Deven frowned. "It would be hard to know exactly what they were trying to find, but if I can look again at what they used to make the spell, I might be able to limit the focus."

Elia motioned toward the box. "Everything with a spectral trace is in here, except for the dead birds. We saved a sample of the collection in the morgue if you need those."

Deven rifled through the box. He removed the bloodletting cord and the remnants of burned papers. He tried to unfold them, but they broke apart in his hands.

He sorted through the material until he found a small fragment of bone. It glowed faintly, not enough to be noticed in a bright room but enough that when Deven cupped his hands he could see the faint light.

"Aztaws always glow?" August asked.

Deven nodded.

"No wonder Jaguar wanted you as an assassin. You could hide in the dark."

"They can see in the dark," Deven clarified. "In fact, most lords have the power to quench all light, natural or mechanical, since it hurts their eyes. But it still proved an advantage." Deven swallowed, thinking of Jaguar's training, then shook his head. "This is all we need." He gathered the bone and the cord and the dented copper bowl for good measure.

August grabbed a small medical kit from the counter, then waved to Elia. "We're done. Thanks."

She nodded back shyly. "You have my condolences, for Carlos." She touched August's sleeve.

August's jaw clenched tightly. He nodded.

Elia smiled. "At least he died doing something he believed in."

August eyes narrowed. "What?"

Elia looked embarrassed. "He was doing important work. And he—"

"Do you know how Carlos wanted to die?" August interrupted. "The same way I do. Old, in my bed, asleep."

"Of course." Elia had flushed bright red.

"His life was taken from him in violence. That's about as awful as it gets." He yanked open the door. "Come on, Deven."

Deven followed, with a sympathetic look from Klakow.

"Don't be his bitch," Klakow muttered.

Deven said nothing in return, but he really wanted to tell the agent to fuck off. Instead he followed after August, who stormed down the long hallway like a man on a mission of murder. Deven hurried to catch up with him, anxious about getting lost in the labyrinth of similar-looking corridors.

As Deven fell in step alongside him, August said, "Don't say *anything* about it."

"Why would I?" Deven asked.

August ran a hand through his hair, causing his dark curls to stand on end, making him look wild. "I'm sick of people justifying what happened to Carlos as *part of the job*. That's bullshit. I'm not willing to die for *work*."

Deven said nothing, and this seemed to anger August more. "What? You agree with them?"

Deven shrugged. "Where I come from life means nothing, because the afterlife matters more. I saw humans murdered by the hundreds. I saw Aztaw soldiers killed in endless combat. I took their lives. And at any moment, I expected them to take mine." Deven thought for a moment. "None of it meant anything there. But here, I think I see your point. Life is the only sure thing. It's *known*, which makes it all that matters."

August stared down at Deven with an expression similar to the one he'd had in the morgue the day before. His eyes were a little glassy.

"Come on," Deven said, echoing what he was discovering were August's favorite words. "Let's find a nice, dark, quiet place to summon a vision serpent."

August seemed to pull himself together. He nodded. "Dark, quiet place."

"Preferably bigger than a closet," Deven added.

August gave him a sideways glance. "Why, afraid of standing in the closet with me?"

Deven laughed at that. "No. Afraid the deodorant I stole from you this morning may be wearing off and you'll find my smell offensive again."

August smiled. Deven again marveled at how something as simple as a smile could bring such light to his eyes and completely transform his face. He really was quite gorgeous.

"I said you smelled, I didn't say you smelled *offensive*." August lowered his voice. "Quite the contrary. I like your smell."

Deven felt the words sink into his stomach and roll there, warm and heavy.

August resumed his quick pace. “One stop at the armory, and off we go.”

Deven got to meet the odor-sensitive pixie August had mentioned the night before. Deven had never seen a pixie and was surprised by his size, having assumed he would have been small enough to fit in his hand.

Instead, the pixie was nearly Deven’s height, although his ageless body was thin and his skin nearly blue in color. He wore only a small loincloth and had iridescent wings, which increasingly flapped the more annoyed he got.

And annoyed he was. He begrudgingly shoved a set of freeze balls at Deven only after Agent August cut him off mid-curse and threatened to call in Director Alonsa, the head of the Mexican branch office. August grabbed a weapon for himself from an arms locker that was labeled “shard pistols.” Freshly armed, Deven wanted to test his new weapon, but August was determined to do the vision serpent spell as soon as possible.

72 drove them to a warehouse in an industrial part of the city. The boarded-up building appeared condemned; rusted and dented metal garage doors barred the entrance and a large *Se Vende* sign was nailed over the narrow windows.

72 opened the heavy padlock on the door and they stepped inside, where the building was revealed to be in good condition, brightly lit and clean. The large open space had little furniture, only a few folding chairs and a table set up in the corner, holding a flat of bottled water, a coffee maker, and what looked to be some dirty coffee mugs. The rest of the concrete floor was bare, although markings had been scrawled in a circle at one end and another end was scorched black with burn marks.

“You working for Agent Ortega today?” August asked 72, who nodded. August turned to Deven. “How long does this take?”

“About fifteen minutes to conjure. If we use our blood, the vision will last no longer than an hour.”

August nodded to 72. “Pick us up in two hours.”

72 nodded, his gaping, vacuous mouth echoing screams and chilling Deven. He relaxed once the driver was out of the building.

“Where are we?” Deven asked.

"Practice studio." August shrugged out of his suit jacket. "It's a safe environment for conjuring with wards around the facility to contain effects. The agency tries to set one up in every city they have a field office." He threw his coat over the back of a folding chair. He leaned forward and sniffed at the coffee maker. Something about the odor made him back away. He nodded to Deven. "It's your show, pretty boy."

Deven scowled at the name but nevertheless pulled out what he'd taken from Carlos Rodriguez's evidence box. He also removed conjuring papers from his pocket and matches.

He held out the thorn-threaded cord, a moment of nausea quickly pushed down after years of experience.

"You need blood, right?" August asked. He pulled out the pocket medical kit he'd taken from the forensics lab and rolled up his sleeves.

"Not from your arm." Deven stopped him. "More effective from the tongue."

August looked a little queasy at that. "Disgusting."

"Aztaws usually take the blood from the penis."

"No thanks."

Deven handed August the copper bowl. "Hold this under my mouth." He didn't think about it. He tore the thorned cord quickly over the center of his tongue and pain choked him. Blood filled his mouth. He spat into the bowl and took it from August, holding it under his chin as he let the blood drip from his tongue.

August had a look of extreme distaste, grimacing at the bowl. "You don't need that much blood to do a spell, you know." He pulled a needle from the medical kit and examined it as if making sure it was clean. He pricked his finger, then took the bowl from Deven's hands. "Our research department has shown most traditional spell casting uses far more blood than necessary. In actuality..." He squeezed the tip of his finger and several drops of blood fell into the bowl, mingling with Deven's voluminous contribution. "Half a teaspoon will successfully fuel any magic and with less consequences." He squeezed a few more drops into the bowl, then handed it back to Deven.

Deven glared. "You might have started that speech a minute earlier." His words were garbled as he spoke around the swelling of his injured tongue.

August laughed, his eyes twinkling as he pulled a bandage from the kit and meticulously wrapped his index finger. He used his bandaged finger to point at Deven. "Less chance of infection too."

"It was your friend's thorned cord," Deven reminded him.

"Actually, it was most likely Bea's. She was researching links between Aztaw invasions in pre-Columbian Mexico and influences on indigenous culture. She loved old artifacts."

Deven spat more blood on the floor as a response.

August walked over to the table and returned with a bottle of water. He handed it to Deven.

"Thank you." Deven gratefully diluted the metallic taste of blood in his mouth. When the bleeding slowed enough, he held out his summoning papers. "If you're ready, turn off the lights."

August switched off the lights and moved to stand behind Deven. Other than the faint glow of an emergency exit sign in the back of the warehouse, the space blackened completely and Deven relaxed in the safety of darkness.

He poured their mingled blood over the papers, lit a match, and set them alight. At first the smoke sputtered, the paper soaked wet, but then a whiff of the smell reached the underworld and the paper burst aflame.

Deven dropped the fiery sheet into the copper bowl to burn up the rest of the blood. He pushed the bowl away and stepped back. August avidly observed his actions.

Deven had performed little magic in the natural world and for a moment he wondered if he'd done something wrong. Then a burst of smoke mushroomed from the flame and shadowy shapes filled the darkness. White smoke coiled, curling and expanding into a massive double-headed serpent, rearing on its tail from the flaming bowl. Its two skull heads turned, forked tongues reaching out to nearly lick their faces. The serpent grew to the ceiling of the warehouse.

Deven glanced at August to make sure he was all right. Deven had seen human captives faint dead away or go white, screaming at the sight of vision serpents. But August stared intently at the specter, not scared, simply looking like he was trying to figure it out. Deven felt oddly proud.

White smoke clearly defined one of the serpent's heads, detailing each tooth and bone. But the other head wavered in smoke tendrils, barely formed as it peered into another world.

The head facing them hissed. Deven raised the Aztaw bone from Rodriguez's apartment. "Show us what he died to hide," he commanded in English and in Aztawi. He threw the bone at the serpent. The smoke rippled where the bone shot through the vision. The skull in the natural world pulled away and the obscured skull of the supernatural world turned to face them. Its jaws opened and dislocated, revealing what looked to be a filthy, dark Mexican alley. An Aztaw lord walked slowly through this alley, dragging one leg as he moved. His body rhythmically pulsed as if he were a walking heart. The vision of the lord was vivid, even in the dark, flickering only as air currents disturbed the smoke.

He was Aztaw, no doubt about it, but he didn't look like any lord Deven had ever seen. Paper-thin, translucent skin stretched over his luminescent skull and spine, weathered with age. His face bones were painted in black and yellow stripes, and his eyes burned in their sockets, wide and lidless. His lipless mouth opened to reveal teeth sharpened into long fangs.

His left leg ended in a sandaled foot, but the right terminated at an exposed shin bone that scraped along the ground as the monster walked. He wore black and yellow Aztaw armor and carried a tall staff in one hand. In his other hand he held an axe with a handle as long as a man's body. An obsidian mirror was strapped to the back of his head.

All Aztaw lords were terrible in appearance, but this one was particularly unusual because his flesh was so thin it revealed coursing red blood moving underneath the surface, pulsing around his spine. He resembled a fat, transparent tick, swollen on blood. Dozens of red arteries streamed out from his spine and stretched into the ether. The blood vessels hovered above the alleyway pavement, turning the corner as if the creature were the heart of a city-sized circulatory system. As he walked, dragging his right foot behind, his entire body pulsed and the blood under his skin pumped.

"Christ..." August blinked at the vision.

Deven recognized the black and yellow paint from oral legends. "Night Axe," he said. "Lord of Hurricanes."

The lord spun and stared straight at Deven, pupils contracting to pinpricks. His mouth opened wide, revealing sharp, jagged teeth.

Terror rushed through Deven. "He's seen us!" He kicked over the copper bowl, spilling the remains of their blood onto the concrete.

"I thought it was only a vision," August said.

"Somehow he knows we're looking at him." Deven cursed himself for not crafting a jade spell breaker. "Enough!" He waved at the vision serpent. "Turn your face away!"

But vision serpents were notoriously disobedient and the terrible image of Night Axe remained. The lord seemed to smile. His body throbbed as he pointed his staff directly at Deven. He dragged the sharp tip over his own neck in warning.

"Look away!" Deven commanded again, and at last the jaws of the vision serpent snapped shut. Its tongues hissed at Deven, screeching as it dissipated back into the copper bowl. The smell of sulfur and ozone permeated the air and soot scorched the back wall of the warehouse, forming a final, murky image of the serpent.

Deven breathed heavily. Fear tingled down his spine. *Impossible.*

"Shit." He heard August curse somewhere off in the distance. Then the lights switched on. Deven covered his eyes with the palms of his hands.

"Is that what Aztaw lords look like?" August asked.

"No. He's mutated." Deven lowered his hands, wincing at the light.

"Do you know who he is?"

"Yes, but I don't know how he could be here."

August frowned. "Your hands are shaking."

Deven swallowed. "Night Axe...he's the bogeyman to Aztaws. And I've never seen any lord break through a vision spell and peer back at the spell caster like that."

"What does it mean?"

"It means he's here." Deven fumbled on the ground for his bottle of water and took a deep gulp.

"Here?"

"He's not on another plane. He's *here* in Mexico City, hidden by magic but in the natural world." Deven's tongue throbbed angrily in his mouth.

August frowned. "So Carlos and Bea were trying to find out where he was?"

Deven nodded. "Yes, although why I have no idea."

"Who is he?"

"He is the Lord of Hurricanes, although Night Axe is what Lord Jaguar always called him. Almost a thousand years ago, the lords banded together in a rare moment of unity to collectively exile Night Axe from Aztaw. Even by their standards he was considered too evil—reckless in his manipulation and excess. I've heard of him spoken of only in whispers, but he has many names. He's the Trickster, the enemy, the Lord of the Smoking Mirror. His house power allows him to change his appearance, even mimic the shape, movement, and sounds of others. Doing so, he brings discord and deception wherever he goes. The lords exiled him for the unadulterated pleasure he gained by continuing a cycle of destruction. He once burned crops to purposefully bring famine to his own vassals. And when Aztaws suffered, he'd use his smoking mirror to reflect their pain and prolong their suffering.

"But he didn't just hurt Aztaws. Even though all Aztaw lords sacrifice humans for their blood, they treat us respectfully in the underworld until death, because our role is so important. Aztaws truly believe humans will be reincarnated as part of the eternal house powers they die to fuel. But Night Axe showed no such respect. Night Axe entered the human realm and killed en masse, torturing his sacrifices."

August walked back over to the table and pulled on his coat. "If the other lords feared him so much, why didn't they kill him?"

"He was too powerful," Deven said. "He had enchanted armor and he can modify his body, allowing him to hide in plain sight in the guise of animals or other Aztaws. Coupled with his insatiable passion for battle, the other lords lost and were forced to offer gruesome tributes, killing their own people in the dark to be eaten by Night Axe's soldiers. His soldiers were fierce and he had the tzimimi under his will."

"So instead of killing him they exiled him here? To Mexico City?"

Deven scowled. "No! That would have defeated their purpose. They needed him stripped of power. And of course, human blood only strengthens the lords. Since they couldn't defeat him, they worked together to align two tricky calendars and forced Night Axe to the realm of light, hoping he would weaken without darkness and starve without human blood or Aztaw food."

"Clearly it didn't work." August snapped open a bottle of water and took a deep gulp.

"I don't know how he managed to escape the realm of light, but he's here." Deven shook his head. "It shouldn't be possible. There are no natural calendar alignments between the realm of light and anywhere else. It was the perfect prison."

August arched an eyebrow. "The Irregulars have a report on the realm of light. From the way it was described it isn't a prison, rather a place full of peaceful, bodiless beings."

"No body means no blood. That's hell for an Aztaw lord." Deven shook his head.

"What were those veins floating all around him?" August asked.

"I don't know, but it must have something to do with how engorged he was on human blood," Deven said, frowning. "None of this makes sense."

"Night Axe needs sacrifices to fuel his magic, yes?"

"Of course."

"If he's trying to keep a low profile here, it would draw attention to him if he murdered dozens of people to extract their blood," August said.

"You think he's developed another way of collecting sacrifices?"

August shrugged. "Hell if I know. Can you use your mirror to look into the future and see?"

"I can try, although I doubt it will help." Deven pulled his obsidian mirror fragment from his pocket. He unwrapped its cloth and dipped a corner of the mirror into the puddled remains of their mixed blood.

Deven spat on the mirror. He didn't expect to see much. Premonitions were murky at best and subject to change. He'd rarely found anything worth learning when peering into the cloudy uncertainty of the future.

The opaque surface of the mirror shimmered and cleared. He looked at the image. From a pool of darkness glowed the bones of a horde of Aztaw soldiers, running full speed, weapons raised as they charged.

Deven pulled out his knife and shouted to August, "Run!"

Chapter Seven

The air snapped like exploding light bulbs. The corner of the warehouse ripped open to reveal a jagged pool of darkness. At least a dozen Aztaw soldiers poured from the breach between realms, raising dart blowers, swords, and batons spiked with obsidian blades.

Deven caught August's sleeve and pulled him to the front door. Adrenaline tensed the muscles of his body into flight mode.

August stared at the coal black crack in the air, then seemed to finally comprehend the danger. He pulled his new shard pistol from a holster hidden under his jacket.

"Too many! Run!" Deven urged.

"There are civilians out there!" August cried. He grabbed another object from his pocket, a powdery white ball that resembled something for a bath. He hurled it at the soldiers. It hit the Aztaw in front and a fine white powder burst out explosively, shooting upwards to coat all of them in glittering fragments of light.

"What the hell is that?" Deven cried. He yanked open the door.

"Glamour bomb!" August shouted. Half a dozen poison darts flew past their heads, embedding in the door. "We can't have them seen here."

"Go, go!" Deven pushed August out into the street. He broke into a run.

The hot midday sun blinded Deven. He followed August down a narrow side street. Something knocked over behind him and he heard angry yelling in Spanish.

Deven glanced over his shoulder to see what looked like a mob of angry Mexican men charging him.

The masking spell was good—from afar, they appeared rough, unapproachable, but undeniably human. But the masking spell hadn't applied evenly and at certain angles Deven saw their Aztaw bodies poking through the deception.

In their natural form, the soldiers were slightly larger than humans, with pale skin like rice paper stretched over their glowing bones. Skirts of cotton and feathers covered their waists and armor of finely braided, enchanted husks protected their bony chests like bulletproof vests. The fierce black and yellow markings of the Lord of Hurricane's house darkened what could be seen of their skulls underneath the human camouflage. One of them had obviously protected his face from the glamour bomb and his lidless eyeballs rolled in his skull sockets.

They moved as if drugged, slower than August and Deven, but their determination to follow didn't waver.

"We've got to get away from all these goddamn people!" August gasped, sprinting from a busy intersection and down another side road.

The Aztaws continued doggedly in pursuit. Glimpses of raised spears and batons shimmered into sight and disappeared as the masking spell failed under the heavy sunlight. The range was too far for Deven's knives but maybe not too far for his new freeze balls.

But as he pulled one from his pocket, August barked, "No! Too many civilians." He stopped for a moment, concentrating, as if discerning their location. He pointed to the left. "This way. Hurry!"

Deven did as he was told, racing to keep up. Up ahead a temporary fence cordoned off a vacant construction area. Vaguely he remembered it was a Sunday.

But there was a guard for the site, who yelled and rose as if to physically restrain them from entering the property.

"*Corre*!" August shouted at the man. The guard picked up his phone. Then his mouth went slack as he saw the dozen angry men chasing Deven and August. The guard dropped the phone and ran toward a trailer on the periphery of the site.

"Where are we?" Deven panted.

"New subway tunnel drilling site. Come on!"

"Good thing I took up running!" Deven shouted to August. To his surprise, August barked a short laugh.

At the poorly barricaded tunnel entrance August paused to pull out his utility knife and quickly selected a tool that came off the knife. He cradled the small metal sliver in his hand.

The masking spell was wearing off the soldiers. They looked more like a furious attacking Aztaw army. But it wasn't as if Deven didn't have practice running for his life from Aztaw soldiers. He knew what to expect. Aztaw soldiers were fierce but unimaginative; they hunted in formation and never strayed. Normally, Deven would do anything but flee in a straight path from Aztaws. But he was stuck following August into the tunnel.

They entered the smooth, cylindrical shaft, lined with concrete walls. The ground was roughly hewn rock and soil. Dim emergency lighting lined the ceiling, but as they plunged deeper, shadows overpowered the light. The tunnel entrance gaped like a minstrel's mouth, a circle of light in swallowing darkness.

Once the soldiers entered the tunnel, August tossed the sliver he held in his hands and it spun like a propeller. August shoved

Deven hard against the concrete wall and covered Deven's body with his own.

An explosion rocked the tunnel. A blast of hot air knocked both of them over. August held him tightly underneath him as another wave of heat threatened to blow them into the darkness. Deven's nostrils burned with the stench of scorched ozone.

After a moment, August pulled himself off Deven and stood. Deven blinked, feeling stunned. "What was that!"

"Mage grenade." August stared intently at the tunnel entrance.

Deven stood to watch as well, bracing his hands on his knees, catching his breath.

August leaned against the tunnel wall, breathing hard. "Goddamn Aztaws are *scary.*"

Deven nodded, remembering the first time he'd met one, age ten; he'd thought his father had dragged him down to the hell his grandmother had always been going on about.

A shuffling sound directed Deven's attention to the tunnel entrance. Most of the Aztaw soldiers remained motionless on the ground, but several slowly rose to their feet. August looked shocked. "Shit!"

"Can I use these freeze balls now?" Deven asked.

"Yes, yes!"

Deven pulled one of the balls from his pocket. It fit nicely in his palm and was soft and slightly warm.

The soldiers moved toward them, cursing in Aztawi. One's glowing tibia protruded through his skin. Another had lost the bottom half of his jawbone. Still they charged. Deven threw the ball. As it spun in the air it hissed and popped like fire on dry wood. It launched itself at the nearest soldier and slammed into his body. The Aztaw gasped, freezing solid, falling backward from the force of the impact.

The soldier beside him tossed his spear and barely missed Deven's neck. He and August ran deeper into the tunnel. He threw the other two freeze balls in his pocket. Each hit their mark, but the three remaining soldiers were close. Deven tossed one of his knives, but it hit the soldier on his armored chest, causing no damage.

August fired his shard pistol. Thin, needle-like slivers of metal sprayed from the smoking barrel. Several of the thin slivers sliced through the soldier's rib cage and stuck in his bones, but others shot through him and out the other side. The wounds were severe but not debilitating. The soldier's knife was nearly long enough to be a sword and he raised it to cut August down.

Deven didn't know if August had experience with hand-to-hand combat. He wasn't about to find out the hard way. He threw himself between the soldier and August, blocking the blow clumsily with a knife. The blades clashed and his knife clattered to the ground. The soldier swung again. Deven ducked low and threw himself forward into the soldier, knocking him off balance.

He spun and pushed August out of the way as the other soldier swung his baton. The blow landed hard on Deven's arm, sprawling him onto the tunnel floor. Pain radiated up his side. As the soldier raised his baton again, Deven pulled the last knife from his back pocket and hurled it at the soldier. The blade sank deep into the soldier's eye and he screeched, dropping the baton as his hands fumbled blindly at his face.

Two remaining soldiers were nearly upon them, and Deven was out of weapons. Without another choice, he yanked the pen from his hair and frantically started scribing glyphs on the ground. Each symbol brightened, then dulled into deep black, sinking to the underworld. He wrote around himself in a circle, the pen growing colder in his hands. It was a dark, purplish red when full of his energy, but almost immediately the color began to drain from it as he wrote the spell, and Deven felt himself weaken as his energy drained out to fuel it. He could almost smell the stench of corn on Lord Jaguar's breath as he held the weapon between his fingers.

He drew the symbol of a dog eating itself, the pyramid, the black reed. He drew crossbones and a quail feather. He drew the images of the lords who created the house power.

August stood in front of Deven, shard pistol aimed at the soldiers. "What are you doing!" he cried.

Deven finished the last glyph and jumped to his feet, grabbing August and yanking him into the circle as a wall of sparks shot from each glowing glyph and linked to form a fiery curtain around them. The sound of howling wind filled the circle, deafening in volume.

"Is it a shield?" August shouted, covering his ears.

"No! I took us out of time!"

"What?"

The soldiers charged through them into the black emptiness of the unfinished subway tunnel. August spun to watch, gun aimed.

"Don't shoot!" Deven cried above the wind. "We're in a time lock. It won't do anything."

"They passed right through us!" August shouted.

Deven felt sick with exhaustion. The benefit of being able to fuel his own magic without sacrifices was lessened by the fact that it sapped most of his strength. The sucking wind grew louder. They didn't have much longer. "We have to get out."

"They may double back when they reach the end of the tunnel." August watched for them anxiously.

Stepping out of time was a tricky prospect and Deven watched the edges of the time lock sizzle, blacken, and fly away like charred embers. He gripped his pen and drew a symbol in the air, conjuring the image of the grinding wheels of calendars. They had mere seconds before the calendars moved again.

"We've got to go, now!" The roar was deafening. Deven's pen was nearly white, its inky power drained from it. He shoved it back behind his ear and grasped August's arm. He stuck out his foot and smudged one of the symbols.

The floor beneath them split and cracked away in a perfect circle.

"Jump!" Deven shoved August toward the natural world.

August landed on the tunnel floor and spun. He looked back and went sheet white. Deven glanced down and saw the movement of thousands of glowing bones, felt the furnace of heat of the Aztaw world—his world—rumbling below.

Dangling from earth, Aztaw looked like hell incarnate. The smell of burning maize overpowered Deven.

August gripped Deven's arm and jerked him up. The circle of earth beneath Deven's feet crumbled and collapsed into the dark underworld. Everything Deven knew and had cared about was down there in that heat.

No, no, I want down, Deven thought, but August's hand was warm in his and held him tight. As the tunnel floor plummeted into darkness August hauled Deven back into the human world.

Chapter Eight

When they emerged from the construction tunnel, filthy and exhausted, Deven saw city lights twinkling in the darkness. The smell of sewage and lime permeated Deven's senses, reminding him he was in Mexico once more. A sick, nervous grief tore at his throat and left him ragged. If he'd only dropped...

"It wasn't even noon when we entered the warehouse!" August complained, scowling at the soil stains on his designer suit jacket.

"Time locks mess things up," Deven said, too exhausted to explain. The Aztaw bodies littering the entrance had already started to desiccate from the dry summer heat. He felt drained and realized he hadn't eaten anything since last night's burger.

"Food. Now," he mumbled. His tongue still smarted when he spoke.

August nodded. He pulled out his phone, frowning at a new crack across the screen. "Damn it!" He punched numbers angrily. When he got someone on the phone, he issued orders, mentioning the pile of Aztaw bodies at the tunnel entrance, the two that had gotten lost in the darkness, and something about how they could be tracked by glamour bomb residue. Deven heard August's tone change, becoming apologetic as he asked for another cleanup team. August finished his call, gave Deven an irritated look, then led him to the nearest taqueria.

The place looked dirty, but the rotisserie near the entrance smelled wonderful and the restaurant had chairs, which was all that mattered at the moment.

They both collapsed into plastic seats. August ordered two beers.

"Maybe I don't want a beer," Deven complained.

"You need a drink as badly as I do," August replied. He rubbed his hands over his face. "Why, you want a soda?"

Deven waved off the issue. He rested his head on his arms. "If you're going to control everything, order me one of whatever you eat as well." He yawned and closed his eyes.

August spoke to the waiter in broken Spanish, then switched back to English as he made several phone calls. At first Deven listened, but the warmth and delicious smells of the restaurant made him sleepy, and he found himself unable to do much more than long for his hotel bed.

A heaping platter of *tacos al pastor* arrived. August dove into the meal like he hadn't eaten in weeks. Deven took one of the small, soft corn tacos and fell in love with the first bite.

The flavor was hearty, sweet, and tangy with lime and cilantro. It seemed even richer after his brush with the underworld. There was a familiarity about the flavor, something that reminded him of his Mexican mother and his childhood, but like all thoughts of her, he couldn't pinpoint anything more than a generalized good feeling.

He took a sip of his beer and was shocked by how good it tasted when combined with a corn tortilla. And as far as he could remember he'd never eaten a radish. The sharp taste fascinated him, although it caused the cut on his tongue to burn. He loved the radish's colorful pink skin. It was beautiful, really.

"You could have saved us a lot of running, you know." August watched him with half-closed eyes. "You might have done that time lock trick back at the warehouse."

"I shouldn't have done it at all." Deven drank more of his beer. The alcohol warmed his stomach, sent heat down into his kneecaps. "As it stands, that might have been the last mistake I ever make."

"How so?"

"I just showed my hand, didn't I?" Deven reached behind his ear and pulled out his pen.

August took it from him gingerly. The pen had almost returned to its natural rust-red color, but it was still lighter than it should be—it would take more of Deven's strength to feed it what it needed to remain whole.

"Beautiful," August said, studying the intricate carving. It was a remarkable work of craftsmanship, something Deven was proud to be the guardian of.

"This is your house power," August said, understanding dawning. "Why hide it?"

"Night Axe saw us in the warehouse. He no doubt observed the pursuit of his soldiers. And now he knows I have this."

"You think he'll try and take it?"

"I would." Deven yawned again. "Not only will it open the gates between here and Aztaw, but it will give him control over the surviving lords now that their own powers have been destroyed. As for the Aztaw citizens who led the revolt? They're dead as soon as he returns."

August frowned at the pen. "I didn't think time was so malleable."

"Time itself isn't, but the way it's measured is," Deven said. He took the pen back and pulled one of the thin paper napkins from the table dispenser. He drew three cogs of different sizes, showing August how they fit together. "Time works on a series of calendars. Every calendar is unique to a location. There are times when certain moments intersect between each calendar. When that happens, a schism appears between the worlds that someone can pass through.

"Other worlds have their own calendars, although date matches are rarer. Location matters as well. Mexico City has hundreds of calendars, so there are more opportunities to find moments that coincide between the natural and supernatural realms. But in, say, Iceland, there are no calendars that match up with Aztaw. In South America, there are a few, but their cycle is long. It may be only once a century that a date from the South American calendar coincides with the same date on the Aztaw calendar and someone can cross between worlds."

August frowned. "If Night Axe wants to reenter Aztaw, he's going to have to find a place where the dates align and make a gate."

"Right. Unless he has this." Deven wagged the pen. "This is the Jaguar dynasty house power. It rewrites the calendars, so it can force connections between dates. It allows me to slow down or speed up the turning of these wheels."

"In the tunnel, you created a time lock," August confirmed. Deven nodded. "So you basically wrote us out of the calendars?"

"Yes, but you can't exist outside of time for long. As soon as the wheels start turning again, you'll fall between them and disappear."

August paled a little at that. "Good way to kill off your enemies."

"It takes a great deal of energy to do that," Deven said. "It wouldn't be a problem if I had dozens of sacrifices to bleed into the pen, but since I'm the only one fueling it, I have only enough strength to do one or two tricky rewrites before the pen drains of energy and I'm exhausted."

"Could you pass it to another human to use?"

"It would have to be someone with magical abilities, otherwise I'd have to drain their blood. And it would have to be done quickly. If the pen runs out of ink it will starve and die. A house power is like a living object. It must remain fueled to survive."

August was silent for a moment, eyeing the pen. "How many dates intersect between the realm of light and Aztaw?"

"None," Deven said. "That's why he was sent there. Nor are there any dates that intersect with calendars in the natural world."

"There aren't any spatial portals between here and there either. It's why there is such little information about the realm. Information comes to us secondhand, from some being who knew of another realm where someone had once seen an inhabitant there." August frowned. "So a thousand years ago your Lord Jaguar used this pen and forced a connection."

"Yes."

"Is there another pen somewhere?" August asked.

"No."

"Has it been out of your possession at any time?"

Deven smirked. "You sound like the man at the airport."

"I'm serious." August narrowed his eyes. "That isn't a memento from a dead relative, Deven. It's an extremely dangerous weapon. Did you ever lose it?"

"Of course not. It's been in my sole possession since Jaguar gave it to me."

"And when was that?"

"A little over a year ago." Deven swallowed. "As the rebels laid siege to Lord Jaguar's palace." Nausea rushed through him and Deven dropped the remains of his last taco, no longer hungry.

August looked at the pen, seemingly poised to ask another question. Instead he signaled the waiter for the bill.

"For what it's worth, something that valuable should be locked up in the Irregulars' treasury, not perched behind your ear," August said finally.

"It doesn't leave my possession," Deven stated. "I swore to preserve it with my life."

"The one you made the promise to is dead," August said quietly.

"That doesn't matter," Deven replied, feeling his anger rise once more. "Don't you understand? I served Lord Jaguar from the age of ten. I watched him destroy enemy lands with a swipe of this pen. The ability to manipulate calendars is one of the greatest house powers in Aztaw. Time is sacred in Aztaw and this pen represents that great part of their culture. If the rebels succeed in destroying this, they destroy what defines Aztaw society."

"But the soldiers have rebelled against that society." August eyed the pen warily. "If they want to end the domination of the magical lords over them, I can see why they'd destroy the trappings of their servitude."

Deven scowled. "It's too important to be destroyed for politics. Besides, it strengthens their connection to the human world."

"The new Aztaw realm doesn't need connections to the human realm, does it?" August continued. "With the lords dead, and the house powers gone, human blood isn't needed. You said the citizens slaved to support a sacrifice industry that took resources away from their own well-being. This may be exactly what the new, freer Aztaw needs—a break with contact from the human realm. A chance to live without spells and magic."

Deven bit back his angry response and instead downed the rest of his beer. He hated how quickly August had moved to the side of the rebels, although he shouldn't have been surprised. Of course an American would want a more democratic, unmagical world to thrive.

"How did the other lords succeed in forcing Night Axe through the gate between realms?" August asked, changing the subject.

"I don't know. He was in a weakened state where he couldn't change his body when they forced him through a gate."

"Why didn't your precious lord send him between the calendars?"

"He probably had used almost all the pen's energy just to help capture him."

"Well, thanks to his desire to save his little writing implement, that bastard is now back amongst the living."

Deven was too tired to argue against criticism of Lord Jaguar. He clenched his jaw shut angrily.

August leaned forward. "If we have to fight Night Axe, we need to know how they weakened him."

Deven shrugged. "He is mortal, although like any Aztaw his life span can stretch eons. Cut out his heart, cut off his head, stab him in the throat, like a human being. The only catch, of course, is that he can change his form."

August drained the last of his beer. "We need a better way to see what he's up to than your temperamental vision serpent."

"You're the one with all the technical gizmos pouring out of your pockets," Deven said.

For some reason this was funny to August. "*Gizmos*," he repeated. "Haven't heard that word in a while." He waved his credit card at the waiter.

Deven rose slowly from his chair, his body aching from the run and the blow to his arm. "I should cover my half," he offered, but August shook his head.

"It's all going on the agency credit card, don't worry." August flashed him a quick, magnificent grin. "Well, now that you've bared all, I'd prefer it if you whipped out your magic faster next time. My legs are killing me."

Deven walked beside him out to the curb. "You run fast," he complimented.

"It's amazing what the threat of death can inspire." August launched his arm into the air and flagged down a taxi.

Back at the Bristol Hotel Deven wanted nothing more than to collapse on his bed and sleep for an entire day. Instead, August started packing.

"Get your things together," he ordered.

"Why?"

"Because your little Aztaw friend found us with no difficulty, I can't imagine it will be any harder for Night Axe."

Deven forced himself off the bed and did as he was told. It took less than a minute for him to finish packing. August was still carefully folding his shirts.

"You want help?" Deven offered.

"No."

"You sure brought a lot of clothes."

August's cheeks turned a little pink. "How you dress says a lot about who you are."

"Oh?" Deven sat on the edge of his bed, glancing down at his dirty cargo pants and dark T-shirt. "What do my clothes say about me?"

"That you don't have any personal pride." August turned and gave him a discerning look that unsettled Deven.

Deven swallowed. "Yeah? And I suppose if you wear tailored suede suit jackets it says you have a lot of pride?"

"No. It says I'm worried about what people think about me." The corner of August's mouth lifted and he looked almost shy. "Actually, you can help. Pack my computer, would you?"

"Sure." They worked in companionable silence for a moment. "One of these days, can I see your knife? The one you keep pulling out of your pocket?"

"Of course. It's a generation eight magical utility blade, but mine's down to its last refills. I need to buy another, I haven't gotten around to it."

"Doesn't the agency provide your weapons?"

"We get an expense budget, but the new generation ten models are over that. Carlos and I were going to get new ones for each other on Christmas." August frowned. He held the shirt in his hand limply.

Again, Deven was at a loss as to how to offer support. His therapist had once told him, when he felt out of his depth, to offer a person a polite pat on the back. It insinuated good intentions and oftentimes physical touch said more than words ever could. So Deven reached over and patted August's arm, a stiff, awkward movement that didn't look nearly as good as it had in his mind.

August seemed touched by it, however. His eyebrow quirked up and he smiled a little. "Read about patting people in a book or something?"

Deven laughed nervously. "Or something."

August cocked his head, studying Deven. "You know, for someone who grew up in hell and returned to the real world only a year ago, you're doing pretty good, Deven."

"Thank you."

"You're welcome." August swallowed. "And thank you. For what you did in the tunnel."

Deven frowned, trying to remember. He touched the pen behind his ear.

"You saved my life." August sounded a little annoyed that he had to say it out loud. "Twice. The guy with the knife? And the baton?"

"Oh. Right." Deven shrugged. "I wasn't counting."

August stared at him.

Deven felt conspicuous. "You're welcome?" he offered, not sure if there was some sort of protocol he was supposed to engage in after saving someone's life.

Whatever it was that August was trying to say, he gave up and turned back to his packing. It was well past midnight when they checked out of the Bristol and checked in to El Angel Hotel a few blocks away. This one had a modern lobby and the room, while smaller, was more tastefully furnished and less inundated with wicker. Deven didn't bother unpacking. He shut the curtains, lay down on the top of the comforter, and was out before August even started to unpack.

Chapter Nine

The following morning, it was August who woke Deven up rather than the other way around.

August looked refreshed despite the activities of the previous day. He was fully dressed in yet another suit, this one a lighter color, with a cream-colored shirt, unbuttoned at the neck to reveal a glimpse of his pale skin. His hair was clean and impeccably styled. His pale blue eyes stared down at Deven with a look of amusement.

"Wake up, sunshine."

Deven scowled and drew back under the bedsheet he'd wrapped around himself at some point that night. He felt tired and unenthusiastic about his mission now that he knew who was involved. It had been one thing to tackle Aztaw lords he had understood. But Night Axe was out of his league; even Lord Jaguar himself had failed to defeat the Trickster. What luck was Deven going to have with nothing but a few knives in his pocket?

"Come on. Murdering monsters wait on no man." August ruffled Deven's hair. It was a gesture Deven hadn't felt since before his mother died as a little boy and it brought a surge of complicated emotions. He sank further under the sheet to hide his face, afraid what he was feeling would be obvious.

"Do I have time to shower?" Deven's voice was cracked with sleep.

August sighed. "If you're quick about it."

Deven emerged from under the covers and hurried to the bathroom. He showered briskly, taking advantage of the free toiletries provided by the hotel. As he hunted through his bag for clean clothes, he felt August's gaze on his bare back like a hot iron and he wondered if it was inappropriate for him to have come out of the bathroom in nothing but a towel.

He turned. August's eyes were locked on Deven's body as if he were memorizing every contour.

At first Deven felt embarrassed, thinking that August must be staring at the variety of ugly scars puncturing his torso. Stab wounds, burns, and bumps from badly healed broken bones aged him.

But August's cheeks were flushed, his eyes dilated, and as he shifted uncomfortably in his chair, Deven belatedly realized the agent was aroused by the sight of Deven's near nudity.

Christopher, the man Deven had hooked up with four months before, had told Deven that he was beautiful. Deven couldn't confirm if this was true or not, since he was far from objective, but he liked that he had this effect on the agent. He wondered if he should act upon it.

Because it would have been nice to touch August. His body looked so warm and inviting and his heart-shaped lips seemed engineered for kissing. But Deven had never seduced anyone in his life. He had no experience, and for all he knew, this glance wasn't personal. Maybe August watched all semiclothed men this way.

As if suddenly realizing he was flushed and staring, August coughed and stood. He yanked back the curtains. "Hot in here," he mumbled, throwing open the window.

Deven hesitated. He wanted to say something to August. Or would it be better to just touch him?

"You want some cream for that arm?" August asked, voice low and rough. "Looks painful."

Deven glanced at his left shoulder. The skin was darkly bruised and it hurt to touch it, but he could move it well enough.

"I'm fine."

"Then get ready." August turned away completely and Deven realized he'd lost his opportunity. It frustrated him more than he thought it would.

Deven finished dressing. As August transferred his wallet, phone, and other random possessions from his suitcases into his pockets, Deven did the same, although August really had him beat when it came to carrying an arsenal. As he tried to find a pocket large enough for his favorite knife, August leveled his gaze at him.

"What?" Deven asked innocently. August raised his eyebrows.

Deven grinned and removed the knife from his belt, putting it on top of the television. "Better?"

August shook his head. "Cleaning lady will love it."

"After yesterday, I'd assume you'd prefer I carry a knife."

"You have two others in your pockets." August smirked.

Deven laughed, realizing the futility in trying to hide something from someone who spent an inordinate amount of time looking at him. As August went back to loading various charms, electronic devices, and medical objects into his coat, Deven considered the craftsmanship involved in the man's wardrobe. The suit was practically form fitting and yet it somehow managed to hide a ton of gear.

Deven realized he was staring at August's ass and looked away. What did normal people do when they desired another person? For a moment he considered phoning his therapist for advice. It was something she'd know and he suspected she'd be thrilled with the line of questioning, rattling on about the value of intimacy and opening up to individuals.

But then he'd have to admit he was in Mexico City, despite her protests, and he didn't feel like having that argument.

"So where the hell is my temporary masking kit?" August mumbled, rifling through his belongings with increasing frustration.

"What does it look like?" Deven asked.

"Small, black leather case..."

Deven sat on his unmade bed, yawning and wondering if he could catch a few more minutes of sleep.

There was a curt knock at the door. "August, open up." Agent Klakow's voice sounded annoyed.

"Christ!" August yanked the door open and glared at his fellow agent. "What are you doing here?"

"Forensics found a trace," Klakow said, entering the room. His eyes darted to Deven. "Hi."

Deven raised his eyebrows but didn't bother saying hello, more intrigued by the temper August was building toward his personal belongings.

"Fuck," August muttered, "I swear I had it when I left San Francisco..." He tossed an eclectic variety of items withdrawn from his suitcase onto his bed. There was another glamour bomb, some latex gloves, several pens, business cards, yesterday's medical kit, and a bundled set of wires. Not finding what he needed, August grabbed a nylon bag out of the nearest suitcase and began tearing through that before chucking away the bag itself in disgust.

"So, forensics—" Klakow began only to be cut off by August.

"What are you talking about?" August began to go through his pockets, tossing the contents, including his utility knife, onto the bed. Deven retrieved it and pulled out the light. He flashed it on August's shirt. Nothing supernatural revealed itself.

"The tests," Klakow said. He moved farther into the room, frowning at the mess on the bed. "They came back."

"And?" August demanded.

"They found a trace." Klakow closed the door behind him.

"Of what?"

"I don't know," Klakow said, shrugging. "You're supposed to go in to the office and see for yourself."

"When you speak, you offer nothing of value to the world," August muttered. He turned to Deven. "I'll have to get another masking kit from the inventory this afternoon."

"What is it for?"

"For you, in case we run into any watchbirds, soldiers, or underworldly employees trying to find you."

Klakow moved toward Deven with a smirk. Deven noticed his right leg dragging behind him.

"You hurt yourself?" Deven asked.

"I hurt every time I see Agent August," Klakow replied with a cold smile.

"Funny, asshole."

As casually as he could, Deven shone the light on Klakow's leg. As the light hit his leg they both saw it ended in an exposed shin bone.

Horror choked off Deven's cry of alarm.

Klakow lunged. He gripped Deven by the throat. With shocking strength, he lifted Deven one handed and shoved him against the wall, knocking down a picture of sailboats. It shattered on the floor.

Deven pulled a knife from his belt, but Night Axe swatted it out of his hand instantly.

Deven couldn't breathe. He felt the muscles in his throat convulse against the unrelenting pressure of Night Axe's fingers as they pushed into him, cutting off his breathing.

I want the pen.

Deven's body shuddered at the scraping sound of Night Axe's voice. He still resembled the Irregulars agent, but his grin was monstrous. Deven kicked against the wallpaper. His hands grappled with Night Axe's chilled flesh, but he couldn't breathe, couldn't break free.

Night Axe reached for the pen in Deven's hair.

August threw his shoulder into Night Axe. They both fell sideways on and over the side of Deven's bed. Deven dropped to the floor. With shaking hands he grabbed the pen and shoved it down the front of his trousers.

August fumbled his hand over the bed and grabbed the first thing he made contact with, another glamour bomb. He smashed it into Night Axe's teeth. An explosion of glittery particles coated them both and Night Axe retched horribly. His face contorted in rage. With a roar of fury, he punched his fist through August's chest.

August's body shuddered with the force. Nausea swelled in Deven at the image of Agent Klakow's arm rotating deep inside August's torso, as if wringing August's heart.

August went white and his body convulsed as Night Axe shoved him off, yanking his arm free. His fingers closed as if pulling an invisible thread from August's jacket. August let out a breathy gasp and arched his back.

Deven scrambled to his feet and hurled his knife just as the creature's body transformed into that of an owl. The knife hit the hotel wall and clattered to the ground. The owl screeched and took to the air, circling Deven's head.

I'll find you.

His voice shrieked through Deven's consciousness like nails on a chalkboard. Night Axe flew out the window and Deven slammed shut the window behind him, knowing the futility of the gesture but unable to stop himself.

Chapter Ten

"Agent August!"

Deven rushed to where the man had fallen on the opposite side of the bed. He dropped to his knees beside August's body.

August's appearance was warped and distorted by the glamour bomb. He looked Mexican, with dark black hair, a full beard, and brown eyes. His suit glimmered with powder that made it appear like he was wearing jeans and a pale blue dress shirt. The fragments disoriented Deven and he had to blink several times, straining to concentrate and see what was actually August.

August writhed in pain and his breath shuddered out of him. It was obvious even through the illusion that he was bleeding. Deven brushed off the masking spell glitter, trying to get to the man underneath. His fingers touched hot, wet blood even though he couldn't see it.

Deven had no idea what to do now; saving people was not something he did. He'd watched hundreds of them bleed to death and die, and he'd never lifted a finger to their aid. He hadn't even bothered to try and save the lives of fellow soldiers in Lord Jaguar's army; death was something you let happen.

But now he felt terror at the prospect of August's death, coupled with the guilt of knowing *he* had been Night Axe's target.

He ripped the sheet off his bed and used it to brush away the particles of masking spell glitter covering the agent's face and torso. When he got enough of the spell off he saw August's true face, contorted in pain.

The front of his suit was a mess of blood. Deven unbuttoned August's coat and struggled to work open the slippery buttons of August's shirt. But as he pulled the shirt open he saw no wound. He ran his fingers over August's pale, hairless chest, terrified this was still part of the masking spell's illusion. Although blood coated everything, it was already coagulating. Only a perfectly circular bruise marred his skin, directly over August's frantically beating heart.

Deven recognized the mark. It was the same one they'd seen on Carlos and Beatriz Rodriguez's bodies. But it didn't look immediately fatal and Deven felt relief. August wasn't going to die.

Yet.

"Can you sit up?" Deven reached behind August and cradled his head to help him up. His fingers tangled in August's damp, sweaty hair. Once he was sitting up, August opened his eyes and glanced down at his chest. A look of panic crossed his eyes.

"Oh God," he said, his voice weak.

"I think we can guess why Carlos and Bea were searching for Night Axe," Deven said.

August glanced to the door. "Is he gone?"

"He flew out the window."

August's eyes widened. "He can *fly*?"

"He turned into an owl."

"Aztaw lords can do that?" He scowled.

"Transformation is his house power." Deven glanced at the closed window. "As soon as he gets that glamour bomb out of his mouth he'll be back, you know."

"I know." August breathed heavily, wincing. He rested his shaking hands over his bruise. "How does he even know who Klakow is?"

Deven frowned. He had no answer to that.

There was a knock on the door. August's muscles tensed under Deven's hand.

"I doubt he'd knock twice," Deven commented.

"Probably not." August nearly fell as he attempted to stand and his face went sheet white.

"Are you in pain?" Deven asked.

"I just feel weak." August slumped onto Deven's unmade bed. A bruise was beginning to form over his right eye, where he'd slammed into Night Axe's hard skull.

The person at the door knocked again. Given the destruction of their room, Deven hoped it wasn't housekeeping.

He picked up his knife from where it had fallen and peered through the door's peephole.

Agent Klakow stood there, looking pissed off.

"Hold your ID up," Deven ordered.

"You have to be kidding me." Klakow grimaced.

"Do it!"

"Fine, fine..." Klakow muttered as he fumbled with the identification in his back pocket. Instantly, Deven relaxed. Night Axe might be able to mimic the look and sound of a person, but he wouldn't know one's habits or gestures.

Still, he waited until Agent Klakow held up the badge before opening the door.

Klakow stepped inside and gaped at the disarray. "What have you two been doing in here?"

At his entry, August leaped to his feet, looking stunned. Klakow glared back at August. His eyes caught the bloody mess of August's clothes and remaining particles of glamour, and his haughty expression faltered. "Jesus Christ, what happened to you?"

"Had a visitor," August growled, sitting back down. His body slumped against the wall. "Looked like you, actually. Have you been downstairs in the lobby long?"

"Fuckin' ages. The front desk wouldn't tell me your room number, no matter how many times I asked. I had to call the field office to get the info."

August's eyes closed. "And you came directly from the field office, I presume."

"Of course." Klakow moved to August's side. "You sure you're okay? You look like shit."

"I just got fisted in all the wrong ways."

Klakow grimaced. "You're a perverted fuckhead." Despite his tone, however, he looked concerned. "I'm calling a field team ambulance—"

"Not yet," August interrupted. "We've got a lord of the underworld in the form of a bird who plans to flap back here and finish the job he started five minutes ago." He endeavored to sit up and then gave up, slumping back against the wall. "Deven, you still have your pen?"

Deven reached his hand down the front of his trousers and pulled it out.

Klakow made another face. "You keep *stuff* in there?"

Deven put the pen back in his hair without commenting.

"Would you hand me a clean shirt?" August asked.

Despite not fully unpacking, August had still managed to hang up all his clothes the night before. Deven picked out a dark-colored dress shirt in case blood seeped through the fabric. He also chose a pair of trousers, because it made Deven's eyes hurt interpreting what was his suit and what was leftover glamour residue.

He fetched a wet washcloth and handed it to August. The agent offered him a weak smile. "Thanks." He started undressing and cleaning himself off, moving slowly.

Klakow stared out the window. "You want me to see if we can trace the glamour trail?"

"He'll come back for us, we don't need to look for him," August replied. "What are you here for anyway?"

"Elia in forensics sent me. She ran further tests on the filaments attached to the obsidian particles from Rodriguez's sister's and identified the visual spectrum." He handed August a small card with a barcode on it. "The monster's hidden lair, revealed."

"About fucking time." August's hands still shook and he struggled to button his clean trousers.

Deven found himself staring and looked away. "What about the ambulance?" Deven asked.

"The doctor is next. I'm not a masochist. But I'm tired of being surprised by this bastard. Let's see what he sees, without relying on moody serpents." August finished dressing and, with a bit of exertion, stood and squared his shoulders. His change of clothes improved his appearance. But the bruise darkening his right eye looked garish against his deathly pallor and there was blood in his hair. Still, he winked at Deven. "Let's make some magic, shall we?"

"Oh brother," Klakow groaned.

❧

Over the next hour, Deven developed a new respect for the talents of Irregular agents, if only for their ability to memorize proper procedure.

He never thought bureaucracy had a place in magic, but that was the indissoluble effect of government, it seemed. The Irregulars had converted the supernatural into a set of standard operating procedures.

"Wrong!" August slapped a wire from Klakow's hand. "Damn it, didn't you ever read the *Occult Agency Guidelines*? You can't transfer energy until all safety bindings are in place."

Klakow's hand made a fist, but otherwise he didn't respond. The three of them sat on the floor, gathered around a piece of bone Deven had extracted from his sacred bundle, August's computer, and the wires from August's pocket. They programmed the bar code spectrum into the laptop, wiring the bone to the machine. Blood was needed to seal the spell, but Deven had learned his lesson and didn't volunteer to go first. He nearly laughed at the regimented procedure by which both Klakow and August calmly produced sanitized needles and small plastic receptacles, extracting only a few drops from their fingers.

August handed Deven a clean needle. "Leave your tongue for more pleasant uses."

Klakow shook his head. "You know, Deven, this qualifies as sexual harassment and you can file a complaint."

"Maybe I like it." Deven's face flushed with the admission and he didn't miss how August's eyes snapped to him. Deven jabbed the tip of his finger and let a few drops of blood mingle with the agents'. He accepted a bandage from Klakow.

Definitely less painful than dragging a thorned cord across his tongue.

The blood was collected on a thin slide that had a USB port and fit into his laptop. August rustled around in another of his bags and withdrew a box of small, half-dollar size disks.

"Quartz, you think?" August asked Deven. "Or jade?"

"What?"

"What stone works better for Aztaw magic?"

Deven shrugged. "Jade is everywhere in Aztaw and used in nearly every spell. Obsidian is predominantly for weapons, although it does have reflective properties."

August selected a several small green disks and fed them one by one into his hard drive, burning the spell onto them. Deven found the entire process fascinating. They truly had distilled the ethereal qualities of magic into a universal form.

"Nice gizmos," August mused.

"Housekeeping!" A loud knock at the door startled all three of them. Deven tensed, holding his knife.

"We're busy!" Klakow shouted back. "Come back later!"

"*¿Qué?*"

"*Volver mas tarde,*" August called out. All three of them froze, as if waiting for the door to break down.

After a moment of silence, the woman said, "*Sí, señor,*" and they heard a cart squeak as it rolled away.

Deven felt the tension drain from him. "This is the busiest hotel room I've ever been in."

August still looked panicked, even after the woman had left. "Let's get these on." He fumbled through his belongings once more.

"What are they?" Deven asked.

"Spell projectors. They work with special glasses, adding visual spectrums to what your eyes naturally see." August held a small plastic device, no bigger than a credit card, and slipped one of the green jade disks into a thin slit at the top.

"Put it in your pocket, then put these on," August ordered, handing Deven the device and a pair of sunglasses.

"Why do you carry two projectors?" Klakow asked, shaking his head. He had his own device in his hands and snapped another of the jade disks inside, clipping it to the side of his sunglasses.

"This one's Carlos',s" August said softly, holding a pair of sunglasses in his hands. "He'd left it in my car." August shook his head. "He always left behind the most important equipment."

"Well, he was on vacation," Klakow countered, but there was no bite to the comment.

Deven put on the shades and looked around the room. Nothing noticeably changed at first, although his eye muscles strained as they adjusted. He caught the faint whiff of ozone.

As he turned his head he saw something trailing out the closed window like a maroon streamer. As the image solidified, he saw it was a thicker than ribbon, circular, and it pulsed. It went straight through the closed window and into the room. Liquid surged through it.

Deven moved closer but didn't touch it. The texture looked rubbery. He realized he was looking at a blood vessel, which stretched out down the road as far as he could see.

His eyes followed the artery to August's chest and understood that it was connected to the agent about the same time August did. But August's reaction was quite different.

A look of revulsion crossed August's face and he gripped the artery in both hands and pulled.

"Get this *off* of me!" His hands grappled with the floating artery, yanking. His face went deathly white as he did so, but he didn't stop pulling. "Pull it out!"

August's panicked breaths were shallow as he twisted the blood vessel stretching from his heart.

"Stop—don't tug on it!" Deven gripped August's hands, pinning them down to the carpet. "Just relax. Breathe!"

August's head fell back against the foot of the bed. A sheen of sweat covered his features. "Oh God." He look down at his chest again and shuddered. "I'm fucking attached to him, aren't I?" His arms tensed, but Deven kept hold of his wrists.

"We'll figure this out," Deven told him.

"God," August said again. He licked his lips and swallowed, clearly trying to bring moisture to his dry throat. "This is what happened to Carlos and Bea." His voice was cracked. "They were feeding their blood to Night Axe. They were fucking *sacrifices*."

Klakow had ripped off his glasses and dialed someone on his phone. Deven wanted to examine August's chest and assure himself he wasn't bleeding out, but he was afraid of letting go of August's wrists. "If I look at your chest, will you stop trying to pull yourself free?"

August breathed through clenched teeth but didn't answer.

"You can't rip loose. You could bleed to death," Deven said, sounding far more calm than he actually was. "Night Axe's house power made this connection, so it can also disconnect it. We'll figure out how."

"Disconnect it?"

"House powers change the world around us but can also reverse those changes," Deven said. He wasn't exactly *lying*—he was, however, simplifying, since it would have to be Night Axe himself who would reverse his own spells. Deven didn't think that level of detail would be welcome at this moment. "Until we figure this out, you need to not hurt yourself. All right?"

After a moment, August nodded. Deven slowly let go of August's wrists. August didn't try and grab the artery again.

"I promise we'll cut you loose," Deven said, although he had no idea how he would keep that promise.

Fury rushed through Deven at the thought of Night Axe doing this. It should have been *him* laying there, bleeding into Night Axe's body. He had been Night Axe's target. August had saved Deven and this was what he got in return.

"We'll cut you loose," Deven repeated. He unbuttoned August's shirt.

With the spell projector glasses on, Deven saw how the circular bruise was the location where the artery connected August's body to Night Axe. The rhythmic pulse of August's blood flowed through the semi-transparent surface of the blood vessel, but none leaked, and the flow seemed small enough not to kill August outright.

August grimaced.

"Like it or not, this does give us an advantage," Klakow said. "Now that you are linked to him, we can find him."

August didn't respond. Deven carefully buttoned August's shirt for him.

"We need to find out more about Night Axe's arrival," Deven told Klakow. "We must know how long he's been here, how much time he's had to develop his network of sacrifices."

"Network of sacrifices?"

"Night Axe apparently has replaced killing human victims on sacrificial altars with bleeding them slowly, consuming their blood through a network of these." Deven motioned to the throbbing artery, pumping August's blood out the window and down the street beyond. "But this requires great effort—it must take half the power he harvests to fuel the spell alone. At some point he'd have to have first fueled his mutation with murder. If we can trace how long ago he came here, we can start to estimate how connected he is through the city and understand how hard it'll be to kill him."

Klakow scowled. "Deven, NIAD doesn't condone the killing of individuals, even if they're from fucked-up realms. We police movement and goods but we don't execute—"

"Shut up, Klakow," August said. "You can lecture Deven on the rules later."

Klakow looked ready to argue, but then his expression softened and he knelt beside them, pocketing his phone. "They're waiting for you at the clinic. I'll take you there, then go back to the office and see what I can find out about Night Axe's recent history."

August nodded. When Deven handed him back his sunglasses, August gripped them tightly but didn't put them back on.

Deven and Klakow both helped him stand, although after a few steps he shoved them both off and walked on his own. "I'm not a fucking invalid," August complained.

Deven considered disagreeing but kept his mouth shut as they made their way to the elevators. August's complexion was deathly white and the surges of blood that drained out of the artery were clearly taking their toll. Even though he walked on his own, August leaned against Deven for support and didn't stray far once they reached the lobby.

A large tour group had arrived; the lobby overflowed with loud people wearing even louder clothes. Luggage spilled out to the elevator and created tripping hazards. The moving mass confused Deven and he had to take a deep breath and work to identify individual objects: a fake Grecian pillar, wrapped in plastic ivy; a chubby woman in a pink-striped skirt, watching over a pile of black suitcases; a small, black-and-white-dotted bird, hopping under one of the coffee tables.

Deven blinked. He removed the glasses and stared at the bird, who had attracted the attention of a group of women. They laughed and cooed at the little creature, snapping their fingers at him.

"Stay here. Don't move," Deven ordered. He held his hand against August's chest and pointed at Klakow. He put his glasses back on and slunk to a large potted plant beside the open front of the hotel and hid behind it as he scanned the street.

Over a dozen Montezuma quail, far from their countryside habitat and hopping down the urban core of the city, peered into buildings and chirped as they dodged footfalls and honking cars.

Deven hurried back. August must have known something was wrong by his expression, for his mouth curled into an angry sneer. "Now what?"

"Watchbirds." Deven pointed to the quail inside the building, skittering between furniture.

"Are they Night Axe's?" August asked.

"No. They must belong to whatever lord has them assigned to track Night Axe's movements. If they're here, that means Night Axe has soldiers in the vicinity."

August rolled his eyes. "This is ridiculous." He angrily yanked his phone from his pocket. "Klakow, pull the car around to the service entrance and meet us there."

Klakow nodded and headed out to retrieve the car.

"Why send him alone?" Deven asked.

"I don't want anyone following you. You're the prize, remember? Don't forget it." He started texting furiously, maneuvering through the lobby toward the elevators without looking, as if he knew the place like the back of his hand. "Damn it! Now we're hiding from wildlife."

The staff in the back of the hotel gave them strange looks but didn't stop them as they made a beeline for the service entrance and waited on the curb alongside several employees who appeared to be taking an extended cigarette break. Klakow brought his car around and Deven helped August climb inside, wincing as he shut the passenger door through the floating blood vessel.

As Klakow drove around the corner and past the front of the hotel, Deven noticed watchbirds were everywhere. But they weren't the only thing that caught his eye. As they passed the hotel awning he thought he saw an Aztaw soldier, visible one moment, invisible the next. The soldier reappeared, but as they turned the corner, he disappeared again.

But then the car plunged into the heavy onslaught of downtown traffic, bright signs, and blinding sunlight, and Deven pushed his new sunglasses tight against his face and closed his eyes. The soldier at the hotel would have to wait.

Chapter Eleven

In the basement of the Sanatorio Espanol hospital, Dr. Ramos from the NIAD medical team admitted he lacked experience with invisible, floating, city-wide circulatory systems.

"I'm not severing the artery," Dr. Ramos told August. "The likelihood of you bleeding to death is too great."

"Why would I bleed to death in a hospital?" August complained. "You sever arteries all the time." He looked healthier than he had that morning. After his examination they'd let him shower the blood from his hair and skin and given him fluids to rehydrate. His black eye and damp curls lent him a defeated appearance, but his expression was defiant as he glowered at the doctor.

Dr. Ramos scoffed. "We don't go around chopping off aortas."

"What about heart surgery?"

"I don't do heart surgery," Dr. Ramos insisted. "Besides, we don't even know how this blood vessel is formed. It could connect to multiple systems. Unless absolutely necessary, I can't in good conscience recommend amputating it until we understand it better."

August's mouth curled in an angry sneer. But the fight seemed to abandon him. He slumped against the exam table and limply took his projector back, along with pain tablets and anemia pills, without further argument.

The medical office was deep in the bowels of the hospital, sandwiched between the laundry room and several storage areas, so they had to navigate a labyrinth of squeaky-clean hallways to make their way back up to the hospital proper and outside.

The dry air and sunshine left Deven aching for the darkness of Aztaw, but it seemed to put August in a better mood.

"At least it's a beautiful day," he commented. He pulled on his glasses and frowned down at the blood vessel that floated through the air from his chest.

Deven still wore the sunglasses, finding them not only helpful in seeing Night Axe's realm but also in coping with the agonizing brightness of the city.

They were in a much nicer neighborhood than Beatriz Rodriguez's home, with a grass median separating lanes of traffic and well-tended, tree-shaded sidewalks lining the curb. The multistoried houses had elegant, decorative wooden garage doors.

They both followed the line August's artery formed as it floated down the center of the street and turned a corner up ahead.

"We could follow it, see where it leads," Deven suggested.

August shoved his hands in his pockets and started walking. "We can't confront him until we have a method of defeating him." As they walked, August's artery retreated into his body, shrinking as he closed the distance between him and his parasitic attachment, lengthening as he walked the other way. It floated through the heads of a cheerful-looking young couple they passed on the street, and for a moment it looked as though August would be sick.

He ripped his glasses off and shoved them in his pocket, wincing at the sunlight.

"Don't you want to see?" Deven asked. He couldn't imagine voluntarily giving up an advantage.

August grimaced. "You have them on. Give me a heads up if you see someone walking around with a shin bone for a foot."

"But—"

"Deven, I can't look at it right now." August looked queasy. "*Feeling* it is bad enough."

"You sure you want to walk?" Deven asked. He almost placed his hand on August's back in support, but it seemed too intimate a gesture. He kept his hands rigidly at his sides.

August nodded. "The safe house is only a mile up the road and I'm sick of Klakow's company."

Once the director of the Mexico field office had discovered August had been injured the same way Carlos had, she'd ordered him to a division safe house for the duration of the investigation into Rodriguez's murder.

"What makes this house so secure?" Deven asked.

"I haven't stayed in Mexico's, but the safe house in San Francisco has wards and masking locks, as well as top-of-the-line digital security systems. There's one official entry and it's guarded by trained personnel twenty-four hours a day."

Deven slammed to a halt.

In front of him, August's artery branched off in two distinct directions.

August tensed beside him. "What is it?"

"Put your glasses on," Deven said.

August pulled them out of his pocket and put them on.

"Following this to Night Axe may not be as easy as we thought," Deven said.

August clenched and unclenched his jaw but continued forward. A block later it happened again; another Y in the circulatory system led in opposing directions, but this time they saw where the blood vessel terminated.

It ended in the body of a middle-aged woman, who was tending a narrow strip of garden behind a black wrought-iron fence in front of a large, showy house. As she knelt on her lawn she wheezed and it was clear by her ashen complexion and the weak pulses of blood through the blood vessel that her health was frail. August looked at the woman with a stricken expression.

The woman eyed the two of them suspiciously. They started walking again.

"I have to help her," August said quietly.

"We will. Killing Night Axe will free her."

"You don't know that. What if killing Night Axe kills all his sacrifices?" August clenched his jaw. "We have to find out how many there are. Are we talking six people? Six hundred? We need to monitor them when we confront Night Axe." Suddenly August changed direction, following the thick branch of his artery east.

Deven hurried to follow. "What about checking in at the safe house?"

"That can wait. Come on!"

They spent the rest of the afternoon following trail after trail of blood vessels, connecting one sacrifice to the next. Sometimes it was difficult; the arteries traversed direct routes, which often led through structures. They had to circle buildings until they found the exit point and could continue their hunt. Other times they couldn't tell one branch of the circulatory system from another. Sometimes it thickened, wide as a football and branching off half a dozen times; some were thin ribbons of rubbery cord, linked to sickly bodies. The vessels stretched for miles, claiming victims all over the massive city.

There didn't seem to be any pattern to the sacrifices. They saw several young men; then they'd turn a corner to find an artery terminate in the soft side of an infant. Some victims were out of sight, as the vessel led into locked apartment complexes or behind closed office doors. But it was unavoidably apparent that Carlos and Beatriz had not been Night Axe's first or last victims.

"Why do you think Night Axe had Carlos and Beatriz killed?" Deven asked. They'd stopped for lunch and to rest their legs, having walked all over the city. August had his glasses perched up on his head, held in place by his thick black hair.

August attacked his eggs ferociously. As he ate, the color of the blood in his artery seemed to enrich, as if Night Axe was sucking the nutrients straight from his body. Deven didn't relay this to August.

"I think once Carlos realized they both shared the same strange mark, he decided to investigate," August said. "Unlike the rest of these citizens, Carlos had the tools to research it, and Bea knew the vision serpent spell."

"So Night Axe must have realized they were getting too close and sent his tzimimi after them."

August nodded. Despite eating, he remained pale. Deven didn't think it was a good idea for him to continue wandering the city on foot.

"You should return to the safe house and rest," he told August. "As long as we give the local agents the jade disk they can use a projector to follow Night Axe's circulatory network, yes?"

"But it isn't their investigation. It's mine."

"And you look ready to fall over." Deven feared he'd have to argue further, but to his relief August nodded, slumping against the back of his seat, his eyes heavy.

"Yeah, I'm beat." August wiped his mouth with a paper napkin. "If we could just rest for an hour or so—"

"Not me."

"What?"

"I need to return to El Angel Hotel."

"Bad idea. Remember the watchbirds? You'd be a fool to go back. Besides, all our stuff's already moved to the safe house."

"There's someone there I need to speak with," Deven said.

"Who?"

"An Aztaw soldier standing guard at the entrance."

"What?"

"I think I know who it is and he may help us find a way to beat Night Axe. Even if he doesn't know himself, he's still well-connected in Aztaw."

"And why do you think he's going to help you?"

Deven grinned. "Because if he doesn't, I'm going to kill him."

"This is a stupid idea, Deven."

"You have a better one?"

August ground his teeth. "The safe house is for both of us. Don't forget it's your little pen the bastard is after, not just my blood."

"I won't stick around long enough for Night Axe to discover me. I need to talk to the soldier."

August's expression remained dark.

"Look, I'm being paid to help you, right?" Deven laid his fingers on August's hand. August's skin was colder than Deven's, but it still felt marvelous, just that little human contact, so much more comforting than the ossified touch of an Aztaw. "I can't help you tucked up in the safe house. But I can use my connections and get some answers."

"Your 'connections' want you dead." August stared out the restaurant's open window. "I don't want anything to happen to you."

"I can take care of myself." Deven smiled. "Besides, if it really is the soldier I'm expecting, he's more afraid of me than I am of him."

August turned his hand over, so Deven's fingers rested in his palm. "Oh yeah? Why's that?"

"Because I killed all four of his sons."

August shook his head. "I told you. Assassins are the worst." But his fingers closed on Deven's, holding his hand.

He didn't let go, even when the check arrived.

Chapter Twelve

Outside El Angel Hotel, Deven paid his taxi driver with the cash August had shoved in his pocket before they had parted ways at the safe house. As the taxi pulled away, Deven glanced around. Few watchbirds remained, and those on the street were scattered apart, scratching at a trail that had gone cold.

Deven scanned the environment for any signs of Night Axe's presence, but the glasses revealed nothing that wasn't visible in the natural world. The flickering Aztaw he'd seen beside the revolving door had apparently gone.

Deven leaned against the opposite wall. He wished he could twirl a knife through his fingers, something to occupy his hands, but that would make him look even more conspicuous. Luckily, a large group of American tourists exited the building, standing on the sidewalk as they debated dinner options. Deven maneuvered himself into their midst.

Moments later, the Aztaw soldier appeared from thin air. He stood by the entrance of the hotel and spun around, taking in his surroundings. He wasn't dressed in formal combat garb and he'd removed his large traditional headdress in lieu of a mismatch of human clothing. He wore an oversized dark blue sweatshirt with the hood pulled tightly over his paper-thin flesh, hiding his glowing skull. From the depths of the hoodie, however, his eyeballs rolled fiercely and his hands ended in skeletal joints. He gripped a knife in each hand.

His trousers were odd, a faded brown corduroy that belonged in another century. The color was atrocious in the harsh sunlight of the city.

None of the pedestrians seemed to notice the soldier's sudden appearance, ugly attire, or skeletal form. Deven removed his glasses, but he could still see the soldier, which meant the other people could if they bothered to look.

But those around him avoided looking at that corner entirely, and Deven realized the Aztaw must be wearing an icon enchanted with an anonymity spell, something used by soldiers that didn't make them invisible, only unremarkable. Nothing about the soldier's appearance attracted attention—rather his presence was completely unremarkable, something the human eye instinctively glanced over and disregarded.

And before anyone could remark on the soldier, he was gone, vanishing once more into thin air.

Deven threaded through the tourists to stand closer, smiling to himself. He'd recognize the movements of his greatest adversaries anywhere, regardless of their chosen disguise.

He pulled the pen from behind his ear and hunched over in the crowd to scribble on his open palm. The calendars closest to this point were interesting; the soldier was in one of the fastest cycles he'd ever seen. Clearly the calendar had been chosen for location, not for convenience, because days flew by there, realigning every thirty seconds for a period of five seconds before moving to the next day. Deven had only a few more seconds before the realms would once again align and the soldier would breach through.

The soldier flickered back into existence. Deven gripped him by the sweatshirt and hurled him into the street. Cars honked and several drivers swore at the soldier, who rushed to the opposite side of the road in terror. He'd dropped one of his knives in the middle of the road.

Stupid, Deven thought.

Deven waited for a gap in the traffic before crossing after the Aztaw. As he closed in, the soldier's eyes widened and he raised his knife.

"*Hello, Fight Arm,*" Deven said in Aztawi. He held his own knife close to his body. Unlike the soldier, Deven had no distraction spell to encase him. "Shall we go for a stroll?"

"*Human Jaguar.*" Fight Arm's mouth curled into a snarl. "*I'm not surprised this was your work.*"

Deven didn't know what he was talking about, but he wasn't about to admit that. "*Tell Lord Knife I said hi. I can't decide if I'm more surprised you're still alive or that you've been demoted to the position of a spy.*"

Fight Arm growled and moved closer. Deven dropped his hand onto his blade and closed the distance.

At once, Fight Arm put his knife into a hilt at his belt and held up his empty hands. "*I did not come to fight, only to observe.*"

"*That's why you're armed?*"

"*I wasn't sure who I'd find.*"

"*You found me.*" Several people had stopped to watch them. One gawked, open-mouthed, at the gaping dark hole where Fight Arm's face was supposed to be. Deven's conversation with Fight Arm damaged his illusion. "*We must walk.*" He turned and strode toward the nearby park.

After a moment's hesitation, Fight Arm followed. Deven's back crawled with the sensation of having his enemy behind him, but they both knew who would win a knife fight, and Fight Arm, despite his animosity, seemed unwilling to die to prove Deven right.

"*Where did you find that portal?*" Deven asked.

"*Dark corner of reeds where Lord Black Dog once had his house.*"

"*Lord Black Dog is dead?*" Deven asked, surprised. He thought he'd be one who'd survive until the end.

Fight Arm inclined his head briefly in response, but his expression was still one of rage. There was too much bad blood between them to engage in idle conversation, no matter how events had changed their roles.

There was a remarkable stink to Fight Arm's human clothing, suggesting endless hours of being lived in. What had been one day in the natural world would have taken weeks of Fight Arm's life.

"*Lingering in that gate was a waste of your talents,*" Deven commented, and he meant it. Lord Knife had other, lesser vassals —why send one of his best fighters?

"*Not all of us have the power to choose when and where we appear.*" Fight Arm eyed Deven's pen almost hungrily.

Deven resisted the urge to pocket it. "*I've a message for your lord.*"

"*My lord wants to hear nothing about you other than you're dead.*"

The walk up Paseo de la Reforma led to a large expanse of parkland in the center of the city. They passed by the Museum of Modern Art and Deven steered toward a park bench, where he sat down, keeping Fight Arm in his peripheral vision.

After a moment's hesitation, Fight Arm sat beside him on the bench. "*Lord Knife sent me to discover your intentions in Aztaw.*"

"*I have no intentions. I left.*"

"*Then why did you kill Lord Knife's watchbirds?*"

Deven suddenly understood why Fight Arm had been summoned. "*You think it was me that did that?*"

"*They are trained to follow lords. Only you have a house power here.*"

"*Not only me. Night Axe has returned.*"

Fight Arm jerked back. "*Who says this?*"

"*I say it. I've seen him. Lord Knife's birds have seen him too, which is why they're dead.*"

Fight Arm sat silently as he processed this. The park was busy, but few paid them notice. Deven noticed something streaming out of the corner of his eye and watched as a teenage girl entered the museum, a thin ribbon of artery trailing out her back. Deven thought how she was consequently connected to August; if the purpose and effect hadn't been so nefarious, the concept was almost poetic.

"*The birds would not follow him,*" Fight Arm said slowly, as if unwilling to believe his own words. "*Night Axe is only legend to the birds.*"

"*They were not following me,*" Deven repeated. "*You need to return home and warn your lord of Night Axe's impending arrival. I'm the least of your concerns.*"

But Fight Arm snarled. "*Give us your house power and I'll believe it.*"

"*No. You know what'll happen if you bring it back down there.*"

"*We can't win this war without the house powers.*"

"*You've lost the war already. I'm surprised any lords are left.*" Deven shook his head. "*And all of Aztaw is like an unprotected child now that the Lord of Hurricanes is at your door. He's fueling himself on live sacrifices—people walking around, living and breathing, feeding him blood directly from their own bodies. He's coming for Aztaw next. And with only half a dozen lords alive and fewer house powers, you'll all be destroyed.*"

Fight Arm said nothing. Deven knew he was considering his words and he found himself grateful Lord Knife had sent him rather than one of his other vassals. Fight Arm could be trusted to think for himself.

At last Fight Arm spoke. "*How did Night Axe escape his prison in the realm of light?*"

"*I don't know,*" Deven admitted.

"*Only Lord Jaguar could have done that,*" Fight Arm said. "*Lord Jaguar or his pathetic human vassal.*"

"*It wasn't me, and Lord Jaguar is dead,*" Deven replied. "*I need to know what the lords used to weaken Night Axe.*"

"*Why? What is your role in this?*"

"*I came to help. I can track and kill Night Axe before he reaches Aztaw.*"

"*You will fail.*"

"*Better I try here, where he's weaker, than in Aztaw, where he'll have his full strength.*"

"*Why would you help us, revolting human?*"

"*Aztaw's still my home.*" Deven swallowed, feeling a wave of nostalgia crest over him. "*I don't want to see it destroyed. I fled only to keep my promise to my lord.*"

"*Lord Jaguar was a worthy adversary,*" Fight Arm said quietly. Deven didn't miss the insult in his own name's omission, but he didn't feel it. He was suddenly too grateful to be sitting with someone who knew Lord Jaguar, even if it was in the role of antagonist.

Deven's heart hurt as he realized he had more in common with the opponent he'd been at war with since his childhood than any of the passersby in the park. Loneliness and regret filled him.

"*The more you tell me how to defeat Night Axe, the more likely my chances I'll succeed,*" Deven said.

Fight Arm hesitated.

Deven sighed. "*I'm your enemy, offering to risk my life to defeat a greater threat. Helping me helps you. How did the lords defeat Night Axe and send him to the realm of light?*"

"*They poisoned him,*" Fight Arm said.

"*How?*"

"*Night Axe needs sacrificial human blood to fuel his manipulations. Without it he can no longer transform. If you poison the blood he uses, he will weaken enough that you can destroy him.*"

"*What kind of poison?*"

"*It was a concoction Lord Crane created. That is all I know.*"

Deven felt a surge of hope. NIAD's advanced technology had to be able to recreate whatever concoction the lords had created thousands of years ago.

"*I'll find out what I can about the poison and how they administered it and report back to you. In exchange for your house power.*"

Deven shook his head. "*I give it to you, the rebels will have it within weeks, and it will be broken, just like your lord's staff.*"

"*These destructions are terrible crimes.*" Fight Arm made a fist. "*We have lost time, our history. There is nothing of meaning in Aztaw anymore.*"

Deven felt a strange bond to Fight Arm. They were both soldiers of an older war, a time forgotten by the fighters of newer battles. They were remnants of a culture that no longer existed.

"*Lord Jaguar's palace...*" Deven hesitated. "*Is it still standing?*"

"*Yes. Despite the war, your lord's house is still intact.*"

Relief flooded Deven as well as a sudden, aching desire to return. But then he noted the dark look in his enemy's eyes.

"*And Lord Knife's palace?*" Deven asked.

"*Destroyed, like the others,*" Fight Arm said. "*Curious, isn't it?*"

Not really, Deven thought. The rebels only had interest in lords that were still alive. Lord Jaguar's palace was a mausoleum now, an empty shell harboring the memories of a dead lord and a missing house power.

"*I miss the old war,*" Fight Arm said, echoing Deven's earlier sentiment.

Deven nodded. "*But there's no point dwelling on the past. If we can't stop Night Axe, Aztaw has a very ugly future.*"

Fight Arm glanced around. "*He's more powerful in darkness and will detect my presence. I'll meet you at the fast gate tomorrow at dawn and tell you what I've learned.*"

"*Thank you.*"

Fight Arm grimaced. "*Don't thank me, repulsive human. As soon as Night Axe is gone, you're next.*"

"*Of course.*" Deven smiled, however, knowing the chances of Fight Arm outwitting him, especially here, were slim.

Deven watched Fight Arm attempt and fail to orient himself in the strange day-lit city. He looked for the hotel but seemed unwilling to admit being lost to his foe.

Deven moved to the paved sidewalk and started drawing with his pen. Weakness shuddered through him as he wrote each glyph, and the pen lightened and grew colder. Several passing pedestrians gathered to watch, as if he were an artist, but moved on once they had dismissed his simplistic, scrawled imagery.

He finished all but the last icon of the gate. Fight Arm stepped inside. He tilted his head slightly.

"*You could write me anywhere.*"

"*Yes.*" Deven had his pen poised to draw the last image. "*But I need your help, almost as much as you need mine.*"

"*I'll return at dawn, at the fast gate.*" Fight Arm hesitated for a moment, then jutted out his jawbone in a soldier's salute. It looked oddly informal when gestured by someone in a hoodie and corduroys, but its implication was still powerful. Despite years of animosity, the damage Deven had done to Fight Arm's family, or the four-inch scar on Deven's back from Fight Arm's blade, there was a temporary peace between them.

"*Age well,*" Deven said. He drew the last symbol, a spear. Light seared upwards from the ground. A couple walking by gasped and stared, but then Fight Arm was gone, dropping in his ancient form into the underworld from which he came.

Chapter Thirteen

Returning to the safe house took longer than Deven had intended. Although he'd learned Spanish from his mother, his reading skills were paltry at best and he spoke at the level of a child. He misdirected his taxi driver and ended up being dropped off at the Tecnología Educativa Galileo instead of Galileo Street, in a different part of town. His phone had long since died without recharging and he didn't have the local Irregulars' office number anywhere else.

He couldn't find another empty taxi so he started walking, asking after Calle Galileo and being directed in a vague, northerly direction.

The endless traffic, colorful buildings, graffiti, and billboards merged with the noises and subway smells to make a chaos that gave him a headache and hurt his eyes even through the sunglasses. The walk was the second long trek of the day and nearly five miles. He felt exhausted from the simple effort of distinguishing street signs from advertisements.

A sense of displacement filled him as he walked, worse even than those first disorienting weeks on San Juan Island. Fight Arm was part of a life he'd left, and the fact that Deven had spoken with him and would see him again filled him with a nervous grief that summed up his suffering since leaving Aztaw.

After all, when he'd first left, he'd fled for his life. But within a hesitant truce between himself and Lord Knife lurked the possibility of return, as mad as the idea was. He knew it'd still be dangerous—even if he managed to ally himself with Lord Knife's dynasty, there were rebels to fight and other lords to conquer—but the comfort of the known tugged at his gut, an unpleasant but undeniable urge, destructive and powerful in nature.

In the daily hour of television prescribed to him by his therapist, Deven once watched a show on addicts, fascinated and confused by why a person would consistently and consensually take something that made them violently ill and ruined their life. But how was that different than this urge? Aztaw was a living hell, he was friendless there, and still he longed for its hot familiarity. He wanted to be back where things were logical—where his eyes didn't hurt all the time, where people didn't expect him to say the right thing. Back where he had a purpose and had known how to do it.

Who was he kidding, anyway? Replacing his knives for freeze balls wouldn't change Deven's nature. He'd been raised to kill the enemies of those he was allied with. That was all he knew. How could anyone expect someone as fucked up as him to grow accustomed to a peaceful life? It was hopeless. And Deven only disappointed those around him by allowing them to cling to the belief he could someday be retrained into a proper human being.

By the time he approached the well-enforced gates of the safe house he'd made up his mind. He would help August and kill Night Axe, secure Lord Jaguar's house power somewhere here in the natural world where it would remain protected from Aztaw revolutionaries, and return home. It would leave him more vulnerable—once again he would be a guardian without a house power, a target for Aztaw soldiers. But he would also no longer be the threat the other lords perceived him to be with his easily fueled house power and he would be keeping the promise he had made to his lord. He would never betray that promise—but he could no longer pretend to be normal.

The safe house blended in with the well-fortified luxury mansions and embassies that lined the shady streets of the Polanco neighborhood, but there was a definite air of impenetrability to the structure. The guard at the house carefully examined Deven's identification before allowing him past the first gate.

At a second gate he was examined with a strobe light he imagined was similar to August's flashlight. After passing that test, he waited as the burly guard dismantled wards and magical shields. By the time the guard finally unbolted the front door and Deven stepped into the light and spacious living room, he was emotionally and physically spent. His feet ached; his heart felt like a gaping wound in his chest.

"You okay?"

Deven spun, shocked he'd been taken by surprise. Agent August's ability to sneak up on him was another sign of his exhaustion.

August's naturally pale coloring was white as death and the dark bruise on his right eye looked nearly black against his skin. He was clearly sicker than he'd been when Deven had left. Still, his expression lifted a little as he offered Deven a tired smile.

"You can take the glasses off," August told him. "They have a disk at the front and Night Axe will be spotted if he tries to enter."

Deven folded the glasses and put them carefully in his pocket. "You look tired."

August shrugged. "It's hard to sleep when you feel like part of you is being sucked away."

Deven didn't like the anxious look in August's eyes so he changed the subject. "Did the local agents find other sacrifices?"

August nodded. "Ortega and Zardo located twenty-nine people so far who're attached to Night Axe."

"Why don't they trace the network to Night Axe and drop a bomb on his lair?"

August snorted. "Nice idea. Unfortunately there's this thing about innocent casualties that the agency tends to frown upon."

"Right, simply killing him would be too easy, wouldn't it?" Deven heard the fatigue in his own voice. Obviously so did August. He gripped Deven's arm and led him to a plush cream-colored sofa and urged him to sit down. Deven collapsed back, sighing as his body sank into the cushions. August sat close beside him.

The room was expansive, the ceiling two floors up with wood fans lazily stirring the air. The room and all its furnishings were exclusively white, the only color coming from the bright red area rug under a white, glass-topped coffee table.

Deven leaned his head back, staring up at the fans. Only the occasional chirp of the security system broke the silence of the house.

"Is anyone else staying here?" he asked.

"Other than night staff, no. You're free to molest me without witnesses." August smirked at his innuendo, but the obvious exhaustion in the agent's eyes belayed any hope that he might have been serious.

"What did you find out from the Aztaw?" August asked.

"He'll discover what he can about Night Axe's vulnerabilities and meet me at dawn. He's confident we can poison him, making him weak enough to subdue."

"Good." August nodded. "I'm coming with you."

Deven frowned. "You don't look up to it."

"I'll be fine. I slept a little and dinner will revive me. Speaking of which, I went ahead and ordered something for you."

"What a surprise." Deven sank lower into the couch and closed his eyes. August said nothing for a bit and Deven had nearly drifted off to sleep when he felt August's fingers touch his shoulder.

"What did he say to you?"

"Who?"

"Your contact."

"I told you." Deven kept his eyes clamped shut, afraid his tumultuous thoughts would show, so close to the surface.

"He said something that's upset you. You're tense and unhappy."

Deven cracked open an eyelid. "I'm hunting the Aztaw bogeyman armed with two knives and aided by an injured asshole of an Irregulars agent. Why should I be happy?"

August snorted. "I'm not that much of an asshole."

"Yes you are."

"You like me anyway." August closed his own eyes and slid down to match Deven's height on the couch. His long legs sprawled out in front of him, limp.

Deven decided not to answer that. He didn't need to complicate matters with his feelings about August.

"You want to return to Aztaw." August said it; it wasn't a question.

Deven opened his eyes. "What does it matter to you? If I finish the job I've been paid for, I can do whatever I like."

"Of course." August clenched his jaw. "But you're making a mistake."

"You don't know what it's like," Deven said.

August scowled. "What? Being lonely? Feeling out of place? Not being able to relate to anyone around you? Welcome to the fucking Irregulars club, Deven. The difference is that here you have people who will help you. Friends in the division who understand that isolation. Occasionally even lovers." Something dark crossed August's eyes, but he blinked and cleared his expression before Deven could read more into it.

"You left Aztaw because everyone was trying to kill you," August continued. "You think that's changed?"

"I left Aztaw to keep a promise to my lord. If I preserve his house power here I can return."

"And serve what cause? Show your affection to whom?"

Deven opened his mouth to speak, but someone coughed in the doorway and both he and August turned to look over the back of the sofa.

One of the front security guards stood there, holding two plastic bags of takeout. "You order this, Agent?"

"Yeah, thanks." August winced as he stood but walked straight-backed, offering no hint of weakness. He took the bags from the guard and set up their meal on the coffee table.

Deven watched this little domestic routine, his throat feeling thick.

He pulled the pen from his hair and stared at its intricate carvings. He had not necessarily been happy back when he'd served Lord Jaguar, but he'd known who he was at least.

"Here." August's voice was gruff and he shoved a paper plate onto Deven's lap with no finesse. Deven returned the pen behind his ear and steadied the plate on his knees. The food looked unfamiliar—and to his surprise, it was cold.

"Eat up," August ordered. He dug into his own meal, which steamed with heat and was wrapped in corn husks.

Deven had to hold the soft, folded taco in two hands. It was stuffed with diced vegetables and what looked like seafood and a creamy sauce. He had no expectations, so when he bit into the sour, fatty, cool creaminess of the seafood ceviche he was startled by the complex flavors and textures. His mouth watered and he instantly craved more, stifling a groan of delight as he bit into avocado that mingled with the lime and onion and snapper so perfectly Deven thought he was in heaven.

He polished off the meal with hardly a breath between bites, and when he was done, he turned to see August had barely started eating, his gaze focused on Deven, eyes glinting with mirth.

"What?" Deven asked, clearing his throat. Some juices from the taco stained his fingers and he licked them clean.

August smiled but didn't say anything. A contentment sank through Deven's tired bones as he leaned back against the couch and relaxed into his calorie high. He watched August's long, beautiful fingers deftly manipulate the husk wrapping his tamale. He made mundane gestures look elegant.

His fondness for August must have shown, because August stopped his gestures and gave him an open, curious look. The two stared at each other for a long moment, and something warm and tremulous tugged at Deven's heart, made him flush with contentment.

Just this, he thought. *Maybe this could be enough.*

August reached out and tucked a loose strand of hair behind Deven's ear. The touch vibrated through Deven's body, sharp and shocking as a wound and almost equally as painful in its brevity.

August turned back to his dinner and Deven glanced at his empty plate, wishing there was more. He might even consider abandoning his new plan to ally with Lord Knife for the prospect of a second ceviche taco in his future.

This shows why people become obsessed with food, he thought, and then he corrected himself.

More likely, this showed that he wasn't entirely convinced he wanted to return, if it took only a taco to convince him otherwise.

❧

Deven slept solidly for several hours, luxuriating in the secure setting and the privacy of his own room for the first time since he'd arrived in Mexico. He charged his phone and its alarm awoke him an hour before sunrise.

He expected he'd have to rouse Agent August so he was surprised to find him awake, dressed impeccably as ever in a pressed suit. He sat at the kitchen table with a steaming cup of coffee, flipping through screens on his phone, the odd greenish tone of the screen contributing a ghastly shade to his already pale face.

"Trouble sleeping?" Deven asked, yawning. He shuffled into the dark kitchen. Only a dim light over the oven was turned on.

"It's uncomfortable," August admitted, and Deven didn't need to ask what "it" was.

"You sure you feel strong enough to meet with Fight Arm?"

"Is that his name?" August smirked, but there was no warmth to it. "I'm fine. 72 is waiting outside."

"Don't the starys ever sleep?"

"They have a hibernation schedule." August refilled his coffee and handed a cup to Deven.

"Thanks."

"Stay alert," August ordered.

It was still dark outside and Deven nervously fiddled with the knife at his belt. He wondered what Lord Knife's reaction had been to the news of Night Axe's return and Deven's presence. He couldn't imagine what Aztaw was like now—the revolution had radically changed the place in only a few years. For all he knew, every dynasty seat could have burned to the ground, the villages eradicated, the fields left untended.

Or something more positive could have sprung up in the place of destruction, as August would have hoped, although what such a reality would look like was unimaginable to Deven. Aztaw had always been endless dark, punctuated with grand palaces for the lords, pyramids of sacrifice, and the frightening tombs where humans waited to be bled. With all those elements under siege, Deven suspected anything could rise up and take its place.

72 parked his black sedan behind El Angel Hotel. Although Deven's spectrum-enhanced sunglasses altered the colors of the world around him, he still saw pink in the sky as daylight broke. A murky smog hovered over the city. August and Deven passed once more through the service entrance toward the lobby.

Inside the hotel, all was quiet. A solitary, bleary-eyed woman attended the front desk, watching a *telenovela* with the subtitles turned on and the sound turned off. She offered a disingenuous smile as they crossed to the front doors.

There were no watchbirds. There were no people. At that hour only a few cars passed by, the rest of the city sunk in sleepy early morning silence.

They stepped through the revolving hotel doors. Deven turned and recognized Fight Arm as four tzimimi lowered torches to his trussed-up body and set him afire.

Chapter Fourteen

Fight Arm's screams shattered the serenity of the morning. His body whooshed, covered in accelerant. He was bound in traditional Aztaw funerary style in a squatting position, rope binding his thighs and arms tied behind him so he was unable to flail.

Deven rushed forward. He threw one knife at the nearest flying spirit, but all four of them took flight, talons clenching at the morning air as they streaked into the dawn.

Deven tried to help Fight Arm, who shrieked as he struggled. Heat rolled over Deven's body, and August grabbed him by the shirt and wrenched him back. It was already too late. With a last howl Fight Arm's efforts ceased and the flames charred his paper-thin translucent skin to ash.

"My God! I call police!" cried the hotel lobby clerk, breathless from her run outside.

"I'm with the police," August told her, flashing his Irregulars badge. Deven hovered helplessly over Fight Arm's burning corpse, the glow of his bones hidden under the flames and blackening ash. Deven glanced up, but the tzimimi were long gone. He saw no signs of any of Night Axe's minions, and it looked as though nothing remained of what Fight Arm might have brought with him to their meeting. The only unnatural presence he could detect with his sunglasses was the thin ribbon of blood coursing out of August's body and hovering down the road.

"Go back inside!" Deven heard August yell. He saw the hotel clerk rush indoors, fearful. August mumbled something under his breath, then came to Deven's side.

"She's going to call the cops."

"Didn't like your badge?"

"Didn't like my attitude." He glanced upward, his sunglasses reflecting the early light. "Did you see where they went?"

"The tzimimi? It doesn't matter." Deven leaned down and picked up his knife.

"We have to fucking capture them," August growled. Deven remembered that August still held them accountable for Carlos's death.

"They'll no longer be a threat once we get Night Axe," Deven assured him. He glanced back at the clerk. "Should we stop her from calling?"

August was already texting furiously on his phone. "Too late. I have to preempt the police force. Damn it!"

Deven kicked through the smoldering remains, hoping some piece of Fight Arm was left to save. He found his enemy's jade necklace and lifted it carefully with the toe of his boot, separating it from the wreckage. He glanced at the glyphs carved on the jade. It was covered in a distraction spell, the one that had been keeping him unnoticeable. Deven pocketed it, fury throbbing through him. Fight Arm and Deven had spent thirteen years fighting for their lords and had survived war, assassination attempts, famine, and a brutal revolution. For Fight Arm to have died on a simple fact-finding mission on Deven's behalf made Deven sick to his stomach. But he needed a clear head. He would kill Night Axe, at all costs. He didn't care about the official Irregulars policy.

Given the lack of traffic at that hour, the Irregulars' clean-up team arrived quickly and consoled the hotel clerk with their more authentic-looking Mexico City police identification. August spoke with one of them at great length, leaving Deven crouched beside the smoking remains of his nemesis, feeling a greater sense of loss than he should have, given the situation.

On the drive back to the embassy, Deven said, "There's another way we could attempt to weaken Night Axe. We could bleed him."

August seemed distracted. It took a few seconds for him to focus his attention on Deven. He scowled. "What?"

"Night Axe. If we bleed him out, he'll lose the blood he needs to fuel his transformation house power."

"Bleed him? How?"

"We cut loose the other sacrifices. Losing blood from twenty-nine severed arteries would weaken him. Then we use the connection to you to hunt him down and behead him."

August looked disgusted. "Are you fucking nuts?"

"It would work, August."

"No. I'm not sacrificing two *dozen* civilians, Deven. Think for a minute!"

August turned back to the window, angry. Deven swallowed, realizing he'd fucked up again. In a vague sense he understood August's protests, but honestly, those other people were strangers, and meaningless, just casualties of a war.

But August was worth saving.

At the embassy August was immediately called into the office of a woman who looked as finely dressed as August and equally as pissed off. Deven made to follow, but the woman in the pinstripe suit held out her hand and stopped him.

"No. This is a private conversation, no consultants." She slammed the door. Deven noticed the window was marked Director's Office and realized that, indirectly this woman had hired him. He wondered if he should thank the person who gave him a job. He doubted the traditional Aztaw gift of a pulsing human heart would be welcome, but honestly, he had no idea what kinds of gifts were exchanged in the natural world, and other than distant memories of Legos and toy trucks for Christmas before his mother died, he hadn't received any gifts except from Lord Jaguar.

Deven wandered the halls of the NIAD branch office, unsure how to occupy himself. Across from the director's office he found a staff kitchen and ate several sticky pastries, putting one aside for August. He then considered visiting the armory but assumed the pixie would be as welcoming as the director.

A tired-looking older agent with an attractive profile and impressively shiny white teeth entered the kitchen and watched Deven for a few moments. He had a trim, graying moustache and pepper-gray hair. He didn't wear a suit, but the badge clipped to his belt showed he was also an agent.

"You the Aztaw consultant?" the man asked, his accent thick.

"Yes."

The man poured out two cups of thick black coffee. He offered one to Deven. "I'm Agent Rafael Ortega."

Deven took the coffee. "Thank you." It tasted like burned tar and he had to grimace a smile to stop from spitting it out. "You located the other sacrifices?"

Agent Ortega nodded. "Zardo's bringing them to the hospital now."

"Won't that alert Night Axe that we're on to him?"

Ortega shrugged. "Agent August texted me. He seemed worried something might happen to them. He wants them all monitored until the investigation closes."

Fear curled inside Deven. He suspected it had been his threat against the others that made August act to protect them, which meant he didn't trust Deven not to act without permission. Deven was surprised how much the idea that August didn't trust him hurt.

"What did you tell them to get them to come with you?" Deven asked.

"They all think they've been poisoned by a toxin."

Deven nearly asked another question when the director's door opened and August stormed out, for once a little color showing on his cheeks. He looked ready to commit murder. He glanced around and zeroed in on Ortega.

"You got them all?" August barked.

Ortega nodded. "Thirty-six total. A few have to be pulled from job sites, but otherwise, yeah, they'll all be tucked up safe and sound by this afternoon."

"Where the fuck is Klakow?"

"He was in the library last I saw him."

August started down the hall but suddenly swayed and nearly crashed into the wall. Deven rushed to his side. August immediately righted himself.

"I'm fine!" he snapped, but he didn't look it. His lips were almost blue.

"You're going to pass out," Deven said.

"No. I just can't make sudden movements." The fingers of his right hand trailed along the wall for support.

Deven and Ortega both watched him slowly make his way. Ortega sipped his coffee and smacked his lips. "That man is going to fall down."

"I'll keep an eye on him," Deven promised.

The library was nothing more than three computers clustered around a printer and mountains of files. Clearly at one point someone had attempted to organize things but gave up halfway through, because some of the contents were color coded to match file cabinets, but other piles remained unsorted.

Klakow looked small in the middle of it, sweating despite the air conditioning and clearly out of his comfort zone.

He shoved an open, crumpled city map toward August. “Here. The circles were drawn by Zardo. It shows where the sacrifices were located.”

“What did you find out about Night Axe?”

“Not much. There isn’t any mention of him, although older references mention sightings of Tezcatlipoca, an Aztec god who was missing a foot. Thirteen years ago, eight bodies were found with their throats cut outside this building,” he said, pointing to one spot, “and another ten over here.” Klakow turned to Deven. “What did you find out from your Aztaw contact?”

“He’s dead.”

Klakow’s eyes widened. “How?”

“Burned by Night Axe’s minions.”

“Before he could tell you anything?” Klakow asked.

August rolled his eyes. “Obviously. Don’t be an idiot. Move over.” He urged Klakow out of the room’s solitary chair and sat down rather inelegantly, sprawling in the seat as if his body was no longer able to support itself. “I honestly don’t know how you ever became an agent.” August started digging through the paperwork spread out on the table. “Give me your damn pen.”

Deven reached behind his ear, but Klakow handed him a Sharpie, which seemed to be what August was after. Deven felt a little foolish and stepped back into the shadows.

August marked the locations where the bodies had been found, which were nearly central to the locations of the living victims.

August typed quickly on the computer in front of him. Deven, who still struggled with basic spelling and who found keyboards slow torture devices highlighting his lack of education, was amazed at the speed at which August typed.

“What are you looking for now?” Klakow complained.

“Information on poisons.” He studied the screen.

“What are you thinking?” Deven asked.

"You said we have to poison his blood to weaken him, right? Well, I'm connected to Night Axe, so if I ingest something toxic, it will affect him. We need a substance that'll weaken him enough to incapacitate but with a fast enough working antidote to save me and the other sacrifices."

Alarm zinged through Deven. "That sounds dangerous."

"You got a better idea?" August smirked, but Deven now knew August's sarcastic looks well enough to recognize he was faking it. Clearly this idea frightened him as much as it did Deven. "Klakow, call R&D in DC and find out what they have on toxic chemicals affecting otherworldly beings."

"I don't work for you, remember?"

"You are an assistant on this investigation from internal affairs. You work for me until we resolve Carlos's death."

"Help him, Agent Klakow."

All three of them turned. The director stood in the doorway, watching the men. Behind her stood Agent Ortega and another shorter, bored-looking man who Deven assumed to be Agent Zardo.

"Yes, ma'am," Klakow mumbled. He shuffled past the director. Deven noticed that August didn't bother to look at the director. He kept typing on the computer.

"I'm Director Herlinda Alonsa." The director held out her hand to Deven and he shook it awkwardly. She turned and faced August. "Why do you want a toxicity report?"

"Deven learned Night Axe needs to be poisoned in order to be weakened enough to be captured. I can poison him. I'm attached. We find something that I can survive with a timed antidote and this may be the best way to subdue him."

The director shook her head. "You're too weak already."

"I'm fine," August grumbled. "Why doesn't anyone believe me?"

"We'd have to detach the other sacrifices," Agent Ortega said. "Otherwise we risk poisoning them as well."

"Dr. Ramos wouldn't do it for me," August said.

"That was before we were considering poisoning three dozen people with a toxic substance strong enough to bring down an Aztaw," Zardo said.

The director nodded. "Zardo and Ortega, go to the hospital and get Dr. Ramos up to speed. We'll attempt a separation on a healthy volunteer. We need to move quickly."

Deven worried that detaching victims, while offering the benefit of draining Night Axe's blood, would also alert him to their plan. But he didn't say anything. Director Alonsa didn't look like the kind of person who was open to suggestions from strangers, and besides, at her command the rest of the room dispersed until it was only August, Alonsa, and himself.

"One more day, Silas," Director Alonsa said, lingering in the library doorway. "That's all you get. Then I'm putting you on medevac back to LA."

She left the room and August's mood seemed to dampen further. He slumped in his seat and rubbed his eyes.

"She's taking you off the investigation?" Deven asked.

August nodded. "She thinks I'm getting careless because I'm sick. But it isn't me. It's this fucking case..." He pushed at the map angrily, tossing it to the floor. August covered his eyes with his hands.

Deven sighed and walked around the table and picked up the map. He studied August's markings. He grabbed August's marker and put a check next to one of the locations.

August uncovered his eyes. "What are you doing?"

"Night Axe is there."

"How can you tell?"

"He'll be based at a crossroads. Crossroads are sources of malevolent energy for Aztaw lords and can enhance their house powers. Night Axe would rely on this additional source of power to fuel any wards or protection spells he has around himself."

"Do you know how to dismantle his wards?"

Deven shrugged. "There are basic wards around locked rooms in Aztaw that I can pick, but more complicated ones require magic more powerful than I have."

"There's a ward pruner in the armory I can borrow," August said, sounding more enthusiastic. "Whatever you can't handle I'm sure the pruner can."

Deven shook his head. "But it won't be wards alone. We've already seen that Night Axe has soldiers."

"The director will issue a raid," August said. "It's usually for cases where a dangerous artifact is located but is occasionally applied when apprehending a threatening suspect."

"We should go to the hospital, so if the separation works, you can be detached as well."

August shook his head. "As much as I love the idea, we need my connection, not only for the poison but to find him. The map gives us an idea of his general whereabouts, but I can still zero in on his location."

"You've seen how powerful he is," Deven cautioned. "There'll be casualties."

"This morning you didn't seem to care about casualties," August said, but he didn't sound angry, only curious.

Deven shrugged. "I *don't* care, but you clearly do. I recognize my sense of morality is...skewed."

August barked a short laugh. "One way of putting it."

August's phone rang, and when he glanced down at the screen a look of fear quickly crossed his eyes before he blinked and took the call. He crossed to the corner of the room farthest from Deven, which peaked Deven's curiosity. August hadn't needed privacy for other calls.

While August was on the phone Deven returned to the Irregulars' kitchen and brought the pastry he'd saved for August back to the library. August had finished his call and took the pastry with a nod, looking wrung out. "That was Teresa."

"Teresa?"

"Carlos's girlfriend. She hadn't heard from anyone and wanted to know what was going on." August pocketed his phone. Deven noticed his hands were shaking again.

"Did you tell her he was dead?"

"Of course. No benefit in lying to her." He ate the pastry quickly and looked around as if hoping there'd be another. Deven felt guilty for having eaten the rest.

"Did you tell her how?" Deven asked.

August glanced down at him. "No. She's aware of the Irregulars and what we do because she works in the San Francisco branch office, but I'm not going into details. That's something no one wants to hear about the person they care about." August angrily reached into his pocket and mouthed a handful of pills.

Deven considered what it would be like to date someone who worked in the same office. It was an unusual situation. In Aztaw, male and female couples led different lives. The women had their own society, their own hobbies and rituals and world outside of soldiering. Only in the temples did the two sexes work together, honoring their lords.

"Do you have a girlfriend?" Deven asked curiously.

August quirked his eyebrow. "Do you think I'd be flirting with a man if I did?"

Deven smiled. "Boyfriend?"

"It's been several years since I've been in a relationship," August admitted. He busied himself with folding up the map he'd drawn on. "The last one ended badly."

"Why?"

"Because of the job."

"Why would that matter?"

August gave Deven a look like he was being an idiot again. "Honestly, how big do you think the pool of prospective homosexual men at NIAD is?" He waved his hand over the office. "The few gay employees in the division are stationed all over the world. And the few at the San Francisco branch are not appropriate dating material."

"Why?"

"I have no interest in screwing goblins, even if they're trans-goblins. Way too much goblin family baggage to deal with."

"So you're the only homosexual human in San Francisco?"

August rolled his eyes. "Obviously not. But my other options in the division are an old bum with frightening fashion sense and a vegetarian." August said this last word as though foregoing eating meat was even more unattractive than being a goblin. “You may have met the goblin at that Christmas party they made you attend.”

The only person Deven remembered at the Christmas party was an attractive man who had been eating cigarettes right out of the pack. Considering that, he could see why August might not date inside the agency.

“What about people who aren’t agents?”

“Dating outside of the Irregulars is too difficult.”

“Why?”

“It’s hard to constantly lie to someone you love. You can’t explain what you do, what challenges you face. They don’t understand how different the world seems, and when something bad happens and you need to talk about it, all you can do is make up some excuse about lost visa applications and hope they buy it.” August’s eyes suddenly got glassy and Deven wished he hadn’t brought up the topic.

August cleared his throat. “Let’s get something more substantial to eat, then check in on the sacrifices.” It took him two tries to get out of the chair, and as he stood, the little color in his cheeks drained once more. Deven walked beside him in case he lost his balance. August leaned into him, their arms brushing as they made their way down the hall.

August lowered his voice. “What about you?” he asked. “Have you dated much?”

“When would I?”

“You’ve been back a year. You could have met someone.”

“No.”

“So no one?” August looked at him, curious. “You’ve never been with anyone?”

Deven quickly determined that his experience with the woman Lord Jaguar had offered ranked low on the morality scale, so he skipped that story, proud of his growing sensibilities.

“A man seduced me a few months ago,” Deven told him.

August grinned. “Did you like it?”

Deven nodded. “It was nice. A little hard to concentrate.”

August threw his head back and laughed so loudly four employees ahead of them in the hallway turned and scowled. Deven was more distracted by the pale expanse of skin exposed when August arched his neck.

When he glanced back at Deven, August's eyes were wet with tears of laughter and he looked genuinely happy. "That's the point, Deven. I'm sure the gentleman involved would consider it a compliment."

Deven felt his cheeks turn red and looked away.

Outside, it had started to rain. Unlike showers in the Pacific Northwest, which were cool and refreshing, this was a hot, sticky rain, combining with the heat to add a muggy layer to the normally dry climate.

Still, the rain reminded Deven of Friday Harbor with its bone-colored sky, sea, and air and its salty breezes, and windy woods. The novelty of homesickness washed over him again.

Director Alonsa was also interested in visiting the sacrifices in the NIAD ward at the Sanitorio Espanol hospital, so they drove together, stopping at another taqueria for lunch. Deven discovered that Director Alonsa and Agent August were friends, having both worked in the San Francisco branch a few years prior.

As they discussed familiar colleagues, Deven watched people stroll by outside of the restaurant window. It hurt less now to distinguish colors and objects as he visually adjusted to the urban scene. Nevertheless, something always came up that he couldn't make out. A bright fiasco of flapping vinyl and metal wheels made him squint and he had to concentrate to figure out what it was, until August leaned over and touched his knee.

"It's a fruit cart," August said quietly.

"Oh." Suddenly his interest perked up. "Oh! I want to try a watermelon."

August gave him an indulgent smile. "Right now?"

Deven shrugged. "Well, sometime. I like fruit." He felt the director's sharp, inquisitive gaze on him, so he looked away and kept silent as they loaded themselves back into 72's sedan and drove to the hospital.

They made their way through a hectic entrance where close to a hundred people lingered in the crowded, hot reception. The rain had brought everyone indoors and an earthy, unpleasant odor of humanity filled the space. Several babies were crying and Deven felt claustrophobic.

Fortunately, they didn't linger there for long. Director Alonsa flashed a badge and they descended into the bowels of the hospital. The laundry churned out heat and chemical odors. But next to it lay the smaller waiting area and a narrow hallway of the NIAD hospital rooms.

Director Alonsa checked in with Agent Zardo, who reported a young man named Honesto had volunteered to have the risky surgery. He had been told the procedure would facilitate removing the toxicity in his blood. The other living sacrifices huddled in frightened groups, speaking in whispers. They were strangers to each other, scared or angry at their forced separation from the rest of the world. Only Deven and the other sunglass-wearing agents could see the remarkable weavings of arteries that entwined them all. The blood vessels tangled as they flowed between bodies.

"Night Axe might sense that," Deven said, pointing to where all the arteries bundled and exited the heavy stone foundation wall.

"Sense what?" August pulled on his sunglasses. He frowned at the exit point. "Not much we can do at this point."

As they waited for the results of the surgery, August volunteered to venture out in the rain and fetch watermelon from the nearest fruit stand. Deven stood to follow, but August held out his hand, holding him back.

"No, stay." He eyed the cluster of arteries in the wall. "You know what to be on the lookout for if Night Axe comes."

Deven nodded and sat back down on a hard bench. He lost track of time in the fluorescent-lit basement. He wondered how far August had wandered.

Agent Ortega approached Deven with a toothy grin. "It's done," he said. "Honesto survived. They had to cauterize the wound with an energy burn, but his bleeding is under control."

"Can I see?" Deven asked. Ortega nodded and the two of them walked down the hallway toward the operating room.

The hairs on the back of Deven's neck stood on end. Deven watched the arteries streaming around them for movement hinting at Night Axe's presence, but they neither tugged nor changed direction.

A smell of rotten flesh filled his nostrils. He reached for one of his knives.

"Something's wrong," he told Ortega. "Get everyone in their rooms. Now!"

Ortega studied Deven's expression for only a second before nodding and bursting into action. He shouted a flurry of Spanish and people began to move, first slowly and then in greater urgency as Agent Zardo rushed down the hall, echoing Ortega's command.

The smell intensified and Deven glanced up. The ventilation shaft grate burst open and clanged to the floor, inches from his head. The four tzimimi shrieked into the hallway, their loose, leathery breasts flapping as they flew. One swung her obsidian-studded baton at Deven's head. He ducked out of the way and she didn't linger for another attempt. All four shot through the window of the door of the operating room, shattering the glass. A scream burst out of the room. It sounded like someone was thrown against the wall.

Deven ran forward and yanked open the door. One of the night spirits slashed at Deven's face with her clawed hand. He pulled back and threw his knife upward, hitting one of her shining eyes. She fell to the floor with a crunch of breaking bones.

Deven leaped upon her, plunging his second knife between her ribs and deep into her black heart. He saw Agents Ortega and Zardo run past him, firing needle-thin shard bullets at the other night spirits.

The one beneath him cursed in Aztawi and writhed as Deven drove his blade deeper. The serpents between her legs hissed and tried to bite at him, and with his last plunge, the spirit contorted, raking her taloned foot down Deven's spine. Her glowing skin shriveled and burned like paper around his blade.

Once her struggles stopped and she died, Deven clambered to his feet. A sharp ache pulsed from his bleeding back. But there were still three more of the monstrosities, and even though Ortega and Zardo were on the offensive, he could see they were all too late. Honesto lay shredded on the bloody hospital bed, his eyes, nose, and mouth ripped from his body to expose his bare skull underneath.

Thin bullets strafed the tzimimi. They retreated to the corner. One threw a jade glyph on the hard hospital floor and fire ignited, licking the bloody bed sheets and spreading up to burn Honesto's fingers.

Deven quickly crushed the jade glyph beneath his bootheel and spat on the fragments. The fire gutted instantly but the odor of burnt hair lingered.

One of the tzimimi crumpled to the ground and another quickly followed. Ortega moved closer to shoot point-blank at the spirits' bodies.

"Aim for the heart!" Deven shouted. He grabbed one of the fallen batons and flung it at the last night spirit, downing her on the bed, on top of poor Honesto.

Deven grabbed her by her grass skirt, dragging her off the patient. He drew his knife across her throat, sawing through her spine and stepping back as she gave one last cry before dying.

Deven turned to confront the other night spirits, but they were dead, shot with so many shard bullets their bodies shimmered metallic with enchanted copper and silver. Ortega's forehead and hair were matted with blood; one of the tzimimi had struck him before dying.

Ortega moved to the beside and checked Honesto's pulse. He quickly dropped his hand.

"He's dead."

The aftermath of the attack reminded Deven of Lord Jaguar's sacrificial altar. The heavy odor of metal and blood permeated his senses, and for a moment he was transported back, kneeling at the feet of his lord, watching in silence as women, men, and children were silently led to the altar to have their throats slit.

He'd learned how tricky it was to walk through slick pools of blood in corn-husk sandals, and now he walked to Honesto's side, treading carefully.

All of the tzimimi must have shredded the man with their claws. Deven picked up his sunglasses, which had come off in the struggle, and he saw the bulging incision where Honesto's connection to Night Axe had been severed. The end of the vessel was charred black.

"Oh Jesus," Director Alonsa said, stepping in the room, sounding breathless. She looked flushed, as if she'd run in from the other end of the hospital. She took in the bloodbath, shaking her head.

"Jesus! Luis," she said. Only then did Deven notice the body slumped in the corner of the room. It was Dr. Ramos, the back of his head smashed in, pieces of obsidian blade glinting in the fluorescent lights between the matted blood and hair.

"Honesto would have lived," Ortega said, panting. He wiped blood out of his eye. "The surgery was a success."

"But it alerted Night Axe," Deven said. He turned to the director. "We can't do more. For all we know, he senses the other sacrifices have been gathered here and is on his way. We must act now."

Director Alonsa looked to Agent Ortega. "Go upstairs and get a doctor to stitch up your head. Zardo, call a cleanup squad." She looked helpless as she stared at the mess. She reached over and squeezed Honesto's ankle, the only part of him that hadn't been raked open.

She then turned to Deven and her eyes narrowed. "Where are you hurt?"

"Me?" Deven remembered the talons in his back and reached around. His white T-shirt was wet with blood. "It's all right."

She hesitated as if she didn't believe him but then nodded. "Where's Silas?"

"Outside, getting me a watermelon." He felt embarrassed admitting it. While innocent people needed the Irregulars, one of them had been out fetching Deven a treat.

Director Alonsa led Deven out of the bloody room and firmly shut the door behind them. Pieces of glass broke from the shattered window and she quickly withdrew her hand to avoid the shards.

"Don't let Agent August see this," she told Deven.

"Why not?" Deven didn't imagine August was the kind of man to be squeamish.

"The way that young man is sliced up looks too similar to how Silas's lover died," Director Alonsa said.

Deven visualized the mangled remnants of Honesto's face, imagining how he'd feel if that face had belonged someone he loved.

"His lover was cut up?" Deven asked.

Director Alonsa nodded. "A faerie assassin sliced him to pieces."

Deven remembered the glassy expression on August's face when he'd talked of hiding his career from his lovers. "Did his lover even know August was with NIAD?"

Director Alonsa looked at him blankly. "Silas *wasn't* an agent. His lover was. Silas thought Jake was an immigrations officer. Only after witnessing Jake's assault did he learn of the agency and was invited to come on board."

That wasn't what Deven had been expecting. "Why was he invited? He doesn't have any magical ability."

"He was a top-notch investigator for the DEA, and we were looking for more expertise in investigation over magical abilities. Equipment can handle magic; it takes intelligence to resolve crimes."

"How long ago was Jake killed?"

"Why, you interested in taking his place?" Director Alonsa asked.

"Not his place as a casualty," Deven clarified.

"Be kind to him," Director Alonsa said.

"He's a jerk."

"Yes. And he is a great investigator and agent, and a friend of mine." Director Alonsa squeezed Deven's arm. "He's not as hard as he appears. He's just damaged and lonely."

"But I make up for it with impeccable fashion sense."

Deven swiveled at August's voice. August's hands were full with two enormous slices of red, dripping watermelon. Deven wondered how long he'd been standing there, listening.

Director Alonsa gave Deven a pointed look and walked off.

"What happened?" August snapped, smile fading as he took in the cries of the other patients and the broken window on the operating room door.

"Honesto's dead," Deven said. "Come on."

"What? What happened?" August strained to look through the window. Deven grabbed his arm and led him away. He snatched one of the pieces of watermelon out of August's hands.

"He survived the operation, but the tzimimi got him."

"What?" August's mouth curled in a snarl.

"They're dead," Deven assured him. "Agents Ortega, Zardo, and I got them all."

"About fucking time." August frowned. "Are you bleeding?"

"A little. It's not bad."

"Like hell it isn't. Hold this." August handed Deven his slice of watermelon and lifted the back of Deven's T-shirt. Deven's skin prickled with the sensation of August behind him, touching him.

"Christ, Deven. This looks awful. Let's find a doctor to sew this up."

"There's no time. We have to go after Night Axe now."

"What about detaching the others?"

"Night Axe knows what we're doing. Besides, the doctor is dead." Water from the watermelon dribbled on Deven's hand and he licked at it. "Thank you for the fruit," he told August.

"Yeah...well, no problem." August still scowled at Deven's back.

Deven took a bite. The fruit's sweetness and watery, crispy texture shocked him. He realized the watermelon had been the first gift he'd been given in the human world since his mother died and felt a sudden, overwhelming rise in temperature as he flushed with happiness. Even with bloody rakes in his back, obsidian shards in his hair, and a renegade Aztaw lord to stalk, someone had voluntarily given him a gift and that, at least, was worth sticking around for.

August's expression was somber, almost haunted, as he took in the marks on Deven's back. Deven polished off his watermelon in four quick bites, then grabbed hold of August's hand. "Come on, let's get Night Axe before he kills anyone else."

August squeezed his hand and, for once, followed Deven.

Chapter Fifteen

It was nearly dark by the time Director Alonsa assembled her raiding party, so Deven suggested they reconvene at dawn, when daylight would weaken Night Axe's wards. Some quiet exchange occurred between Alonsa and August, and she agreed that August could continue another day.

August and Deven returned to the safe house. Deven slept little, his body already charged with the adrenaline rush of impending conflict.

The house was quiet at the early hour, with only the security system humming in the background. Deven showered and dressed, and when he emerged from his room, one of the guards informed him that Director Alonsa had phoned and was on her way to pick them up.

Deven made his way down the hall to August's bedroom. He knocked, but there was no answer. "Agent August?" he called. He received no response.

Fear seized him. He rushed through the door but exhaled in relief when he saw August had merely slept late again, face as pale as the bedsheets on which he slept.

He appeared to be deep in slumber, but he didn't look peaceful. He twitched and jerked in his sleep, hands drifting unconsciously to his chest and the connection that linked him to Carlos's killer.

Deven sat at the edge of the bed and gave in to his urge to run his hand through August's dark curls. He'd never seen such a thick, chaotic, beautiful head of hair before. It was wild and almost childlike in its resistance to order.

August's eyes slowly opened as Deven stroked his fingers along his scalp. August appeared confused for a moment, but then the confusion disappeared and he simply stared into Deven's eyes.

Desire, sharp as an electric charge, sparked through Deven. His breathing hurt. He stared back, heart racing, terrified and elated and unsure what to do next.

August seemed to be waiting for something. He froze, unmoving, as Deven continued to stroke his hair. His lips parted and he took in a hitching breath.

The sight of his soft, wide lips was too much to resist and Deven leaned down closer. His heart hammered in his chest. He still feared he had misread the agent, up until August closed the distance between them and kissed him.

Deven gasped and opened his mouth and August plunged his tongue inside. The feeling was like a shock, pleasure bolting down the nerves of his spine, pooling in his groin. Hot pulses of desire flooded him and he opened his mouth wider, pushing his tongue back into August's mouth.

Who would imagine such a strange, wet, and slick sensation could be so intoxicating? August tasted like toothpaste and sleep. He wrapped his arms around Deven and pulled him down, flush against his body. Despite the thrusting urgency of his groin, August's touch was surprisingly gentle.

But the moment Deven's hard cock rubbed through his pants against August's a flare of need dismantled all other thoughts and he began gracelessly rubbing against him. Their kiss intensified, mimicking the pulsing of their hips, August's hands deftly moving to Deven's belt, unbuckling it without looking.

Deven had been nervous when touched the first time by Christopher, but he wasn't anxious now. The slow, simmering arousal that had built all week burned through any fear. He brazenly ran his hands down August's slender body, stroking the contours of his hips, drawn to the hard heat between them.

August pulled Deven's trousers and underwear down and quickly divested his own. His long, slender fingers grasped hold of Deven's cock and Deven shuddered, his body blazing with a solitary, driving need—to be inside August, to fill him.

Their fingers intertwined as they grabbed hold of each other, rubbing for delicious friction as their mouths met once more.

He was drowning, drowning. He heard August gasp for air and he pulled back, worried he was too forceful, given August's injuries. But August seemed oblivious to his own body's torments—he pumped both of them together in a palm slickened with their mingled pre-ejaculate.

"Yes," August mumbled against Deven's lips. "Yes, yes, yes." He kissed him once more and then turned, writhing out from under Deven to bend down and pull Deven's cock into his mouth.

It felt like the place where craving and satisfaction met, a slick, hot enveloping world summoning him deeper, and Deven arched himself into August's mouth, delirious with gratification. Nothing had ever felt like this and he knew he was completely lost now—only this would ever inspire him.

He glanced down at the site of August's sweat-kinked hair, his lips drawn taut around Deven's flesh, and Deven shuddered and came, muffling his cry by clenching his jaw shut.

He lay there, panting, recovering from what surely was some form of magic. August lay half on top of him, hot breath grazing Deven's hip bone as he pumped himself in his own fist.

Curiosity and affection emboldened Deven, and he forced his heavy, sated body to turn so he could return the gesture as he assumed would be appropriate.

August watched with a fragile expression, both wary and hopeful. Deven had no idea what he was doing, but this wasn't hard science either. It was easy to swallow flesh, to respond to the look of surprise and desire that transformed August's face, to go faster when August's fingers rubbed a rhythm into Deven's hair, to pull him deeper and see how far he could go.

August suddenly jerked and his hot release filled Deven's mouth. When Deven swallowed, he thought it tasted bitter and earthy, and it grounded him, here in this world and in this moment, so much that he smiled with relief.

Deven sat up and wiped his mouth with the back of his hand. August stared, almost agape.

"Christ, that's the hottest thing I've ever fucking seen." He pulled Deven in for a sloppy kiss.

"Time to go!"

Both men jerked at the intruding loud knock against the door.

"Director's outside!" the guard shouted.

"We hear you!" August cried back, reluctantly letting go of Deven. His hands shook and his hair was mussed. His cheeks showed a little color and his lips were finally back to the red Deven had first noticed, swollen from their kisses.

Deven touched his own lips, swollen from August's cock and raw from August's short stubble.

"God damn it!" August said, shaking his head. He steadied his hand on Deven's shoulder as he sat up. "I can't believe I slept in again."

Deven's heart raced. The last thing he wanted to do was leave that bed. "You needed the sleep," Deven said, surprised by the huskiness of his voice.

"I needed what we just did more." August offered Deven a crooked smile. He found his underwear and winced as he pulled the fabric over his wilting erection. August glanced at him with a sweet expression. "You okay?"

"Sure." Deven felt out of breath. He wasn't sure how to describe his feelings. Elation? Fear? Anticipation of next time? A little of everything.

August leaned down and kissed Deven once more, briefly, then clambered out of bed.

"Need help getting ready?" Deven offered.

"Yeah, want to dress me?"

"I prefer the opposite," Deven said, feeling his ears flush red.

August laughed. "Nice to see you're getting the hang of flirtatious banter. Klakow's going to lose his mind." With impressive speed given his weak state, August changed into a dark blue shirt and black suit, mumbling about alarms all the while.

Deven dressed quickly as well, smoothing the palms of his hands over his trousers, anxious some trace of what they'd just done lingered on the carelessly tossed fabric. But August didn't seem to be worried so Deven reassured himself that this was all okay.

Besides, more pressing, and dangerous, matters awaited them out in the predawn gloom.

Parked outside the safe house was a long white van with a gas company logo stenciled on the outside. Inside sat nearly a dozen Irregulars agents, crowded on seats and on top of boxes of what looked to be ammunition and computer equipment. Everyone other than Director Alonsa in the front seat was dressed in identical blue overalls with the same gas company logo above the breast. But underneath those overalls Deven saw the width of bulletproof vests and didn't miss the noticeable bulges in their pockets. Judging by the number of objects dangling disguised in black pouches from their utility belts, they were well armed. The firepower and sheer number in the operation relieved him but irrationally left him angry. Where the hell had they been when he was pawned off by a lunatic diplomat? He'd spent years imagining rescue from topside agents dressed in fatigues swooping in to carry Deven back to safety.

But they'd never arrived and he'd learned a valuable lesson: never again to rely on anyone else to save him. So while he was grateful for the additional eyes and weapons, he kept his knives close since they were all he really put his faith in.

He pulled on a spare pair of overalls and transferred his knives, obsidian mirror, Fight Arm's necklace, and his jaguar skin into the large pockets, where they'd be easy to reach, as August more slowly pulled on his own overalls.

Director Alonsa made introductions as Deven and August dressed. Deven recognized Agents Ortega, Zardo, and Klakow, but the rest of the names flashed by too quickly for Deven to learn them. The only name he caught was a woman called Dr. Ruth Hansing, who'd flown in from DC the night before to take Dr. Ramos's place as the medical advisor for the mission.

"I have liquid cyanide here," she told August, holding out a small vial of yellow fluid, capped with a plastic top. "Drink it all. You're going to have trouble breathing and experience seizures before you drop into unconsciousness."

"Great." August took the vial and pocketed it in his overalls.

"The antidote comes in three parts," Dr. Hansing said, holding a syringe. "I'm going to have to give you amyl nitrite, sodium nitrite, and sodium thiosulfate in rapid succession as soon as the poison has taken effect, so stay close to me for the duration of the raid. If something happens to me, Agent Ortega has a full antidote kit as well."

August nodded. The overalls made him appear younger, his curls forced into order, his black eye garish against his pale skin. He didn't look like the sneering, domineering man Deven had met only a few days before.

He looked scared, and Deven couldn't blame him.

The van lurched into gear and Deven struggled for a handhold against the corrugated wall of the vehicle. He jostled against August. Deven wanted to hold August's hand again, to feel even just a fraction of the connection they'd shared less than an hour ago. But he worried it might look bad in front of the other agents so instead he reached out for one of the weapons piled in the center of the vehicle.

Director Alonsa leaned over the back of the front seat. "Put that down," she shouted. "You aren't going on the mission. You're staying in the van with me."

"*What*?" Deven and August both exclaimed.

"This is an NIAD operation. No consultants."

Deven's stomach dropped. "But—"

"I need him," August snapped. "He's the only one here who even speaks Night Axe's language."

"We take only vetted employees on high-risk operations," the director said. "You know that."

Deven felt something close to panic at the idea of being left behind. He'd finally found a role for himself in the natural world. The irony of being cut from the team because something was "too dangerous" was bitter.

"How do you plan to surprise Night Axe?" Deven asked, trying to sound more assured than desperate.

Director Alonsa shrugged. "We're armed well enough that we don't need surprise. But we should be able to move quickly enough to take him unawares."

"The same connection to August that you're using to find him will alert Night Axe to your approach," Deven said. "He's bound to have security wards protecting his lair. And you'll be up against Night Axe's soldiers. Remember what happened at the hospital."

There was an uncomfortable silence. Deven pressed on, "But I can get you into his lair, without detection, even with the connection to Agent August."

Director Alonsa narrowed her eyes. "How?"

"I can transport you through a portal. You'll appear out of thin air."

August frowned. "I thought you could only use the pen to travel between calendars, not between portals in the same realm."

"Yes, but I can move your entire force down to Aztaw and back up using the calendars."

Only the sound of the van's engine could be heard as everyone digested the idea. No one looked like they cherished the concept of traveling to Aztaw.

"I don't like it," the director said.

"It would only be for a few seconds. I write very fast."

"How do you know he has a portal in his lair?" Klakow asked.

"Most Aztaw lords don't move far from them," Deven said. "Time is sacred in Aztaw and temples and places of power are built around calendar intersection points. Besides, the evidence of the original victims' locations, and the proximity to crossroads, suggests this is where Night Axe operates. There must be a portal nearby."

The director studied Deven, obviously considering his proposal.

"You would have the element of surprise," August said. "It may be the advantage we need."

"I'd be putting a lot of trust in you, Deven," Director Alonsa said, sighing. "My hesitance to bring you along isn't only about liability should you get injured. I'm still not convinced your loyalties are where they need to be."

"I'm not moving back to Aztaw." Deven didn't realize he meant it until he said it and felt surprised by the statement. He clenched his jaw. "My loyalties are here. I won't let anything happen to Agent August."

August cocked his head slightly. He gave him a small smile. "Good choice."

"Thought you'd like that."

August grabbed Deven's hand.

Klakow moaned. "Please stop before I puke."

Director Alonsa nodded toward the pistols. "Take one. But you follow August and Ortega's orders and stay out of the way. You open the portal, get them through, and stay under cover until Night Axe is apprehended."

"Yes, ma'am," Deven said, mimicking Klakow's words to her the day before.

"And this is for all of you: timing is critical and coordination essential. We have a five-minute window. August drinks the cyanide, the team apprehends the target, and the success is radioed to our doctors at the hospital, who will immediately administer the antidote to the rest of the victims. Dr. Hansing will inject the antidote into August. If we screw up our timing nearly thirty people will be poisoned, and we'll lose an agent." Director Alonsa eyed August meaningfully.

"Don't look at me," August said. "I'm not letting that syringe out of my sight."

"Good. This isn't the time for heroism, Silas. Show us where he is, take the poison, take the antidote. Nothing more."

"I get it."

"We'll watch over him," Ortega promised. He looked tired from the day before, a black-threaded gash on his forehead showing where the tzimimi had clubbed him. Still, he held a pistol tightly and looked ready to fight. Deven felt better about their chances.

Someone handed him a gun, ozone-like odor gassing out of the thin barrel.

“You ever fire a shard pistol, amigo?” one of the agents asked.

“No.”

“They’re illegal in the US,” August commented. “So don’t try to bring it back with you.”

Deven nodded.

“Hold down the trigger and brace yourself for recoil,” the agent told him. “And don’t fire on any of us, got it?”

Deven wished he had a belt to hook the gun on. He was about to pocket it when August wordlessly snatched it out of his hands, flipped a switch near the trigger, and handed it back.

“Safety,” August said.

“Thanks.”

As the van made its way through the city, Deven kept an eye on August’s artery. It pulled forward, then yanked to the side as the van turned the corner. The connection tightened as they moved to the center of the city.

“We’re close,” Director Alonsa told them. “Glasses on.”

The rest of the agents donned their sunglasses and made final adjustments to the small projectors in the pockets of their overalls.

It was the first time many of the agents had seen the artery emerging from Agent August’s chest, and an enthusiastic debate started about the nature of the blood vessel and the implications of something fleshy existing simultaneously in two realms.

The agents around Deven spoke excitedly and pointed at the artery. August seemed embarrassed by the attention, leaning against the wall of the van and resting his chin on his chest as if sleeping.

When the van stopped, Deven stumbled onto the street after the agents, blinking at the soft dawn light. He glanced up at the ruins of Templo Mayor and felt a moment of wonder that something so old could remain so very beautiful.

Spanish colonial-style buildings of grand stone and columns lined the streets and the entire neighborhood felt regal, important, and vacant at that early hour. Only a pair of police officers were in sight, leaning against their car beside the temple’s tourist entrance.

Despite the hour, the smell of the subway wafted over the city and Deven wrinkled his nose.

The NIAD team followed the taut line of artery leading from August's chest. The neighborhood grew more residential as they moved between the stone blocks of buildings. Deven pulled his pen from behind his ear and drew the cogs of the calendars on his other palm. There were dozens of calendars interlocking here, time gates piled upon each other in a dizzying array of options. It was no surprise that Night Axe had centered himself here.

As they walked, the team concealed their weapons but prominently displayed the props that accompanied their gas company uniforms. Agent Klakow carried an emission monitor and another agent wore a tool belt.

Deven noticed Agent Ortega's clipboard. He tapped the agent's shoulder. "Can I borrow that pen?"

Ortega handed it to him. Deven slid the pen behind his ear and pocketed his house power. The ballpoint wouldn't fool anyone close, but from a distance, he hoped it would serve as a temporary ruse.

If he hadn't needed the pen to create the gate, he would have left it behind. Watching how August's artery thickened and pulsed as they drew closer to Night Axe's lair set Deven's heart racing faster. He'd brought what he valued the most to his enemy. He began to have doubts about his plan.

As they turned a corner, the artery led from August down into the pavement in front of them. August's heart rate soared. At first Deven thought it was their proximity to Night Axe. Then he realized August's heart was just beating fast. His hand rested at his pocket, hovering over the butt of his pistol.

Klakow pointed to where the vessel disappeared beneath them.

"What does that mean?"

"Most of these older neighborhoods were built on top of Aztec ruins," Agent Ortega said. "And many ruins have never been explored. Perhaps there's something buried under this neighborhood that Night Axe is using as his lair."

Deven drew his calendars again. A powerful calendar tied the spot to numerous locations. "This is where we'll leave." He dropped to the sidewalk. As he started drawing glyphs, the other agents watched. Someone made some comment too quietly for him to hear, but several laughed until August growled back a response. They stopped laughing.

*Dog, arm bone, reed, star, death, lizard...*Deven drew symbols that had been ingrained in his memory as deeply as the spelling of his own name. He concentrated on the formation of each figure, knowing any error could create an alternate glyph and change calendars, sending them somewhere unexpected. As each symbol completed, the image sizzled, burning in his nostrils and making his heart race faster with thoughts of home.

The rushed, excited conversations of the agents around him hushed into whispers and silenced altogether as Deven crawled around them, drawing a large circle to enclose a dozen people.

Fatigue coursed through him. The pen grew cold in his hands as it drained of ink. The symbols shot a curtain of light upwards, drawing around them like a circle of fire. Deven finished all but the last symbol and paused, glancing up to ensure everyone was inside the circle and August was safely surrounded by the others.

"Ready?" he asked. August gave him a small nod.

Deven took a second to fully accept that, despite everything, he was returning to Aztaw. He was going home, even if only for seconds. Nervous excitement and fear percolated in his throat.

Before he lost his nerve entirely, he quickly drew the symbol of the jaguar. The last beam of light shot upward from the symbol, blinding him in a blaze of white light. The ground dropped from beneath, his stomach lurched upwards, and the party tumbled down into the eternal darkness of Aztaw.

Chapter Sixteen

Suffocating, vice-like heat pushed against Deven's body. He gasped to draw the thick, burning air into his lungs. Each breath felt like swallowing fire and he coughed, his lungs protesting.

Around him, the coughing gasps of his companions sounded above the distant roar of a black river. His eyes adjusted to the utter darkness quickly, the enchantment spell bringing contour and depth to their surroundings. The agents huddled, reaching out to touch each other in the dark.

"Deven." August sounded angry. "I can't see you."

"It's fine. We'll be leaving shortly," Deven reassured him. He recognized the glow of approaching bones and suspected a raiding party had sensed the portal opening. In the distance he could make out the old palace of Lord River, a massive stone compound at the raging water's edge, where a prominent pyramid used to stand. But even from afar Deven saw that the pyramid had been destroyed, its masonry pillaged and broken. Above the fortress wall a banner displayed a bony fist, the symbol of the rebellion, hanging limp in the stagnant, dry air.

Aztaw wasn't large. For a moment, he entertained the idea of returning to Lord Jaguar's compound. He needed to reassure himself that Fight Arm hadn't been lying, that despite all odds, Jaguar's legacy remained. The need to do so nearly overwhelmed him.

But there were fields nearby, Deven noted, and a settlement of civilian Aztaws. Life continued for the general populace, even if the great temples were gone. The heavy air stank of hot corn and cooking fires instead of heated blood and he heard neither crashing armies or human screams—only the murmur of the river and the pleasant hum of distant Aztaw children chanting rhymes.

Maybe being surrounded by humans altered his perspective, but Deven recalled his first impressions as a child. *This is not a place for me*, he had thought long ago, and after thirteen years, the sentiment held.

"Hurry," August hissed. Deven snapped back to the task at hand.

He drew a calendar in the air. It burned brightly against the blackness, flush with the magic of the Aztaw world. Even the agents could see it and someone cried out.

"That's me drawing," Deven reassured.

"I can't breathe!" someone complained.

"Take slow, even breaths," Dr. Hansing suggested.

"I lived here for thirteen years," Deven reminded them. "There's enough oxygen and nitrogen in the atmosphere to survive."

The glowing bones drew closer.

"Who's coming toward us?" August asked, his voice low.

"I don't know. Probably a raiding party." Deven studied the calendars. He found the one he'd noted near Night Axe's lair and began his connection. "No one move," he said. "I'm drawing around you."

One of the agents pulled out a utility knife that resembled August's, and a beam of light shot forth from the end, scanning the area.

At once, Deven heard the shout of the Aztaw party. They broke into a run.

"Turn that off!" Deven hissed. "They know humans are here now!" He wrote faster, hand trembling and he scored the pen deep into the hard, burned soil. *Heart, pig, mirror, crane*...his brain struggled against growing exhaustion to remember the intricate pattern of the smoke symbol, which he'd only drawn a few times in his life. His pen lightened in weight and grew icy to the touch. He worked his way around the clustered bodies of the agents, gasping for breath and praying that he had enough strength to fuel the pen for the journey back to the natural world. Sweat broke across his brow and his hair grew damp and heavy. For a moment, he considered using his knife to bleed one of the agents to give his pen the extra power it needed to finish rewriting the calendars. The old Deven wouldn't have thought twice about it.

But he saw August's grim expression, heard the way he struggled to breathe in the fetid air, and changed his mind. August would hate Deven for doing such a thing, so Deven continued the spell fueled with his power alone, feeling sick with weariness, the pen dangerously brittle in his hand.

"*Who is there*?" demanded the tallest of the soldiers.

"*Human Jaguar*," Deven said. He didn't stop drawing.

"*You have brought your power to ruin us*," the soldier said.

"*Take his pen and string him up*!" cried another. His glowing bone face came into focus, eyes dark and rolling. One of the agents swore loudly.

"*I am taking these humans and leaving,*" Deven told them. He nearly dropped the pen to reach for his knife. But he wasn't sure he had enough strength to defend himself, let alone the other agents. He kept writing. "*We mean you no harm.*"

"*Strange, since your brothers are already mounting a force,*" the large soldier said, coming to a halt beside Deven. His thin skin and skull bones were painted with the blue-green color of the rebellion. He bore no symbols of dynastic allegiance, but deep scars etched ruts in the bones around his eye sockets, showing he'd spent many years serving under one lord or another.

Deven looked at the agents. Many had indeed drawn weapons, but the soldiers weren't giving them second glances, staring only at him.

"*Brothers*?" Deven asked.

"*The House of Jaguar stirs,*" the large soldier said. "*A barricade is erected. They have begun an assault.*"

"*I have nothing to do with it.*" Deven's mind struggled to make sense of the information as he drew. *Paper, blackfish, feather*...His hand shook as it scored images into the ground. His other hand gripped the hilt of his knife.

But the soldiers didn't attack.

"*Night Axe, the Lord of Hurricanes, is on his way to destroy you,*" Deven warned. "*I will try and stop him, but you must prepare yourself. You have greater enemies than the House of Jaguar.*"

"*The Houses of Jaguar and Hurricane are one and the same.*"

Deven felt something sick twist in his gut. He finished the symbol for fire and stepped into the circle.

Light burst from glyphs and the ground lurched beneath him. Vomit rose up his throat as they moved through contorted time.

Darkness shattered with a blaze of red light and Deven shielded his eyes, muffling his cry of pain. The air was pulled from his lungs.

The portals were mismatched and they dropped from a height of a few feet. Deven landed hard, falling to his knees. Behind him, someone cursed.

The place they had traveled to was very cold, especially in comparison to the suffocating heat of Aztaw. Faint red light emanated from a tunnel to the side of the chamber, but otherwise it was dark.

Deven felt too weak to do more than kneel, breathing hard. The air was chilly and stale but still felt rich with oxygen and moisture compared to Aztaw. He was back in the natural world.

August hovered over Deven, fumbling with his hands out. "You okay?" He blindly felt Deven's body as if searching for injuries.

No, Deven wanted to say. A sense of betrayal overwhelmed everything.

"Deven?" August sounded worried.

Deven gripped August's hand and pulled himself up. "I think I know how Night Axe escaped the realm of light."

August looked as if he were going to ask a question, but then he squinted as someone turned a flashlight on directly into his face.

As if choreographed, the other agents simultaneously switched on a variety of flashlights and other small illuminating devices.

"Where are we?" Klakow asked.

"Underground." Deven returned his brittle, nearly white pen to an inside pocket and put on his projector sunglasses.

They were in an old temple, sunken underneath what appeared to be crumbling cement foundations. The air was stagnant but cool; the ancient stone walls of the temple could be glimpsed through centuries of crumbled earth and mud. The old stones oozed rust-colored water that made the walls appear as though they were bleeding tears.

The space was large, perhaps as wide as a football field, but the low, precariously uneven ceiling made the dark space feel cramped. There was a circular stone well in the center of the temple.

"It has a cenote," Agent Ortega said.

"What's that?" Deven asked.

"A sacred well, important in Maya and Aztec rituals."

As Deven's eyes adjusted to the light, he made out other familiar Aztaw features scattered around the room—a pile of human bones, stacked to show the remains of a meal; a jade statue of the stars to draw power to the location.

Dr. Hansing stepped over the putrefying remains of some small animal, looking like she was going to be sick. She moved to August's side. "You ready?"

The stench of blood overpowered even the odor of putrefaction coming from somewhere in the corner of the temple. And all around, visible through his glasses, Deven saw thick, braided networks of arteries, throbbing as they pulsed to a great heartbeat, gorged with blood. They were strung through the low cavern like vile party streamers, drooping low and forming tangled knots, all leading directly into a darker corner of the temple.

"Night Axe," Deven whispered.

"Where?" August's body tensed beside him.

"Corner, ten o'clock," Ortega said, swiveling to face the threat.

The Aztaw curse for darkness sank through the air and at once their lights extinguished. The blood vessel emerging from August went suddenly taut and all the arteries strewn about the temple shifted.

"Stay close to me," Deven whispered to August, drawing his knife. "Dr. Hansing—"

August flew forward as Night Axe yanked the artery connecting them. August's hands and face slammed against the uneven stone floor and Deven watched in horror as August was dragged toward Night Axe, his fingers raking the stone in an effort to stop.

Night Axe appeared from the shadows, grinning as he reeled August in, hand over hand. He looked directly at Deven.

Then he jumped into the cenote.

"No!" Deven shouted, rushing forward.

August was dragged to the lip of the well. He cried out in surprise as he was yanked into the well after Night Axe. His shout echoed down the stone walls.

Deven jumped into the well after him.

Only once he was in free fall did he realize how stupid that was.

This is going to hurt like hell.

Chapter Seventeen

Deven stretched out his arms to try and slow his descent. His knuckles grazed stone, but the well was too wide to brace himself. A protruding stone snapped his ring and middle fingers and he instinctively jerked them back. A moment later he hit the water hard. The noise of his crash echoed through the vast, cold chamber. The impact sucked the air from his lungs and shocked his senses, and he floated, stunned for several seconds, forcing himself to breathe and assess his injuries. His back ached and nausea welled if he tried to move his left ring or middle finger. His boots filled with water and his feet sank to the sandy bottom of the cenote. But he could stand—the water level was no higher than his ribs.

The water was icy cold. His eyes adjusted to the dark. He heard splashing at one end and focused, hoping to find a sign of August. The chamber was wide underneath the mouth of the well, revealing a cavernous water table with a jagged limestone ceiling. Part of the well tapered to a low-ceilinged passageway where water dribbled from the rock. The remains of some long-ago human sacrifice huddled on the high ridge of the limestone. He searched the dry platform and the surface of the water. He'd lost his sunglasses in the fall so he couldn't see the connection between Night Axe and his sacrifices.

He felt water churn around him and turned. The hard impact of Night Axe's fist jarred him and he fell back into the water. Blood filled his mouth. Night Axe lunged again, but Deven sank deeper into the water, darting under the surface to the opposite edge of the pool.

He reemerged and gasped for air. His face ached from Night Axe's punch.

Night Axe's body was fat with human blood, his thin skin purple-colored in the cold. His striped black and yellow face paint had smeared in the water, making him appear even more menacing. Deven recognized the shriveled flesh of children's tongues, forming a necklace around Night Axe's bony throat. Water droplets pearled on the matted straw surface of his enchanted armor, making it look as though he were sweating.

Even from across the well Deven's skin burned as Night Axe's mirrored headpiece reflected back his own sensations, amplifying the ache in his fingers and his face. Blood dripped from Deven's nose. He still couldn't see August.

"You want this one?"

Night Axe lifted Agent August out of the water by his hair.

August gasped for air. His face was white with shock. Deven wondered if he too had broken something in the fall.

Before he could speak, Night Axe pushed August's head back down under the water. August struggled underneath the surface, but Night Axe forced his head down, drowning him.

Fear filled Deven. "*Here*!" he shouted, grabbing the pen from behind his ear and holding it out with his uninjured left hand. "*Take it. Let him go*." He gripped the hilt of the knife in his right pocket.

Night Axe greedily surged forward. He let go of August and grabbed the pen, clenching it tightly.

Night Axe's face contorted the second he touched the obvious plastic. Deven grabbed his wrist and yanked him forward. He shoved his knife into Night Axe's left eye, dragging the blade to split the eyeball open.

Night Axe jerked himself free, shrieking. The sound echoed through the cavern, amplifying his fury. Deven dropped beneath the surface of the water and kicked off the wall, aiming for August. He grabbed him by the arm and towed him to the raised limestone ledge, heaving him upward. August was conscious. He scrambled to the middle of the rock, sodden overalls and suit making it hard for him to move. Blood oozed from a wound on the back of August's head. Deven saw that it formed a steady red stream, even when diluted by the water.

Bony fingers clamped Deven's ankle. He was yanked under the water with great strength. He clenched shut his mouth and kicked out but hit nothing but armor. Panic seized him as he struggled to breathe.

Night Axe lifted Deven, throwing him hard against the rocky wall.

Pain blossomed across his back and his vision darkened. He fell back into the pool and choked for air.

Agents above them shone their lights into the well, forming circles of illumination in the cold water. They shouted Deven's and August's names, but before Deven could even draw a breath to respond, Night Axe was on him again, shoving him against the wall and punching him in the face.

Deven nearly passed out. Pain filled his senses, made it impossible to think. Blood filled his nose and mouth. He writhed as Night Axe tore through his overalls with sharp fingers, searching for the pen.

Tiny whispers of slivery metal shot past Deven and filled Night Axe as an agent from above fired a shard pistol. The slivers pierced Night Axe's engorged arm and it burst open like ripe fruit, spilling the blood of his victims. The water turned murky red. Deven's consciousness faltered.

Another round from the shard pistol flung Night Axe back and Deven fell into the water. The lord growled the command to summon his army in Aztawi. Urgency overwhelmed even Deven's pain. He had to warn the agents above him. They didn't know what to expect.

Night Axe ripped a bead from his necklace, shattering the string. He threw the obsidian bead upward and growled the Aztawi curse for a dark ward.

The opening of the well sealed shut with an oily pool of dark liquid, blocking the light from the agents and the world above them. Deven's heart sank. Dark wards took heavy magic to build and dismantle, and Deven's own abilities weren't enough to rip a hole in it.

Desperation filled him. Neither he nor August would survive, that was obvious at this point, but he had to stop Night Axe.

He reached for his knife, but Night Axe was stronger and

faster. He grasped Deven's wrist and twisted, breaking the bone with ease. Pain shocked through him. He tried to move away, but Night Axe kept hold of him, jerking his knife free with one hand as he bent Deven's broken wrist backward.

Deven gasped and shuddered, unable to concentrate on anything but trying to move away. Night Axe tilted the mirror in his headpiece. Deven's pain reflected back to him and he cried out in agony. Every sensation multiplied, reinforced by the echoing mirror.

Night Axe split open the front of Deven's overalls with Deven's own blade. The tip sliced through Deven's clothes and skin, and the pain magnified, built and repeated, growing until he could no longer contain it.

Night Axe searched through Deven's inside pockets with bony fingers. He held the pen aloft in triumph. A primal instinct forced Deven to breathe past the blinding pain.

Night Axe let him go. Deven fell back into the water. He forced his aching body to move, using his undamaged hand to push water and distance himself. But to his surprise, Night Axe didn't follow him.

Instead, Night Axe began to convulse. His uninjured eye rolled. He roared and gripped something invisible at his waist and pulled, twisting furiously. He thrashed in the throes of a seizure.

Deven turned to see August slide down the wall of the well, dropping the empty vial of poison onto the limestone. Blood began to stain August's overalls.

Deven started swimming toward August, but hesitated as Night Axe thrashed, gurgling water.

This was his one chance to end Night Axe. But he wanted to be beside August. August motioned toward the Aztaw weakly, and Deven didn't need a second request. He pulled the last of his knives from his back pocket and forced his injured body into movement.

It was difficult, holding his knife in his left hand. Night Axe resisted him, even as his body trembled with affliction. Deven wrenched his pen free of the creature's grasp, put it back behind his ear, and sawed his blade deeply into Night Axe's neck. Rage filled him. August couldn't reach his antidote and would die in this fetid well. Deven chopped inelegantly with his left hand. Blood burst from the engorged Aztaw and stained the water. He cut until Night Axe's vertebrae were visible. He severed Night Axe's spine and wrenched the bastard's head clear off. Only then did he fall back, exhaustion and pain making it impossible to continue.

Deven crawled up the bank of the well. He dropped his blade and climbed over August's writhing body. "You idiot!" He grabbed August's sodden lapels with his left hand. "Why would you do that!"

August wheezed in response. Sharp shudders wracked his body as if he were jerked by marionette strings. Blood oozed from his chest.

Deven's throat tightened. "You said you wanted to die old in your bed!" Tears burned his eyes. "Old in your bed, not here!"

August smiled weakly, his eyes closed. "Don't always get what we want," he whispered. "I wanted you to slowly make love to me this morning. That didn't happen either."

Deven leaned down and kissed August. It hurt his bruised and bleeding mouth, and August gasped for air as his body shook, but Deven didn't care. Regret overpowered everything. He'd lost more than his chance with August—he'd ended up killing him with his terrible plan.

Deven broke the kiss and August struggled to intake air, his body convulsing rapidly. His eyes rolled back in his head and Deven realized he had to stop this, at any cost.

To keep the poison from killing August, he had to suspend him in a time trap, just like Lord Jaguar had done to him all those years ago.

He scored the tip of his pen into August's neck, writing clumsily with his left hand. Time traps were different than locks, and he struggled to remember the subtle differences in the glyphs. He finished the time trap and rolled off. August froze mid-gasp, fingers rigid as claws, back arched mid-spasm. He didn't move, frozen in the suspended animation of the trap.

Time traps sapped power unlike anything else and Deven lay alongside August's frozen body, utterly spent. The pen lay limp in his grasp, bone white and ice cold. Only a small amount of inky color remained at the very tip.

Deven weakly tapped August's frozen side. "Help is coming," he whispered. He glanced up at the sealed well, wondering how long it would take the agents to defeat Night Axe's soldiers, find a way out of the sunken temple, locate a ward pruner, and lift them out.

Now that he had a moment to pause, he realized how badly he was injured. His face felt pummeled; his broken wrist and fingers hurt unlike anything he could remember. The cut down his ribs was shallow, but it oozed blood. The only thing staving off the worst of the pain was his numbness, the cold water evaporating off him as he lay, bare chested, on the hard ledge of the well floor.

He closed his eyes. Maybe he could rest a bit until the Irregulars came to rescue them. There was, of course, a part of him that was near panic; the badges had failed him before. What indicated he could trust they'd save him now?

Something trembled in his trouser pocket.

Deven held his breath in the dark, senses coming back to full alert. He moved his left hand slowly, feeling in the remains of his overalls. He pulled out the sodden scrap of jaguar skin.

It writhed in his hand, alive.

No, Deven thought, slowly sitting up. He dropped the jaguar skin on the rocky surface and watched it writhe into the water.

He glanced up, past the floating remains of Night Axe. He saw nothing but the wet contours of the cavern.

A faint glow moved into the cavern from the narrow well passageway. Water lapped against the rock.

Deven carefully replaced the pen behind his ear.

Lord Jaguar entered the cavern. He'd been hiding in the wells for some time—his luxuriant jaguar skin skirt and gold breastplate were drenched with moisture. Lord Jaguar's black dotted face paint had streaked in the water. His headdress was simplified— instead of the magnificent jaguar skull with obsidian jaws and long tail of human finger bones, he wore a gold and jade feathered crown spiked with jaguar teeth. Carved human knee bones clanked together around his neck.

"*My lord*!" Deven knelt on instinct, breathing fast. His entire body shook from adrenaline and cold.

"*I see you've kept my house power safe in your own stupid way.*" With his bony fingers Lord Jaguar snatched the pen from behind Deven's ear. Panic seized Deven as the pen left his possession. Lord Jaguar's touch sent a shiver of repulsion through Deven's body.

"*I thought you were dead, my lord.*" Deven gripped the hilt of the knife beside him. There was only one way Lord Jaguar would be able to refuel his pen and use it.

"*No, not dead. I traveled undetected to the realm of light to free the Trickster.*"

"*But why*?" Deven stared at Lord Jaguar, the creature he had been willing to die for, over and over. Nothing but fear filled him now.

"*No force left in Aztaw can defeat the rebels. It takes a lord of a different caliber to bring order to such disloyal chaos. The Lord of Hurricanes and I could have easily defeated the rebels. Now you have ruined all of that.*"

"*You should have confided in me,*" Deven cried.

Lord Jaguar reached forward and cradled Deven's chin in his skeletal fingers. Deven's flesh crawled. "*To make my death appear to be real, you, more than anyone else, had to believe it.*"

Deven didn't know why he continued to kneel, face in his lord's bony grasp. Years of instinct kept him obedient, despite everything.

Lord Jaguar's glance flickered to Agent August's frozen body. "*You nearly destroyed my power saving that worthless human. I think it is only fitting that his blood will be the first to fill my pen.*"

"*Don't touch him,*" Deven growled. He'd never spoken a command to his lord. But he'd also never had anyone he wanted to protect more than Lord Jaguar himself.

He jerked free of Lord Jaguar's grasp.

"*You will not take him.*" Deven took a shaky breath. "*And you will not return to Aztaw. Things have changed there. They no longer need you.*"

Lord Jaguar stared, stunned. "*You order me*?" His mouth contorted in rage. "*Shut your mouth and bow down*!"

Years of training made it hard to disobey Lord Jaguar's commands. Instead he reached into the shredded remains of his overalls and clutched Fight Arm's distraction-enchanted beads.

Deven kicked Lord Jaguar's knee. The thin skin broke as the glowing bone underneath bent awkwardly. Deven dashed out of the way and threw the beads over his neck.

Lord Jaguar spun, searching for him. Deven's heart raced in terror. He felt too tired to fight, but he reminded himself that Lord Jaguar was Aztaw, and therefore slow. He waited until Lord Jaguar turned completely in a circle, trying to locate Deven in the obscurity spell.

Once Lord Jaguar's back was to him, Deven rushed forward and snatched the pen back. He darted to the edge of the pool and Lord Jaguar splashed through the water after him.

Something heavy clunked against Deven's thigh and he remembered his own shard pistol. He unlocked the safety and fired. The powerful recoil slammed him backward as it sprayed metal into his lord. Lord Jaguar howled in agony and ducked under the water.

Deven had only seconds. He started to write, his left hand scratching the glyphs imperfectly, drawing figures in the water. The water turned to steam in the shapes of the symbols. *Seven, gold, fox, clove…* He scrambled to surround Lord Jaguar.

Lord Jaguar resurfaced, his bones shimmering with fragments of silver. Deven knew he wasn't invisible, just unnoticeable, so he kept moving. But Lord Jaguar could see the glyphs steaming and knew what Deven was doing.

He growled a curse and shoved his hand over the surface of the water, dispelling one of the glyphs and breaking the pattern. Deven kept writing.

"*Faithless human*!" Lord Jaguar roared.

Deven shot him in the mouth with the pistol. Lord Jaguar fell back, moaning and clasping his jaw with his hand.

The pen was a feeble thing in Deven's hand, drained from writing the time trap. Guilt and regret flooded him, even as he kept writing. Such a beautiful thing, really. The last of the house powers. The last of the age of magic in Aztaw and he was killing it.

It needs killing, Deven told himself.

"*Deven...*" cried Lord Jaguar. His hand clutched his ripped jaw. "*You swore an oath to protect me. An oath*!"

Exhaustion brought tears to Deven's eyes as he drew. Every symbol took more from his body, made it harder to keep his eyes open. Deven tried to write faster, but he physically couldn't. As it was, he crawled, half in water, half out, body shaking with the effort. The pen was so thin and brittle part of its tip crumbled and broke in his hands. He kept writing.

The pen splintered further. He drew with the pieces, scorching glyphs into the water, making substance of liquid and shooting light through the deep, chilly darkness.

With the last fragment of his pen, he finished the circle and rolled out of the way as the wall of light encased Lord Jaguar and dropped him out of time forever. The light flare receded; only a crumbled fragment of the pen remained, cold and lifeless in his palm.

But the darkness didn't continue.

Sudden sparks burst from above. A flare burned brightly as the ward sealing them beneath the world was dismantled. The Irregulars were breaking through. They were going to be rescued after all.

"Thank you," Deven muttered, realizing how grateful he was to see light shining down, piercing the darkness.

Chapter Eighteen

Deven wasn't the first to be discharged from the NIAD ward of the Sanitorio Espanol hospital. The younger, healthier sacrifices who had been administered the cyanide antidote on time and had their connections surgically removed had left before him.

The rest of the sacrifices were discharged later, after being fully cleared of any lingering effects of the poisoning. They lost one person in the exercise, an older woman who had suffered cardiac arrest when Night Axe had died.

Deven saw them leave the hospital. But he still waited, because the last one to leave was the person he wanted to see most of all.

As it was, he almost missed Agent August completely.

Deven had been sitting outside the doors of Sanitorio Espanol hospital for hours, scanning the crowd of admissions and discharges for sight of the agent. But when August finally emerged, Deven barely recognized him.

He looked like a new man.

His dark, thick hair was cut short, probably to lessen the appearance of the shaved patch and stitches behind his left ear. His hair was less curly when short, more tamed, lending him a rakish, movie-star appearance.

But more noticeable was the rosy pink hue to his cheeks and the sparkle in his blue eyes. He looked rested and healthy, healthier than he had before becoming Night Axe's sacrifice. He moved with energized urgency, as if late for something. He walked right past Deven, who'd been sitting on the pavement near the door.

"Agent August!" Deven cried, standing up quickly.

August turned in surprise. For a second Deven worried he'd made a mistake in hanging around for August to finally be well enough to leave.

But August's mouth curled up into an inviting smile and his eyebrows lifted.

"Deven."

"After they released me, I wasn't allowed back in your ward since I'm not a relative or an agent," Deven explained, rushing his words in his nervousness. He felt his cheeks flush. "So I thought I'd just wait and—"

August gripped Deven by the shoulder, pulled him close, and kissed him. Deven opened his mouth and August's tongue surged inside, filling him. Warm heat pooled in Deven's groin and spread through his body. He pressed himself against August's lean body, feeling a matching hardness that promised more than mere words ever could.

But Deven sensed the gaping children and disapproving glares of several older ladies in the waiting room, and he pulled back.

"I'm very happy to see you," August said at last, grinning. His lips were red and swollen from the kiss, almost obscene, and the look of them drove a surge of need through Deven's belly, recalling the sight of August's beautiful lips wrapped tightly around him.

"Are you feeling all right?" Deven asked belatedly.

"Like a million bucks." August reached for Deven's right hand and examined the brace on his wrist and bandaged fingers. "You?"

Deven shrugged. "I'll live."

"And aren't you glad about that?"

"Yes, I am." Deven grinned. "As much as it pains me to say it, you were right, Agent August."

August took his hand and said, "Call me Silas."

THINGS UNSEEN AND DEADLY

Ginn Hale

The dead are selfish:
They make us cry, and they don't care,
They stay quiet in the most inconvenient places,
They refuse to walk, and we have to carry them
On our backs to the tomb...
Diatribe Against the Dead
— Angel Gonzalez

In the predawn gloom the phalanx of armed NIAD agents threw dull reflections across the wet sheen of the narrow streets. A fine rain diffused the glow of the streetlights, making their black-clad figures look like shadows cut loose from the creatures that cast them. They moved swiftly, silently toward the innocuous stone front of a three-story antiques shop.

From the hidden recesses of the shade lands, Henry watched the young agents fan out behind him, filling the narrow San Francisco street. His old trench coat and patched pants hung from his long frame, utterly at odds with the sleek garb of the homogeneously clean agents behind him.

They carried mage pistols loaded with laser-etched incantation ammo. Henry wore masking tape and ink-stained rubber bands around his nine fingers and was currently loaded with whiskey and a sweet, nameless poison. His straw-yellow hair smelled like roadside brambles and the dark soil where he'd spent so many nights.

For all that, Henry easily strode through the shade lands while at his heels younger, far more keen agents crouched and scampered across the earthly ground, no more able to enter his world than could the rain or wind.

Three hours earlier their operation commander—a slim, athletic woman with cropped black hair who answered to the name Carerra—had informed Henry that her San Francisco agents ranked among the top three internationally for execution of Irregular assault operations. They'd all been on raids before; they'd busted illegal goblin markets and shut down soul trafficking rings. They were toned, trained, and supremely experienced at keeping magic artifacts from coming to light while simultaneously ensuring the general public remained in the dark about their very existence.

Between the spritz of holy water in Henry's direction and her cool tone, Commander Carerra had made it clear that her state-of-the-art strike force did not need the assistance of some shabby relic from an age when Irregulars' operations had been run on half-assed witchcraft, peyote spit, and blood sacrifices.

Henry had slumped in the commander's straight-backed chair and assured her that he'd have been happy to leave her and her enthusiastic crew to their modern devices, but he'd been dug out from the field and sent back to San Francisco by Director Hehshai herself. Neither he nor Carerra would defy the director. And they both knew Hehshai wouldn't have dirtied her claws exhuming Half-Dead Henry if his presence wasn't in some way necessary. Though in exactly what way Hehshai hadn't said. Oracles never did.

Still, Henry didn't doubt that he could make some kind of difference, because really even the smallest thing, an icy step or a missed letter, could save or end a human life. Henry knew too well that it took only one mistake to strip all the swagger and confidence from even the best agent and reduce him or her to a cold lump of meat. And somewhere deep in him he still cared about human lives, even those of these strange, modern agents who seemed so much more like machines than women and men.

But they were human enough, certainly, to err.

Most of the young agents hadn't noted the thin filaments shimmering through the soft rain all around them. The two who had simply brushed them aside like cobwebs. The threads were hardly visible and appeared to break at the touch of a hand, but that fragility was itself a weapon, producing countless poison needles.

Henry held up a callused hand and Commander Carerra, watching him through spell projector glasses, signaled her agents to a stop. Henry glanced back at them only briefly. Two swayed, glassy eyed, their skin tarnishing blue black as mage poison infiltrated their organs through thousands of needles.

They were already dead. They hadn't hit the ground yet, but that would be only a matter of seconds. Henry couldn't save them. The best he could hope for was to keep the rest alive.

He turned back toward the antiques shop.

Millions of the gold threads cocooned the quaint facade of the gentrified Victorian storefront and cascaded down over the door like a tangled glass tapestry.

He focused on the delicate filaments in front of him. This old spell was probably the reason Director Hehshai had tossed his ass on a Falcon 7X jet in the dead of night and shipped him back to San Francisco. He might look like a battered hobo and smell like a cold night in a fresh grave, but old magic saturated his blood. Ancient incantations ringed the chambers of his scarred heart and etched the shrapnel of the other men's bones that he carried beneath his skin.

Carefully, he reached out and stroked one gleaming thread with the rubber band ring wound round his thumb. The filament sparked and Henry felt a chill shudder through his guts. But he was gentle and slow, never allowing the thread to break, even as he drew it back and caught another around the band of heavily defaced masking tape on his forefinger. Steadily, he chose and captured other strands, until all nine of his fingers were ringed with luminous gold threads. His breath felt cold as nitrogen on his tongue.

Slowly, turning first one strand aside then another, he twisted and unbound the tangled tapestry, playing a game of cat's cradle, reweaving the web.

At last, just in front of the shop door, he found the knot at the heart of the immense tangle. A ruby nearly the size of his fist but cut into the form of a spider: the guardian of this gate set here to keep other magicians from entering its master's domain. It glinted and flashed as it caught hints of the power within Henry.

And as Henry drew closer, the scarlet limbs twitched. The gleaming threads that encased Henry's fingers pulled taut—almost brittle.

If he'd been as sober and focused as the clean agents waiting behind him, he would have tensed in an instant and the guardian at the web's center would have known him to be something powerful, something dangerous. Instead, Henry went slack as any hapless drunk, staggering unaware into a doorway. Around him the countless strands trembled but didn't break. Not yet.

Henry averted his gaze from the twitching ruby legs and fat orb belly. He closed his eyes and let his mind wander where it would as he unconsciously searched for the words that the jeweled guardian needed hear before it could return to its deep sleep.

What absence kept it from rest? Random words floated through Henry's mind, as did half-forgotten promises, old regrets and pleasures. He blew out a soft breath across the ruby spider and faint words echoed back to him. He blew out a second breath and listened more intently.

Henry tilted his head, hearing something fragile and faint. Perhaps an old nursery rhyme, but not one of his recollecting. And then the words came to him.

"This cuckoo's a fine bird; he sings as he flies. He brings only good news and tells only lies," Henry whispered to the spider.

Deep within its body something seemed to shudder. A tremor passed through the threads binding Henry's fingers. It felt almost like laughter.

Yes, this was the way to reach her.

"My spider's a sweet girl," Henry crooned to the guardian. "She rocks and she spins. She waits on the doorstep to catch her dear friends."

Henry felt another laugh escape the guardian. Gleaming threads all around Henry sputtered out like spent candle flames.

"Cuckoo comes calling, a lullaby he sings. And spider she's sleeping all curled in her strings."

Henry fell silent, feeling only the tingle of tiny flames on the back of his tongue. Then slowly the ruby spider curled her legs closed and dropped into Henry's extended hand. He held the jewel for a moment, marveling at the craft of its design, feeling the slightest pulse pass through it, as if it harbored real life. And he knew that once it had.

Then he turned back to Commander Carerra and stepped out of the shade lands into the crisp air of the world of the living.

Several agents jumped back at his sudden appearance.

In his right hand he held the gray cinder that had once been some unlucky child's heart and, in another world, still longed to be sung a lullaby and laid to rest.

"Door's open," Henry informed Carerra.

She pushed her spell projector sunglasses up from her eyes and scowled at him. "You're certain? We've got two down already."

"I never said you wouldn't lose agents, just that I'd get the door open for you. It's open. You may lose more once you step inside." Henry gently slipped the hard little cinder into one of his deep pockets. "You want me to go ahead and clear the way?" Henry asked.

"We can handle it from here," Carerra responded. She clearly didn't want him taking credit for the capture of the site. That glory belonged to the San Francisco branch. That was fine with Henry; he'd found glory an overrated commodity. Didn't keep a body whole or even make for good company through the lonely evenings that followed its capture.

Commander Carerra signaled the first six of her agents ahead through the door. They marched in like windup toy soldiers.

"I could follow them through the shade lands—"

"You let me worry about my agents, all right, Falk?"

Carerra gave him a hard glare and didn't wait for his response. "HQ informed us that you could create some kind of dimensional split. Make this whole place disappear to the common populace. Is that the case?"

"I can call the Lost Mist and lay wanderers' wards to keep anything from getting out of that building." Henry shrugged. "It won't help your people inside there, though."

"You just concern yourself with keeping civilians from getting past our police lines," Carerra told him. "The last thing we need are more pictures of bat boys popping up on the Internet."

Henry heard something squeal and hiss from beyond the open door. He smelled the tang of human blood rushing up to the open air. They were already dying in there.

But these men's deaths weren't his business; if they were lucky, they never would be.

Henry gave Carerra a sloppy salute. Then he stepped back into the shade lands, where Carerra and her agents looked like shivering little shadows at the door of an immense, coiling darkness. He called up a white, rolling mist and it covered them all like a shroud.

❧

The wheels of Jason's battered green bike hissed against the wet pavement. He veered past braking cars and banked a sharp right turn despite the blazing red light. He couldn't have stopped if he wanted to, not at this speed. Iron balconies and painted Victorian houses blurred as he plunged down into the sea of fog that lay across the streets below. Dull shadows and the haze of red brake lights were his only warnings of imminent collision. Jason swerved, darted, and narrowly missed a speeding police car.

His heart pounded and sweat drenched his chest, but he didn't slow. Instead he threw himself into the momentum of the steep San Francisco hill, racing into the cold fog. The whole city narrowed to the white mist, the slick black road ahead of him, and the knowledge that he was late and not getting any earlier.

He was only twenty-four, but he already knew that time forgave nothing. Not a single second could be begged back, not for pity, love, or money. Two minutes too late to save his father might as well have been two years.

He felt the immutable past as if it were growing behind him. He felt it like hot breath at the nape of his neck, drawing closer to him, hungry to overtake him. And he saw it too, wavering at the corner of his vision, those long white creatures with their grasping spidery limbs and gaping rows of bloody teeth.

A chill deeper than the damp fog sank through Jason.

He didn't want to think about his father's murder. He couldn't keep his head on straight when he did. Because all those horrific details that he remembered so very clearly couldn't have been what happened. Those long-limbed, gape-mouthed creatures that had crouched over his father's prone body, feeding on his organs—they simply did not exist.

"They weren't real. It never happened. Don't think about it." Jason repeated the words like a mantra, pacing them with the fast rhythm of pumping pedals. But the surrounding mists haunted him with creeping white forms, and that old fear twitched through his nerves.

Somewhere ahead, on Van Ness maybe, an ambulance siren wailed and distorted with speed.

"Never happened. Don't think about it. Not real…"

It would have been so much easier to forget those red-slit eyes and bloody saw-blade mouths if he was still on ariprazole. But antipsychotic medications weren't cheap and without insurance Jason hadn't been able to fill a prescription in nearly two years. Most days he kept himself calm by averting his gaze and doing his damnedest to ignore what he knew was crazy. But this morning between the stress of traffic and this strange creeping fog, his brain was sputtering like an engine misfiring on all eight cylinders.

It shook Jason to realize just how quickly he could lose his grip on reality again.

He needed to keep his head together for a little longer, he tried to assure himself. Soon he'd be eligible for medical insurance; it was just a matter of maintaining steady, legal employment. Which was nearly as impossible to find as Brigadoon for anyone with a history like his. A brutal murder and years spent in and out of psychiatric hospitals and foster care weren't winning resume builders.

All of which made Jason's current job precious to him, an almost miraculous promise of a normal life. He still marveled at the sheer luck of it.

A month ago he'd ducked out of the rain and into the gilded warmth of Phipps's Curiosities and Antiques. Among carved camphor cabinets brimming with glittering baubles and scattered across the displays of ornate furnishings he recognized several familiar musical instruments. Out of nostalgia he'd picked up a clay ocarina—not much larger than a human heart, he thought. When an older woman in a fashionable maroon suit inquired about it, Jason obligingly demonstrated the sweet, tremulous notes, playing an old melody he remembered from his childhood. The woman listened, her expression softening from cool interest to rapt delight.

"It's so beautiful..." The woman gazed at the small ocarina with longing and Jason handed it to her. She cupped it close to her chest as if she were a little girl cradling a bird.

Then, while purchasing the small ocarina as well as an ornately carved Chinese bed, she gave Jason a bright smile and complimented the elegant silver-haired storeowner on his charmingly knowledgeable staff.

If the owner, Mr. Phipps, was surprised by the woman's assumption it didn't show in his serene, aristocratic expression. "We do our best."

After the woman departed Mr. Phipps approached Jason and made polite but pointed inquiries concerning his musical training. Jason kept his answers brief and somewhat honest. He'd studied ethnomusicology at UC Berkley—at least as long as his scholarships had lasted. He loved old and odd instruments.

Mr. Phipps considered Jason for a few moments. His keen gray eyes seemed to take in every detail that Jason wanted hidden—his clothes slightly too loose to fit him properly anymore, his hair a little too shaggy to pass for stylish.

"Why don't you show me what you could make of this?" Mr. Phipps led Jason to an oak cabinet and handed him the lute-like body of an aged oud. Jason took the instrument like a elderly animal. The small pear-shaped body and short neck felt fragile in Jason's hands, but as he carefully examined the oud he found that the wood was still strong and the tuning pegs fit well enough.

"It should be restrung and properly tuned," Jason said. "Mostly it needs to be played. Otherwise it'll get brittle…"

Glancing up through shaggy brown bangs to Mr. Phipps's amused expression, Jason realized that the majority of antique buyers only desired instruments to grace their display cabinets, not be performed upon. And yet the lean older man indulged him, allowing him to pluck and tune the old oud. Soon it felt warm in Jason's arms and its notes sounded rich and sweet as they rang through the shop.

An hour later when Jason handed the oud back, Mr. Phipps offered him a position.

Jason wasn't sure if his employment had been an act of charity or actual need. But either way Jason had worked hard the last month, wanting to prove, if only to himself, that his skills and knowledge were worthy of more than pity. He'd removed anachronistic steel strings from Vietnamese moon lutes and replaced them with lengths of twisted silk. Over lunch he cleaned cobwebs from the hollows of bone whistles and porcelain bells. He spent several of his days off repairing the delicate bamboo membrane of a lovely jade dizi, so that after sixty years the flute's resonant melody once again filled the air.

Mr. Phipps had actually broken into a wide grin when Jason played the flute for him.

"You're quite a find, Jason."

Jason had flushed with pleasure at the compliment.

Then Mr. Phipps had inquired if he could get to work early to demonstrate the sound of a chelys lyre for a very valuable customer. Jason had been ecstatic at the prospect. He'd assured Mr. Phipps that nothing would keep him away.

Now Jason swore at the grinding stitch in his side as well as the morning traffic. Why, today of all days, did every road seemed clogged with stopped cars?

Twice he'd been detoured by traffic cops wearing neon vests. He was so close, only a few blocks away, but every route he tried seemed closed.

Jason swerved aside as another police car wailed past. Its lights flared through veils of fog like strange lightning. That had to be fifth police car he'd seen this morning.

Something very bad must have happened. Something very close to Phipps's Curiosities and Antiques…The alarming thought of Mr. Phipps alone and injured came to Jason.

He peered into the walls of fog. No sign of a fire. A robbery? But why so many police? What could have happened?

As Jason drew in a deep breath, he recognized the pungent floral scent flooding his lungs. His heart gave a wild kick against his chest. The air had smelled strange that day too. And there had been a deep fog as well—cold but perfumed, as if it were the smoke of an alien fire. He remembered all too clearly the way his father's voice had broken as he'd screamed.

Suddenly the closed streets and blinking police blockades meant nothing. Jason had to know that Mr. Phipps was safe.

He shot past a traffic cop and swerved down the alley that led to the back door of the antiques shop. He dodged trash cans and seagulls and narrowly avoided a vagrant in a tattered trench coat. Behind him, piercing police whistles sounded and someone shouted for him to halt.

But he couldn't, not with the memory of his father's murder growing stronger than reason in his mind.

He couldn't let it happen again. The white mist rolled and swirled around him, brushing his face with dank fingers. The red brick of the back of the antiques shop loomed before him. Five concrete steps led up to the oily black back door.

Then, like one of his nightmares made real, two white, long-limbed creatures stepped out from the door. Toothy spears crowned their heads; the slits of their eyes and nostrils flared wide and scarlet. One held an unlit cigarette between its alabaster talons. The other flicked a silver lighter. Both wore dark uniforms with some sort of government insignia on the chests.

Jason lurched back, slamming his brakes instinctively. His bike skidded across the slick blacktop and swung out from under him. In a crash of wheels and metal frame, Jason hit the ground and rolled into a trash can. The adrenaline flooding his body brought him up to his feet instantly. His arm was bleeding, but he hardly registered the pain. All he saw were the two creatures on the steps above him.

They couldn't be here. They were just delusions. Figments of imagination that several psychiatrists had agreed were Jason's way of dealing with witnessing his father's brutal murder.

They did not exist.

This whole morning had just gotten the better of him; he had to get a grip before it spiraled out of control.

They're not real. They can't be real. But Jason's terror coursed through him with a power far beyond logic.

Both the creatures regarded Jason. Then the one holding the silver lighter pocketed it and took a step down toward Jason.

"Just hold it right there, kid." Hundreds of piranha teeth flashed from the vast gash of its nearly lipless mouth as it spoke. Oddly, its pronunciation was perfect, its words carrying through in a smooth, masculine tone.

It took another step and Jason reflected its advance with a retreating step.

"You don't want to run, kid."

But that, in fact, was all that Jason wanted to do. When the creature took a third step, Jason bolted, racing blindly for the mouth of the alley. He heard the creatures coming after him and somehow he managed to pour on more speed. His muscles flexed and sprang, burning through every gasp of oxygen he pulled into his lungs; his heart pounded like it was going to burst out of his chest. He bounded over two empty milk crates. Seagulls shrieked and took to the air as he came running at them.

Suddenly a tattered beige trench coat enveloped his field of vision and he slammed into the shockingly solid chest of the vagrant he'd nearly hit on his way into the alley.

They both stumbled. Jason flailed out, the back of his hand grazing uselessly across the rough stubble of a hard jawline and through shaggy blond hair. The vagrant caught him in a firm grip and pulled him to his feet. Jason tried to push past him, to keep running, but all the strength seemed to drain from his body as the man held him. His legs felt like broken rubber bands. His lungs were raw. Only the big hand at his back kept him upright as he gasped and floundered like a fish pulled from the water.

"Steady there, speedy." The vagrant's deep voice seemed to resonate through Jason's chest. His tone struck Jason as warm—almost amused––despite his harsh features. As Jason bowed his head, catching his breath, the mineral scents of clay and the tang of juniper drifted over him from the other man's coat.

"They're coming. They—" Hearing the wild panic in his own voice, Jason stopped short. He fought to get control of himself—to drive back the terror pounding through him and think clearly. Unless he wanted to end up in another psychiatric hospital, strung out on haloperidol, he needed to get a grip. Or at least pretend that he had a grip.

Having another human being beside him reassured him and offered him a means to reassess the situation. If there were two nightmarish creatures charging down the alley, certainly this big, blond guy would have reacted with alarm. But he seemed perfectly calm. He clearly didn't see them.

Because they aren't there. They aren't real.

Jason managed to push back from the other man and turn to face his pursuers. He wanted to see nothing, or barring that, two normal human beings—but they remained monsters. Scarlet nostrils flared to deep pits, eyes narrowed to red crescents. An unlit cigarette hung from the ugly mouth of the one nearest Jason.

Jason started back, but the man behind him caught him and stilled him once more. And Jason wasn't sure if it was just a trick of the light or his imagination, but the vagrant suddenly seemed strangely luminous. With his free hand the vagrant flipped an ornate pocket watch from his coat and held it open as if he were displaying a badge. The two creatures pulled to a halt.

"Henry Falk. Shipped in from the field," the man identified himself. "I've got this one."

"Yeah, thanks for that." One of the creatures nodded while the other flipped his cigarette into the toothy chasm of his mouth and swallowed it.

"Henry? My God, it's good to see you again. It's been ages." It shook its ugly head. "The commander didn't mention you were the one they sent out to us. Nice work on the door earlier."

"Gunther?" The vagrant's tone warmed. "I didn't know you were on this operation." The blond man offered an easy smile.

"Yeah, all part of the recent promotion," replied the creature, Gunther—though Jason could hardly reconcile the monstrosity in front of him to such a normal name.

"Good for you." The blond man glanced to Jason and Jason felt suddenly aware that he was gaping. He closed his mouth and the blond man returned his attention to the two creatures in front of them. "How are things in there?"

"Pretty hairy for a while, but the first floor is secured. It seems like the strike force is getting control of the second."

"Good," the blond man responded. "Could one of you tell Commander Carerra that I've closed the mist and all the wards are in place?"

"Will do." Gunther's companion gave a sharp salute with a heavily taloned hand. Then the creature headed back towards the door. Gunther turned his attention to the spill of wheels and spokes that Jason's bicycle had become.

Jason watched the monsters move while his brain seemed to lurch in his skull. He took in his fallen bicycle and the smear of blood where the alley gravel had ground up his forearm. It was starting to hurt badly now. The pain, at least, felt real.

Then he stole a glance to the tall blond man behind him. The man cocked his head, watching Jason in return and giving him a crooked smile, like he was thinking of a joke.

"There's more here than meets the eye, isn't there?" The man's low voice rumbled through Jason and this time Jason saw the silver flames dancing inside the man's mouth. He felt a surge of heat flood him and then his muscles and mind went limp and empty.

Chapter Two

Henry considered the unconscious young man. His pallid face shifted between pretty and plain under the flickering florescent security lights. His body felt too lean for comfort, but he wasn't so slight that lifting him came easily. Henry was glad to flop him down on an absurdly lavish divan. The young man sprawled in his oversized brown suit with the grace of fallen lumber.

Gunther followed them, walking the battered bicycle into the antiques shop. Green trails of spent dampening dust powdered the wood floor. Strips of red exorcism tape closed off the foot of the nearest staircase, and from the noise Henry guessed that Commander Carerra and her agents were still fighting through the balconies that made up the second floor. As if hearing his thoughts, Carerra appeared and peered over the wrought-iron railing. She regarded Henry and his unconscious acquisition with suspicion, then returned her attention to something dark and snarling just beyond Henry's line of sight. A moment later, a deafening staccato of gunfire muted the bestial roars to a whimper and then quiet.

Henry turned his attention back to the young man spilled across the red silk cushions of the Indian divan.

"Who is he?" Gunther leaned the bicycle against the abandoned sale counter and stepped closer to Henry's side.

"Not sure," Henry admitted.

"When he was looking at me..." Gunther tilted his head so that a lock of his black hair shadowed his eyes. He frowned as he studied the unconscious man but said nothing more.

Henry simply nodded. He'd met Gunther's parents when they had just emigrated from goblin lands and were still uneasy in their new human forms. They'd worked as translators in the old San Francisco office where Henry had often crashed between his assignments. Over the years Henry had become a regular at their holiday dinners.

That had been decades before Gunther had been born, and as far as Henry knew, Gunther had never worn the flesh of his ancestors. He'd been made tall, dark, and handsome while still a toothy embryo in his mother's womb. The only hint of his unearthly heritage remaining was his taste for tobacco laced with straight butane, but otherwise not even Henry could discern a flaw in his human appearance.

And yet it had seemed that this inert young man on the divan had looked directly through the strongest and deepest spells of transformation. More than that, he'd broken through the Lost Mists and breached Henry's wards to reach this place.

"A witch, you think?" Gunther asked. "Maybe he's disguised. They haven't found Phipps yet. Could be him."

Henry scowled at that. Back in his day a dealer like Phipps would have been their first target. Securing the treasury of talismans and stolen magics that Phipps had hoarded here in this shop would have come last. But the Irregulars were all about reappropriating and neutralizing trinkets these days. With so many wars of sovereignty raging across the unearthly realms, every nixie prince and kelpie queen was looking for the symbols of power and legitimacy to prop up their claims to the ancient thrones.

"Could he be extra-human?" Gunther's expression conveyed his skepticism of even his own suggestion.

"He certainly doesn't look the part. Doesn't feel eldritch either, but maybe." Henry held out the black nylon wallet he'd lifted off the young man in the alley. It contained three dollars, a cracked BART pass, and a forlorn-looking identification card.

"ID says he's Jason Shamir. This home address mean anything to you?" Henry handed the wallet to Gunther.

"Just off the Tenderloin." Gunther arched a dark brow. "Skid row. Could be a junkie? Maybe that's why he freaked out when he saw me and Tim."

"It's possible," Henry conceded. Clearly Gunther had been shaken by Jason's reaction to him. "That still wouldn't explain how he got through the mists."

Gunther scowled but said nothing.

Henry crouched beside the divan and leaned very close. He studied the fine skin and simple, clean features. Too simple, really. Natural skin bore freckles and moles, tiny imperfections that made individuals so very singular. Jason's skin was smooth as a newborn's and devoid of anything that might serve as a distinguishing feature. At a glance he could have passed for anyone and no one.

"Something's not quite right about him, that's certain." Henry watched the rhythm of Jason's steady breath and slowed his own. As Jason exhaled, Henry drew in all that he gave up.

Dark coffee and hints of cinnamon toothpaste rolled over Henry's tongue. He tasted exhaustion and hunger. As he held the breath in his lungs he felt the electric crackle of longing and the suffocating cold of fear. But nothing more. None of a faerie blood's violet perfume nor even the faint dank of black cat bones that clung to most young witches. Not even so much magic as a lucky rabbit's foot was on the boy.

Absolutely average—less than average, in fact, since most young people still carried those tiny charms of a mother's kiss on their cheeks or a father's best wish upon their brows. But this youth lay devoid of even the smallest blessing to protect him.

Only when Henry released the breath did he hear the faintest whisper of something unearthly. For an instant the sweetest, saddest melody drifted from his lips like a whisper. Wordlessly, it promised Henry something gentle as salvation and stronger than hope. It felt like sure hands stroking his weathered cheek as if he were handsome again. It warmed him like sunshine and for just a moment it made him believe that Frank was still alive, standing just behind him.

But he knew it couldn't be Frank's hand brushing the ragged collar of his coat just now, because most of Frank's finger bones lay like shrapnel beneath Henry's skin.

Henry recoiled at once, bounding up and away from the prone young man. He nearly collided with Gunther, who'd moved closer and stared at Jason with rapt fascination.

"Shake it off, Gunther!" Henry elbowed Gunther's chest and Gunther suddenly snapped upright as if he'd just woken.

"Henry…Where am—" Gunther looked around in confusion and then his gaze settled back on Henry. "What the hell was that?"

"Not sure, but I think—" Henry stopped short as he realized that at least a dozen agents had been drawn to the balcony railing above them and were now staring down in varying states of confusion. Only a few feet from Gunther, two winged snakes that had previously camouflaged themselves on a carved bedpost hovered in the air, their gilded wings beating softly as they stretched toward the divan. They crooned like hungry doves and circled, as if searching for something that they had suddenly lost.

A dirty-looking brownie, standing no more than two feet tall and wearing only a pair of black dress socks, also seemed to have been drawn out from where it had been hiding in the dark corners of the shop. Now the gaunt, leathery creature swayed less than a yard from Henry and stared at Jason with its bony hands lifted like it was about to receive a precious gift.

Just as awareness lit the brownie's expression, Henry bounded forward and snatched hold of it.

"NATO Irregular Affairs Division," Henry informed the brownie before it decided to bite.

"Aw shit," the brownie mumbled.

"Do we have a situation down there?" Carerra's voice carried down from the second floor. She shouldered between two of her stunned agents and glowered down at Henry from the wrought-iron railing.

"It's under control, Commander," Henry assured her.

Carerra turned on her own agents, ordering them back to their positions. Just as she began to move away, the brownie let out a howl and jerked against Henry's grip. It kicked at Henry's crotch, landing a hard punt into his thigh. Henry swung it up off its feet and dangled it by its wrists at arm's length.

"Put me down, you hog twat!" the brownie shouted. "Criminal brutality, that's what this is! Not one of you dirty badges has got goods on me! I was here square and legal to do proper business for my master. I got rights!"

"I suppose you've got a passport and the sales documents to back you up?" Henry asked, and despite himself, he smiled at the savage little brownie. There weren't many of this kind left. Nowadays most dolled themselves up like little butlers and played hurt or obsequious when they were collared with counterfeit bills or sacks of severed hands. It had been decades since Henry'd encountered a filthy, cussing brownie, swinging its withered little prick around like it could piss acid.

"I got that an' more for you, dick wadcutters. It's in my fine boot!"

"Dick wadcutters?" Gunther repeated the words as if they were from a foreign language. "What does that even mean?"

The brownie simply thrust out its stocking foot. Henry kept his right hand firmly clamped around the brownie's tiny wrists and used his mutilated left hand to peel down the brownie's sock and pull out a wad of reeking papers.

He tossed them to Gunther, who made a face at the dank fungal aroma but quickly flipped through them.

"Well?" Carerra called down. She sounded tired of the matter already.

"The passport's legal," Gunther announced. "The bill of sale looks shady, though."

The brownie shrieked an obscene protest.

"Them papers are clean as a unicorn's snatch, you screw! My master paid for that boy half up front, a troll's skull of gold dust!" The brownie kicked its foot toward the divan where Jason lay.

"I just came to collect the property. But seeing how you dirty badges banged the boy up, I want a discount!"

"This just gets weirder and weirder," Gunther commented softly. He frowned at the young man.

"So, we can add human trafficking to Phipps's crimes," Carerra pronounced from the balcony. "We'll need the paperwork on this filed before I get back to the station."

A brief burst of gunfire sounded, followed by the voices of alarmed agents. Carerra glanced over her shoulder and obviously did not like what she saw among the antique canopy beds and exotic gilded statues. A smoky serpentine shadow swayed against the high ceiling, growing steadily more solid by the moment.

"Right now we've got bigger fish to fry up here." Carerra turned her attention to Henry. "You handle this, Falk. Figure out what the hell is going on with that boy."

"Yes, ma'am." Henry saluted, though Carerra had already turned away.

Chapter Three

Jason woke to the awareness that he lay prone atop a firm surface. His feet dangled slightly and his right forearm throbbed with a dull ache. For just an instant he thought he'd fallen asleep on his narrow futon and dreamed something terrible.

But he knew instinctively that this wasn't his home and he hadn't been dreaming. His memory roiled with images of pale monsters in dark uniforms and a strangely luminous vagrant with a silver flame flickering in his mouth.

Crazy stuff, he thought in frustration. The kind of crazy that had gotten him locked up before and could get him locked up again...maybe already had.

He flexed his wrists, testing for the resistance of restraints. He encountered none and opened his eyes to take in the small beige room and the two other occupants seated at a cheap looking table. One of them took a swig from a metal flask while the other held a white paper coffee cup to the bloody gash of his gaping mouth.

Jason closed his eyes again immediately.

"Back among the conscious, Mr. Shamir?" He heard the rustle of clothes as the big blond vagrant moved closer to the white vinyl couch where he lay.

"He's awake?" The second voice was smoother, younger. He sounded so calm, so human. Jason recalled him answering to the unremarkable name of Gunther. Still, Jason kept his eyes closed. He didn't think he could bear to look at that gaping mouth again.

"Yes, I'm awake." For a moment Jason tried to imagine what the other two men made of him, of the entire situation. He probably seemed insane. Jason didn't allow himself to consider that they might be right to think as much. "I crashed my bike…"

"Yes, you did," the vagrant said. "Banged up your arm too."

"We had a medic clean it up for you," Gunther told him. "It's scraped up, but nothing's broken."

"Thanks," Jason replied, but then he didn't know what else to say. He wanted to demand to know where he was and who these two thought they were, holding him here.

But, God, he didn't even know if he was really here with them. All of his senses told him that he was in the grip of reality: the slight tack of the vinyl against the bare skin of his arm, the smell of stale coffee, and the noise of an overhead fan.

And yet when he cracked his eyes just enough to glimpse the two men, horror gripped him and everything became unreal. It wasn't just the toothy, slit-eyed monstrosity of Gunther. The other man, too, grew stranger and stranger the longer Jason studied him.

He flickered slightly like a florescent light that hadn't come up to its full burn. A haze like the tracers of taillights built around his eyes until they seemed to blaze beneath the dark shadows of his lashes.

As he shifted, his rumpled coat fell open, and steadily, strange luminous symbols began to glow up through the threadbare material of his undershirt. The rubber bands ringing his long fingers twitched like reviving centipedes. And something in his coat pocket pulsed with the rhythm of a beating heart.

Jason clenched his eyes closed. He hated this uncertainty, despised the sense of reality slipping out from under him like quicksand. He didn't want to be afraid to just open his eyes. Why couldn't his mind just work? Why couldn't he stop seeing monsters and weird creatures all around him? Why couldn't he just be normal?

"I imagine you have a lot of questions for us." The vagrant's voice was soft, but somehow Jason thought he could feel the warmth of the man's breath against his ear, whispering other words.

You haven't gone mad, Jason. Just hear me out.

"I'm Agent Henry Falk and the striking gentleman with me is Agent Gunther Heartman. We work for the NATO Irregular Affairs Division and we're hoping that you might be able to help us in apprehending a criminal."

None of this was anything Jason had expected. Reflexively he sat up, staring at the two.

"What did you say?"

"We'd like you to help us out, if you can." Agent Falk offered him another of his easy, crooked smiles and his whole body seemed to throw off a radiant light. He didn't look anything like a government agent, but Jason didn't feel certain enough of his senses to point that out.

"According to your W2 you'd been employed by Mr. Phipps for close to two months." Gunther set his paper coffee cup aside and as he did so Jason noticed that his taloned, bony hand cast a weirdly human shadow. Jason wondered if it was a little glimpse of reality. The rest of Gunther's shadow fell in a pool at his feet but seemed smooth and benign in comparison to his jagged white body.

"Mr. Shamir?" Gunther prompted.

"Uhm…yes, that's right. Seven weeks, come Wednesday." Belatedly, Jason realized where this might be leading. "Has something happened to him? Is Mr. Phipps hurt?"

"As far as we know, he's fine." Annoyance sounded through Agent Falk's gravely voice. "You're the one that nearly disappeared."

"What?"

"Phipps brokered a deal with a foreign entity to sell you," Agent Falk told him. He took a quick swig from his flask and the blaze of his eyes seemed to dim.

"To sell me…That—that's got to be some kind of a joke."

"It's not," Gunther informed him. "If our agency hadn't raided Phipps's shop when we did, you would have been handed over this morning."

"No…That's crazy," Jason said, though he felt weird, looking at these two and calling anything crazy. Still he went on, "Who on earth would want to buy me?"

"Someone who knew what you could do," Falk replied.

"What I can do?" Now this really did have to be some kind of elaborate joke, didn't it? "The only remarkable thing I can do is survive for two years on nothing but dry breakfast cereal. That and collect loose change from parking lots—"

"You can see through transformations, through spells and even glamours, straight to the truth," Agent Falk cut him off. "That's what you're doing right now, as you're looking at me and at Agent Heartman. You're seeing what no one else does. The truth at the core of us."

Jason went very still, though his heart pounded frantically in his chest. No one had ever suggested anything like this to him before and it had to be madness…and yet it felt like a revelation, like an assurance, at last, that he wasn't insane. He wanted to believe it so badly that it terrified him, because it was just the kind of delusion that would lead him to a complete break from reality.

"I don't know what you're talking about," Jason said carefully.

"Yes, you do," Falk replied softly and with certainty.

"I don't." Jason could hardly force the words out of his clenching throat.

"All right." Falk shrugged. "Tell you what, I'll drop the whole thing if you just tell me what color Agent Heartman's eyes are." Falk flashed a wide, wicked smile and Jason glimpsed the silver fire dancing behind his teeth. "Just tell me the color. Easy peasy, yeah?"

Jason gave a stiff nod.

Gunther closed the distance between them in quick steps and then bent so that his face was only inches from Jason's. Jason fought against the instinct to recoil.

He could smell the tobacco on Gunther's breath and see the fine striations in the hundreds of jagged teeth protruding from his deathly white jaws. His scarlet eyes gleamed like fresh wounds.

Jason forced himself to stare hard into those red slits, searching for any sign of human eyes. A faint reflection of his own strained face floated up to him but nothing else. A cold sweat beaded his brow.

"Brown…" Jason guessed at last, because brown was the most common color of human eyes—the color of his own eyes.

Gunther drew back, stole a quick glance at Falk, then returned his attention to Jason.

"You really can't see me, can you?" Gunther sounded both puzzled and awed.

"His eyes are blue," Falk supplied. "Bright blue."

Somehow that was the last straw. Jason just didn't have the strength to fight anymore. He stared down at the shadows on the floor. "I couldn't see them."

"Not at all?" Gunther asked.

"Not the way other people do…" Jason admitted.

Gunther cocked his grotesque head. "What do I look like to you?" he asked in a tone of idle curiosity.

Like a monster, Jason thought. *Like the things that murdered my father. But he didn't want to say as much.*

"I'll bet he sees the snow goblin you would have been if you hadn't been transformed," Falk stated as if anyone would draw such a conclusion.

Gunther scowled like he'd just stepped in dog shit. Falk fished through one of the deep pockets of his trench coat and brought out a small black book, which he tossed to Gunther.

"Page twenty," Falk instructed. "See if I'm not right."

Up close Jason could see that the book cover was badly scuffed and the binding had split in several places. Gunther turned through the pages and then stopped.

"Talk about your old-school goblins," Gunther commented.

He turned the book to Jason, exposing a page of tightly packed print and a hand-colored illustration. Jason instantly recognized the gaping creature depicted with a human skull gripped in its talons.

He stared at the picture with the same kind of wonder that he'd felt the first time he'd read a stanza of his favorite music and had realized that many people had known this melody before him.

"That's it exactly," Jason admitted.

"I don't look anything like this woman," Gunther muttered. He took the book and scowled at the open pages before handing the book back to Falk.

To Jason's surprise, Falk laughed.

"The truth hurts, Gunther. But on the bright side, if this job ever goes south, you could make a killing performing drag with that pretty goblin face of yours."

"Yeah, that's great to hear. Remind me to thank my parents for choosing such a sensitive man to be my godfather."

Falk simply shrugged, then plucked a pair of cheap plastic glasses from his breast pocket and spat on the lenses. His saliva gleamed like mercury as he smeared it across the lenses with his thumbs. Then he stepped to Jason's side and thrust the plastic glasses out at him. "Try these on and tell me what you think."

Jason accepted the black-framed glasses gingerly. The plastic radiated heat against his fingers.

"Go on," Falk told him. "They can't make Gunther look worse than he already does."

Gunther shot Falk a sinister look, but then Jason thought that any expression would appear sinister on such a face.

"They'll allow you to see the world in all its illusions, just like the rest of us do," Falk told him.

"Some kind of reverse spell projectors?" Gunther asked.

"Something like that." Falk nodded.

Jason slid the glasses on and for a moment he simply stared around himself in wonder. The room changed only slightly—one of two doors evaporating beneath the bare surface of a beige wall—but both Falk and Gunther were considerably altered.

Jason gaped at the tall, tan man Gunther had become. With his strong build, handsome face, glossy black hair, and brilliant blue eyes he looked more like a film star than a government employee. He offered Jason a dashing smile and Jason felt a flush spreading across his cheeks. He was beautiful.

Embarrassed, Jason turned his attention to Falk.

His transformation was more subtle but in a way stranger, because Jason had grown almost used to the luminous quality of the man. Now his eyes and mouth looked like dull shadows beneath the harsh angles of his sharp brow and crooked nose. Blond stubble mottled his jaw and his pale hair jutted out as if it hadn't been brushed or washed in days. He stood several inches taller than Gunther, but where Gunther looked toned and healthy, Falk seemed rangy and hungry.

Above all else Jason noticed that, devoid of his radiance, Falk seemed worn—not gray haired or wrinkled—but weathered and scarred like the rundown rooms of the flophouse where Jason slept these days.

Jason took a few more moments, allowing himself to accept the full impact of these plastic glasses and the new world he viewed through them.

I'm not crazy. It's just the way I see…

It seemed almost too relieving to believe.

"Mr. Shamir?" Gunther prompted and then he glanced to Falk. "Did you do something really weird to him?"

"I'm fine," Jason said quickly. "I just…This is unbelievable."

"But true, all the same," Falk said with a certain finality. He lifted his flask but then dropped it back into his coat pocket without drinking from it. Jason absently wondered what else he secreted in those pockets.

"Having true sight probably hasn't been all that useful to you," Falk said. "Most of the folks with it end up in mental institutions."

Jason felt the color drain from his face at the memory of St. Mary's. If either of the agents noticed, they didn't remark on it. Falk went on speaking.

"But the ability to see the truth can be valuable when it comes to magics. It's particularly useful in dealing with the sidhe, the fae in particular, who traffic in illusions and glamours. Even the best technology we have can't pierce the faerie glamours that you could see past at a glance."

"Faerie glamours? Like magical litltle faries?" Jason tried not to sound skeptical because he was wearing what appeared to be some kind of magic glasses. But still…faeries?

"Nah, not just faeries." Falk replied. "I mean not unless you'd call a troll or a goblin a faerie."

"We prefer to be called the Luminous Ones," Gunther commented. Falk smirked at that.

"Yeah, and I'd like to be called Prince Charming, but it isn't what I am." He scratched the blond stubble of his chin. "The point is that you, Mr. Shamir, have a great talent and value. Your employer, Mr. Phipps, made it his business to trade in such things, and when you fell into his hands, he put you up for auction—"

"For auction?" Jason wished that he could stop feeling shocked and out of his depth.

"Yes. He sold you," Falk said as if this sort of thing happened every day and warranted no more surprise than a parking ticket.

"And someone actually bought me?" Jason asked. He couldn't imagine them paying much.

"Someone certainly tried to." Falk nodded.

"Who?" Jason asked.

"That we don't know," Gunther admitted. "The buyer paid in gold dust—half up front, apparently—but we can't reliably track it back to a source. And the brownie sent to retrieve you and make the second payment is too infected with spells to be able to tell us, even if he wanted to."

"Which he doesn't," Falk added.

"No, he really doesn't," Gunther agreed and he looked oddly grim for a moment. Then he picked up his coffee cup and frowned into the depths of its contents.

"So, it boils down to this," Falk went on while Gunther drank, "we're pretty certain that Mr. Phipps made previous illegal sales to this same buyer—possibly previous employees. We need to track the buyer down before he can find a new supplier or, if the goods exchanged were human beings, before he decides to dispose of them to hide his crimes." Falk's shadowed gaze settled on Jason. "We'd like you to help us."

For just an instant Jason stole a glimpse over the top of his glasses. Falk's eyes shone like the blue flames of a gas stove.

"How?" Jason asked.

"We're betting that Phipps will attempt to turn you over to his buyer; he'll want the second half of his payment. We've shut down all of his accounts. He doesn't have any other source of revenue open to him and he'll need money if he hopes to relocate to another realm."

"So..." Jason considered this as best he could without getting caught up on the idea of faeries and gold dust and brownies. "Are you asking me to let him abduct me?"

"You'd be protected the entire time," Gunther said quickly. "We'd have agents tailing you and at least one planted with you."

"But that's what we're asking," Falk replied.

Jason scowled down at his hands. Flecks of his own dried blood pebbled his right palm.

"You're free to refuse," Falk told him with another of those crooked smiles, though now the expression looked dark and cynical. "But the fact remains that Phipps is likely to come after you whether we're protecting you or not. If you were smart, you'd invite us along."

Jason nodded, not because he agreed so much as he couldn't disagree. He could hardly process all of this. And it felt suddenly like the first night he'd spent in St. Mary's, half out of his mind with horror while soft-spoken doctors and nurses had told him what would be best for him and locked him in a small room where the bed was bolted to the floor.

He wondered how it could be that, in discovering that he wasn't insane and never had been, his life had actually become more unbelievable and farther beyond his control? At least before there had been a real world where monsters didn't exist. A real world that he could hope to one day belong to. Now that was lost to him.

Jason closed his eyes and for a moment cast his thoughts back past all this confusion to the moment he'd first woken this morning, when everything had been calm and hopeful. He thought of the melody that he'd planned to perform for Mr. Phipps's special customer. The soothing refrain played through his memory and Jason let it calm him.

At last he forced himself to look up and face the two agents in front of him. "So, how will this work? You guys stake out the place where I'm staying and I wear a wire or something?"

"No wires." Falk shook his head. "They're too unreliable where magic is concerned. Too conductive to outside influences."

Gunther nodded in agreement with Falk and then went on, "We'll place agents around you, and since Falk's with us, we'll also be able to have him shadow you through the shade lands."

"Should I ask what the shade lands are or will it just confuse me more?" Jason inquired. "Because I'm feeling pretty close to my limit of confusion right now, but I need to know what's going to be happening to me."

Gunther looked slightly concerned, but Falk just gave a rough laugh.

"Have you had anything to eat this morning?" Falk asked.

"I didn't have time—"

"Why don't we go grab us a couple sandwiches or something?" Falk suggested. "Maybe somewhere a little more comfortable. And NATO will foot the bill."

"Sure." The suggestion struck Jason as relievingly mundane. "I'd like that."

"Carerra hasn't gotten back in—" Gunther began in a low whisper to Falk.

"Just tell her I felt I needed to relocate to a point of greater personal geomantic power. She's already sure I'm a kook." Falk smiled in that oddly knowing manner. "And who knows, it could be true."

"What geomantic location are you thinking of?" Gunther asked.

"Mac's joint." Falk sounded almost wistful. "Is it still around?"

"No. Mac passed five years back." Gunther shook his head. "His diner's a Starbucks now."

For just a moment the shadows of Falk's face deepened. Then he turned his attention back to Jason. "Why don't you pick. You got a favorite spot?"

"I like the HRD Coffee Shop, just off Third and Tabor Alley," Jason suggested. Despite what Falk had said about paying, he thought he should keep things in a range he could hope to afford. Maybe someday he'd eat somewhere as exotic and refined as Michael Mina, but right now he just wanted to escape to cheap, cheerful, and above all, familiar surroundings.

Falk gave him a nod. "All right then. Let's go get some grub."

Gunther and Falk escorted him out of the small room through a rather dull corridor of what looked like offices. When Jason kept his gaze straight ahead, he encountered only beige walls cement floor, and ordinary men and women dressed for business.

But occasionally, he glimpsed a flare of brilliant color or a strange, beastly countenance just over the frames of his glasses. And once, when he glanced up at the ceiling, the periphery of his vision filled with thousands of arcane symbols, blazing like stars against a fathomless darkness. Looking directly through his glasses, he saw only a yellow Casablanca ceiling fan wheeling in slow circles beneath a white plaster ceiling and banks of florescent lights.

Tellingly, he couldn't hear a hint of traffic or the busy street life that usually filled the city.

"Where are we exactly?" Jason asked.

"San Francisco headquarters," Gunther replied.

"Underground," Falk added.

"You mean we're in tunnels under the city?" Jason asked.

Falk just nodded.

Jason remembered fellow patients at St. Mary's whispering about the vast system of tunnels supposedly lying below San Francisco, but he'd never really believed any of their stories. At the time the descriptions of secret subterranean bunkers and missile control rooms had struck him as paranoid delusions. Now, walking these immense corridors where the elongated silhouettes of black cats and red-eyed goblins slunk through his peripheral vision, it struck him that a secret military base was actually rather mundane—even a little unimaginative.

As they progressed, passersby laden with black folders and stacks of files greeted Gunther warmly but took in Falk's presence with an odd uncertainty, as if he was someone they knew of but never imagined they'd meet, like Santa Claus or Jack the Ripper.

One pretty young woman admitted that she'd thought Half-Dead Henry had gone over to the other side, while a plump, bald man recalled his superior officer disappearing for a week while he supposedly attended Falk's funeral.

"But that was back in the weird old days, you know, when all the monarchies were being overthrown and none of our agents would say what they were really doing out in the other realms." The bald man stopped in front of a door marked Lower Incantations. "It must be nice to be back now that things have straightened up."

"Sure," Falk replied, but he didn't linger on the subject or in the other man's company. Instead he turned away. Gunther and Jason followed after him.

The gold plaques designating each door they passed offered Jason an almost surreal sense of the types of work that went on behind them—Sacrifice Licensing, Enchantment Residue Analysis, Transformation Vaults, NATO Irregular Affairs Division Payroll—but none proved to be their destination.

As they walked farther, he began to wonder if they were lost. And he almost asked, but then they turned a corner and came to a halt where the hallway abruptly ended in a wide expanse of gray concrete. The air smelled of the subway and someone had stenciled a mishmash of city transit routes, street maps, and timetables across the concrete wall in front of them. To the far left stood several steel bike racks where—among mountain bikes, ten speeds, and a few brooms—Jason's battered green bicycle leaned at an expectant angle.

Aside from a few additional chips in the paint, his bike looked to be in good shape, which Jason found relieving. It had been his one reliable form of transportation since he was sixteen.

He gripped the handlebars and took a kind of comfort in the solid reality of them. Nothing strange or hidden here, just simple machinery laid bare. For just a moment he could pretend that the world was still the same as it had been yesterday.

When he looked up from the bike, he saw Falk take a piece of white chalk from one of his pockets and scrawl something on the cement wall. Beneath that he drew the tall rectangle and simple circle that a child might have used to depict a door and its knob.

A delighted smile lit Gunther's handsome face.

"I've always wanted to see how they used to do this back in the day," he commented to Jason, as if Jason could have any idea of what he really meant.

"The door's the easy part, really. The trick is deciding whether you trust yourself enough to walk through it." Falk dropped the chalk back into a pocket of his stained trench coat and glanced to Gunther. "Are you coming or staying?"

Gunther looked torn but then shook his head.

"I've still got paperwork and background files. Commander Carerra will skin me alive if I wander off on a hobo adventure just now. But I'll catch up with you later. No doubt Carerra will have orders for me to deliver to you."

"Sure." Falk gave the response in an offhanded manner as if his attention was already far away. Then he spat into his own palm and smacked his hand against the chalk doorknob.

Jason felt the hair standing up on his arms and along the back of his neck.

Then Falk blew out a long slow breath.

It was hardly anything, and yet Jason's stomach flipped as if he'd suddenly dropped twenty feet. For just an instant he thought he saw a white mist rising at the edges of his vision. Peering over the frames of his glasses, Jason saw Falk blaze to a silver brilliance. He looked radiant, almost beautiful, but far too bright to keep gazing at.

Jason shifted his attention to the concrete wall and realized that the outline of the door wasn't just a line of chalk anymore.

Bright white afternoon light poured in at its edges. A warm beam fell across Jason's arm as he walked his bicycle closer.

Falk pushed door open and blinding sunlight poured into the dim hallway. Jason smelled frying onions and noticed the noise of street traffic rumbling over pedestrian conversations. A car alarm went off and then stopped.

Falk stepped out into the light and Jason blindly followed him out of the dark into the mundane squalor of Tabor Alley. When Jason glanced back he found nothing remained of the door but a few scratches in the graffiti tagged across the brick wall behind him.

Chapter Four

The HRD Coffee Shop was not a coffee shop, Henry noted, but more like a greasy spoon diner that had collided with an Asian taco truck back in the seventies and was still reeling with dark wood paneling and flecked Formica. The sweating cooks behind the grill served up pancakes, turkey dinners, fried rice, pork tacos, kim chiburritos, and Mongolian cheesesteaks to a throng of seedy customers.

As he and Jason worked their way to the counter, Henry noted that several burly cooks seemed to know Jason by sight and greeted him warmly. The Hispanic girl working the register offered him a sisterly grin and judged his new glasses to be "very smart". Jason laughed at that, then after a moment of consideration, ordered a kimchi burrito.

"I love that there's so much to choose from here," Jason commented to Henry. "It's like free will on a menu board."

"Certainly more exotic than most coffee shops from my day," Henry agreed. Still he chose to play it safe his first day back among the living and ordered the Mongolian cheesesteak.

"It's not all that spicy," Jason assured him and Henry tried not to smirk at the young man's concern.

They seated themselves at the narrow bar. While Jason mulled over the variety of hot sauces, mustards, and soy sauce on offer, Henry studied the place more closely. It was cheap, run down, and certainly quirky, but for all the exotic menu items and condiments, it remained utterly human.

Not a trace of otherworldly magic hung in the pungent, oily air. Not a single nixie lurked among the newly delivered boxes of napkins. No restless ghosts lent their unearthly chill to the wheezing beverage cooler. The place was clean, at least in terms of supernatural activity. The countertop seemed a little on the sticky side.

Still, Henry could understand why Jason felt comfortable in this cramped dive. It was entirely free of illusions. And in a city like San Francisco, seated atop so many portals and populated by such a diverse variety of both the unearthly and undead, Jason probably tripped over a displaced ogre, a slumming djinn, or an out-of-work kelpie every time he stepped out his front door. After only one supernatural encounter the average man generally flipped his lid. More than a few ended up on the evening news, wearing nothing but tinfoil beanies and screaming at invisible pixies.

Hell, a good fifth of NIAD's recruits were picked up en route to psych wards.

But somehow Jason had eluded detection for years. It could have been a coincidence, but Henry didn't think so. Too much about Jason seemed designed to be overlooked, misfiled, and forgotten. Henry didn't think he'd ever met a man who better embodied the average nice-guy qualities that so easily melted from memory. Just one more in a sea of boys next door who claimed no fixed address in anyone's awareness.

Henry stole a sidelong glance at the young man as he briskly anointed his burrito with bright red sriracha sauce. A subtle dexterity played through his long hands. The speed of his motions brought to mind a few of the genuine magicians Henry had known—not those flashy con men on darkened stages, but the rare people whose bodies pulsed with magic.

And yet, Henry couldn't catch even a whisper of power from the young man. So, either he was the best fake Henry had ever encountered or the power within him had been hidden very deeply indeed: carved into his bones and then buried beneath layers of anonymity spells. Jason was definitely too young and too inexperienced to have done such a thing himself.

"You have much family here?" Henry asked.

"Me?" Jason glanced to Henry as if he expected him to be addressing someone else.

"I wasn't asking myself."

"No, sorry." Jason flushed a little and Henry recalled that in their questioning earlier Jason had also seemed surprised to be regarded with any importance. Most men his age would have betrayed a trace of excitement at discovering they were so unique.

"I'm pretty much alone. I moved here with my dad..." For just an instant something like fear flickered through Jason's expression, but then he just shook his head. "He's gone. So it's just me now."

"Yeah, same here." Henry remembered his childhood dog better than any of his surviving relations. "So you grew up in the city?"

"Yeah. My dad and I moved here when I was seven and I've lived in the Bay Area ever since." Jason supplied the answer with a telling kind of tension in his voice. This was painful for him, Henry thought.

"Never wanted to travel?"

"I don't know." Jason relaxed a little. "San Francisco's familiar. I like that." He took a bite of his burrito, effectively evading further questions. And Henry decided to let it go for now.

He sampled his Mongolian cheesesteak. His silver tongue drew in far more of the slaughterhouse from the succulent meat than Henry would have liked to swallow. That was always a problem with fresh food, traces of memory persisted in the flesh.

Beside him, Jason ate like a neat machine. Even after he'd finished his food Jason's furtive gaze flickered over other men's meals.

"You want these fries?" Henry offered. It wasn't his habit to let other people eat off his plate, but he'd never cared that much for the common french fry.

"You're sure?"

"Yeah. Have 'em." Henry pushed the fries to Jason and watched in fascination as Jason drenched them in hot sauce and disappeared them like so many gangland snitches going into the East River.

Either the guy had a tapeworm for a dietician or he was half starving. In that, he reminded Henry a little of Frank but not so much that it hurt. They'd all been hungry young men back in the day.

"Can I ask you a question?" Jason glanced up at him from over the rim of his glasses. Henry wondered just what he saw.

"Sure, you can ask anything you like," Henry replied.

Jason smiled slightly at his response.

"But you might not answer, right?"

Henry shrugged.

"Well, either way," Jason replied. "There was something kind of fluttering in your coat pocket earlier. I've been wondering what it was all morning."

"Can't you see it?" Henry lowered his voice. "If you take the glasses off?"

"Not through your coat," Jason responded as if Henry were dense. "I don't have X-ray vision."

"Good to know." True sight was so rare that not even Henry knew exactly how far it extended and, as a rule, those who possessed it—and didn't go crazy—generally kept the limits of their vision secret to protect the value of their services. Jason seemed oddly sane and forthcoming.

"So what is it?" Jason took a swig of his coffee. "The thing in your pocket."

"It's the remains of a little girl's heart," Henry replied. Jason blanched and set his coffee down.

"Why do you have…that?"

"Because she was murdered to create a curse. She died so alone and so terrified that her heart became a grasping, poisonous little thing." Henry kept his tone neutral and low. "She needs be carried and kept company before her terror will fade and let her pass through the shade lands."

Henry considered showing Jason the tiny cinder that remained of her. The girl would probably have liked to be held by someone as gentle as Jason. But Henry wasn't sure of just how terrible her visage would be to Jason.

"Gunther mentioned the shade lands earlier. He said you could watch me from there, didn't he?" Jason kept his voice low. "You never told me what they were."

Henry frowned. All around them the clatter and rumble of more earthly pursuits rose and fell. Two construction workers debated their fantasy football picks. A scrawny Asian boy tried to convince the plump white girl next to him to come clubbing with him later tonight. And over it all the cooks at the grill kept up a steady stream of conversation and bursts of song as they shouted along with the classic rock drifting down from decades-old speakers.

And here was this fresh young man sitting beside him, so obvious in his longing both to know the truth and also to belong to a warm, mundane, human existence.

But the truth could change everything in this little sanctuary. It would make this diner—this whole city for that matter—seem like a world of happy insects frolicking on a fallen leaf as it drifted over the surface of an immense sea.

"Is it bad?" Jason asked quietly and Henry realized that the truth had to come out because it wouldn't do anyone any good to keep it hidden. But it didn't need to be grandiose. The hungry dead and the voracious darkness that held them weren't Jason's concern.

"The first thing you should know is that there are lots of other realms. The guys up in the labs like to call them infinite dimensional planes, but as far as I'm concerned they're realms. Some are very small, others vast enough to contain countless worlds folded up within them. Some are nearly too far to reach, others sit right on top of our own. Irregulars deal with interactions between the populaces of those other realms and our own earthly realm."

Jason nodded.

"I sort of got that idea with all the talk about faeries and the work being done in those offices." Jason had the good sense to keep his voice down but not to draw attention by whispering. Nothing was quite so suspicious as the sound of whispers.

"Yes, but it's not all just faeries, and not all of what we think of as faeries are the same race. The sidhe alone make up a solid fifty different tribes. Infinite worlds of infinite variation and all that, you know."

"I…I think so." Jason nodded. "So, these shade lands?"

"It's not a realm where anything lives. It's the place of the restless dead. The hungry dead," Henry replied quickly. He hunted there, spent years at a time in those murky depths, but he didn't like to talk about the place all that much. "The shade lands lie just under the skin of all living worlds. When you see a ghost here, its spirit is trapped in the shade lands and usually trying to break back through to the living world because of something unfinished, something it needs or fears or loves that it's still holding on to, even in death."

Jason was very quiet for a few moments.

"Are there a lot of ghosts?" he asked at last.

"Fewer than you'd think, if you believe in them," Henry answered. "A lot more than you'd expect if you don't."

"That's not really an answer."

"It's the best I can give." Henry shrugged. "It's not like they fill out census forms. And the shade lands aren't a clear, bright place. They're murky and filled with currents like the deep sea. They stretch infinitely out as far as death reaches."

Jason nodded, but he wasn't looking at Henry. He hardly seemed to be listening to him.

"If someone was murdered…violently, would he end up trapped there? Would he still be suffering?" The anxiety in Jason's expression was obvious.

"No. Not necessarily." Henry wondered just who Jason had lost. The father he'd mentioned earlier or the mother that he didn't mention at all? From the way his face drained of color Henry guessed that it had been someone close to him and the end had been very ugly. "The vast majority of souls pass through the shade lands, no matter how they died. It's generally when magic is involved that they remain. But most streak through instantly. Like shooting stars." Sometimes they even made the gray darkness seem beautiful.

"My dad was murdered…" Jason looked away from Henry, down into his coffee cup. For an uncomfortable moment Henry feared that the young man might cry, but to Henry's relief he pulled himself together. "He was torn apart by monsters—snow goblins. And I just need to know if he could be trapped in those shade lands?"

"How long ago was this?" Henry asked.

"Seventeen years." Jason's gaze remained on the dark liquid in his cup. "He suffered…"

It didn't take a mathematical genius to figure out that Jason would have just been a child when his father had been murdered, and it sounded like he'd witnessed it.

"No. Your dad's not trapped. See, unless they're political refugees, snow goblins only come to the earthly realm as mercenaries, not magicians. They can be brutal, but they don't bind souls or break them with torture," Henry assured him. "Whatever your old man suffered, it ended with his life. By now he's been reborn. More than likely he's kicking up trouble as a surly teen somewhere."

Jason at last lifted his gaze to meet Henry's. He was a plain young man, but there was something so hopeful and relieved in his expression that he seemed rather handsome at the moment.

Henry felt loathe to ruin Jason's happiness, but the fact that his father had been murdered by snow goblins didn't bode well for Jason himself. While a few of their clans lived as political refugees, most served the powerful rulers of other unearthly realms. And a man didn't make an enemy of any of them by accident.

"What did your father do?" Henry asked.

"He was a musician. He could play pretty much anything with strings." Jason answered this easily and with more than a hint of pride. "My mom too. She played the flute and the mandolin. I still remember the songs she taught me."

"Yeah?" Henry encouraged Jason to go on. Smiling and animated, the young man took on a charming appeal.

"'Suite Romantique', 'Syrinx', 'Carmen Fantasie', 'The Stone Of Fal'—"

"Stone of Fal?" Henry knew the name well enough but was surprised that Jason did.

"Yeah, I think it's Irish or something."

Sidhe actually, Henry thought but he didn't say so. "So what's it about?" Henry inquired.

"According to the ballad the Stone of Fal must be possessed only by the high king of where-ever-it-is." Jason cracked a shy smile. "So when a usurper murders the rightful king and rapes the king's daughter, the princess steals the stone from the usurper's bedroom before he can claim the throne."

"Yeah?" Henry asked. "And how does that work out for her?"

"Kind of weird and sad. Most old ballads are like that," Jason replied, at ease with his subject. "According to the song, the only way that the princess can hide the stone is to swallow it. When she gives birth to the usurper's child, the stone is in him. But the usurper, fearing the princess's child will have a legitimate claim to the throne, hurls the child into the sea and thus loses the stone forever...It's pretty dark, but the tune is really beautiful and the chorus is fun to sing."

"That's the case with a lot of those old songs," Henry commented, but his thoughts were on the ancient magics hidden so often in music. Sidhe in general—and the Tuatha Dé Dannan in particular—favored spells woven through simple melodies. Supposedly one of those songs—a cheery tune that unleashed a merciless slaughter—had stripped them of their humanity and gotten them banished to an underworld by a band of Milesian magicians. "Are you and your mother still in touch?"

"No. She left us when I was seven..." Jason looked a little sad but not as anguished as Henry had expected. "Dad always said that she was a free spirit who couldn't be kept in one place. She had to go, but at least she left us with each other so we wouldn't miss her so much. That's what my dad said anyway. He was sort of a sap, really, but a good guy. I guess my mom's probably in Timbuktu playing guitar with Tuareg nomads or something by now."

Henry nodded. He wondered if she might not be even farther away.

Seven years would have been more than enough time to bind a truly immense magic to a child's bones. That, added to the seventeen years that had passed since, would have placed Jason's birth right around the time of the revolts against the Tuatha Dé Dannan regent, Greine the Usurper, as many called him. Greine still maintained rule over the Tuatha Dé Dannan Islands, but the theft of the Stone of Fal had prevented him from claiming both the title of high king and the power the stone conferred.

The thief had never been discovered as far as Henry knew.

"Do you recall much about your mother?" Henry tried to make the question sound casual.

"Her first name was Fionn…but I don't think I ever heard her maiden name. I just called her Mom. She had bright red hair and long hands." Jason spread his own fingers and smiled a little wryly. "I think I inherited her hands. I'd like to think I inherited some of her musical skill as well. She played beautifully."

"So you share your parents' disposition for music?"

"Yep." Jason smiled. "Both sides of the family. No getting away from it."

"Are you any good?" Henry asked.

"I think so." Jason flushed slightly.

"Maybe you can play something for me? What's your instrument of choice?"

Jason colored a little more, but Henry was certain why.

"I'm pretty good with most any musical instrument. I like woodwinds best. I have a fife that belonged to my mother that I've written a few melodies for."

He took another drink of his coffee. "It's really old-fashioned music, though. You probably won't like it."

"Nah, I'm pretty old-fashioned myself," Henry replied. "My socks are the most modern things I own and they date back to 1962."

Jason cracked a grin at that but then cocked his head thoughtfully and studied Henry, his dark eyes peering over the rims of his glasses.

"You can't be that old—" Jason went silent mid-question as his gaze jumped to something behind Henry. He gripped his coffee cup tightly and the pink flush drained from his face.

Henry glanced back but only saw the three big men in bike leathers pushing their way into the diner. He glanced back to Jason, who was still staring at the men from over the edges of his glasses. He looked terrified.

"What's wrong?" Henry asked quickly.

"Goblins," Jason whispered. "They're staring straight at me and they don't look happy about what they're seeing…"

"Don't look at them," Henry ordered, but it was already too late.

The men shouldered past the startled young cashier, intent upon Jason. Henry noted that the bald guy in the lead looked like he was packing a pistol. The bruiser on his left was shorter and thicker, while the thug to his right stood a head taller and sported a thick black beard.

Very briefly, Henry considered the number of bystanders and the tight confines of the diner. The fastest way to get out would be through the plate glass window at the front of the diner. But it would mean risking Jason being cut all to hell and Henry would also have to turn his back to an armed attacker. He hated being shot in the back.

He dropped his hands into his coat pockets. His fingers brushed over his flask, a piece of chalk, and then found the smooth surface of his switchblade.

"Jason Shamir, you want to keep breathing, you come with us," the bald guy snarled as he drew alongside them. Jason kept his head down, his eyes fixed on the coffee cup that he gripped with trembling hands.

"Who exactly are you?" Henry asked.

"Fuck off, revenant. Or we'll put you in a grave for good." The bald guy snorted like an enraged bull.

Up close Henry tasted the black magic on his breath and smelled his hidden goblin body. All three of these guys had been transformed very recently and they still wore their human flesh like ill-fitting suit coats. Chances were, they weren't yet familiar with their new bodies' weaknesses.

The shorter goblin reached for Jason, and to Henry's surprise, Jason slammed his coffee mug into the goblin's face, knocking the guy back a step. The bald goblin went for his gun.

So much for buying a little time with small talk.

Henry bounded forward before either of the other two goblins could lay their hands on Jason. His switchblade glinted like it was grinning as it sliced through the tall goblin's carotid artery and jugular. Blood sprayed and the goblin stumbled, then fell, bleeding out across the floor.

Henry saw the gun muzzle flash and felt a bullet punch into his chest. The impact kicked the breath from his lungs but didn't slow his momentum. Behind him, one of the cafe windows exploded as the bullet tore free of his body and shattered the glass.

Henry's switchblade flipped from his fingers and sank to the hilt into the bald goblin's right eye. Henry jerked the blade free and the goblin shrieked like a baby in a fire. It crumpled back into a booth, convulsing.

Henry staggered for the third goblin, but it grasped Jason by the throat. Jason clawed at its thick fingers, but his pale face was already darkened to an alarming violet.

"Just let up a little there and I won't hurt you." Henry held up his hands for the goblin to see as he quickly folded his knife closed.

Distantly, Henry was aware of the people around them staring in horror. The cashier shouted into her cell phone for help. One of the cooks gripped a cleaver, his expression caught between determination and confusion. Henry's own strength ebbed, but he fought to remain in the living world for a few minutes more.

The wet heat of blood seeped down his shirtfront as a deep pain spread through his chest. *It wasn't really any better than being shot in the back, come to think of it.*

"You don't want to kill him." Henry had to concentrate to get the words out. Already the Lost Mist was rising off him like steam; very soon the shade lands would reclaim him. "Just let Jason go. We can work all this out without anyone else getting hurt."

"Fuck that," the bulky goblin spat. "The runt's better dead than back in the tyrant's hands." His meaty fingers clenched tighter around Jason's throat. Jason jerked against the goblin's grasp, but his strength was obviously fading in the grip of suffocation.

Better dead it was, then.

Henry lunged forward and grasped both Jason and the goblin. He pulled them through the broken window and down into the dark murk of the shade lands.

❧

The goblin let out a shocked cry as it was wrenched from the living world. Jason thrashed against Henry like an eel submerged in alcohol.

A hazy, dank atmosphere enfolded them and the diner faded to shadows. As they sank deeper into the depths all sign of the living world disappeared. A twilight gloom surrounded them and black currents swirled over their bodies like rafts of rotting kelp. Jason shuddered reflexively at the contact. The goblin choked and coughed as its lungs rejected the deathly air, but it didn't release Jason.

Henry seized the goblin's hands and tore them from Jason's neck. Jason fell, coughing and gagging, to Henry's feet. The goblin made a dazed attempt to reach for Jason, but Henry shouldered it deeper into the darkness. The goblin staggered and then doubled over, heaving as if it were attempting to vomit its true body from the tortured shell of human flesh restraining it.

Not that it would have done him any good. The shade lands eroded all life, regardless of form.

Henry dropped to his knees. Jason stared up at him, white faced with the pain that every living being suffered in the shade lands. Fortunately, the atmosphere alone didn't kill quickly; it drained life the way a pitcher plant ate through the struggling bodies of drowning flies.

The dark atmosphere even fingered the edges of Henry's wound and lapped at his warm blood. But the dark didn't worry Henry. The voracious hunters lurking within the gloom were another matter. Ghosts came in many forms and some were ravenous.

Slowly, dozens of luminous forms drifted out from the murky depths. They shone, translucent and tangled as jellyfish, all faint light and endless appetite. Some bore recognizable features while others had long ago melted into strange colonies of the hurt and hunger. Countless broken souls fused by a desperate need to reclaim even a sliver of life. Hungry ghosts.

The goblin flailed and screamed a long distorted howl as three ghosts clasped it in their tentacles and sank their needle teeth into its flesh, ripping away pieces of its muscle and drinking the living warmth from its blood.

Henry remained on his knees at Jason's side. Reflexively, his bloodied hands found his flask. He slugged back a deep drink of his old poison as the ghosts closed in around him.

His tongue felt like ice and his throat tightened to a frozen trench as he swallowed. The poison spread through his bloodstream, chilling his veins like liquid nitrogen. Agony flared through Henry's bones and ground into his muscles. But it felt so familiar he hardly noted it.

He'd died so many times now.

As one long swaying ghost extended a tangle of luminous tentacles toward Jason, Henry caught it in his frigid grip. It fought him, but the ghost's need for life was only that of one young man lost in terror and still praying for salvation. Henry's grasp was the void of a black hole, a chasm of emptiness torn in him by the countless souls he'd held and his own multitude of demises.

Henry drew the power from this ghost as well, drinking in its anger, fear, and even the faint spark of hope that had trapped it in the shade lands. Henry tasted the sick bitterness of love betrayed and a body tortured in the embrace of an iron lady. He felt screams rock through him and heard laughter answer his pleas for mercy. He took those memories and many more.

He drained away every agony from the trembling soul, taking them for his own, until the ghost ceased its struggle. Its fury dulled in his hands. Its cold light dimmed and at last it lay, no more than a helpless cinder, in his palm.

"Your rage is mine now and I will not forget the wrongs done you," Henry whispered to the ghost. "Leave this place and let your sorrow be mine."

He spat on the cinder and slowly it kindled to a hot gold light. Then Henry hurled it upward and it ignited like a firework, tracing brilliant streaks across the gloom as it tore free of the shade lands. And for just an instant, the darkness fell back, exposing a rolling landscape as white as bone.

Then the dank atmosphere closed in again.

The remaining hungry ghosts drew back from Henry's reach, receding into the darkness. The goblin's remains were stripped nearly to its skeleton. At Henry's side Jason lay as still and wide eyed as a corpse.

Henry touched his cold cheek and Jason blinked.

"It was beautiful for a moment," Jason murmured. He looked hollow and haunted. Then he asked, "Can I go home now?"

Chapter Five

A searing acidic sensation flared through Jason's muscles and then both darkness and pain rolled back from his prone body. His eyes watered as if burned by chlorine, but he still made out the familiar expanse of pale blue sky above him.

Falk's silhouette loomed over him, seeming almost black against the sudden flood of sunlight.

"You're safe, Jason." Then Falk staggered and crumpled to the ground like a slack sail.

For one moment Jason simply lay in the narrow alley beside Falk, reeling between horror and disbelief. He didn't even know if he could move his arms or legs. His entire body burned and tingled with numbness.

The sweet, rotten stench of trash surrounded him and black flies darted between a nearby dumpster and Falk's prone form. Jason clenched his eyes closed. He wanted to howl from the turmoil that this day had made of his carefully balanced life. He'd wanted to sob like a seven-year-old boy. Anger, pain, and fear churned through him with a force that sent tremors through his body. Or maybe that was just shock, he thought. Maybe he was just going to have a nervous breakdown right here and now.

But he fought to keep his terror down—fought to keep a grip on himself and regain the control that he'd spent years mastering. This entire day had been strange and frightening—he didn't even understand half of it—but falling apart wouldn't make anything better. It never did, he knew that.

With an effort, he pulled himself upright. He'd lost his glasses somewhere in the HRD Coffee Shop, but as he gazed down at Falk, the battered man looked dull, as if a shadow had fallen over him, blotting out that luminous quality that Jason had grown accustomed to. The front of his coat was dark with blood and his limbs seemed oddly stiff, as if rigor mortis had already set in.

Horror welled through Jason at the thought.

Agent Falk couldn't be dead, Jason told himself. But he'd seen corpses before and instinctively recognized the lifeless slump of Agent Falk's form. Still, he didn't want to accept it, because he'd just met Agent Falk—just started to warm to his rough looks and crooked smile. And if he was dead, then it was Jason's fault, because he'd fought to protect him; there could be no doubt that those three goblins had come after Jason.

He can't be gone. He can't be...

Despite the clumsy numbness of his limbs, Jason groped at Falk's throat, feeling for a pulse. When at last he registered a faint kick beneath his fingers, the relief that washed over him was out of all proportion, verging on pure joy.

"Agent Falk?" Jason's voice sounded as rough as his throat felt. "Agent Falk?"

Falk opened his eyes. His gaze seemed far away and Jason couldn't tell if he could see him or not.

"Agent Falk?"

"Yeah..." His response could have been a low groan, but then he dragged in a rough breath and went on. "I'm with you...Give me a minute..."

"Should I call an ambulance?"

"No...Waste of their time. Just give me...a minute." He pulled in another ragged breath and a little color seemed to come back to his cheeks. He blinked and his gaze rolled to meet Jason's stare. "I should be able to walk the worst of this off."

"There's blood all over your coat—"

"It's nothing. Most of it isn't even mine." Falk rolled to his side and then slowly pushed himself into a sitting position. "I don't know what's worse sometimes, going or coming back."

Jason wasn't certain he wanted to know exactly what Falk meant by that. He didn't think he could stand too many more revelations today. He already felt so helpless against the onslaught of weirdness that this day had been.

Falk scrubbed at his face as if he were just waking up. His fingers left bloody tracks across his cheek, but he didn't seem to take note of it.

"What about you?" Falk asked. "Are you all right? You think you can walk?"

Jason would have laughed at the question coming from Falk in his condition, but in truth he wasn't sure if he could even stand.

When he tried, he discovered his limbs were alarmingly clumsy and weak. Still, he managed to rise to his feet. He swayed slightly and then steadied himself against the hard edge of a dumpster. "I'm just a little dazed and bruised, but I think I'm okay."

"Good," Falk replied, but he hardly moved. "We'll need to get you holed up and call this into HQ as soon as possible."

"I don't have a cell phone—"

"Not secure in any case," Falk cut him off. "I'll worry about that once we get to your place..." One of Falk's legs twitched, but he didn't rise. He glanced up to Jason and a faint blue flame lit his eyes. "Give me a hand with this old sack of bones, will you?"

Jason knelt at his side. Up close he could see the gleam of fresh blood seeping through the front of Falk's coat. His body felt hard and cold as ice as Jason wrapped an arm around him and helped him up to his feet.

"It's going to be all right," Falk told him. "Just trust me a little, you'll see."

There was absolutely no reason to believe that anything would be all right. Jason's entire world had been altered and as far as he could work out he'd become some kind of commodity to goblins and magicians. And yet Falk's words did ease him; maybe it was that tone of experience or maybe some spell, but Jason nodded and steadied Falk as they stumbled forward.

They staggered out from their shadowy alley into the bustle of the post-lunch rush on Turk Street.

Fortunately, they didn't have far to go.

The weathered Victorian sprawl of the Avalon Apartments slumped over a dingy liquor store and a concrete laundromat like the remains of a wrecked ship. Decorative woodwork and paint had long ago weathered away and the rickety fire escape looked like it had been thrown on in a windstorm. Two ground floor windows were boarded over and the entryway reeked of urine from the number of drunks who had pissed themselves after passing out on the stoop.

"Avalon." Falk's voice was little more than a whisper, but Jason still noted the tone of irony. He'd thought the same thing on earlier occasions.

Inside, the grimy yellow wallpaper displayed a Rorschach test of water stains. The cage elevator bore a perpetual "out of order" proclamation and for the first time Jason resented it.

In truth, there were only three things to recommend the Avalon Apartments at all. First, the rent was cheap. Second, the locks worked. Third—and most importantly, this afternoon—it was not the sort of place where anyone took much note of two beaten, bloodstained men staggering up the stairs together. With so many drunks, junkies, outpatients, and social outcasts in residence, the sight of him and Falk merited little more response than a bloodshot glance from a half-dressed transvestite traipsing down in the opposite direction.

"I'd throw that one back, honey," the transvestite informed Jason.

"Damn. If I'd known we'd be meeting the queen on the stairs, I'd have worn my tux," Falk replied gamely and received a laugh in passing.

Jason smiled despite his exhaustion.

Together they fought up another flight of stairs. When Falk's boot caught on a step they both swayed. For an instant Jason thought they would fall, but he didn't let go of Falk. To his relief, Falk caught the handrail, steadying them both.

Falk seemed to be getting stronger. At least Jason hoped he was because he was himself on the verge of collapse.

His muscles trembled with exhaustion and a raw ache scraped through his bruised throat with every breath he took in. Still, it was a relief to feel anything at all.

By the time they reached Jason's rooms on the third floor, Falk was taking most of his own weight and Jason could feel living warmth radiating from his lean body.

❧

"So here it is, Chez Shamir." Jason unlocked his door and followed Falk into his tiny studio apartment. He guessed that Falk wasn't the type to give a damn. Still, he felt slightly embarrassed by the single room, bath, and kitchenette that made up his home. It had to look miserable to a stranger. Falk couldn't know just how much of an achievement it represented to Jason to live free of mental institutions and halfway houses.

A shelf made of cinderblocks and planks stood beside his narrow window. It overflowed with sheet music, instruments, and CDs. His stereo and speakers perched on a second shelf on the other side of the windowsill. Jason's folded clothes and paired socks occupied a stack of two milk crates beside his futon. A third crate displayed his alarm clock, a battered lamp, and a history book he'd been trying to read.

The barren kitchenette stood open just past the door to his bathroom. From the doorway Jason could see his frying pan and coffeemaker sitting beside his empty sink.

"Clean." Falk said it like he'd expected as much. Then he glanced over his shoulder to Jason. "Close the door and lock it, will you?"

Jason did both quickly. Then Falk reached out and laid his bloody right hand against the door. He flexed his fingers and silver light gushed up from his chest, lighting him like a halogen filament. His eyes shone bright. His hair and clothes moved as if caught in a breeze.

"I name you sanctuary." Falk leaned close to the door, almost pressing his mouth to the white paint, and whispered, "Let none pass who mean him harm."

Blazing light flashed up from Falk's hand and spread like frost across the door and walls of Jason's apartment. Jason stared as the crystalline patterns climbed his window and curled across both his floor and ceiling. He thought he saw florettes of blades and glinting forms that reminded him of skulls and he wondered if the markings were the letters of some strange spell. They moved as if they were almost alive.

At last the luminous filigree closed and the entire apartment glowed so intensely that Jason squinted against the flashing brilliance. He stole a glimpse back to Falk and found the man's figure strangely dark in the midst of so much light, as if it had drained him completely.

Then Falk lifted his hand from the door and the symbols sank away beneath paint, plaster, and flooring. Only Falk's bloody handprint remained, a wet crimson smear on white planks.

Again Falk swayed on his feet but didn't fall. He met Jason's worried expression with a crooked smile.

"Just got a whiff of myself. Nearly floored me," Falk commented. "You have a private tub and toilet in this joint?"

"Yes, right through there." Jason pointed to the bathroom door. Falk strode in without bothering to close the door after him. For a very awkward moment Jason wondered if he should follow the other man in to make sure he was all right or give him his privacy.

"If you have any salt, bring it, would you?" Falk called. "And a felt marker. Mine's getting dry."

"I've got a ballpoint pen." Jason pulled it out of his jacket pocket.

"That'll work." Falk's reply rose over the sound of rustling cloth.

"How much salt do you need?" On his way to the kitchenette Jason stole a glance in at Falk and found the man bracing himself against the small porcelain sink as he stripped off his bloodstained clothes.

"A cup would be good, but anything you have will help."

Falk's coat and vest lay in a heap on the floor. His button-up shirt hung open, exposing the solid expanse of his bare chest and abdomen. Jason remembered how strong and hard that scarred body had felt against his own. The memory was immediately eclipsed by the sight of a bloody bullet hole gaping over Falk's heart. A sluggish stream of blood seeped down his chest.

Jason stared in horror at the wound, feeling amazed and sick at once. How could Falk even be standing?

Falk glanced up and, meeting Jason's stare, offered him an almost sheepish smile.

"I know, blood's a bitch to clean up. I'll pick up a new set of towels for you as soon as I can." He shrugged off his shirt and Jason noted a second massive stain from the exit wound in Falk's back.

"How can you still be alive?" Jason's words came out in a horrified whisper.

For just a moment Falk went still. He glanced down at the stream of blood pouring from his torso and seeping into the fabric of his pants as if he'd just noticed it.

"No other option," Falk replied offhandedly, but he didn't meet Jason's gaze. Instead, he wadded up his shirt and wiped at his bloody chest almost self-consciously. "You gonna grab that salt?"

"Ye—yeah." Jason tore his gaze from Falk's chest and bolted into his kitchenette. For a moment he thought he might throw up in the sink, but then he regained his composure.

He'd seen worse—much worse. But there was something so disconcerting about the combination of Falk's easygoing manner and those ugly, gaping wounds. How could a man be so deeply injured and just keep moving?

The sound of water running in the bathroom brought Jason back to the task at hand.

"Is kosher salt okay?" Jason called.

"Better actually," Falk replied between splashes of water. "But anything you've got will do."

Jason brought the entire box of Diamond Crystal kosher salt and his ballpoint pen.

Falk sat on the edge of the claw-footed bathtub, naked, with a roll of masking tape in one hand and a towel in the other. The water in the tub swirled with currents of deep red and dilute pink. Falk had clearly made an effort to wash away the blood. Water glistened in his blond chest hair and droplets slipped down the line of his lean abdomen. He was a big man, and stripped of his ill-fitting clothes, he looked more savage, muscular, and tattooed than Jason would have expected.

A black star shone against the pale skin of his hip and tiny golden symbols stretched like constellations across the scarred lengths between his right thigh and his broad shoulders. Amidst the arcane markings a black block letter *F* stood out on his right shoulder like a brand.

He held one of Jason's white towels against the wound in his chest, as if shielding Jason from the sight, though, he seemed utterly unaware of the disarming effect of his nudity.

Despite himself Jason felt a flush rise across his cheeks.

"What should I do with—"

"Just leave them on the toilet seat." Falk didn't look at Jason. "You don't have to watch this. I can manage it myself."

Suddenly Jason felt like an ass. Falk had suffered these wounds protecting him. More than likely he'd saved Jason's life. The least he could do was help the man.

"The bullet hole in your back looks like an awkward reach for you on your own," Jason commented. "It would probably be easier if I helped with that."

"You sure?" Falk glanced to him questioningly. "'Cause it won't do either of us any good if you lose your lunch trying to patch my ugly ass up."

"I won't," Jason assured him. "No way am I giving up my free meal."

"All right then." Falk held out the roll of masking tape to him and Jason took it. For just an instant he expected to see something strange on the surface of the tape—some swirling magical script—but it seemed to be nothing more than mundane beige masking tape.

"What should I do?"

"Just tape me up."

Falk turned so that Jason could see his bleeding back. Just below his shoulder blade streaks of scarlet blood seeped from a ragged exit wound.

"You don't have to look at it," Falk told him. "Close your eyes and just concentrate on the idea of healing. Try to hold the thought while you make a mark on the masking tape with your pen and then slap the tape over the wound."

"What kind of mark?" Jason frowned at his pen and the tape.

"Doesn't matter," Falk replied. "It's the thought that counts, not the wrapper, if you know what I mean. The faster you do it, the less likely you are to overthink it, though."

"Right." Jason responded automatically to Falk's terse tone. The man was probably in intense pain; Jason could ask questions later. He gripped the tape and pen, closed his eyes, and thought of what healing meant. Smooth skin marred by only the shadow of a long faded scar. Health and well-being. Unbidden, a melody came to him and he wrote the simple notes on the masking tape.

Then he tore off a length and taped it over Falk's back. He half expected the piece of tape to just fall off. But it adhered instantly to Falk's flesh. As Jason watched, the inky notes dulled from black to red to the shiny white of scar tissue and the beige strip of tape melted into Falk's flesh, taking on the color and texture of his skin. Only Jason's musical notations remained as the faintest scars.

"That's good." Falk sounded both surprised and relieved. "Really good. Can you keep going?"

"Yeah…It seems kind of easy actually."

"Easy..." Falk repeated as if he found it ironic. "Where have you been all my life?"

Jason's cheeks flushed at the remark. He glanced away before Falk could notice and returned his concentration to the next strip of tape.

He expanded his melody, writing the notes nearly as quickly as they came to him. He laid each new strip next to the last. Soon the wound in Falk's back was entirely closed. Jason stared at the pale scars and expanse of healthy skin, hardly able to credit that he'd played any part in anything so amazing. Pride swept through him.

"Shall I take care of your chest as well?" Jason offered.

"Are you sure you're up to it?" Falk asked. "I don't want you dropping dead of exhaustion."

"I'm fine. I actually kind of enjoyed doing it." Jason stole a glance to Falk's disbelieving expression. "Is that a weird thing to say?"

"No more weird than closing a bullet hole with masking tape is in the first place," Falk replied, but then added, "Though it's pretty damn impressive that you haven't even broken a sweat."

Falk turned to face Jason and the regard in his expression made Jason flush slightly. Slowly Falk lifted the white towel away from the gory hole in his chest. The sight of it still unnerved Jason, but he pushed past that. Here was something of real value that he could do, something that made him feel a little more in control.

Already the gentle notes of his healing melody came to him and he wrote them across lengths of masking tape in a flurry. He closed Falk's chest quickly and then just stared at the new skin.

Falk too stared down at the phrases of tiny notes that lay like pale scars over his chest.

"A song?" Falk asked.

Jason nodded.

"Any tune I'd know?"

"No. It just came to me, when you said that I should think of healing."

Falk contemplated his chest for a moment more, perhaps attempting to decipher the pattern of scars, and then shrugged. "As long as it's not 'Love for Sale', I think we're fine."

Jason smiled. He liked Falk's dry humor and calm demeanor. Somehow he made even this strange, bloody scene seem reasonable. Then he realized that he was staring and self-consciously lowered his gaze before Falk could take note.

"So what do you need the salt for?" Jason asked.

"Ah yes, that. Add it to the water in the tub," Falk directed him.

Jason dumped the salt out and watched as the large white crystals melted into the still, red water. Beside him, Falk remained motionless, slowly recovering his natural radiance. Finally, he leaned over the heap of his discarded clothes and dug into a pocket of his trench coat. He cupped something between his hands, plainly hiding it from Jason's view.

"I have a proposition for you, my girl," Falk whispered over his own hands.

Jason tried to not to stare, but there wasn't anything else in the tiny confines of the bathroom that he could even pretend was more interesting. He remembered that just before they'd been accosted Falk had told him that a girl's heart lay hidden in his pocket. Was that what Falk cradled so gently in his big, scarred hands?

"I can give you a living body, but in return you'll be bound to my will by my blood." Falk spoke softly over his hands. His expression was gentle and his deep voice struck Jason as disconcertingly charming.

"It's your choice," Falk said, as if responding to a question. He smiled wryly at something and shook his head. "No, not as a princess…Who do you think I am, the gnome king? Nah, you wouldn't like him anyway, would you?"

"Are you talking to…her ghost?" Jason asked.

Falk glanced to him and gave him a quick nod but then returned his attention his hands.

"A kitty? You're certain? Sure, I can manage a cat. Easy peasy…" Then Falk looked up at Jason and his eyes shone like blue flames. "She wants to know if you'll sing her a lullaby. She says she heard you singing to yourself when we were in the shade lands. She likes your voice."

"Oh that..." Jason resisted his reflexive embarrassment at having been caught doing something so strange as humming to himself when he was terrified—the quiet melody came unbidden in moments of fear. He hardly knew when he was doing it anymore. Compared to the bizarre sights and actions he'd witnessed today, it hardly seemed worth note.

"I'd be happy to sing a song. If you want," Jason offered.

"A lullaby," Falk clarified. "That would be great." His intense blue gaze had already dropped back to his cupped hands.

As Jason sang, "Hush Little Baby", Falk leaned over the tub and slowly submerged his thick, scarred hands in the bloody water. Something wriggled from between his fingers. Jason fully expected to see a little heart. He'd almost begun to imagine the pink symmetry of a valentine. But the shape beneath the murky water looked leggy and insectile—like a spider but big. The sight gave him a pause. He didn't like normal house spiders and the thing creeping across the bottom of his tub was nearly the size of one of Falk's fists.

"Keep singing," Falk reminded from where he crouched beside the tub.

Jason continued the lullaby, though he watched the shadowy form beneath the red water warily.

Falk stroked his mutilated left hand over the water, producing a series of ripples. Below, the spider's silhouette broke and distorted. Falk glared down, his expression going hard and commanding. He spat out a rasping low word and Jason saw silver light burst from his lips. The water flashed as if reflecting the light. Then Falk slapped his hand down into the tub.

Waves sloshed and crested as Falk agitated the water further. Strangely, the blood seemed to settle out of the water and Jason realized that he could now see the scarlet shape distorting below the frothing water. What had been a plump ruby spider stretched and twisted like a length of red kelp caught in storm surf. The sharp peaks that Jason had thought were huge mandibles rolled and resolved into two little ears. The legs folded and bent from hard insect angles to supple mammalian limbs. A tail flicked through the water and then a yowling feline head broke the surface.

It was a kitten, Jason realized, though, he'd never seen a cat with such a brilliant crimson coat or such dark eyes before.

The kitten sank its claws into Falk's hand and wrist as it scrambled to escape the water. Falk scooped it up and cradled the shaking creature in the crook of his arm.

"You're all right, Princess. I've got you. See, you're fine." Falk stroked the cat's head and began drying its tiny body with the clean corner of one of Jason's bloodstained towels.

"So, she's the ghost girl you told me about earlier?" Jason stared at the kitten.

"One and the same." Falk shrugged. "Give or take a few legs."

"But she's…alive now?"

"Princess here wasn't really all that dead to start with. Her body was gone, but her soul was intact and her will was strong. By my count that made her two-thirds alive already. I just built her a body to inhabit."

Disconcertingly, the kitten studied Falk as if contemplating his explanation. Then she nodded.

"But she looks like a cat to me," Jason said. "Shouldn't I see something else? Her true ghostly form or something?"

"Not anymore. This body is her genuine flesh now." Falk stroked the kitten's ears. "This isn't some transformation of her original flesh or a glamour disguising her. She's a kitten all the way to her bones."

"A normal kitten?" Jason asked skeptically, because looking at her closely, he noticed that the toes of her front paws strongly resembled fuzzy fingers and he could almost make out a darker patch of fur on her foreleg that looked remarkably similar to the *F* tattooed on Falk's shoulder.

"I didn't say that," Falk replied. He stood with the kitten and snatched up his stained trench coat, then started out of the bathroom. "You ever heard of familiars?" he asked over his shoulder.

"Like witches' familiars?" Jason pulled the plug from the tub and then followed Falk as the water drained out.

Falk tossed his coat over the doorknob, then strode to the window, apparently unconcerned about displaying his nudity to the world. He released the kitten onto the windowsill, where she set straight to licking her ass.

"Exactly like a witch's familiar." Falk gave the kitten one of his brief, crooked smiles. "A spirit pulled from another realm and bound to a witch's will by blood and flesh."

"So Princess is your familiar?" Jason inquired. Then after Falk's quick nod, he asked, "Does the *F* on her shoulder stand for Falk? Like your tattoo?"

"Hers might. Mine doesn't..." For the first time since they'd met Jason thought Falk actually looked taken off guard. But then he shook his head. "No. It stands for Franklyn Fairgate."

He gazed past the kitten and out the window, with an oddly distant expression. Jason guessed that was the end of the conversation, but then Falk turned back to him. "Franklyn brought me into the Irregulars, way back during the war. They were desperate for grunts and guinea pigs and I fit the bill for both. I spent four years catching bullets and testing black poison for him."

"That sounds terrible."

"Those were the times. People were dying by the thousands in the trenches. We had to do everything we could to end it." Falk shrugged. "You got spare pair pajamas or something by any chance?"

Jason accepted the abrupt change of subject. Though the mention of people dying in trenches made him wonder just what war Falk was talking about.

"I have a pair of sweats that might fit you."

Jason easily located the faded blue sweatpants from among his few other clothes. Falk, in the meantime, steamed the windowpane with his breath and then drew a small square on the glass.

"Here." Jason handed him the pants.

"Thanks." Falk took the clothes and pulled them on quickly.

Normally the sweats looked rumpled hanging off Jason's slim frame, but on Falk they clung to the muscles of his thighs and stretched to accommodate his groin. Falk turned his attention back to the kitten. He stroked her head with one finger.

"You go to Gunther, Princess. Tell him about the ambush at the coffee shop and that I've secured Jason at his residence but that I think that this is bigger than just Phipps. We might be dealing with the sidhe. Tuatha Dé Dannan."

The kitten rammed her nose into Falk's palm.

"Yeah, you're pretty as anything. Now get going," Falk told her.

The kitten butted her head lightly against the square that Falk had drawn on the windowpane. The glass swung out like the flap of a cat door. Beyond it Jason glimpsed the corner of a door. Then the cat darted through, the glass swung closed, and the view returned to the familiar expanse of surrounding buildings, power lines, and the darkening sky.

Falk briefly studied the sky, then commented, "Looks like rain again tonight."

Jason just stared at him. He made all these truly unreal things seem so simple…so normal.

"You're amazing…" The comment escaped Jason before he could think about it. "How do you just do something like that as if it were nothing?"

Falk simply shrugged, but Jason thought there might have been the slightest flush to his tanned face.

"I mean, you're magic. Really magic." Jason wished he could think of any other words to convey exactly how astounding everything Falk did seemed to be. The man walked through walls and brought animals to life from bathwater. He always seemed to have a solution for any situation.

Earlier, Jason had been too disoriented and then too terrified to truly appreciate any of it. But now it struck him just how incredible Falk was. Like some magician out of a movie, only so much more soft spoken and subdued that no one would have ever have suspected.

"You're one to talk," Falk replied.

"Me?" Jason shook his head. "I could never—"

"You could," Falk cut him off. "Why else do you think those goblins wanted you? Why do you think Phipps sold you?"

"Because I can see things," Jason supplied. "But that's not really doing anything except opening my eyes. And most of what I see isn't useful to me. It's weird and creepy. It's not like I can change anything by seeing it."

"Maybe not yet, but everything begins with perception. No one can alter what he can't perceive. The more perfectly you see, the more accurately you can work magic." Falk gave a wry smile. "Most of us have to build spells based on myths, superstitions, and guesswork. Believe me, all that can go to shit fast." Falk lifted his mutilated hand and very slowly closed his fingers into a fist, then dropped his hand back down to his side. "You're far more rare and powerful than you realize, Jason."

Jason contemplated his shelf of musical notations. He didn't feel powerful and rarity just made him a freak. His true sight had screwed up most of his life and now it made him a target for attacks from monsters.

"None of that did me any good when those goblins came after us at HRD." Jason dropped his gaze to his own pale hands. "I would have died if you hadn't been there. And you got shot protecting me..."

"All part of the service," Falk replied easily. Then he cast Jason a scrutinizing glance. "I suppose I could teach you a trick or two, but I don't know if I'd be doing you a favor or just getting you in deeper."

"I'd like to be able to protect myself." The idea appealed immensely to Jason. "I don't see how that could hurt."

"You wouldn't, would you? But I've seen it happen more than once." Falk leaned back against the wall. "A guy picks up a few moves and he starts to think he can take on the world. Then, when he should be running for his life, he stands his ground and ends up butchered." Falk scowled and turned his gaze to the stained walls surrounding them. "Sometimes a little magic is worse than none. And on top of that, learning magic isn't like taking up the trombone. It's dangerous. And if you're going to take on a teacher it should be someone you know and trust. Someone who isn't going to skip town in two weeks."

Jason felt a flare of disappointment at the mention of Falk leaving, but it didn't alter his situation. If anything, it exacerbated it.

"That may be," Jason replied. "But you're the only person I've got right now and I need to learn now. I mean, Mr. Phipps is still going to come after me and there may be more of those goblins as well."

Falk looked uncertain and Jason decided to press his point.

"You already showed me how to close a wound."

"That's not even remotely the same as engaging in a battle using magic."

"I'm not going to engage in a battle," Jason snapped. "I'd just like to know enough to defend myself or have a chance of understanding what people around me are trying to do to me…I want to have some control of my own life."

Jason waved a hand at the sparsely decorated room around them in frustration. "You know, it took me nearly a decade to achieve this much freedom from the doctors, psychiatrists, and therapists who were all trying to keep me safe and thought they knew what was best for me. The last thing I need is to have a new bunch of well-intentioned people making all my choices—"

"I'm not—"

"Maybe you don't think you're taking my choices away, but you are. And maybe you're right about what would be best for me. But this is my life and I have the right to live it for myself. If I make a mistake, that's my right!"

Jason glared at Falk only to catch the other man contemplating him with an unnerving gentleness. Jason suddenly felt his face warming with embarrassment at his outburst.

"You spent a lot of time locked up?" Falk asked quietly.

"Yeah," Jason admitted, though it was the last thing he wanted to discuss. Falk nodded but didn't inquire further. Instead he yawned and stretched his long arms.

"All right, I'll show you what I can," Falk said at last.

"Really?" Jason wondered what had changed Falk's mind. He hadn't expected Falk to relent, at least not so easily, and for a moment he just stood there, feeling a little stunned and grateful.

"Yes, really," Falk replied. "But not right now. I'm bushed and you look like you just got cut down from a noose. First thing tomorrow I'll show you a couple moves. In the meantime I'm thinking that we ought to put this bed of yours to use."

Falk dropped down onto the futon and then looked up to Jason. "Come here. Sit down and let me see what I can do about your neck. Just looking at those bruises is making my throat sore."

Jason sat beside Falk, feeling overly aware of the easy sprawl of Falk's long limbs. If he moved just a little closer his thigh would brush against Falk's. The room seemed too quiet.

"How do you want me?" Jason asked.

"Now there's a leading question." Falk grinned and Jason suddenly flushed.

How had Falk known? How had he given himself away?

"I didn't mean—" Jason began, but Falk's low laugh cut him off.

"I know, I know. I'm just having fun with you," Falk assured him. "This would work best if you faced me straight on."

Falk laid one hand on Jason's shoulder, leading him just slightly. Jason moved to sit cross-legged on the futon across from Falk.

"What are you going to do?" Jason almost flinched at how much excitement rang through the nervous question.

"Just heal up those bruises. I won't hurt you," Falk promised.

He reached out and gingerly traced two of his thick, callused fingers across the delicate skin of Jason's throat. An electric tremor shivered through Jason and his heartbeat quickened.

"That's all right, isn't it?" Falk continued to stroke him. Waves of heat seemed to radiate from his hands. It had been so long since anyone had touched him so carefully or so tenderly.

"It's nice," Jason admitted. Though, it was more than that. His whole body hummed with the pleasure of this simple human contact.

Falk drew him a little closer, and for an instant Jason thought he might kiss him. His gaze was so intense—his expression so searching. Jason knew he ought to stop him. He hardly knew Falk. And his life was already too complicated right now. But at the same time he couldn't bring himself to resist. He craved the comfort of another body desperately, even if only for a few hours.

But then Falk bowed his head to Jason's neck. His blond hair tickled Jason's cheek. He smelled of earth and juniper.

Falk whispered a low, soft word against Jason's skin. The sensation of his warm breath sent another thrill through Jason's body. One of Falk's big hands cradled the nape of his neck; the other rested against his back.

"This next part might seem weird, but trust me, okay," Falk whispered. "I won't hurt you."

"Okay."

Jason felt as though he might be in the hold of some greater spell. He closed his eyes and relaxed in Falk's grip.

Falk drew him closer and ever so lightly pressed his lips to Jason's neck. Arousal fluttered through Jason's loins at the contact and he started to draw back, if only to save himself the humiliation of popping a boner like a twelve-year-old. But then warmth flared through the muscles of his neck, eclipsing all other sensations. A molten heat coursed from his throat down to the scabbed bruises of his forearm.

As Falk opened his mouth and touched Jason's bare skin with the tip of his tongue, the heat intensified to the edge of pain. Jason felt like his arm and throat were burning up. In a moment flames would erupt from his mouth; dark smoke would rise from the gash in his arm.

It took all of Jason's willpower to remain passive in Falk's grasp.

And then Falk lifted his head and the waves of heat dulled to a lingering warmth. Falk released him and flopped back onto the futon. He looked exhausted.

"Are you—" Jason began.

"Fine. Fine," Falk replied. "Just drained. How's the arm?"

Jason peeled back the dirty bandage from his forearm. Not a trace remained of his injury.

"Better?" Falk asked.

"Much," Jason replied.

"Good." Falk closed his eyes. "Don't go anywhere, okay."

"Ever?"

"Until I wake up," Falk replied with a smirk, but he didn't open his eyes. "Get some sleep. You've had a hell of a day."

Jason was about to ask if Falk minded him sharing the futon, but then he realized that Falk had already fallen asleep.

Jason slid off his own shoes and after a moment of consideration, stripped off his stained clothes, and then lay down alongside Falk. He stretched a blanket over them both. He felt certain that he wouldn't sleep long or deeply, but in an instant he slipped free from any further thought.

Chapter Six

Henry felt the living heat of a man's body pressed against his own. He didn't open his eyes—didn't really wake—just caught the scent of masculine sweat and traces of ancient blood magic. He registered the rattle of water pipes and the hiss of a radiator, and old memories stirred.

It should have alarmed him, but somehow he still found comfort in the sensation of a lean body pressed against him, wanting so much in silence. For just an instant, Henry was certain that it was Frank lying next to him again, just as he'd come to him their very first night together.

If only time could have stopped right there, in that perfect moment of knowing they'd found each other.

If only Henry could have kept from remembering how it all fell apart three years later. He didn't want the memory of Frank's engagement to Director Walton's daughter. And he would have gladly forgotten all those terse arguments in dank hotel rooms that followed Frank's many relapses into desperate sex with him. More than anything he wanted to forget that sick knowledge that he had become a liability to Frank's ambitions.

But not even death stopped time. Events flowed from cause to effect like a fuse burning to a bomb.

And in an instant Henry had gone from knowing that Frank had given him the short straw to fighting the leather restraints on the steel table and biting back a howl of agony as Frank's assistants severed his finger and used the gory digit to dedicate his flesh to life within death, to the eternal that lay beyond mortality.

On the edge of shock, Henry had looked to Frank. Maybe it had just been reflex or perhaps he'd harbored some desperate hope that Frank would call it all off. It had been so long ago Henry didn't remember anymore. What had been burned into his mind at that moment had been Frank's countenance.

Henry could see him even now.

His face was pale as candle wax, his eyes wide with terror, and yet his expression was pure determination. The smell of vomit clung to him and sweat had soaked through his clothes and lab coat. Still, he took Henry's severed finger in one hand and lifted the long bronze knife in the other.

In that moment Henry knew there would be no reprieve. Not even an angel of Abraham could still Frank's hand. He'd convinced himself—and too many of his superiors—that this was the right choice, the only choice. A single human life and, in return, mastery over the shade lands: a key to death and immortality. This war and every one after would be theirs to win. And what was one life lost when thousands were dying pointlessly in filthy trenches?

This single sacrifice would promote Frank to the highest ranks and open the gates of the most profound power for him. And perhaps there had even been a part of him that had felt relieved to be free of the exposure that Henry had come to represent. Henry thought he saw as much in Frank's face as he leaned over him, his clammy skin glistening with sweat.

The surgical lamp flared like a halo.

Frank's hands trembled as he lifted the knife over Henry's heart, but he still brought the blade down fast and hard. It struck deep to the very core of Henry and agony bloomed through him.

Henry knew he was dying and almost welcomed it, if only to stop seeing that sick, broken expression spreading across Frank's face…if only not to witness Frank cry out in horror and crumple over his body sobbing—now that was all far too late.

Henry just wanted it to end.

But the pain only intensified as Frank tried hysterically to jerk the bronze blade out of Henry's body. Henry felt every motion as Frank's sweating hands slipped on the blood-slick hilt.

At the edges of Henry's vision the Lost Mist rose and then the dark depths of the shade lands opened. He'd thought it had been all over then. But he'd been wrong.

They'd all been so wrong.

Back then, they hadn't understood the real nature of sacrifice nor the price of true power. It had all seemed so simple when depicted in neat little rows of pretty runes. They'd blindly reenacted rituals pilfered from ancient tombs and then expected easy glory. They'd been stupid as kids playing tag in a minefield.

Their incantation had opened the shade lands before them all, but the dead within that vast darkness did not suffer the living. And suddenly only Henry, with a blade in his jerking heart, no longer qualified as a living sacrifice. But every other man and animal in the military laboratory had been.

With each of their torn bodies, the ritual had bound Falk to life in death: fed him their deaths, armored him with their shattered bones, and burned away his promise of mortal respite.

Eighteen hours later, in the gore-spattered ruins of the lab, Henry's heart had started beating despite the bronze blade impaling it. Henry had taken a breath and choked on pain and blood. And then he'd realized that it would never be over, not for him.

Henry came fully awake, but the warm body in his arms hadn't fled along with his dreams.

Jason lay pressed against him, his long hands curled against Henry's belly and his breath tickling through the blond hair of Henry's chest. His morning erection thrust up against Henry's thigh with the excited optimism of a teacher's pet waiting to be called upon.

Henry's own arousal intensified from a dim flicker to something much harder and hungry. As gold pools of morning light spread across the bed, Henry shifted, slipping his big hands down Jason's body, stroking the length of him.

Jason's eyes opened and he smiled, groggy and shy. But he didn't pull away. He nuzzled his face into Henry's chest and murmured a soft encouragement. Henry almost laughed at this sleepy lust, but somehow he found the honesty of it too moving to deny. As he stroked and teased Jason's flawless, young body fully awake, Jason shyly returned his attentions.

Jason's hands drifted to the waistband of Henry's sweatpants and slipped past the elastic. Anticipation thrilled through Henry. Just the first brush of his fingers felt electric. His sure caress and knowing grip assured Henry that Jason might be young and sweet but he was no virgin.

With that knowledge, Henry abandoned his restraint. He nudged Jason's legs wider, feeling an almost predatory pleasure at the trusting access Jason offered him to his body. Henry slicked his fingers with saliva and incantations. Then he applied himself to discovering just what touch where would bring the young man off. Henry's hands were large and rough, but Jason soon responded to his motions with wanton thrusts and urgent, eager gasps.

All the while, Jason's encouraging caresses rocked through Henry's body, like the rush of life returning to his flesh. Whether by instinct or experience, he knew almost too well what he was doing. Sweat beaded both their bodies and their breaths came in fast gasps. Jason gazed through his lashes, his face flushing. Henry watched him with hungry fascination.

They worked each other almost as if it were a contest of pleasure. Henry drove Jason's taut body to crests of ecstasy with calculated control, while Jason gasped and quivered, using both his sweat-slick hands to pump and please Henry's thick erection.

At last Jason came with a muffled cry into Henry's chest. As if inspired by Jason's exuberance, Henry's own body climaxed, spilling semen across Jason's belly.

Jason smiled and lifted his face to meet Henry's gaze directly. He looked both vulnerable and proud, like he had just won a marathon and wanted to be congratulated. He'd looked the same way briefly last night, just after he'd patched up Henry's chest… flushed and tender, like he was waiting for true love's kiss.

It was only then that the stupidity of this entire thing struck Henry. He was nobody's true love. Hell, he was hardly decent enough company for the hustlers in the Tenderloin. Jason was probably too inexperienced to recognize it, but a man like Henry would be worse for him than letting a vampire loose in his living room.

He should have known better than to even lay a hand on someone as kind, clean, and young as Jason.

Henry broke away from Jason's gaze and sat up.

"What time is it?" Henry asked, though he could see the clock easily.

For an instant Jason just lay there, looking stunned. Then he too quickly sat up. He turned so that Henry couldn't see his face.

"Six a.m." Jason didn't look back from his study of the clock.

"We should probably get a move on…" Henry commented, but without any real intention. He just didn't want this to become some kind of a scene.

"Right," Jason agreed. But he still didn't look back at Henry. Bright morning light shone across the planes of his straight back and tense shoulders.

Henry felt like a bastard, but he couldn't let Jason start thinking that they were having a romance here. Jason would only end up hurt worse.

"Unless you need to use the bathroom first, I'm going to take a shower," Jason stated.

"Sure, go ahead."

Jason stood quickly, snatched some clean clothes from the crate beside his bed, and fled into the bathroom. Henry heard him lock the door behind him.

"Well, shit," Henry muttered to himself. This was exactly why Henry spent more time with the dead than the living.

From the windowsill a tiny meow sounded as if in agreement with him. Princess lay in a patch of morning sunlight, watching him from over her scarlet tail.

Henry tugged his sweatpants back up and then stood.

"Did you get word to Gunther?" Henry inquired of the kitten. She gave him a curt nod, then hacked up a damp wad of paper.

"Nice," Henry commented and he thought that Princess looked embarrassed, but then she busied herself cleaning the unnaturally long toes of her front paws.

Henry unfolded the wet paper to find a note written in Gunther's neat, cramped script.

Good to hear you're ok. HRD looked nasty. PR division cleaned it up. News will report a biker brawl if anything.

Trolls posted bail for the brownie we nabbed. Ten minutes later the Tuatha Dé Dannan regent unleashed his ambassadorial corps. They went straight for Carerra's throat—demanded disclosure of all properties and persons seized during the Phipps raid. Cethur Greine's definitely after Shamir and he's got legal on his side. Carerra's still holding out. Keep him on the down low for as long as possible. And just a warning: the guys in R&D to want a look at Shamir before anybody else gets a hand on him.

Take care.

G.

Henry didn't like the idea of Research and Development getting involved with Jason, though he knew he should have expected as much. He certainly wasn't any happier about the sidhe regent's interest.

Absently he registered the noise of the shower running in the bathroom, but his thoughts were far away. Princess butted her head into the back of his hand. He scratched her and frowned at the note in his hand.

He'd already suspected that the attack on Jason's father and this latest grab for Jason were linked and that both would lead back to the Tuatha Dé Dannan court. Though, it struck him as strange that Greine would bother to dispatch ambassadors when he'd already loosed assassins. And if he'd known enough about Jason to hunt him down at his favorite coffee shop, then why had he drawn attention by confronting NIAD and demanding information about Jason?

It wasn't like the bronze-skinned sidhe regent to fuck around with two radically different tactics.

Cethur Greine threw everything into his ambitions, whether that meant amassing an army of snow goblin mercenaries to assassinate a legitimate king or shoring up his claim to the throne by dragging the murdered king's daughter to his bed. Greine wasn't the type to relent or rethink his approach.

That uncompromising character was also largely responsible for the fact that even now, nearly thirty years since he'd assumed power, his snow goblin mercenaries still had to suppress violent protests and enforce curfews in every city of the Tuatha Dé Dannan Islands.

Henry had dispelled the furious phantoms of hundreds of Greine's enemies over the last twenty-five years. And he suspected that if Greine ever did lay his hands on the Stone of Fal and claimed the famed power of the high king he'd be dispelling thousands more. Only the theft of the Stone of Fal limited Greine's hold over his subjects.

At the time of the stone's disappearance, agents and sprites alike had suggested that Greine himself had been behind the theft, removing it to ensure that the stone couldn't reject him. It was said that the relic would only answer to the bloodline of the true high king.

But Henry had never swallowed that line. The stone had responded to usurpers before and there were always ways to cheat blood magic—particularly when Greine kept the daughter of the true king on hand to bed and bleed as he needed. No, Greine would want the stone badly enough to kill for it without a doubt.

But when Henry thought of the attack in the coffee shop, he scowled.

He'd seen the ruins of Greine's enemies. They were murdered with brutal efficiency. Killed in an instant by assassins as silent and merciless as shadows. Greine wouldn't have dreamed of hiring the messy, rough thugs that Henry had dispatched at the HRD Coffee Shop.

Henry would have bet his right thumb that those boys had been backstreet toughs serving a cause. Talented amateurs, but amateurs nonetheless.

Which meant the real soldiers were still to come. Automatically, Henry felt for the wards he'd placed around Jason's flat. All still in place, but not untouched. Something had brushed over them and then withdrawn.

Then Henry noticed that Jason was singing something to himself very softly. The melody just carried over the spit and hiss of the shower. He had a beautiful voice. Princess tapped her front toes in time to the tune and purred.

"You like him, don't you?" Henry commented.

Princess nodded.

Henry shook his head.

"You don't even know him," he muttered. Princess gave him a dark, assessing look, which Henry decided to ignore.

He listened to Jason's song, feeling almost as if it were waking something in him, then scowled at his own drifting attention. What was he, an infatuated fifth grader? So Jason had a nice voice. It wasn't going to do him any good when Greine's assassins showed up.

Henry needed to think.

He read Gunther's note again and this time the implication that Greine held some legal claim over Jason struck him with greater force. That alone disturbed Henry, but coupled with the events of the previous day, it also made one thing very clear.

If the law were truly on his side, then Greine wouldn't have bothered to purchase Jason through Phipps. Greine would have done just what he was doing now—manipulated the NATO Irregular Affairs Division do his dirty work and hand Jason over to him. So Greine hadn't been the party Phipps had auctioned Jason off to, but whoever employed those angry goblin thugs seemed likely.

And if Greine had only just recently unleashed his ambassadorial liaisons, then he hadn't known about Jason until after

Phipps's original deal had gone sour. Henry could think of only one person who possessed the time, knowledge, and character to have passed on information regarding Jason—for a fee, no doubt. He realized that he needed to get his hands on Phipps.

The water went off, and a moment later Jason leaned out from the bathroom door, looking a little shy and very wet.

"Would you mind tossing me a clean dishcloth from the kitchen? There should be two of them in the drawer."

Then Henry remembered that he'd left Jason's bath towels, damp and bloodstained, on the bathroom floor. He quickly located the dishcloths and handed them to Jason.

"Thank you." Jason took the cloths and held one over his groin, still shy despite the fact that Henry had already seen and touched every inch of him. Or maybe shy because of that.

"No problem…" Henry felt an uncharacteristic heat flushing his cheeks. "Look, Jason…I need to go somewhere—"

The disappointment in Jason's face stopped him as he realized how this was coming off, like he'd screwed Jason and was about to bolt.

"I guess you don't have time to teach me anything, then." Jason dropped his gaze and Henry silently cursed himself for fucking this all up and making the kid feel used.

"We've got a little time, but we'll need to be out of here before noon."

Jason looked up at him in surprise. His entire countenance lit up as he smiled.

"You want me to come along?"

"I wouldn't be much of a bodyguard if I just left you on your own, would I?" Falk replied.

"I'll get dressed right away." Jason was already pulling on a pair of blue jeans. Henry had to suppress a laugh as he realized that the yellow T-shirt Jason shrugged on proclaimed him to be a "treble maker".

"You want coffee?" Jason bounded out from the tiny bathroom.

"Sure. That'd be nice," Henry said. He collected his trench coat from where it hung on the doorknob, and while Jason padded into the kitchen, Henry cleaned himself up and dressed in the bathroom. When he stepped out, Jason handed him a mug of hot black coffee.

"How did you get all the blood out of your clothes?" Jason asked.

"Enchanted threads—Gunther picked up the shirt and pants for me at a local goblin market ages ago." Henry took a swig of the black coffee and wondered if Jason had added a little cinnamon to the grounds. "Blood dries, then flakes right off."

"There's still the bullet hole in the chest, though," Jason commented over the rim of his coffee cup. "You sure you don't want to borrow one of my shirts?"

Henry felt pretty certain he wouldn't fit all that well into anything of Jason's, not his clean shirts or his tidy life.

"Thanks for the offer, but when you're known as Half-Dead Henry, a bullet-riddled wardrobe isn't really a problem." Henry glanced down at the tattered fabric of his shirtfront. "Anyway, the hole offers me a rare opportunity to tan my nipple."

Jason almost choked on his coffee as he tried to stifle a laugh. Henry gave him a gentle slap on the back.

"Thanks," Jason said, though he looked inexplicably flushed. Then Henry realized that his hand still lingered on Jason's back, making the contact seem like a caress; the heat of Jason's body radiated across Henry's palm. He drew back, turning toward the cramped kitchenette.

"You don't keep much of a pantry, do you?"

"There's cereal and milk," Jason replied, as if that constituted all the sustenance anyone could ever need. Henry supposed that, being a man who regularly ate cold chili beans straight out of the can, he couldn't criticize. The shredded wheat cereal reminded him of old army mattresses, which probably meant it was good for him.

After he and Jason had both eaten, Henry decided to get down to work on Jason's defenses. While he showed Jason a proper stance, Princess jumped down from the windowsill to lap the remaining milk from Henry's bowl.

Henry wasn't really the teaching type and his first few attempts to ascertain the extent of Jason's power seemed to result in nothing. Whether he called a burst of cold blue flame or the tendrils of Lost Mist, he couldn't seem to provoke the slightest magical response from Jason. Though, Jason certainly looked uneasy enough.

"Am I doing this right?" Jason asked. He eyed the guttering blue flames on his left suspiciously.

"You're doing fine." Henry tried not to sound annoyed. Normally, even the weakest nixie would throw off a few sparks in response to geysers of blue flame, but Jason demonstrated no discernable defensive reflex. If Henry hadn't known better, he would have sworn there wasn't a shred of power in Jason's entire being.

He did note that each time he spat a blazing spell out at Jason he missed his mark by farther than he had intended. Henry'd never been one to miss his target, particularly not at this range and certainly not three times in a row. Some deft magic worked to deflect his assaults with a subtlety that aggravated him.

Standing at the foot of the futon, Jason looked nervous but utterly unaware of the forces surrounding him. He watched Henry with wide, dark eyes. His long fingers lightly tapped an uneasy rhythm against his legs.

"Let's give it one more go," Henry decided and Jason nodded his assent.

Just as Henry drew the burning power of an unformed spell into the hollow of his mouth—felt it flickering across the tip of his tongue—he saw Jason's mouth move just a breath. Henry went still, straining to catch the word on Jason's lips.

Henry felt, as much as heard, a bittersweet melody wash over him like the promise of redemption. Beautiful and definitely magic. Henry swallowed his burning spell back into his gut instead of wasting the energy.

"Do you know what you did just now?" Henry asked.

"Me?" Jason looked startled. "Nothing. I was just standing here like you told me to."

"No, there was something. I felt it. Tell me what you were thinking about a second ago."

"Nothing." Jason shook his head. "I just had a little tune in my head but—"

"What tune?" Henry moved closer to him, drawing in the faint whisper of power before it could dissipate with Jason's exhaled breath. Penetrating the camouflage of warm domestic tastes—coffee and milk—Henry discerned that spark of fire that he'd mistaken twice for cinnamon.

"It's just a little song that I sing when I get nervous. My mother taught it to me."

"Yeah? Like that song she taught you about the Stone of Fal?"

"That, and 'Greensleeves,'" Jason replied.

Henry smirked. Jason definitely hadn't been singing 'Greensleeves'. No, an immensely potent magic fueled that other little tune of Jason's.

"I need you to think about that tune—don't sing it, not even a whisper. Just think about it, will you?"

"Sure."

For a moment Jason simply looked thoughtful, his gaze distant and his fingers absently tapping in time to an unuttered melody. Then Henry felt the wards he'd set begin to shimmer and shudder with a kind of excitement. As he watched, his glinting, serpentine wards slithered and wriggled closer to Jason. They wove around him like love knots. Henry's own damn spells. No wonder he couldn't come close to hitting Jason.

"Fuck me," Henry whispered under his breath. Then he raised his voice. "You can give it a rest."

"Okay." Jason looked nonplussed and Henry felt his wards slipping back into his control. "Did it help?" Jason asked.

"It cleared a few things up." Henry studied Jason. "Tell me, when you were thinking of that song, what were you imagining—I mean, did you see anything?"

"It always makes me think of being safe…" Jason shrugged, but then added, "Anytime I hear music I sort of see the shape and color of the melody. With that particular piece I imagine the notes are weaving a shining gold orb around me…Sounds stupid, doesn't it?"

Henry shook his head. "You see the orb when you're thinking of the tune?"

"Yeah, but I see all kinds of shit—" A look of realization suddenly lit Jason's features. "Is it really there?"

"Yeah, it's there all right," Henry assured him. "Your mother taught you a powerful protection spell. Clever, too, because it manipulates the powers around you so that someone watching for magic might not even notice that the spell is coming from you."

"My mother knew all that?" Jason asked.

"I imagine she knew quite a bit more," Henry responded. "How many songs in all did she teach you?"

"Dozen and dozens, but most of them are just normal songs. You know, 'Do-Re-Mi' sort of stuff…" Jason frowned at the small bone fife on his shelf. "Though there was one that was very strange…"

"Yeah? Strange how?" Henry prompted.

"I never got to play it," Jason replied. "She made me memorize the fingerings for the melody on my fife but insisted that I never play even a note of it aloud…'Amhrán Na Marú.' I think that was the name of the piece. I'm not sure. It's been a long time since I've even thought of it."

Henry didn't recognize the name of the song, but he did know what *marú* meant in the sidhe language. Slaughter.

"When you were practicing the fingerings on your fife, did you ever see anything?" Henry asked.

"Not really…" Jason responded slowly and Henry could tell that he was rethinking those pure, simple memories of his childhood. How different were they now that he knew his mother had been secretly training him to perform spells?

"One time, when I was about six, I'd gotten all excited about reading and writing music. I remember trying to write down the melody of 'Amhrán Na Marú.' I could hear it as I wrote it and then I started to see it...It scared me, all those white shining notes, razor sharp and spinning around me like saw blades. My mother caught me and tore the notations to shreds. She spanked the hell out of me. And after that I couldn't forget about 'Amhrán Na Marú' fast enough."

"Quite the lady, that mother of yours," Henry commented.

"What do you mean?" A strain of offense sounded in Jason's tone, but Henry ignored it. Jason needed to be told the truth—or at least as much of it as Henry could work out—but he didn't imagine that Jason would thank him for it…He supposed that there wasn't much Jason would thank him for.

Princess eyed him from the windowsill.

"Do me a favor, Princess. Keep Gunther company at the office and keep your ears pricked for any news concerning Jason," Henry told her. "Find me if the sidhe court makes any more demands."

Princess gave a quick nod and then slipped out the window. Henry turned his attention back to Jason.

"We should get a move on as well."

"But I thought you were going to teach me how to defend myself?"

"You already have more skill than I could teach you in a single morning. You've just got to commit to unleashing it. The next time someone corners you, don't just whisper that song under your breath, belt it out."

"I'm supposed to sing to them?"

"Music soothes the savage beast, isn't that what they say?"

"You're serious?" Jason seemed caught between incredulity and amusement.

"Dead serious," Henry replied. "You might want to bring that fife of yours along as well."

"Of course." A hint of sarcasm colored Jason's voice as he snatched his fife from the shelf. "I can always knock someone over the head with it if serenading fails to produce an effect."

Despite himself, Henry laughed and Jason's annoyance seemed to dissipate.

"So where are we going?" Jason asked.

"The Grand Goblin Bazaar," Henry informed him. "And while we're on our way we need to have a talk about 'The Stone of Fal' and all those other songs your mother taught you."

Jason looked apprehensive but tucked his fife into the pocket of his hooded sweatshirt and zipped it up. Then he followed Henry out the door.

Chapter Seven

Jason wasn't certain if the events of the last day had simply depleted his ability to feel shocked or if he was somehow becoming accustomed to the surreal. A week ago he would have reeled with denial when Falk informed him that, in all likelihood, he harbored some mystic relic in his bones—the very Stone of Fal he'd described to Falk only a day ago. Falk played it easy and offhanded as he mentioned that there really was a usurper, Greine, who wanted the stone as well as a group of sidhe revolutionaries who were desperate to keep it from him.

More than likely the woman who'd raised Jason hadn't been his biological mother but her lady-in-waiting, Fionn.

Jason wished he could dismiss it all as crazy, but he no longer possessed that capacity. Instead Falk's words resonated through him with the inevitability of truth.

"Nobody's going to get to you." Falk's blue eyes seemed to blaze against the gray morning mist. "Soon as we track Phipps and find out what he's sold Greine, we'll be ahead of the game." He left much unsaid, Jason knew, just from the careful way he chose his words.

Ahead of them the crosswalk light flashed. And for the first time Jason noticed that the icon of the walking man looked like the chalk outline of a murder victim: his head severed from his body, his hands and feet missing.

"Do you know if it was Greine or the revolutionaries who killed my father?"

"No way to know for sure." Falk glanced quickly to him and Jason thought he read worry in Falk's expression. He probably thought Jason was going to start bawling, but Jason had cried about all he could over his father's death a long time ago. Not that he didn't still feel the hurt and horror, but it wasn't the open wound it once had been. He certainly wasn't going to go to pieces in front of Falk.

Then Falk reached out and pulled Jason to him with an awkward but oddly comforting squeeze of his shoulder. An instant later Falk released him, but they continued to walk closely. Jason could feel the heat radiating off Falk.

"If I had to put my money on one or the other," Falk said, "I'd bet Greine was responsible for what was done to your dad. Revolutionaries would have torched the entire house to cover their tracks and keep Greine from knowing where they'd been looking for you. The way your father's body was left, that strikes me more as a message from Greine to the revolutionaries. He'd want them to know he was close to reclaiming the stone and just what he'd do to his enemies."

Jason wasn't violent by nature, but in that instant he wished he could lay his hands on this bastard Greine. He'd be more than happy to loose the razor notes of the 'Amhrán Na Marú' upon the man.

"If it's revenge you're thinking about, don't," Falk told him with an uncanny insight. "Trust me, no good comes from stewing on all the wrongs of the past. There are just too many to ever reach the end once you start down that road."

"So what do you suggest?" Jason retorted. "That I just pretend nothing ever happened?"

"I didn't say that." Falk shook his head. "I'm just telling you that it's easy to lose sight of your future when you're caught up with the past."

"My future?" Jason almost laughed at the idea. He'd lost the only promising job he'd had in years, he was being hunted by monsters as well as a supernatural megalomaniac, and the closest he'd come to a romantic encounter had been a morning-wood pity fuck from Falk—which Jason couldn't even think about right now without feeling disheartened. Really, the idea of his future should have depressed the hell out of him, but there was something about Falk's company that kept Jason from pitying himself; he certainly wasn't going to whine about his job prospects and sad love life to a guy who just shrugged off bullet wounds.

"You said yourself that you've spent years trying to have a normal life and you obviously have a future as a musician." Falk gave him another of his quick, piercing glances. "What I'm trying to tell you is that this world around you here and now is full of possibilities and hope. That's what you should be living for, not some dank, dead past...You don't want to end up as a haunted, half-dead relic like me, I promise."

"You're not so bad," Jason responded.

Falk just snorted at that.

"I think you're kind of charming," Jason admitted because it was obviously true, otherwise this morning wouldn't have started the way it had. Falk might not want it to be so, but Jason wasn't going to lie, at least not to himself.

"Yeah?" Falk actually laughed. "That's me all right, Prince Charming."

Jason flushed but then shot back, "What would you know about it? I'm the one who can see people as they really are, not you."

To his surprise, Falk didn't have a response. Jason wasn't certain, but he thought a faint flush might have darkened Falk's tanned cheeks.

"We'll want to turn right up here." Falk quickened his step and Jason moved swiftly to match his long strides. As he walked alongside Falk through the damp morning mist, he picked out a plump man with the face of a carp selling cut flowers to a couple of tourists. A day ago the gaping jaws of the flower seller would have terrified him; he would have interpreted them as a sign of his disassembling sanity.

But now he knew he wasn't out of his mind, and as he surreptitiously studied the flower seller arranging a bouquet of peonies, Jason noticed how the scales on his hands and face glinted iridescent gold in the passing breaks of sunlight. Across the street two young girls chatted. Tiny wings fluttered and flashed like butterflies on their shoulders.

The world was stranger than most people would ever know, he realized, but also more beautiful.

When Falk showed him to a blue port-o-let near the harbor, Jason wasn't surprised to discover rolling green hills and a cerulean blue sky beyond the door. He followed Falk out onto an oddly serene and empty hill. Countless tiny flowers carpeted the ground and perfumed the warm air. Sunflowers the size of Jason's little finger bowed over even smaller sprays of scarlet poppies and white roses. The brilliant blue port-o-let seemed to be the only notable landmark as far as Jason could see.

"This doesn't look like a grand bazaar," Jason commented.

"Nah, this is just a layover." Falk fished a pocket watch from his trench coat. "The portal to the bazaar won't be aligned for twelve more minutes. All the portals have different schedules. Nowadays, of course, computers track most of them and set up layovers like this one. But back in the day we had to do it by memory and feel. It took skill and balls, like jumping trains."

"You sound like you miss the old days."

Falk appeared troubled by the idea.

"No, they were rotten times, really. People died—sometimes badly—and nobody could afford to give a crap because that was just the price of knowledge back then. I'm glad all that's gone now." Falk closed his pocket watch and slipped it back into his coat pocket. Then he offered Jason one of his self-conscious, crooked grins. "I'm just a codger who misses the man he was before all those good old days took their toll."

Jason considered him: his ghostly, luminous quality and his rough appearance, all those scars, his missing finger, and that tattoo like a brand left on him by the man who'd recruited him.

"Something really bad happened to you back then, didn't it?" Jason asked.

"Something bad happened to most everyone back then. At least I'm still walking," Falk replied. He watched Jason almost warily. But Jason wasn't about to force him to talk about anything he wasn't ready to share. He'd endured too many mandatory psychiatric sessions himself to treat another person's private history so cavalierly.

"So where is this place?" Jason asked instead.

"Remains of the Elysian Fields after the bombings of '42," Falk replied. "Eight square miles of dwarf-flower preserves. A community of faeries settled here about fifty years back. Whatever you do, don't swat any of them." Falk thumbed up at the sky.

Jason gazed up to see a single, colorful cloud rolling slowly closer. As it drifted near, Jason realized that it was composed entirely of pale moths and butterflies. The majority of them settled across the carpet of flowers but several of them fluttered only a few feet from Jason.

A faint haze surrounded each insect with what looked like the silhouette of a human body. Then suddenly the haze around the nearest moth grew solid and in an instant the moth was gone and a dainty woman with oddly yellow hair, eyes, and lips stood only a foot from Jason. The faintest shadow of a moth fluttered over her heart. Jason didn't scrutinize it too closely, since it did nothing to clothe her small, bare breasts.

"A new face to our sunny fields!" The woman cocked her head back to beam up at Jason from just above his belt. "Have you come to dally among the flowers, fair traveler?"

"No. We—we're just passing through," Jason replied quickly. The woman's flirtatious gaze and nudity unnerved him far more than her sulfur-toned mouth.

"He's with me, Buttercup." Falk took an almost proprietary step closer to Jason. Buttercup's lemon brows rose and she peered up at Jason.

"You don't look like one of the dead." She leaned so close that her cheek brushed his arm; her skin felt as cool and powdery as cornstarch. She flicked out her shockingly orange tongue as she drew a deep breath of Jason's chest. "You don't smell dead either…Oh, not at all! In fact, you smell sweet and fiery and young, like cinnamon bark and semen!"

An embarrassed flush heated Jason's face.

"Give it a rest, Buttercup. He's spoken for." Falk gently drew Jason back and Buttercup stared at him.

"Oh! That's how it is?" She raised her brows.

"Yeah, that's how it is," Falk stated firmly, though he shot Jason an odd glance. Then he went on talking to Buttercup. "But I have a different proposition for you, my girl."

"Of course you do! But what could a tiny starving faerie offer you, Half-Dead?" Buttercup smiled brightly at Falk and batted her long yellow lashes. "Not my helpless little body?"

"Your little body's about as helpless as a black widow's," Falk replied. "I'm looking for three pinches of dust." Jason wasn't sure what exactly that meant, but Buttercup nodded.

"What you got for it?" Buttercup eyed Falk speculatively, though Jason noted that she never drew too near him.

"Treasure from another kingdom." Falk reached into his pocket and drew out what looked like three red-and-white-striped straws.

"Pixy Stix!" Buttercup's entire expression lit up. The shadowy moth floating over her heart beat its wings wildly, as if attempting to fly to Falk's hand. Jason noted several other moths rise from the flowery carpet at their feet, but Buttercup swung her arms out, waving them away.

"Mine!" she called out and the moths fell back. When she returned her gaze to Falk, Jason thought her eyes might actually be sparkling. "Three for three."

"Three for three," Falk agreed. He extended both his hands, proffering the paper-wrapped candy to Buttercup with his right. "A trade fair and true, says I."

"Fair and true, says I," Buttercup echoed. She flicked her right hand from her chest to Falk's empty left hand three times. Each time Jason saw her fingers brush through the shadowy moth at her heart, collecting a velvety gray dust from its wings, which she brushed across Falk's palm. The instant she made the third exchange she snatched the candy from Falk and bounded back as if she expected to be pursued.

Falk closed his hand into a fist and then slipped it into his coat pocket—where Jason was beginning to suspect he kept an inordinate number of odd things.

Buttercup tore open one of the red-striped straws and tossed back the contents. An instant later she let out a crow of joy and danced back to him and Falk. Her cheeks flushed bright orange and her feet hardly touched the ground as she skipped around them gleefully.

"What was in that thing?" Jason asked softly.

"Colored sugar, citric acid, and all the anticipation of a six-year-old on Christmas morning." Falk's expression softened slightly as he watched Buttercup. "The bright packaging doesn't hurt any."

"More beautiful than phlox, sweeter than honeysuckle, sharper than lemon blossoms!" Buttercup paused a moment to hold the straws to the cloudless blue sky. "I would wed you, sweetness, if I weren't going to devour you instead!"

Falk gave a quiet laugh and then asked offhandedly, "You haven't heard anything of a bauble-snatcher called Phipps lately, have you, Buttercup?"

"Passed through early yesterday, sweating and swearing. Left word that buyers could find him at Red Ogre's." Buttercup glanced away from the bright candies for only an instant. "Be careful doing business with him, Half-Dead. He's just your opposite, a handsome hollow wrapped around a rotten pit."

"I'll keep my head up. You take care as well, beautiful." Falk flashed her a smile, then turned to Jason and beckoned him toward the port-o-let.

"It's about time for us to go. But first, there are a few things I need to tell you about the bazaar. Most importantly is that our human laws have no authority there, so be careful and stay close to me. Law in the Grand Bazaar is a force unto itself. Definitely don't accept anything unless you've paid for it, even if it seems like it's being offered for free—nothing is ever free at the bazaar. And don't give anyone your real name. Your identity in particular needs to be protected. So today you're Agent August, got that?"

"Agent August," Jason repeated, though he doubted that anyone would mistake him for an agent of any kind. "What should I call you?"

"Most everyone knows me as Half-Dead Henry." Falk sounded tired of it, but then his tone lightened. "You could just call me Henry, if you like."

"Sure, Henry it is." Jason didn't know why, but he felt almost touched to be on a first-name basis with Falk. Then he scowled at his own sentimentality. Fortunately Falk had turned to return Buttercup's farewell wave.

"I don't really look the part of an agent," Jason commented as Falk's attention turned back to him.

"But you will." Falk raised his dusty left hand and lightly traced a symbol across Jason's brow. Then Falk leaned close. Jason smelled the earthy aroma of his skin and saw silver light flash between his lips as he whispered, "Faerie dust, deceive all eyes. On this stately form lay August's dour guise."

Jason tensed, feeling the tingle of a spell pass over him. But it faded in an instant. He glanced down at his hands and arms. Nothing seemed different. But then how would he know, he wondered.

"Did it work?" Jason asked.

"Like a charm. Now you just have to remember to keep looking unimpressed—" Falk lifted his head slightly as if catching a scent on the air. "I think our ride is rumbling into the station. Let's leg it." Falk drew Jason through the port-o-let door. When he opened it again, an entirely new world spread out before them.

❧

Jason did his best not to gape at the vastness of his surroundings. He stood only a foot from the edge of a dark, watery canal that flowed between long alleys of densely packed and ornately carved stone buildings. Brilliant banners and strings of gold bells hung from the upper floors of the buildings. Below, crowds of odd, eerie, and beautiful creatures hustled past Jason, conversing in a cacophony of strange languages. The air felt hot, smelled exotic, and pulsed as if filled by hundreds of foreign radio stations.

Two small creatures that looked very much like goats from a children's book—complete with beribboned aprons and prim bipedal gaits—bleated loudly in Jason's direction. When he glanced to them, they lifted their aprons to display bulbous pink udders. They both let out shrieks of laughter at his shocked reaction but then raced away when Falk turned his attention to them.

"The Pepper Sisters," Falk told him. "I think you just got an eyeful of the new ad campaign for their dairy."

"Were those the owners or the producers?" Jason asked.

"Both. It's an employee-owned co-op. Chemical-free too now that Pickle's quit smoking." Falk moved ahead into the tight confines of the crowd. Jason followed him, still trying to take everything in.

Overhead a cluster of gold birds took wing from a windowsill, and higher in the clouds, Jason thought he sighted something that looked like a fighter jet—but with wide, gaping jaws. Rays of light flashed off its silvery body and fell across the cobbled streets like streams of sunlight.

Despite the sinister coils and huge, serpentine heads of sea creatures breaking the surface, a fleet of small boats skimmed across the deep, dark canal waters. As Jason watched, three beautiful youths lifted their faces from the waters and then hefted their muscular torsos and long fish-like tails onto the deck of a moored boat. They pulled nets filled with wriggling eels up after them.

Commerce fueled it all, Jason soon realized. Beneath every banner and in every doorway displays of ludicrous, luscious, and glittering goods abounded. Jason glimpsed pungent fruit, gaudy baubles, skeins of feathers and fabric, oily bicycle chains, and steel cages brimming with glassy-eyed teddy bears. Merchants called from both the surrounding streets and the canal waters and shoppers bartered with them through a din of competing transactions.

Only the ubiquitous flocks of tiny, bright gold birds seemed to have nothing to buy or sell. They flitted between buildings and watched the populace passing below with dark indigo eyes. What Jason could catch of their songs sounded like quiet laughter.

"Do you know what kind of birds those are?" Jason asked.

"Birds?" Falk glanced between a large raccoon selling blood sausages and two plump women offering a variety of felt hats.

"The little gold birds flying all around us." Jason started to point one out, but Falk caught his hand.

"It's not polite to point," Falk said. Then he dropped his voice to a whisper. "Especially not at spies no one else can see."

A nervous thrill rushed over Jason and he quickly averted his gaze from the nearest of the birds. Falk quickly drew him down a narrow, dark alley.

"Spies?" Jason asked under his breath.

"Shadow Snitches, they're called," Falk replied. "Are any of them following us?"

"No. They're fluttering around all over the place, but none seem interested in us." Jason tried to appear casual as he scanned the lichen-crusted bas-relief of the surrounding walls and peered up at the azure sky. "Who do they spy for?"

"Anyone with a few pounds of pumpkin seeds," Falk replied quietly. "The bazaar's famous for its gangs of invisible informants. Some may even be on the lookout for you. I should have mentioned them, but I didn't think it would matter with the glamour protecting you."

Jason felt the blood draining from his face. He didn't think he could stand another encounter like the one that had taken place at the HRD Coffee Shop yesterday.

"Don't look so worried," Falk told him. "As far as anyone here can see, you're an Irregulars agent who dresses far too nicely for the company you're keeping. That's all. The only thing that might give you away is if you started pointing out Shadow Snitches and the like."

"Right," Jason agreed, though he wasn't certain how he was supposed to know what everyone else wasn't seeing.

"Here. These should help." Falk dug down into his coat pocket. "They're pretty scuffed up, but I think the glamour on you will disguise the worst of it." He held out a pair of plastic sunglasses that looked much like the ones he'd given Jason when they'd first met. One of the lenses bore hairline cracks along the edge and the black frames were scratched, but otherwise they appeared to be intact.

"You lost them in the shade lands and I picked them up before we left."

Jason slipped them on and all at once the stone walls lining the alley took on the luster of abalone shell. The flocks of gold birds blinked out of sight, as did several doors and windows. Bright signs filled with flashing gold script popped into existence over numerous doorways. Simple boats bobbing in the canal transformed into resplendent gondolas.

Jason also noted his clothes—yellow T-shirt, hooded jacket, jeans, and old sneakers—had upgraded into a tailored charcoal suit, a white dress shirt, and tastefully expensive-looking leather shoes.

Beside him, Falk dulled. His eyes cooled to a washed-out blue; wrinkles and shadows weathered his naturally luminous flesh. For the first time Jason wondered why Falk disguised himself in such a manner. Had he, like Gunther, been transformed?

"Are you wearing a glamour too?" Jason asked.

Falk snorted derisively. "I don't know just how bad I look to you without the glasses, but I promise you, if I bothered to doll myself up with a masking spell, I'd certainly aspire to be better than hobo handsome."

"But there is something..." Jason insisted quietly. "It's like a shadow over you—"

"The long dead leave their mark," Falk cut him off briskly and then started walking. "Red Ogre's isn't far, but we'll want to get there before the tide comes in."

"All right." Jason let it go and followed Falk in silence down ever narrowing alleys and across a series of badly eroded bridges, until they reached a slum of dank, half-flooded catacombs, crumbling temples, and what looked like the wrecked remains of a fleet of galleons. Strange figureheads of monstrous creatures leered from the deep shadows of the surrounding buildings while huge, glossy red centipedes sheltered beneath cracked portholes and under the eaves of roofs. Heaps of tiny bird bones littered the moss-damp ground and barnacles studded the flagstones of the largely abandoned streets.

The air smelled oddly fragrant. Jason recognized the scents of malt and yeast but couldn't identify the clean floral perfume that drifted to him from what looked like rotting masts and collapsed rafters.

A glance over the rims of his glasses revealed not only the golden corpses of Shadow Snitches in the jaws of several centipedes but also a sea of ghostly pale flowers cascading over the wrecks and ruins.

"You take me to the weirdest places," Jason commented.

"All part of the service." Falk stopped in front of a white tower that looked to Jason like a cross between a lighthouse and a Hindu temple, replete with carved figures in various states of naked frolic decorating the walls and staircase that wound up some seven stories. Whelks and drooping strings of emerald kelp encrusted the lower levels of the stairs, making the images difficult to discern, but by the time Jason reached the heavy hatch-like door on the fifth floor, he'd realized that the carvings presented a far too detailed parade of mermaids, unicorns, satyrs, and griffins indulging in pornographic gymnastics with a variety of slender men and women.

If it was advertising, Jason was pretty certain he wasn't up to making any transactions. Something pink blurred past the tiny fish-eye porthole set in the rust-red door.

"So what exactly is this place?" Jason asked just as Falk raised his scarred right hand to knock.

"Depends on what you're looking for when you come. They have rooms to rent and don't ask questions about the kind of company you might like to keep," Falk replied. "But most come to the tower for the drinks. Red Ogre and her wife have been brewing their own beers from all the way back when this district served as a shipyard for the Atlantean Navy. You can still see their influence in the art." Falk gave a nod to the lewd menagerie decorating the walls and staircase. "The most perverted culture I've ever encountered." With that he gave quick rap against the door.

The scarlet handwheel spun, and then with a hiss, as if releasing some foreign atmosphere, the heavy hatch door swung open.

❧

Few places remained just as Falk remembered first seeing them. But as he dropped down onto one of the wooden stools at the bar and took a deep breath of the smoky speakeasy atmosphere, he felt as if he'd stepped back to the first weeks after Frank's death. It all seemed the same: the close proportions of the circular chamber, the shadowy patrons with their odd mix of races and lowered voices, the faint drone of an antique phonograph playing a scratched record of Selkie torch songs. Hell, even the dark stains defacing the oak counter looked like the ones Henry remembered drunkenly tracing with his one good hand.

Henry touched a deep gouge in the wood, noting against his will how it cut and curved to form a rickety *F*.

In an instant, ninety-four years seemed to roll back. He felt swallowed by recollection. An ache flashed through his chest and flared across his hand with the intensity of a raw wound. Reflexively, Henry curled his arm against his chest as if he could shield himself from injuries inflicted so long ago.

How could mere memory hurt so badly, Henry wondered. How could entire empires rise and fall and all the while part of him still remained lying there on that cold steel table with Frank's knife buried in his heart? Why couldn't it ever just be over?

"Lucky number seven?" Jason swung onto the stool beside him and flashed him a warm, charming smile. His cologne of cinnamon and coffee pushed back the dull, dead taste in Henry's mouth.

"What?" Henry asked.

"Carved into the bar counter. It's a seven, isn't it?"

"It—" And suddenly Henry realized that Jason was right. He'd been looking at the carving upside down and misread it. "Yeah. Probably left by one of the famous dwarves."

Jason gave him an uncertain look, then laughed.

"You nearly had me there," he admitted easily.

Henry almost laughed himself, seeing such a friendly expression animate the guise of Agent August's normally grim face. Watching Jason peer at the beer pulls and study the colorful array of liquor bottles behind the bar, Henry felt as though he could almost see Jason through the glamour disguising him. Jason caught him staring and flushed slightly.

"I'm gawking, aren't I?"

"Not more than anyone new to the place would," Henry assured him.

"I was just wondering if this is where Arrogant Bastard Ale really comes from?" Jason inclined his head toward the large crest of a scowling gargoyle that hung behind the bar. "Or is it an import?"

"It's made here. Red Ogre must have finally gotten an export license for the United States..."

Henry wasn't certain of why, but now with Jason sitting beside him he suddenly took notice of all the little ways in which Red Ogre's tower had altered since he'd last cared enough to really look around him.

The gleaming amber light fixtures with their sleek chrome fittings could have come from an IKEA catalogue. Photos of faerie celebrities and kelpie queens hung on the walls where once there'd been only yellowed etchings. Even the melody that he'd initially recognized revealed itself to be no more than a catchy sample cut into a modern remix.

Jason tapped his fingers across the bar in time to the new, jazzy bass line.

Red Ogre herself was nowhere to be seen; most likely she was somewhere below, tending her hops and oak barrels. However, her pale wife, Sorcha, moved behind the length of the bar with all the assurance and musical grace of a full-blooded sidhe; even though she'd been cast out from Tuatha Dé Dannan society for her passionate love of Red Ogre, she still wore her golden hair in a courtier's braided crown and held her head high as she glided silently up to them to take their orders.

"Half-Dead." She inclined her head in easy acknowledgement but then paused as she caught sight of his companion. Jason offered her a winning smile, which looked utterly out of place on August's sardonic face and brought the faintest crease to Sorcha's brow.

"Here on business?" she inquired softly.

"Not officially, my beauty," Henry replied. "But there is a fellow here we'd like a word with."

"Red Ogre won't be happy if you've come to drag one of her regulars out."

"Nah. You know me, Lady Sorcha, I wouldn't—"

"Yes, I know you, Half-Dead, but your companion has a rather different reputation, I think." She settled a firmly disapproving glower on Jason.

"I'm just along for moral support and a good drink, ma'am," Jason replied. Then he turned the pockets of his jacket inside out. "See, I'm not even carrying my badge. It's my day off."

Sorcha gave a little laugh at that but then seemed to catch herself. She raised a gleaming golden brow and peered at Jason a little too intensely for Henry's liking.

"The man we're looking for isn't a regular." Henry drew Sorcha's attention back to himself. "He'll only just have arrived. Goes by the name of Phipps."

"Him." Sorcha's expression lifted immediately and she nodded. "Red suspected that he'd have a few visitors tracking him down…" Sorcha lowered her satin-soft voice. "Who in this day and age pays with gold dust, really? Hasn't he heard of American Express?"

"Mind telling us which room he's rented?" Henry inquired, though he knew what the answer would be.

"Mind ordering a drink to make it worth my while?" Sorcha returned.

"My pleasure, Lady Sorcha. I'll have a Rotten Rye whisky and my associate—"

"A pint of the Spartacus Hard Cider," Jason decided for himself. Henry shot him a warning glance, but Jason just appeared all the more pleased with himself.

When Sorcha moved away to procure their drinks, Henry hunched a little nearer to Jason.

"The cider you ordered is made from goblin fruits—"

"I know. I was reading about it up on the menu board. It says I'll never taste better." Then Jason lowered his voice and glanced meaningfully to Sorcha. "She looks human."

Henry simply nodded.

"All the Tuatha Dé Dannan clan look human. Her, and you as well. Your ancestors were human once but also very ambitions as a people. They stole immense powers from other realms and used them without understanding the cost." Henry wasn't one to recount old legends, but he thought that this might be something Jason would need to know. Because one day he might very well find himself in the position of his ancestors, calling up murderous forces. "Claiming and wielding great power—the kind that sunders seas or drains the lives from entire armies—it changes you."

"Like it turns you into a giant snake or something like that?" Jason asked. He appeared to be only half joking.

"Well, I can't say that it hasn't ever happened," Henry conceded. "But I'm not talking about a superficial transformation. I mean a more fundamental change, an effect that reaches all the way down to your soul and slowly distorts your whole being. You already know that magic can alter how you perceive the world around you. It can show you things that almost no one else can even understand."

Jason's expression went serious. Yeah, Jason understood that part all too well.

"Wielding that power removes you from the rest of humanity even further. You do it long enough and you can become alienated from all those mundane experiences of life that allow people to understand each other. The things that make us feel connected to each other and help us give a damn about our fellow human beings. And once you stop caring, once the only thing left in your life is power itself, you become capable of sacrificing even those people who you once thought you loved just for the sake of more power." Henry tried not to sound bitter, but it was hard. "Believe me, the greatest magic always comes at a cost. Often as not, what you sacrifice is your humanity."

"Something like that happened to you, didn't it? You had to pay a price for your power?" Jason asked suddenly and softly.

"What? No—I mean, sort of, but not like you're thinking." Henry shook his head. "I wasn't the guy who went questing for power over life and death. I wasn't so smart or ambitious. I was just too naive to realize that he'd kill me to fulfill his aspirations."

Jason blanched slightly at Henry's words but then asked, "But you're alive now. So what happened?"

"It went wrong." Henry hadn't spoken of that cold April morning since his debriefing ninety-four years ago; it had always seemed too soon. He wasn't really certain why he was talking about it now, except that Jason made it feel like such a long time ago. "The officer in charge, the one who wanted to claim power over death—"

"Franklyn Fairgate, right?" Jason asked. "The man who recruited you."

Henry hadn't expected Jason to remember that. How strange it seemed to hear Frank's name spoken by someone else, and in that unconcerned tone.

"Yeah, that's right." Henry couldn't meet Jason's interested gaze. He stared down at the stained counter in front of him. "Frank was no slouch. He just got one little detail of the ritual wrong. The incantations, the bronze knife, the symbols of binding—he had all that dead on. But he hadn't understood what it meant to make a willing sacrifice of precious life. He hadn't realized that immense power only gives itself to those prepared to lose everything for its sake. He figured that it would be enough to sacrifice his…friend."

Henry swallowed hard against the tight feeling in his throat. He wished Sorcha would hurry up with his drink. "Long story short, he miscalculated and ended up getting himself and about a hundred other guys killed. I was the only one of Frank's crew that walked out of the compound more or less alive."

"That must have been really hard..." Jason sounded at a loss. "I'm sorry."

"Yeah, well, everybody's got a sob story." Falk glanced across the bar to see Sorcha gliding silently toward them with their drinks. Last thing he needed was for her to see him going soft and self-pitying.

"Looks like we've got company," he warned Jason. Then he raised his voice in greeting to Sorcha. "And speaking of angels. Sorcha, you're a vision of lovely mercy for a thirsty man."

"If flattery were cash, you'd have made me a wealthy woman a hundred times over, Half-Dead," Sorcha replied with an amused smile.

Jason accepted his pint of luminous gold cider. Henry exchanged his blood-red whiskey shot for a gold goblin's coin and didn't ask for his change. In return, Sorcha told him a room number and withdrew to tend the other patrons gathered around the bar and slouching at the shadowy tables.

"Here's to walking away." Falk lifted his whisky.

"More or less alive," Jason finished.

Henry tossed his Rotten Rye back and felt it burn down to the pit of his belly.

Jason took a more measured taste of his cider, but after his initial swig, his face lit up like he'd just discovered jacking off. Then he all but dived into his pint.

"This stuff is amazing. It's got to be the most delicious thing I've tasted in my life," Jason informed him. "Have you tried it?"

"I'm more of a whisky man, myself," Henry replied. That was when he wasn't swigging back poison to keep himself on the brink of the shade lands.

"Yeah, but this is...I can't even think of a word beautiful enough to describe it. It's like drinking Vivaldi's 'Autumn Allegro.'" Jason clutched the glass between his hands, cradling the last inch of radiant liquor. Then he thrust the glass toward Henry. "You have to try it."

"Don't you want it?" Henry asked.

"Of course, but I want you to taste it more." Jason slid the glass over to Henry.

There had been more than one story of drinking buddies beating each other nearly blind over a bottle of this goblin cider. And yet here was Jason, willing to relinquish it to him.

"Don't tell me you're weirded out by drinking out of the same glass because—"

"That's it exactly. I'm a clean freak." Henry actually laughed at the idea. Then he lifted the glass and drank.

Jason was right. It was delicious, beyond mere taste. Golden light of a fall afternoon spread through Henry. He smelled sweet, ripe fruit and brilliant fallen leaves. He faintly heard a bird singing. And in the midst of it all, he tasted just a hint of Jason's warm lips. Henry allowed himself to savor it for only a moment.

He wasn't here to daydream about Jason's mouth or the comfort of his company. And it wouldn't do him or Jason any good to linger on either thought.

"It's good. Probably too good to be true," Henry said and set the glass aside. "Now come along, Agent August. There's a man in room ten we need to talk to."

❧

A narrow stairwell led them down what felt like fifteen floors and then opened into a hall cramped and corroded enough to look like it had come from a sunken submarine. The air felt thick in Jason's lungs and tasted like seawater. Out of the corner of his eye Jason even thought he saw a school of silvery fish drift by. Above them, clustering around the lights fixtures, clouds of jellyfish appeared to be feeding on the insects drawn to the diffuse light.

Suddenly Jason wondered if he could be drowning and not know it. He crushed the thought. Falk wouldn't let that happen to him.

Still, only a decade of practice in halfway houses and psychiatric assessments allowed him to keep calm and simply follow Falk through the curving hallway while green-eyed sharks swam past. Keeping his gaze focused on the vision his glasses offered, Jason saw only a series of heavy hatch doors, each bearing a painted red number.

They reached ten, and Jason realized that they weren't the first ones to come after Phipps. The heavy metal door bore deep dents had obviously been forced. A thick fungal stench poured out into the hall. The voices that rumbled from behind the battered hatch sounded as low and deep as an avalanche.

"Troll," Falk mouthed and he moved quickly between Jason the door. He dropped one hand into his pocket and Jason wondered if he was going for his badge or his knife. But Falk just pulled out his flask and took a swig. Then he edged the door open with his foot. It swung in, exposing the cramped room within and its three occupants.

A withered, leathery man the size of a child spun on them. He wore nothing but a pair of knee-high black socks and held what looked like a soldering iron in his bony fist.

The other two occupied a half-collapsed bed. Jason hardly recognized Phipps from where he lay, gasping beneath what looked like a rockslide. Then the lichen-speckled, stone-gray creature holding Phipps turned its head to glower at Falk and Jason. Its eyes were pits, and when it opened the ragged chasm of its mouth, a sound like cracking boulders rolled out. Jason guessed that was the troll.

"Now here's a picture for the scrapbook," Henry commented offhandedly. He addressed the leathery little man standing closest to them. "Do you always get up to these kinds of hijinks right after posting bail?"

"God's twat! What hole did you dirty badges crawl out of? If you haven't been told, you got no authority here, you dick wadcutters," the little man spat. "This is my personal business."

"Looks personal enough," Falk replied. "The thing is, I've got private business of my own to discuss with Phipps there."

"I got him first. You can have him when we're done!"

"We all know he won't be doing any talking after you and your troll moll have rammed that soldering iron up his ass."

Jason's stomach lurched at the thought.

"He owes me—"

"He owes everybody," Falk cut the little man off. "But he isn't going to be able to pay no matter what you do to him. His accounts have been frozen by NIAD."

"Sez you."

"Yeah, sez me," Falk agreed. Almost casually, he pulled his switchblade from his pocket. "So, you can believe me and move along or we can knock heads and see who goes home with a bloody nose."

The bed groaned as the troll rose from it. The creature's jagged skull gouged furrows in the metal ceiling as it straightened to its full height.

Jason's heart lurched and then started pounding like a jackhammer. A sudden cold sweat dampened his skin. This was going to be just like the fight in the HRD Coffee Shop—only that troll looked far too big and hard for a mere switchblade to penetrate.

That familiar calming melody rose in the back of his mind, but he resisted it. If Falk needed his help, he couldn't just huddle in a corner humming to himself like a hapless basket case. For the first time since he'd been a child, he sought the blade-sharp notes of a different melody. He held them ready but couldn't bring himself to unleash them.

"Nice knife, badge." The little man sneered at Falk. "What are you gonna do, clip my nails?"

In response Falk growled a throaty word and spat on the blade. Even with his glasses on, Jason saw the white flame that gushed up from the silver spittle.

"Whoa!" The little man dropped his soldering iron and hopped back to his troll companion's rocky shins.

"Nothing to fear here." Falk stepped into the room, smiling like he was delivering a punch line. Wisps of white mist rose in his wake and Jason felt the difference in the atmosphere like a sudden frost in the air. Black shadows churned at the edge of his vision.

"I just thought you two might want a night-light for the dark when I open the shade lands." Falk blazed as brightly as the flame of his blade.

Phipps issued a weak, sick groan from where he lay, spilled across the broken bed. A weirdly childlike screech escaped the troll and it shook its rumpled head wildly. At its feet the leathery little man blanched to dull gray.

"No need to turn nasty, badge." He gave Falk a terrified grin, displaying teeth as ragged as bottle caps. "Linda and me believe you. We'll just be moving along."

"You got till the count of three to scram," Falk replied coldly. "And I'm already on two."

They bolted through the door. Jason had to step back to avoid being rolled over. He watched them race to the stairs and clamber up in a racket of metallic scrapes and odd curses.

When he stepped inside the cramped room, he found Falk straightening Phipps up to sitting. Not even a hint of the murky darkness of the shade lands remained. The overhead light cast bright white illumination across Phipps and the squalid little room.

"Thank you," Phipps said to Falk. He brushed his silver-gray hair back from his face and made a hopeless attempt to straighten his torn silk pajamas. A large bruise was already darkening the left side of his face. The holes in his clothes afforded Jason a view of red abrasions.

"No," Falk replied. "Don't thank me. I'm likely to do worse to you myself."

Phipps glanced quickly, searchingly, to Jason and then swallowed like it hurt.

Despite his harsh words, Falk dragged a tiny table to Phipps's bedside and, after rummaging through a couple drawers in his dresser, brought over a bottle of what looked like wine. He produced a tin cup from his coat pocket and set it in front of Phipps.

For his part Jason didn't know what to feel. Half of him still felt indebted to Phipps for the kindness he'd shown him. But that only made him feel all the more betrayed, knowing now that the man had sold him like some knickknack.

Jason leaned against Phipps's wooden dresser, trying to affect an air of indifference.

"Well, you certainly have the advantage over me—I take it that you are Irregulars?"

Falk just gave a curt nod.

"You've come calling to discuss something you discovered after you broke into my business, I suppose?"

"Right again," Falk allowed.

"Jason Shamir…" Phipps nodded to himself as if there could be no other answer. "I had wondered how quickly you'd penetrate the anonymity spell placed on him. I hadn't thought quite so soon."

"You mean not before Cethur Greine set you up with asylum in exchange for the information you gave him, yeah?" Falk's tone remained conversational. It reminded Jason a little of his own interrogation.

"Yes. Another day at least." Phipps sighed heavily, then glanced forlornly to the battered mass of his door. "I really do need to look into recovering my security system."

"You might want to invest in something electronic this time." Falk found a chair and seated himself across from Phipps. "The ghosts of murdered little girls just aren't as reliable as they used to be."

Phipps raised his eyes to Falk.

"I take it that you were the one that got in." Phipps offered Falk a mock salute. "I had wondered how those fresh-faced fascists made it through the door so very quickly."

"Maybe you just left it unlocked." Falk picked up the wine bottle, pulled the cork free, and set the bottle back down in front of Phipps.

"Very civilized of you," Phipps commented. "Or is this to be a last drink for a condemned man?"

"That would depend on how cooperative you decide to be," Falk responded.

Phipps filled the tin cup himself and swallowed the contents in a single gulp.

"Ask what you want." He refilled the cup. "I'll tell you everything I can."

"Let's start with exactly what information you sold to Greine," Falk prompted.

"Everything I knew and a few things one might call conjecture." This time Phipps took a more refined sip of the white wine. "The boy was obviously in possession of the Stone of Fal. I knew that the moment I heard him singing. And once I managed to glimpse past that anonymity spell I realized that he was the spitting image of Cethur Greine himself—"

"What?" Jason couldn't help himself. Falk shot him a silencing glance, then returned his attention to Phipps.

"By that you mean you suspected he was the Greine's son?"

"Exactly," Phipps replied. "There have always been those rumors about the fruit of Greine's wedding night. Born dead, thrown into the sea. Supposedly eaten, if you trust the word of a certain Moth Man—"

"Never have before," Falk replied. "Wouldn't start now."

Phipps nodded.

"None of my informants agreed on what fate had befallen the child, but they all agreed that the princess had borne Greine an heir. And I realized that he hadn't died at all. He'd grown up in the earthly realm of his ancestors. When I passed that on to Greine he seemed quite pleased."

"Why the hell wouldn't he be?" Falk drew his own flask from his pocket and took swig. "You gave him exactly the ammunition he needed to lay legal claim on Jason and the stone."

"If it matters at all, I'd like to point out that Greine wasn't my first choice," Phipps stated. "If your raid hadn't ruined everything, Jason would have been back in the hands of his mother's agents by now."

"You mean those two who just left?" Falk raised his brows. "Because I got it from one of their colleagues that they'd rather kill Jason than chance him falling into Greine's grasp. So you'd be doing him no kindness there. Or did you mean that you tried to sell him back to the mother who hid him away in the first place?"

Phipps pulled a pained face that made Jason want to slap him. "It wasn't as if I were spoiled for choices, was I? I contacted the princess first but heard nothing back. Then I found out that she'd been locked away, sleeping in a tower for the last decade. Shortly after that I was approached by that gruesome brownie about locating the Stone of Fal…And, well, I'd already located it, hadn't I?"

"I—" Jason barely caught himself; he felt so betrayed—and not just by Phipps but also by his revelations. By the fact that some tyrant had claim over him as his father while the man Jason had known and loved…Jason didn't even know who he had been. And his mother— if possible, he knew even less of her.

"I read that Jason Shamir had only been working for you for seven weeks," Jason ground out. "Did you start looking for buyers the minute you hired him, you ghoul?"

"Yes. I knew he was something rare and valuable the moment I laid eyes on him and such commodities are what I deal in." Phipps drew himself up straight as though there was some dignity to be claimed by the admission. He narrowed his gray eyes at Jason. "But don't pretend that you Irregulars are just going to pat that boy on the head and turn him over to his daddy. We all know that's not the case. Your people want the stone just as badly as anyone. Unless Cethur Greine acts very fast, your so-called Research and Development people will have carved the stone out and slapped together some zombie patch job to fob off on him." Phipps sneered at Jason. "You Irregulars like to claim that you're defending us all from ourselves, but isn't it just so convenient that to do so you have to seize every talisman and charm you can impound?"

Jason fought to maintain a neutral expression. He didn't know anything about the Irregulars as an organization, but he trusted Falk and didn't believe Phipps.

Falk scowled but denied nothing.

"For all you know I've done the boy a favor." Phipps took another drink. "At least his own father might not be quite so keen to strip him to the bone."

At that, Falk gave a derisive snort.

"Yeah, Greine's well known for his decency and compassion," Falk replied.

Phipps shrugged, but something like melancholy showed in his expression. He took another slow, measured drink from the tin cup.

"I would have preferred it if Jason had ended up with his mother," Phipps admitted. "I did like the boy, actually. He was the best employee I ever had."

Jason glared at Phipps. Clearly he hadn't liked him enough to resist the temptation to sell him.

"You're such a hypocrite," Jason snapped. "You auction someone off to the highest bidder and then sit around looking morose and making accusations about other people's evil intentions! What utter bullshit!"

"I did what I could for him," Phipps snapped back. "But it wasn't as if I could have kept him a secret! That anonymity spell placed on him may have hidden him through his childhood, but it wasn't going to last much longer. And especially not if he kept singing. I could see it wearing away day by day. In a week's time it would have burned out completely. In place of a plain-faced nobody for an employee, I would've had a shining sidhe prince working my till and enchanting half the city with his songs. How long do you think it would have taken the revolutionaries or Greine to notice him after that?"

"Who knows," Henry answered. "But you didn't try, did you?"

"Oh, go to hell," Phipps replied. He glowered between the two of them, lifted his cup, and then set it down without drinking. "I did try, actually. Not that it's any of your damn business." Phipps sounded almost defeated. "The day after he started working for me I cast a second anonymity spell over him. It should have lasted three years, but he seared through it like a flame through paraffin. An hour after I cast it, the spell had burned off. Even if I'd decided to, I couldn't have kept him."

"I'm pretty sure he wasn't meant to be kept," Falk replied. "Did you provide Greine with means to verify Jason's paternity?"

"Blood. He cut his hand once while restringing a harp for me. I lent him my kerchief but didn't wash it afterwards. Blood like his always has a use."

Jason remembered that afternoon. At the time he'd been embarrassed about letting his hand slip and then bleeding all over Mr. Phipps's work table. He'd also been touched by Phipps's concern for him.

God, he'd been a pathetic sucker.

He had to look away from Phipps's self-satisfied face to keep from giving this whole charade away with a furious tirade of obscenities and accusations.

Not that he wanted to keep standing here, listening to Phipps recount all the ways he'd been deceived and used. What an idiot he'd been. What a fucking idiot.

He didn't want to stay in this dank little room one more minute.

He stole a quick glance to Falk only to catch Falk considering him in return. Whatever Falk read in his expression, it seemed to displease him. He dropped his flask back into one of his deep pockets and stood.

"I think that's about all we need to know for now," Falk told Phipps. "Can't say it's been a pleasure, but you were certainly informative."

Phipps gave a wave of his hand as if he were shooing away flies.

"Don't let the door hit you on the way out," he replied.

Falk smiled and replied, "If I were you I'd be more worried about trolls hitting me on their way in."

❧

Henry saw it coming, though it impressed him that Jason got all the way to the Elysian Fields before he blew his lid. He possessed a remarkable level of restraint for such a young man, particularly one of sidhe heritage.

Though right this moment he looked mad enough to chew nails and spit rivets. The muscles of his jaw worked like flexing fists.

He kept silent and still while Henry called the glamour of Agent August's guise off him; Henry drew the illusion into his own lungs like he was taking a deep drag from a clove cigarette. He swallowed the slight burn, tasting both the sting of faerie dust and the natural spice of Jason's body.

Watching Jason as the glamour receded, Henry wondered how he'd previously failed to notice the subtle bronze luster of his skin or the gold gleaming through his dark eyes. The anonymity spell shielding Jason must have once been truly powerful to render such a presence unremarkable.

But Phipps hadn't been lying about the speed at which the spell was degrading. Little to none of it would be left by the day's end.

Even scowling and bristling with anger, an unearthly grace permeated Jason's motions. The hint of a hot, sweet spice perfumed the air around him.

Jason shoved his battered glasses into the pocket of his red sweat jacket and then wheeled back from Henry, scattering the creamy white butterflies fluttering on the flowers all around them.

"That son of a bitch!" Jason kicked at the ground hard. Clods of soil and miniature lilacs went flying. "Just sitting there looking sorry for himself while he fed us that bullshit about how much it pained him to sell me out! Literally—fucking—sell me out!"

Henry kept his trap shut. No doubt, Jason had been screwed over. Offering him some lip service about how things could have been worse or counseling him to take a philosophical view would only further insult his justifiable anger.

He had a right to blow off some steam. In his position Henry would have probably loaded a pistol and blown off much more.

"And this Greine asshole is not my father!" Jason growled. "I don't give a shit what some blood test says. My father was Levi Shamir—the man who raised me. The man who died—" Jason's voice broke and he sent another clump of earth and flowers sailing through the air. "I don't care if he wasn't my biological father. He loved me and that's all that matters."

"I truly wish that were the case, Jason," Falk told him. Someone had to.

Jason turned back to Henry and Henry wasn't certain if his expression displayed more betrayal or anger.

"The son of a bitch who murdered my father," Jason ground out, "does not get to take his place."

Suddenly Henry wished that they didn't have to have this conversation. But Greine's lawyers could be depended upon to exploit every aspect of the arcane fine print of any number of treaties. Henry could guarantee that they had already pointed out that Jason had been born a sidhe and never legally emigrated. As a sidhe he was a year short of his majority and so technically still under his biological father's guardianship.

If his father had been some shiftless gnome, it wouldn't have mattered. NIAD would have simply trotted out their own retinue of lawyers, filed an injunction, and delayed until Jason came of age.

But Greine commanded a vast army of goblin mercenaries and exerted immense financial influence as a highly valued trade partner. He would be appeased and Jason would be handed over to him—very quietly and very soon.

The knowledge ate into Henry like a shot of battery acid.

"The problem is that he's got the law on his side," Henry said.

"What are you talking about?" Jason demanded.

"Legally, you're a sidhe minor of the Tuatha Dé Dannan clan, not an American citizen—"

"You're saying I'm an illegal alien?" Incredulity almost tempered Jason's outrage.

"It's a little more complex than that, but basically, yeah," Henry replied. "As such, it'll fall to the Irregulars to turn you over to your guardian."

"So that he can butcher me for some fucking mythical rock?" Jason glared at Henry. "What a great law! How about putting dingos in charge of daycares while they're at it?"

"I never said it was right—"

"No, you said that going to Phipps and finding all of this out would help somehow." Jason pinned him with a stare as hard and sharp as a razor. "Has it helped?"

"It's given us warning of what we're up against and a little time..." Henry told him.

"When you say 'us' do you mean you and me or you and your Irregular buddies?"

Henry could read suspicion spreading across Jason's face as Jason belatedly realized how little he really knew of Henry or NIAD.

"It's not the same thing, is it?" Jason asked.

"No, it's not," Henry admitted. Gunther had all but told him that Research and Development wanted a crack at prying the stone from Jason's body before they had to hand him over to Greine. Phipps had been right about that.

"Phipps wasn't just bullshitting when he said your people wanted to carve me up for the stone and turn me into a—a zombie patch job, was he?" Jason stepped back out of Henry's reach, but he didn't run. That showed just how little he truly understood of the danger Henry posed to him. Or perhaps it simply betrayed Jason's desire to trust him even now.

"Phipps wasn't wrong. Gunther sent me a note this morning. R&D wants me to turn you over."

"But you're not going to…" Jason took another step back but then stopped and stood, staring at Henry warily.

All morning Henry'd shied from asking himself what he'd do when the moment came to pack Jason up and hand him over to the dowdy, merciless creatures that populated the R&D laboratories in DC. He hadn't suspected that his own conscience would kick quite so hard. The Irregulars had created, trained, and kept him for nearly a century; the institution was a great gyre that carried his wreckage, making him look alive and full of purpose.

Jason, on the other hand, was nearly a stranger. They'd had sex, but Henry wasn't one to mistake that for anything beyond a momentary respite—more pleasurable but certainly not more meaningful than sharing a drink and a laugh. It'd been a good time but taking it for more than that wouldn't have just been whistful but damn unwise. Yet Jason's gaze affected Henry more than he wanted to acknowledge; the smallest spark flickered in the darkness of his dead heart.

Jason exerted no special power over him—commanded no spells, oaths, or obligations written in blood. Instead he just looked at Henry like he could see the decency in him—like he was betting his life on it. And somehow just that made Henry feel the good, gallant, and foolish man he'd once been awaken within him.

Henry held his scarred left hand out to Jason and Jason came to him.

"When I said 'us', I meant you and me," Henry told him.

Jason nodded, looking relieved but also exhausted. Overhead a flock of smoky blue butterflies swirled across the sun like a passing cloud.

"So what now...Henry?" Jason said his name like it was a secret spell. Silly, really, but still touching.

"We need to find a way to keep you out of both the research labs and Greine's reach." No news there. But Henry didn't feel quite ready to explain all the details of the plan that had been growing in the back of his mind since early this morning. He didn't trust his own commitment enough yet to test it against the hard realities that even words would evoke. "You need to disappear for at least a year."

"Disappear to where?" Jason asked.

"As who might be more important—" Henry cut himself off as the door of the brilliant blue port-o-let swung open. A group of naked, green-haired youths burst out and immediately dispersed into a cloud of emerald butterflies. Princess padded out in their wake. She watched the nearest butterfly flutter with feline interest before trotting to Henry's side.

Henry scooped her up, noting the pretty collar she now wore as well as the silver message cylinder hanging from it like a delicate bell. The note inside told him nothing he didn't already know, except that Gunther had bought the collar for Princess and that Greine had been formally invited to take custody of his son first thing tomorrow morning. R&D were expecting Henry to make a delivery to them within the day.

Princess settled herself on Henry's shoulder but watched the surrounding moths and butterflies with great attention.

"We better leg it," Henry said. "Buttercup won't abide a cat in her kingdom, not even an enchanted one."

"But where are we going to go?" Jason asked.

"Back to where we started," Henry decided.

Chapter Eight

Carerra's strike team had left Phipps's Curiosities and Antiques locked up, taped off, and warded with small gold spheres that looked to Jason like miniature sea mines. Jason's own key and Falk's knife made easy work of the first two obstacles, but after that they both spent nearly an hour dismantling all the security spells with lullabies and curses written across masking tape. At last they slipped through the backdoor.

Inside, the once-tidy shop now stood in disarray. Antique chairs and ivory-inlaid card tables lay toppled and cracked like the remnants of a fire sale. Tapestries had been ripped from the walls and the entire collection of eighteenth-century Japanese umbrellas rested in a heap, tattered with bullet holes, as if they'd been executed by a firing squad.

Most of the valuables were missing. The display cases that had housed Persian and Chinese gold jewelry were nothing more than battered frames haloed by shards of shattered glass.

Falk snorted derisively.

"I knew they'd snatch up the fool's gold and leave the silver goblin's scimitar lying in a pile of tarnished trash." He carefully lifted the sheathed blade from a heap of broken glass and bent bookends. When he drew the blade a few inches Jason noticed red symbols glowing along it.

Princess circled Falk's feet but then bounded away to bite the wings of a stuffed owl that had fallen behind the empty, open cash register.

"Of course they also left a lot of actual garbage," Falk commented. He sheathed the scimitar.

Hints of both gunpowder and camphor scented the air. And a fine white ash drifted down from the second floor, where the incinerated remains of what looked like an immense serpent spilled across three shattered display cases that had once housed jade and carnelian hairpins.

The afternoon light streaming in through the windows dulled to hazy gold shafts as it filtered through the drifting clouds of ash.

Jason found a silk kerchief and tied it over his nose and mouth. He offered another to Henry, who followed Jason's example after only briefly smirking at the spray of silk pansies embroidered across the cloth.

"What do you think?" Falk asked through the kerchief. "Do I look like a proper robber now?"

"It does strike a nice balance between criminal menace and floral extravaganza." Jason grinned from behind his own display of pink roses.

"Sure. We'll set a new trend in criminal fashion. Pretty soon all the young thugs would be swaggering around with their grannies' hankies over their faces."

Together they scavenged and pilfered through gilded cabinets, pungent travelers' trunks, and the dark little drawers of any number of dressers and desks.

Steadily, he and Falk amassed a treasury of arcane weapons, ancient necessities, and petty valuables. Strings of semiprecious stones, silver blades, tinderboxes, leather satchels, two pocket watches, and a variety of old and costly clothes heaped up on the silken divan where they gathered their loot.

Jason's nerves tingled with both excitement and anxiety when he surveyed the assortment of odds and ends and realized that he would have to build a new life in another world with just these supplies. But it would be his own life.

He picked up one of the battered pocket watches and studied the constellation of symbols and additional hands that revealed themselves to him. According to Falk it was a compass for traveling between realms.

Jason wound the hands experimentally. A portal to Atlantis would be active in only twenty-three more hours.

"What about Atlantis?" Jason asked.

"Depends on how much you enjoy the damp. Very pretty, though. Red Ogre's tower was built there. She swears that some quiet nights you can hear the mermaids singing in the lower floors," Henry replied from the balcony above.

Jason remembered his ghostly visions of serene sea creatures drifting through the hallway.

"I'd like to at least see it," Jason decided.

"Not a bad thought. There's certainly wealth there and the inhabitants aren't too keen on either the sidhe or NIAD. There's plenty of glass here to trade with the mermaids and merrows, though crystal would be better..." Falk glanced up and then suddenly swung up onto the railing of the balcony and leaned out to catch one of the crystal chandeliers. He quickly plucked several shimmering baubles from their metal supports as if he were picking cherries. "They love how leaded crystal splinters light into rainbows. Pixies tend to go for prisms for the same reason."

Jason nodded and tried to commit this to memory along with all the other odd and esoteric information Falk had offered him as the sun had sunk outside the windows and the streetlights had flickered into life.

Cold iron downs pixies, nixies, and faeries. Trolls are nuts for coconut sunscreen. Brownies only keep their word when swearing on a sewing needle. Griffins have canaries for brains and go after their own reflections nine times out of ten. Never travel by using Mexican calendars. Don't eat goblin shashlik.

You must name the weapon you use to kill a unicorn so that the curse of its spilled blood will fall upon the weapon and not its bearer. The same held true with silver knives and werewolves...

Jason could hardly remember it all, but he still felt flushed with excitement at the prospect of seizing control of his own life. He wouldn't wait for some government agency or a sidhe regent to decide his fate any more than he would willingly walk back into St. Mary's.

And, despite his fears, the idea of traveling in disguise to new worlds appealed to him. He guessed that Falk was the one who made it appealing in the way he casually mentioned curses and enchanted fountains while neatly wielding his knife to pry the pearls from a Hindu statue. Someday Jason wanted to be that experienced and confident.

Jason ducked beneath the line of a window and crept up the stairs. Princess trailed him, swatting at the fluttering streamers of broken exorcism tape that littered the steps.

"What about this?" Jason held up a blanket embroidered with golden winged lions. When he'd worked at the shop he'd always thought it was a beautiful creation—faded with age and yet still whole and flashing with gold threads.

"Certainly looks like it could keep off the sun or the cold." Henry swung down from the railing and landed with surprising quiet. "How's it smell?"

Jason took a whiff of the thick cloth.

"Like fried chicken." Jason's stomach gave a demanding growl in response to the scent.

"Really?" Falk asked.

"No," Jason admitted. "I think I'm smelling the restaurant down the street. They probably started dinner service."

"Yeah, now that you mention it, I can smell it too." Henry took in a deep breath and frowned at the nearest window. "It got dark quick enough, didn't it?"

Jason shrugged. For the last twenty minutes or so he'd been using the light radiating off Falk to see his way around the shop. It struck him as almost ironic that Falk could shine so intensely and yet be utterly unable to perceive his own brilliance.

"Why don't you pack the bags while I grab us some grub?" Falk suggested. Jason felt more than happy to agree.

Falk handed him a fistful of cut crystal gems. Then he pulled down his kerchief and took a long swig from the flask in his pocket. A moment later the light radiating from him dimmed and he sank back into a darkness that not even Jason's vision could penetrate.

The entire shop darkened in his absence and Jason had to grip the handrail of the stairs to ensure his footing as he descended toward the silken divans and ornate Indian beds on the first floor. He wondered if he could create some small illumination of his own; he remembered how he'd used a melody to close Falk's wounds and decided to try. He let his thoughts fill with the low, warm tones of glowing embers and then the rushing whispers of flames as they burned the air. If anyone but Princess had been with him he would have felt too absurd to open his mouth and release this strange, primal song. But now as the raspy, growl of notes rushed out of him a ball of fire burst up before him.

Princess, who'd been trailing him with a strand of pearls dangling from her mouth, dropped her treasure and let out a startled yowl.

"It's all right. I'm not going to hurt you—or burn the building down…" Jason reassured her and himself. "It's a tiny flame, just enough light to see where I'm going."

Very cautiously Jason lifted his hand and the small ball of flames drifted to his outstretched fingers. It felt warm against his skin but didn't burn. In fact, it hardly felt much hotter than a warm breath against his skin.

Once he reached the divan on the first floor, Jason placed the flame in an empty crystal chalice on a dresser and set to work sorting and packing everything he and Falk had gathered. Princess curled up on an upholstered footstool where she could watch the flame and chew on her string of pearls. Ever so slowly the flame dimmed until only the dull glow of a red ember fell across Jason.

He lowered the full leather packs to the floor and stretched out on the divan. It had been a long, exhausting day and he suspected that only hunger was keeping him awake at this point. In the chalice, the ember's light pulsed and dimmed as if it too were fading into unconsciousness.

Then Falk appeared in halo of cold radiance, carrying a bucket of fried chicken and a six-pack of Anchor Steam Beer.

Jason rolled out one of the many Persian carpets and they ate on the floor in the warm fluttering light of the smoldering ember. Initially, hunger rendered Jason oblivious to everything but devouring hot drumsticks, salty biscuits, and cool beer. But slowly he became aware of the way the Henry watched him as he slowly drank his beer.

"Do I have something on my face?" Jason asked. He wiped his mouth with the back of his hand self-consciously.

"Yeah," Falk replied. He leaned close. "Let me get it for you."

He kissed Jason and his mouth tasted like beer and something earthy and strong that Jason couldn't name but yearned for. He leaned into Falk, kissing back and feeling the sensation of Falk's lips and tongue shiver through his entire body.

He wanted this so very badly and yet he didn't know if he trusted where it would lead. Falk's hand curled around his shoulder and Jason thought he would pull him closer, but he didn't.

Jason drew back. Falk held his gaze even as he allowed him to withdraw.

"I thought you didn't…" Jason wasn't certain of what he wanted to say except that after they'd screwed this morning Falk had seemed so cold, almost angry with him, and Jason didn't want that to happen again. "This morning…"

"I was an asshole this morning. Sorry about that, I wake up surly. But I don't think I ever said anything about not wanting you." Falk's mouth curved like he might laugh, but his gaze remained intense and fixed upon Jason. "What about you? What do you want?"

Jason wasn't certain how to answer that. For such a simple question it asked so much—from his long-ranging romantic ideals to a preference of sexual positions.

In response Jason simply caught Falk's scarred, calloused hand and drew him up onto the silken divan.

They undressed together. Jason felt self-conscious, comparing his soft naked body to the ropey muscle, rough blond hair, and scars of Falk's tall frame. His inexperience seemed so obvious.

But it relieved Jason to see that he wasn't alone in his feverish, flushed skin or excited, shaking hands. Jason tossed his T-shirt aside and Falk kissed his bare chest and then his abdomen, sending tremors through Jason's flesh.

"You're beautiful all the way to your bones, you know that," Falk told him and then he pulled aside Jason's underwear.

Jason gasped as Falk's mouth engulfed him, his silver tongue lashing waves of pleasure through him. He didn't know if it was magic or simply a result of Falk's vast lifetime of experience, but never before had Jason felt ecstasy rock him so powerfully or linger so long after.

As Jason lay, sticky and catching his breath, he noticed that the ember had died out. It didn't matter; Falk illuminated him, bathing him in a glow as radiant as starlight. Jason touched Falk's weathered cheek and he wasn't sure if Falk's expression was sad or tender as he gazed down at him.

"Are you worried?" Jason asked.

"Maybe a little..." Falk stretched out beside him on the divan. "Mostly about rolling off this thing." He pulled a crooked grin.

But Jason could tell he was lying and Falk seemed to realize as much because his expression sobered.

"I don't want you to get hurt," Falk admitted. "But that's life. Sooner or later everyone loses something or someone."

"It's not like I've never lost anyone." Jason searched Falk's angular face. He didn't know how he could look so rough and handsome at the same time. Like one of those tough-guy detectives from an old-time movie: the kind that talked mean and then sacrificed everything to save some hapless heroine in the end.

But Jason wasn't a heroine and he wasn't hapless. And most importantly he wasn't going to let fear of an unknowable future keep him from embracing his freedom now.

"Look," Jason said, "I can't promise that I—or you for that matter—will be safe and sound for all time to come. But we're here together now. And this is good, isn't it?"

"It's very good," Falk admitted. The smile that curved his mouth this time was genuine.

"Then let's enjoy now," Jason suggested.

Falk kissed his brow lightly.

"If we're going to keep enjoying ourselves, I need to get something out of my coat pocket," Henry informed him.

Jason guessed that even magicians needed lube and condoms.

When Henry returned, he lay down behind Jason. His hands felt hot as he stroked the muscles of Jason's bare back and traced curling designs down the length of his spine.

"Is this all right?" Falk asked.

Eight hours ago it might not have been, but now Jason nodded.

He relaxed, allowing Falk to arouse his languid body, while he built a song of passion and rapture in his mind. Falk shifted them both up to their knees. Jason's skin shivered with delight at the sensation of Falk's hair brushing over his back and buttocks. The heat of Falk's skin and the smell of his sweat filled Jason's senses as his hard width filled Jason's body.

Falk moved so carefully, easing into Jason as if he were delicate beyond imagining and in response Jason whispered the first notes of his longing. He felt Falk's entire body respond. His hands dug into Jason's flanks and his hips rocked deep and strong.

Jason's breath caught.

"Don't stop," Falk groaned into Jason's shoulder. And Jason realized that Falk was in his power in this moment and giving himself up to Jason's longing.

Jason called out in the rhythm of desire and coupling bodies. Falk answered him with a primal drive, pinning Jason hard and fast to the power of his own demands. They rocked and thrust, both caught up in the possession of yearning.

Shaking, as ecstatic sensation rushed through his body, Jason whispered only for more, plunging them both deeper into his song of ecstasy.

At last Jason's voice broke in a hoarse moan and Falk called out with him.

Jason collapsed against the cool silk of the divan and Falk fell beside him, breathing heavily and shining like the sun. Jason thought he could feel Falk's heart beating against his back.

"I can die happy now," Falk muttered. "My God, you're… fucking amazing."

Jason grinned. He didn't think he'd ever felt so utterly pleased to be so spent. His eyelids drooped and he nearly dropped off to sleep right then. But he realized that he ought to say something.

"You were great too," Jason mumbled. "Amazing fucking." Falk gave a dry laugh and Jason let himself drift into a contented doze. Falk shifted beside him, but Jason didn't open his eyes. He barely felt Falk's fingers caress his brow.

"Sweet dreams," Falk wished him, and Jason thought he felt Falk's lips graze his feverish skin. He drifted but then came near waking as he felt Henry's hands lingering on him.

"Lend me the grace of his form," Falk whispered as if offering up a prayer. "Let my coarseness keep him from harm."

It seemed an odd thing to say, but Jason could hardly keep the words in his mind. In moments all he recalled were soft comforting sounds floating at the edge of his awareness. He felt Falk spread his tattered trench coat over him and wish him safe dreams and a deep, deep sleep.

❧

Jason wasn't sure how much time had passed. It seemed like only minutes, but a particular feeling of warm sunlight dancing across his closed eyes undermined his certainty.

He managed to crack one heavy lid, but his vision seemed hazy and his sluggish mind felt too slow to respond to anything he saw.

Beams of bright morning light revealed a circle of sharp-featured, stately men dressed in leather and green silk and holding ivory spears. Their features struck Jason as unnaturally handsome and cold. Their skin shone like polished brass. Falk stood before them—

And Jason knew he was dreaming then, because Falk stood barefoot, wearing only Jason's jeans and yellow T-shirt. He held Jason's red hoodie in his hands.

Jason sensed other people there as well: grim men and women in black uniforms standing far back in the shadows. Jason thought Gunther hunched among them, his terrible goblin face distorted further by anger. He couldn't see that, but he sensed it in the way of dreams.

Before him, Falk held out his hands. One of the men in green encircled his wrists with iron chains. Then the rest closed ranks around him and they led him away.

Jason wanted to sit up and call out. He tried to shout, but Princess crouched on his chest. She bowed her scarlet face close to his.

I am sent here to hide you until the regent's guards have taken the bait and flown home like so many swallows carrying poison back to their nest.

Sleep.

❧

Jason woke suddenly and with a cry of alarm. Princess startled off the divan and Gunther—with a cigarette in his ragged, toothy mouth—glared at him.

A dizzy, unreal feeling moved through Jason as he attempted to work out what was going on. Bright afternoon light poured in through the windows of Phipps's shop. Empty beer bottles and the remains of a chicken dinner lay a yard from the divan where Jason sat naked.

Falk's trench coat lay across one of his legs.

"This has got to be a low point—even for you," Gunther growled at him. "How could you let them take him? You know what they're going to do to him when they get him back to the sidhe realm."

"What—" Jason began, but Gunther cut him off.

"They're going to cut him up with rusty razors and shove his remains through a fucking sieve until they find the damn Stone of Fal." The phone in Gunther's pocket sounded, but he ignored it. "If you were going to go ahead and let him get diced, you might as well have handed him over to our people. At least the guys in R&D use anesthesia. At least they would have tried to keep him intact..."

Jason just stared at Gunther, trying to understand what he was talking about and feeling disturbed that he just allowed his phone to keep ringing.

"Where's Henry?" Jason asked.

Then it was Gunther's turn to gape. His phone let out a last tone, then went quiet.

"What did you say?" Gunther moved closer and instinctively Jason grabbed Falk's coat and pulled it around his naked body.

"I want to talk to Henry. Where is he?" Jason asked again.

Gunther narrowed his red-slit eyes, dug into his suit pocket, and pulled out what looked like a small flashlight. He shone it on Jason and then swore in a crackling, grumbling language that Jason didn't need to know to understand.

"Doesn't work. Must be a glamour. A genuine faerie dust glamour. Damn it." Gunther flicked the light off and considered Jason. "If you're here, then who—" Realization showed on Gunther's face and at the same moment a terrible knowledge dawned upon Jason.

Falk had asked for three pinches of faerie dust from Buttercup. He'd used the last two on Jason and himself last night while Jason had dozed.

The whole time that he'd been offering Jason easy advice and helping him pack he'd never intended to leave with him.

"That stupid son of a bitch," Jason snapped.

"Oh yeah," Gunther agreed. He crumpled his cigarette in his hand and then tossed its crushed remains into his mouth. "He could actually get himself killed this time. Damn him."

"Princess can find him, though, can't she?" Jason asked.

"Of course. She's blood of his blood." Gunther considered Falk's familiar, then added, "No one at HQ is going to sign off on this, though. If they find out what Henry's done..."

"No. They can't know," Jason agreed.

Gunther fished a phone out of his pocket and began to dial. His toothy expressions were difficult to read, but Jason thought he looked strained or perhaps furtive. Suspicious fear moved through Jason. He tried to sound casual as he asked, "Who are you calling?"

Gunther turned his attention back to Jason.

"My boyfriend. He hates it if I don't call when I'm going to be late for dinner." Gunther paused, looked Jason over, then added, "By the way, you'll probably want to put some pants on."

Chapter Nine

A stinging salt rain lashed Henry as he raced for the shelter of an overhang. The green-garbed assassins Cethur Greine had sent to retrieve Jason surrounded and led him as they had for the entire day's journey through archaic portals, across the ragged sea cliffs, and now up through the dim twilight to the white walls of the high king's citadel.

They sneered at the pelting rain. Their commander—a lustrous-skinned, dark-haired bastard who addressed Henry obsequiously in English but referred to him as *miolra*, vermin, in his own tongue—caught hold of Henry by the hood of his red sweat jacket.

"You cannot stop here, young prince," the commander told him in thickly accented English. "We must climb to the parapet wall and cross over to the Hall of the Throne before the King's Star rises."

"Why?" Henry asked because Jason would have. He already knew the answer—not that these men would tell him the truth. They planned to murder him under cover of darkness, before word could spread across the Tuatha Dé Dannan Islands that the prince had returned to the sidhe realm.

His armed escorts played at polite only because it suited them not to have to drag him kicking and howling up the high walls before them. And Henry went along because every minute he kept them fooled meant a greater distance for Jason to put between himself and Greine.

Jason might have reached Atlantis by now. Princess would hate the water but love to chase the flying fish.

Overhead lightning cracked at the darkening sky and Henry heard storm waves breaking against the cliffs below.

"You must take part in the ceremony of your father's coronation." The commander raised his voice to carry over the sudden crash of thunder. His gaze moved over the glamour of Jason's face as if he were sizing him up for sandwich meat.

"It would be easier for me to keep pace with you if you removed these bracelets." Henry held out his wrists, displaying the iron manacles and engraved chains that linked them. The binding spells etched into the iron unnerved him. He'd seen them before, written on leather restraints and a bronze blade. Under any other circumstances Henry would never have submitted to the power of these iron manacles—but he'd needed Greine's men to take him before Jason woke.

"They are necessary for the ceremony," the commander informed him.

Yeah, Henry thought to himself. *Necessary as a sack when you're drowning kittens.*

The man on Henry's left—a scarred sidhe who Henry guessed was old enough to just remember the earthly realm—added, almost apologetically, "We couldn't remove them in any case, my prince. Your father holds the key. You are his to bind or set free."

"We must move," the commander stated and he shoved Henry towards a tower of weathered white stairs. Henry climbed and his keepers followed like hungry dogs.

Flurries of wind pelted Henry with rain as he rose to the spectacular heights of the outer parapet. He shuddered in his soaking clothes and swore under his breath. But even so the view before him momentarily absorbed him.

The Tuatha Dé Dannan controlled only a string of verdant islands in all the vastness of the faerie realm, but their audacious defiance of the violent, black sea besieging them testified to the magic at their command.

The high king's alabaster citadel rose from bare stones and jutted over jagged cliffs like the prow of an immense ship. Its towers shot up as straight as vast masts topped with turrets for crows' nests. Above every tower the famous storm banners, emblazoned with the high king's gold crest, billowed in the wind and traced trails through the dark clouds.

Forty years ago, when Henry had last stood on the citadel walls, the high king had held the throne and those storm banners had ensnared the rage of typhoons and hurricanes, raising the entire island so that it sailed across the seas. In the lee of the citadel, the island cities of the Tuatha Dé Dannan, with their exposed fields and golden orchards, had sheltered in perpetual summer.

But now the high king's storm banners merely dragged wind and drizzle down upon their own towers while the stone galleon of the citadel steadily succumbed to gravity and the sea.

Through the rain and gloom, Henry took in the ocean's conquests. Young mangroves sprouted up in flooded courtyards and the amphitheatres of the low-lying carnival district had become stagnant lagoons. Beyond the parapet, huge waves crashed and roared like conquering demons as they relentlessly eroded the citadel's walls.

However, not all the kingdom's magic foundered. Where plumes of sea spray reached the very heights of the white walls they broke into flights of doves.

"Now there's a trick I wouldn't want to see done with rabbits," Henry commented as he leaned over the alabaster stonework of the parapet. He couldn't be certain, but he thought for just a moment he'd seen figures down on the ragged rocks.

He edged further out for a better view and his six sidhe guards bristled like alarmed watchdogs. Their spears gleamed bright as lightning flashed over the dark sea. Again the commander caught the hood of Henry's red sweat jacket.

"Young prince, you must come away from the edge. It is not safe."

The impulse to show him just how unsafe it was flashed through Henry's skull, but he resisted. Jason wasn't likely to elbow a man off the parapet. So not only would it be a damn obvious giveaway but also it would probably result in Henry playing pincushion to five very long ivory spears. And that, in turn, would all too quickly end the entire charade.

"Sorry." Henry met the commander's stony gaze as if he were too guileless to recognize the disdain there. "I've just never seen anything so majestic," Henry gushed.

Jason would have been furious at being played like such a chump, but there were advantages to being underestimated by men as well armed and experienced as these ones. And at this point Henry needed every advantage he could get.

The commander accepted his excuse, obviously expecting little of a youth raised by throwback humans too dim to master the simplest spells.

Thunder crashed through the sky.

"We must not keep your father waiting." The commander nudged him onward. Henry went, shivering and working his frigid, stiff fingers against his shackles as inconspicuously as he could manage. He knew there wasn't any point; he wasn't going to get them off, but it wasn't in his nature to quit. While he wore them he could not retreat into the shade lands; he was trapped here.

Despite Henry's foot-dragging, they soon reached the broad stone staircase that led down to the wide courtyard of the Hall of the Throne. As they descended, Henry noted the large number of goblin mercenaries standing guard in the shadows of the ornamental flowering trees surrounding the hall.

Furtive figures peered from the tower windows surrounding the courtyard and below servants dressed in dull green liveries gawked at Henry as he drew near but averted their gazes when he looked back at them.

Then from some high place Henry heard a man sing out the first phrases of 'the Song of the High King's Return'.

"Blood of our true king,
Son blessed by the stone,
Even the storms will sing
Come claim your throne—"

Two wiry white goblins drew their scimitars and dashed across the courtyard into one of the many towers. Moments later, only the wind raised its voice to welcome Henry as he strode across the alabaster path to the golden doors of the Hall of the Throne. His guards trailed him with a wary tension in their movements.

Snow goblin mercenaries hauled the doors open and Henry had to shield his eyes with his shackled hands against the blaze of golden light that fell across him. The din of hundreds of voices burst over him only to be immediately silenced. Gathered on either side of the long gallery, nobles, courtiers, and ministers clothed in resplendent raiment stared at Henry.

"Son of Regent Cethur Greine, born of Princess Easnadh Naomh." A goblin child, dressed as a page, announced Jason's lineage and bowed before Henry. "Presenting Prince Lasair."

Henry briefly wondered what Jason would have thought of being addressed as Prince Lasair. He probably would've been too disturbed by the thought that some man in a tower had just had his throat slit to even notice. Henry wasn't particularly happy about that himself.

He glared across the sea of beautifully gowned and coifed sidhe. At the far end of the immense golden hall Cethur Greine brooded from atop the dark, decayed stones that had once been the shining gold throne of the high king. Without the Stone of Fal, the throne—like the citadel itself—was dying.

Goblin mercenaries flanked Greine and he returned Henry's gaze with an expression that was like longing but more voracious. Phipps hadn't lied. Greine strongly resembled Jason. Henry's heart gave an unnerving kick as he stared into Greine's dark eyes. Jason had obviously inherited his bronze skin, dark hair, and slim build from his father, but Henry had never seen Jason's face light with a smile so imperious or cruel as Greine's.

"At last." Greine rose and held out his right hand. In his left he held an ivory knife. "Come to me, child."

"Do not trust him, my prince," the little goblin page whispered as Henry passed him. Then he bowed and backed away as Henry's guards followed.

Henry crossed the Hall of the Throne with his head held high. On either side of him silk-robed courtiers and ministers sporting the jeweled rings of office averted their gaze. Not one of them protested; not one even whispered as much warning as the goblin page had. One woman covered her face with her hands and two men turned away, but all of them let "Jason" walk past to his death.

Henry hadn't wanted to get angry—he hadn't wanted to feel anything for fear he would betray himself—but as he glimpsed his reflection in the polished gold walls rage began to smolder inside him.

Because it was Jason who he saw striding past the assembled nobles of the Tuatha Dé Dannan. Slim, soaking wet, and barefoot, he looked too resolute to merit the iron shackles restraining his shivering arms. Too young to deserve the armed guards at his back or the goblins standing before him at the foot of Greine's throne.

"Flesh of my flesh," Greine addressed Henry, "your loyalty and life are mine to claim. For the sake of our kingdom I call upon you to submit—"

"Shut the fuck up!" Henry snapped. "You want to murder me, then come down and try, but don't feed me bullshit about obedience and loyalty, Greine. You don't even know what those words mean."

Shocked gasps echoed through the hall and for just an instant Greine appeared too stunned by Henry's outburst to respond. Far behind Henry someone stifled a nervous laugh.

Then Greine's dismay turned to fury.

"Kill him!" Greine shouted.

With armed opponents both behind and ahead of him, Henry opted to go for Greine. If nothing else, he was going to ruin the regent's white robes.

Henry took one of the goblins off guard, slamming his knee into the patch of soft flesh between its bone-hard legs. The goblin grunted and stumbled back, but others rushed forward.

He blocked a goblin's blade with the chain of his shackles and then smashed the heavy iron manacles across the goblin's skull. It dropped to the floor. Henry's heart raced and sweat began to bead on his brow. He spat the name of pain into a third goblin's red eyes and it fell, howling. The rest of the goblins retreated then.

On his black throne, Greine paled as Henry started for him.

"*Kill him*!" Greine roared.

Two goblins rushed him, one swinging a halberd and the other brandishing a scimitar. Henry lunged aside but still felt the halberd's iron tip punch through his sweat jacket and graze his shoulder. He caught the shaft of the halberd and wrenched the goblin wielding it into the swinging blade of his comrade. The scimitar ripped through the goblin's flank, spilling blood and bowels across the floor.

Henry's hands were slick with sweat as he jerked the halberd from the fallen goblin's dying grip. It wasn't much of a weapon so long as Henry's hands were shackled, but it put fear into the goblin mercenaries before him. Henry smelled it in their milky white sweat and saw it in their wide red eyes. He advanced and the goblin in front of him took half a step back.

For an instant Henry felt a rush of hope; he had only to reach Greine and it could be over. No one else would have to die.

Then two ivory spears harpooned him from behind. Pain ripped through his chest. One spearhead split Henry's ribs and jutted through the front of his jacket. His lungs shuddered and suddenly he was breathing blood.

God, he hated getting it in the back.

"You stupid fuckers." Henry spat a mouthful of blood at the nearest goblin. "You've trapped me here and now you're all going to die with me."

Wisps of white mist drifted from Henry's body. Despite the blaze of gilded torches, the hall darkened. Bound by the iron shackles, he couldn't escape into the shade lands, so now they came here to enfold him. Black rafts like rotting kelp drifted from the shadows and the air turned murky, cold, and acrid.

Henry stepped forward and the goblins before him broke ranks and pelted for the doors. But it was too late. The hungry dead were already descending. Choking screams suddenly filled the hall.

Henry dropped the halberd and staggered to the throne, dragging the ivory spears behind him. Greine stared at him in horror as he drew closer.

When Greine plunged his ivory knife into Henry's chest, Henry hardly felt it for the numb cold spreading through him. He gripped Greine's throat in both hands.

"No," Greine gasped. "The kingdom is yours but have mercy on your father."

Henry had neither the inclination nor the time to tell Greine that this was a mercy. He should have simply left him to the savage appetites of the hungry dead. But there was too much of Jason's visage in Greine for Henry to bear the sight of that. Instead he strangled the life from Greine.

Greine's wide-eyed corpse fell from the throne and Henry slumped to his knees. Darkness enfolded him, but it did not end his pain or the screams surrounding him.

Chapter Ten

Jason felt the difference the moment he stepped out from the rusting shipwreck of a portal onto the ragged rocks of the Tuatha Dé Dannan Islands. A sensation like an electric hum went through his body and the wild winds seemed to sing their names to him. The crash of the waves pounded with the rhythm of his heart. He didn't know this land, but it knew him.

"That's the citadel there." Gunther pointed his long, taloned finger up to the towering white edifice jutting out over the crashing sea. "I told you Rake wouldn't steer us wrong. The man knows how to travel."

Jason simply nodded. He'd grown accustomed to Gunther's lean, jagged visage, but Gunther's retired ex-partner had been another matter: winged, towering, and wreathed in flames. Jason had felt like he was standing on the precipice of a volcano, gazing down into molten magma each time he'd met Rake's gaze. But the man had behaved normally enough, offering Gunther directions and wishing them good luck when they'd left him.

At Jason's feet, Princess let out an annoyed yowl and pinned her ears back against the rain.

"Can you find Henry?" Jason asked her.

She gave a little sniff, then leaped across the ragged rocks toward the jutting white prow of the citadel. Both Jason and Gunther sprinted to keep pace with her. As they drew closer to the huge citadel Jason thought he glimpsed a figure wearing a red jacket at the very height of the wall.

Please let that be him. Let him be all right.

Jason wanted to call to Falk, but he knew his voice wouldn't carry across so vast a distance. Instead thunder boomed across the leaden sky.

And then the figure was gone.

Jason's muscles burned, but his whole being called out to move faster still—to reach Falk sooner. And suddenly storm winds roared over them, lifting and throwing them ahead nearly too fast for them to keep their feet.

"Are you doing this?" Gunther shouted.

"I think so," Jason called back.

"Don't kill us, okay?"

Oddly, Princess appeared delighted, bounding into the gusts and all but dancing on the air. They took the stairs up the citadel wall in the same wild, terrifying manner, springing into the wind as if they could fly as easily as the flock of doves rising above them.

Just as they reached the height of the wall Jason released the winds. He and Gunther staggered a few steps on the rain-slick flagstones, regaining their equilibrium. Princess set down with a hop.

In the courtyard below, dozens of toothy white snow goblins stood at attention, their weapons ready. One yawned and then glanced up to the wall. It gave a shout and pointed up to where Jason and Gunther stood. Jason's whole body went cold as he watched entire ranks of goblins raise their toothy faces to glare at him.

"Crap," Gunther muttered.

Then, with a howling cry, the goblins charged.

Princess dashed down the staircase, straight for them. Gunther drew the scimitar he'd taken from Phipps's shop and Jason let the razor-sharp notes of the 'Amhrán Na Marú' fill his mind.

Then, racing past Princess, he released the cruel melody of bone-cutting blades and merciless flames. Goblins fell, their bodies torn in half, their limbs burning. Gunther defended Jason's back, growling and swearing. Blood from his scimitar spattered Jason as he swung its edge through their attackers' bodies. Soon blood slicked the steps. Steadily, the goblins fell back as he and Gunther advanced.

They reached the courtyard. The white-flowered trees burned before Jason's song, sending plumes of smoke into the pelting rain. One of the remaining five goblins lunged for Jason with his blade drawn. Jason called fire from his heart and the goblin seared to ash as he charged. The remaining goblins turned then and fled.

Princess bounded to the golden doors of an ornate building. Jason followed her and Gunther brought up the rear. Despite the rain, all Jason could smell was blood. His ears rang and his throat felt cracked and raw.

Somewhere across the citadel someone sounded an alarm.

"They'll bring out their archers in a—" The rest of Gunther's words were drowned out by the cacophony of screams rising from behind the set of huge gold doors.

Princess arched and hissed. When Jason laid his hand against one of the doors Princess backed away. The golden surface felt deathly cold against Jason's bare skin.

He remembered this bone-deep cold from when he'd lain in the murky darkness of the shade lands. Suddenly he knew why people were screaming. The thought of going in terrified him. But Henry was in there and he couldn't just leave him.

"You'd better get behind me." Jason's words came out in a hoarse rasp.

Gunther nodded, and holding his scimitar, he stood at Jason's back.

Jason pushed the doors open and stepped into the choking, acid depths of the shade lands. Stinging pain washed over his exposed skin. His lungs caught on the sickly, thick atmosphere and his stomach clenched.

Before him, ghosts rose in an endless a sea of shadows and darkness. They were the dank air and its sticky black drifts. They were the chilling cold and the contorted monstrosities biting, grasping, and devouring every shred of life.

In their midst, the living were few. One tiny goblin only a foot from Jason yowled like a dying kitten as dark, clawed limbs sank into its chest. A bleeding woman crouched with her arms over her face while the man beside her was torn open.

Helpless fear shuddered through Jason.

There were too many of them and he had no way to fight them. Jason couldn't burn the dead or drive them away with wind. They were ghosts—nothing but hunger and hurt.

Then he remembered Henry holding one of them gently and setting it free in a burst of brilliant light.

Jason didn't know if he could do the same, but he'd come too far to give up now.

Jason drew in a deep breath and forced his voice to rise like a blazing light. He beckoned the abandoned and broken, the lost and vengeful with a melody that promised all they desired.

He instinctively grasped what they so craved because he knew what it was to be terrified and abandoned. He understood how betrayal burned inside and how hurt haunted memory. He knew too well how it felt to be locked away from love and life and be left with only a desperate longing.

He called them to him with the notes of blazing joy, building his song from the wonders he'd witnessed in Henry's company, the laughter he'd shared, and the ecstasy that had delighted his entire being.

And ghosts came to him, not just a few but by the hundreds. They rose from the bleeding bodies of the living, flocking over Jason with their grasping teeth and fury.

Jason closed his eyes against their numbers and gave himself up to his song. It blazed inside him and poured out like flames from his lips. He sang with all the strength of his life, offering himself up in shining waves of respite and release. He sensed ghost after ghost reach for him and then burn away in the wake of his song, until at last his whole body felt wasted and hollow and his voice broke.

He struggled for the strength to open his eyes. When he did, he found himself standing in a long golden hall. Lamps blazed overhead and blood spattered the gilded walls. And yet Jason could feel that he still stood in the shade lands as well. Abandoned white hills glimmered like mirages at the edge of his vision. The air tasted sweet and felt empty. Overhead the faint trails of dissipated ghosts streaked the air like shooting stars.

Stunned, bloodied groups of men and women dressed in silk rags gaped at him in silence. Near the doors a small goblin clung to Gunther, whispering in a growling, low language.

Gunther looked to Jason.

"We're going to need nurses and physicians in here," Gunther told him. "Will you be all right on your own if I go with Gnasher to get help?"

Jason nodded mutely. He didn't think he could speak even if he wanted to.

As Gunther pulled one of the doors open, Princess came bounding out of the night. Wild storm winds followed her, rushing over Jason as if they'd missed him.

"Looks like you won't be alone after all," Gunther commented. Then he and the smaller goblin slipped out into the courtyard.

Princess brushed her rain-damp body against Jason's legs and then bounded down the length of the hall to where a dozen bodies—both goblin and sidhe—lay among fallen weapons. At the foot of a broken, black throne slumped three men. One Jason did not recognize. But the second—impaled by ivory spears—was Henry. The third man leaned over Falk, clutching at his heart.

Princess reached them before Jason but only by a moment. She stepped directly through the man who crouched over Falk without seeming to notice him.

Jason studied the man's handsome, translucent features. He hardly seemed to take note of either Princess or Jason. He gazed at Falk with such sorrow and yet he kept his hands buried in Falk's chest as if he were trying to dig out his heart.

"Franklyn?" Jason asked.

The man started in surprise and then very slowly lifted his gaze to Jason.

“How do you know me?” Franklyn asked. His voice was only a sigh.

“Henry told me about you,” Jason replied. He knelt down at Falk’s side. Grief and guilt distorted Franklyn’s face as he met Jason’s gaze.

“I can’t get my knife out of his heart,” Franklyn whispered. “I keep trying, but I can’t get it out. How can he forgive me if I can’t get my knife out of his heart?”

Jason considered the shadow that Franklyn was, the way he clung to Falk.

“The knife came out a long time ago,” Jason told him. “You just have to let go now.”

“I can’t.”

“You must.” Jason reached out and curled his hands around Franklyn’s forearms. They felt cold and as insubstantial as snowflakes melting against his fingers. “I’m going to help you.”

Franklyn looked frightened then, but Jason simply whispered a hoarse, aching lullaby to Franklyn and slowly, gently lifted his hands from Falk’s body.

“I deserve to suffer,” Franklyn said as he rose to his feet with Jason.

Jason shook his head, uncertain if he could force even one more word from his throat. They had all suffered. Wasn’t that what Falk had said? Probably suffered too much.

Jason embraced Franklyn, though it was like holding ice to his bare body. Franklyn melted against him and Jason found the strength to utter a final word.

“Good-bye,” he told Franklyn. And then, in a streak of light, Franklyn was gone.

At Jason’s feet Falk dragged in a slow breath. His eyes fluttered briefly open, seemed to focus on Jason, and then fell closed again.

Jason felt the shade lands slip away.

❧

The doors of the Hall of the Throne swung open and a group of men and women in dull green uniforms gaped in. Despite the horror in their expressions, they entered the hall and immediately busied themselves tending to the wounded. They spoke in a bright language that Jason didn't understand, but he thought that at least a few of them must be doctors.

Snow goblins and tall men in leather armor arrived, bearing stretchers that seemed to have been improvised from spears and blankets.

A pretty young girl with her hair in braided loops spread black cloths over the dead. She approached the throne with a drawn expression, her eyes darting to Jason and then away as if she didn't dare look him in the face. She draped a black cloth over one body, but when she came for Falk, Jason waved her away.

And oddly she obeyed him, bowing and backing from him as she whispered, "Lasair."

Jason felt too done in to wonder what that meant. None of the other sidhe in the hall approached him. Most averted their gazes when he caught them staring at him.

A dozen gold-skinned men dressed in silk arrived at the doors, speaking among themselves excitedly. Jewels glinted from their ornately braided hair and the rings adorning their graceful hands.

Goblins and soldiers carried the injured and dead out past them.

Gunther ducked in through the doors and offered Jason an easy salute before beckoning a man whom Jason had earlier decided was a doctor. It was nearly more than Jason could manage to lift his arm and wave to Gunther in return. But at least Gunther seemed to have things in hand. It didn't look like they were going to have to try and fight their way out of here. That thought alone came as an immense relief to Jason.

Gunther and the doctor stepped out into the rainy courtyard.

Jason gazed down at Falk. If only he would wake up. Jason's gaze suddenly fell on the iron shackles binding Falk's wrists. He knelt, caught them in his hands, and called on them—as he had called on the storm winds—to release Falk. The iron stung his hands, but he didn't let go. He'd fought goblins and conquered a world of furious ghosts; a set of bracelets wasn't going to stop him now.

The metal cracked in his grip and the iron chain fell away.

Jason swayed and stumbled back, nearly delirious with exhaustion. He slumped onto the black throne, wanting only to rest there briefly.

Suddenly a sound like fanfare filled the air and gleaming sparks lit the battered black surface of the throne. If Jason had possessed the strength he would have leaped clear, but as was, he simply watched as gold filigree spread through the dark stone and sprouted up from the back of the throne to reach all the way to the roof of the hall.

Jason scanned the room for Gunther, hoping the agent would offer him some sign of just how badly he'd screwed things up.

He didn't find Gunther, but the view that greeted him seemed almost incomprehensible. All across the hall, men, women, and even goblins stared at him as if in awe. After a moment, some burst out in laughter; others cheered. Many, even those among the wounded, dropped to their knees before him. The girl with her black blankets knelt with her hands raised toward him as if she were warming them before a fire.

"Lasair," called a man in leather armor as he too knelt.

Beyond the open doors the rain seemed to suddenly cease and sunset rays of light poured into the already bright hall. Jason couldn't be certain, but it almost seemed that the entire building was rising upward.

As more people poured in through the great, golden doors only to drop to their knees, Jason began to wonder seriously if he was dreaming.

Then Gunther appeared at the door and sidled his way through the growing crowd to approach the throne.

"I leave you alone for ten minutes and you become the high king," Gunther commented. "Not exactly discreet."

Jason frowned at Gunther's words. Then he realized that Gunther was making fun of the ridiculous scene he'd made. He wondered how long this was going to take to straighten out. Outside the hall, bells rang out and Jason thought he heard distant voices rising in cheers.

"Sorry," Jason rasped. He flopped his hand off the arm of the throne, trying to reach the body sprawled there. "I found Henry."

Gunther's eyes dropped to where Falk lay in the shadow of the throne. He winced at the sight of the spears jutting from his body.

"He's alive," Jason assured him.

Gunther nodded and then crouched down at Falk's side. With what struck Jason as practiced efficiency, Gunther jerked the spears from Falk's body. He groaned.

"Time to wake up, Henry." Gunther stood and surveyed the crowd gathering at the foot of the throne. "You're going to miss the high king's coronation."

Jason mouthed a dry rasp of a laugh at Gunther's sarcasm.

But then Falk's eyes opened. He stared up at Jason for a moment, then offered him a weary smile and clumsily sat upright.

"You aren't supposed to be here," Henry told him. He tugged self-consciously at the sweat jacket he wore, as if he could shield Jason from the sight of the wound in his abdomen.

"Neither are you," Jason replied hoarsely. "Are you all right?"

"Yeah." Henry sounded almost surprised. "I feel better than I have in a long time…You don't look so good, though."

"What kind of thing is that to say to your knight in shining armor?" Jason murmured.

"Nah, you're Prince Charming," Falk told him. He scowled out over the gathering in the gallery of the hall. "Looks like you've got quite the audience."

Jason just shook his head. He would tell Falk all about it later and Falk would probably laugh at him. But he didn't mind that because they were going to be all right now.

That knowledge seemed to release what little energy Jason retained. He leaned back into the throne, hardly feeling Princess's weight as she leaped up onto his lap. Jason let his eyes fall shut.

Outside the hall, voices rose in a song. Jason didn't recognize the words, but it sounded welcoming. He was sleeping when Falk stood, touched his brow once lightly, and then left him.

Chapter Eleven

An unctuous, onion-perfumed steam clouded the view of the world beyond the plate-glass windows of the HRD Coffee Shop. Henry thought that was just as well. The gray December sky and fine drizzle of rain only reminded him of the Tuatha Dé Dannan Islands.

Not that it would be piss and misery there anymore. According to Shadow Snitches and at least one drunk ambassador, High King Lasair had brought blue skies, abundant harvests, and a new charter of rights to his subjects. Apparently Jason was shaping up into something of a populist monarch, despite the opposition of his courtiers and ministers.

Henry tried to picture Jason wearing the golden crown and saffron robes of the high king, but the closest he could manage was a memory of the way he'd looked, satisfied and stretched out, sleeping on a divan with Henry's battered trench coat lying across his naked bronze body.

Not exactly the stuff of royal portraiture.

Certainly not what Henry should be thinking about now that Jason had returned to the nobility of his birth right. A high king didn't need a rangy, half-dead relic for company. But it had been beautiful while it lasted…

Henry took a swig of his coffee and scowled. It was short about four shots of whiskey to really do him much good.

He picked up the festively decorated invitation that he'd been considering throwing away for over an hour now. Inside, a photograph of Gunther and the various poor souls he'd roped into assisting with the social outreach program that he disguised as a Christmas cookie-making party stared back at him. Henry recognized Gunther's current boyfriend—the vegetarian—holding up a snowflake-shaped cookie cutter. Agent August and some feral-looking man made eyes at each other from behind him.

Not Henry's kind of thing at all—too many people, not enough rotgut.

And yet, for the first time since he'd been a young man, Henry found himself welcoming the thought of company, craving noise and novelty. It was ridiculous. After ninety-four years wandering alone and half lost in the desolation of the past, he had no right to turn up at some Cookie Jamboree—or whatever the hell Gunther was calling it—like a repentant alcoholic uncle.

Henry folded the card back closed.

He contemplated his meal, Jason's favorite, the kimchi burrito. He took a bite and found that it tasted odd but good. In spite of himself he wondered if Jason missed it. More than likely he'd discovered something far more exquisite and less messy among the elegant sidhe.

"Jason! Is that you?" the Hispanic cashier called out in delight. "Oh my God, honey, you look great!"

Henry looked up.

And there Jason stood, dressed in a gray army jacket, black T-shirt, and jeans that fit him just right. The cashier grinned at his bronze skin and striking, angular features. He'd always been this handsome. Now with the anonymity spell worn away people were free to take note.

Jason smiled back at the cashier, a friendly, genuine smile. Then he turned and surveyed the crowd of customers at the counter and tables.

Henry met his gaze because it would have been childish to look away. Jason stared hard and too long at him—as if he were attempting to pin Henry to his seat with just the power of his dark eyes.

The cashier gave a little cough. Jason returned his attention to her, ordering his usual and making small talk about the money he'd recently come into and the vacation he'd been on.

Henry tried to pick out Jason's security detail. But either they were invisible even beyond Henry's sensing or no one had Jason's back. The thought disturbed Henry deeply.

"But you're back in town now?" the cashier asked hopefully.

"Yeah, I'm back," Jason stated firmly.

Henry thought it was a little mean for Jason to kid with her like that, but then Jason probably didn't realize how easy it would be for her to get taken with him.

A moment later, Jason strode to Henry's table.

"You can be a very difficult man to find," Jason told him.

"Yeah, well." Henry shrugged, feeling suddenly self-conscious under Jason's scrutiny. "I don't like to get underfoot."

"No, you leave your cat to do that." He placed his order of fries and his kimchi burrito on the table and very deliberately took the seat next to Henry. "She's fine, by the way."

Henry nodded. He'd known Jason would treat her well.

"Does NIAD know you're here?" Henry instinctively lowered his voice.

"Why? Do you want to see my travel visa and diplomatic passport before I can sit down and eat with you?" When Henry didn't respond, Jason shook his head and said, "Yes, they know. I'm all cleared, paid up, and legal."

Henry nodded, but the absence of security still worried him. Unless Jason had slipped away from them for a reason.

"So why did you come here?" Henry asked quietly.

"Because you're here," Jason replied. He picked up a bottle of sriracha hot sauce and squeezed it out over his fries. "I've really missed this stuff, you know."

"As I recall there wasn't much hot sauce in Tuatha Dé Dannan Islands."

"None." Jason ate a couple fries, then looked up at Henry. "You're watching me like you think I'm about to sprout a second head."

"I'm just waiting to find out why you're here," Henry told him. He could imagine too easily the kind of trouble that might drive Jason to seek him out. Nobles infuriated by Jason's reforms. Revolutionaries too long invested in bringing down the throne. There were any number of reasons that Jason might need a man with Henry's skills. "Is there someone you need dealt with?"

"What?" Jason frowned at him. "No. What are you talking about?"

"Your kingdom," Henry stated.

Jason just shook his head.

"It's not mine anymore. We're now officially a constitutional monarchy. As of—" Jason checked his watch. "Three hours ago."

"Are you shitting me?" Henry stared at Jason.

"I shit you not, sir," Jason replied with an easy smile. "Princess Easnadh Naomh took office as prime minister last week and the parliament held its first session yesterday. I have to return once a year to maintain the throne and pick up my stipend, but otherwise I'm out of that place."

"But you're the high king." Henry didn't think he'd ever heard of anything so crazy. Who just walked away from that much power and wealth? And what bunch of idiots let someone like Jason go?

"No, I'm a musician like my father before me," Jason stated firmly. "I wasn't brought up to be a king and I don't want to be king. I know next to nothing about governing a nation."

"But what about your family, your mother?" Henry didn't miss the brief scowl that tugged at Jason's mouth.

"Princess Easnadh Naomh would have roasted and eaten me as an newborn if her lady-in-waiting hadn't secreted me off to her mortal lover. She told me as much to my face. Not exactly the mothering type." Jason shook his head. "Though I think I actually liked her honesty better than all the bowing, scraping, and ass kissing of the courtiers. Even if it was my ass getting kissed."

"I don't know. I recall that you didn't mind when I kissed your ass." Henry couldn't help the remark; it had just been too easy and he wanted to cheer Jason.

Jason colored and Henry hid his smirk behind a sip of coffee.

"I did like it," Jason admitted. "I'd like more and I think you would too."

Henry almost choked on his coffee. Were they really going to have this conversation here?

Jason continued, "I just don't understand why—after everything we'd been through—you left me."

Apparently, they were going to have this conversation, Henry realized, because Jason's tone was too sincere, his expression too hurt for Henry to just pass the whole thing off as a joke.

"I left because I'd done what I'd come to do," Henry told him.

"And offering yourself up in my place?" Jason asked and Henry could see the hurt in his face, though he kept his tone steady. "Was that just part of the job? Was sleeping with me?"

"No," Henry told him, but Jason just bowed his head and scowled at his food.

Henry wished he could find the right words to make Jason happy—to make him understand. But Henry had never been good at talking—not like this.

He reached out and placed his rough, callused hand on top of Jason's. What the hell did he care if a few gawkers saw them? Jason lifted his gaze to him questioningly.

"Look, I'm probably going to screw this up, but just…just hear me out, okay?"

"Okay," Jason agreed.

"I'm no good with lovers. I haven't been since—" Henry caught himself reflexively, but somehow it didn't seem to hurt so much now. He continued, "since everything fell apart with Frank. After that, I went sort of dead inside. I screwed a lot of guys, but I never really gave a damn about them. And then I met you and…"

"And what," Jason asked.

"I don't know…You made me feel like I wasn't such a bastard. You looked at me—the way you're looking at me now. And you made me feel like I was good and decent and honest."

"That's because you actually are all of those things, Henry."

"But I wasn't. That's what you don't understand here," Henry objected. "I went through the motions of upholding the law and keeping people safe because I knew that's what decent people did. But I was like some ugly marionette just miming the actions of the flesh-and-blood people around me because I wanted to be one of them."

Something like understanding lit Jason's dark eyes, but he didn't speak. He just turned his hand to lace his fingers with Henry's. His long fingers felt warm and strong.

"I was walking around and talking, but I was dead inside and I knew it," Henry admitted. "But then I met you and it brought something in me back to life. For the first time since I was twenty, I started to feel like there were things worth fighting for…I wanted to fight for you."

"But then why did you leave?" Jason asked.

Henry didn't answer right away. He didn't want to admit the truth. But Jason had a right to know.

"Because I knew I'd screw it up, just like I screwed it up way back then," Henry said at last.

Jason considered him for a long while before speaking.

"What happened back then was terrible, but that's over. You and me, here and now, we're just beginning."

"Yeah." Henry nodded. "I was starting to realize that…But I'd already left and you…Well, you had a kingdom of better candidates, didn't you?"

"Dear God, no." Jason wrinkled his nose in distaste at some memory. Then he gave Henry's hand another squeeze. "My taste is more for the rough-and-ready type."

"Rough and ready?" Henry laughed and he noticed Jason's cheeks colore just a little.

"Well, I'm not going to lie and claim you won me over with fine dining and long walks on the beach," Jason said, shrugging. "A bucket of chicken and a few beers isn't exactly high romance, you know."

"I suppose not." Belatedly, Henry realized that he ought to have taken Jason out and shown him a good time. He wondered what it would be like to walk beside him and feel proud in the way he never could have been with Frank.

"Not that I couldn't go for a few beers," Jason suggested and Henry guessed he was trying to be sly.

"You doing anything tonight?" Henry asked.

Jason's face lit up like Henry'd offered him a pot of gold.

"Are you asking me out?"

"Yeah, I am. But I won't be offended if you turn me down for this one." Henry handed him the card Gunther had given him. "The Cookie Jamboree isn't all that rough and ready. Though I could always spike the punch."

"It doesn't look so bad. We could pick up a bucket of chicken and a couple of beers and head over to my place after it's over. I have a loft in SoMa now. Plenty of space for equipment and Princess likes the big windows." Jason stopped, seeming suddenly to grow shy. "If you'd like that, I mean."

"Yeah," Henry agreed. "I would like that."

NATO IRREGULAR AFFAIRS DIVISION

ABOUT THE AUTHORS

Nicole Kimberling lives in Bellingham, Washington, with her partner, Dawn Kimberling, and two bad cats as well as a wide and diverse variety of invasive and noxious weeds. Her first novel, *Turnskin*, won the Lambda Literary Award. She is also the author of the *Bellingham Mysteries.*

A distinct voice in gay fiction, multi-award-winning author Josh Lanyon has been writing gay mystery, adventure and romance for over a decade. In addition to numerous short stories, novellas, and novels, Josh is the author of the critically acclaimed Adrien English series, including *The Hell You Say*, winner of the 2006 USA BookNews award for GLBT fiction. Josh is an Eppie Award winner and a three-time Lambda Award finalist.

When Astrid Amara isn't writing, she is either riding horses, goat herding, sleeping, or working as a civil servant. She is a Lambda Literary Award finalist and the author of *The Archer's Heart* as well as numerous other titles.

Ginn Hale resides in the Pacific Northwest, donates blood as a pastime, and tinkers with things. Her first novel, *Wicked Gentlemen*, won the Spectrum Award for best novel and was a finalist for the Lambda Literary Award. She is also the author of the *Lord of the White Hell* books and the *Rifter* series.